# CASTLE GAMES:
# A ROCKY ROMANCE

*Best Wishes!*
*Jan Prestopnik*

## Jan Prestopnik

CASTLE GAMES:
A ROCKY ROMANCE

For my children,
Nathan, Emily, & Adam
-delightful toddlers, excellent adults-

Thanks, kids, for making me laugh . . . a lot.
I love you.

"... please get your rags
And your polishing jars,
Somebody has to go polish the stars."

- Shel Silverstein

# 1

YES, SISTER, I should probably start at the beginning and explain how I end up back at the castle. You should know what it means to me, so you'll understand exactly why I do the things I do and how everything comes about. I do want your blessing, Sister, but I'll settle for understanding. At least that.

I'm going to tell you the whole story, nothing left out. That's the only way you'll get the picture.

How does it start? What possesses me?

◇◇◇

Well, at around eleven a.m. on a warm Saturday in May, I'm chomping on the obligatory wad of gum and slinging home fries at Chez Fred's, when Sir Charles Fitzham Smithson the Second unexpectedly picks me up . . . .

I'd like to say that's how it starts, Sister, but it wouldn't be honest. Even before that, a plan had been lurking in my brain, like a flea beetle in a head of cabbage, peeking out, peeking out, waiting to jump.

You know that I am not a waitress by choice, Sister, and, to be honest, I've been waiting a while for this opportunity, so when I see him come in, I recognize him immediately. I do a double-take and some fast calculating. Here's my ticket out of Chez Fred's and back to the big time, looming large and clear as life. Daddy always told me, "Just polish your own star." Well, I haven't had much in the way of stars for a long, long time, but I can almost see one twinkling on my horizon. Give me a chance and I'll polish with the best of them.

Don't get the idea that Charles Fitzham Smithson the Second is captivated by my efficiency, my clever banter or my seductive, brazen earthiness. He doesn't even notice me, except to give me a wounded expression as he wipes at a spot of grease I missed when I mopped up the booth he's sharing with his eager, chattery friend.

So, The Honorable is grease-shy. Why am I not surprised?

Well, Smithson II may not notice me, but I sure notice him. Tall, good-looking if you like that sort, and that expression of resigned disdain on his pretty face that shows just how he feels about succumbing to Chez Fred's in the first place.

I'd like to spend a bit more time admiring Smithson's beauty, but Old Hank at booth number three is beckoning to me with bleary eyes, and I realize his toast needs replenishing. I always give Old Hank extra toast. Fred doesn't necessarily know, but even if he did know, he wouldn't care. I grab the extra slices as they pop up, slather on plenty of butter, and bring the plate over to Hank. I sit down across from him, slide over the toast, and chat for a minute, asking him about his daughter in Illinois and jawing about the Syracuse Orange. He follows the team, and because he loves them and loves to discuss their stats, I make it my business to know.

"What're you reading, Hank?" I ask. I peer sideways at the page open in the hardcover library book propped up by his coffee cup. Words pop out at me. Lunar crust. Plagioclase. So he's still reading about rocks.

"Trying to figure out about this stuff they found on the moon," he says. "Anorthosite. There's a lot of it around here, too." He pronounces the word carefully. Words don't just slip off Old Hank's tongue. He's a precise speaker, probably because most of his teeth aren't really his. "I just don't know why they have so much more of it up there on the moon," he says.

"Plate tectonics," I say. "It got pushed into the earth's core over time."

"So it's all hiding in there?"

"Or melted."

"Old stuff," he offers. "Been around forever."

"Yep, just like these mountains."

I like to talk to Hank because, like me, he's a reader, and sometimes we even find out that we've been perusing the same books. I read this one on rocks a couple years ago.

We gab on a bit about anorthosite and Hank turns a few pages, showing me photos of rocks that he especially likes.

But my eyes keep roving back to Charles Smithson.

I like his clothes. They're expensive and well-cut, all in muted khakis and browns and blues. And talk about labels. This guy absolutely bleeds labels, little ones, the kind you have to know enough to look for. And believe me, I know enough. I've been studying up.

He looks cool and collected, like maybe he's just stepped off the eighteenth green with a successful score card in his pocket. Actually, it turns out he *has* just stepped off the eighteenth green, which still doesn't explain why he has deigned to sample the sludge we call coffee at Chez Fred's. Our greasy spoon establishment happens to be right down the road from the Tupper Lake Golf Club, right here in the Adirondacks, and The Honorable Sir Charles Fitzham Smithson the Second has probably passed us a million times before with his aristocratic nose in the air, gagging at the reeky, garlicky odors that Fred calls his specie-alities. It must kill this guy to be lowering that trim posterior into one of our cracked plastic booths.

I could just hoot.

Kitty gives her famous half-face smile, the one she uses on everything wearing khakis that happens into Fred's. Her blonde ponytail bounces, and so do a lot of other parts of her as she flips off her cyber solitaire game and brandishes her order pad before booth number six, where these two aristocrats, Smithson and his pint-sized little buddy, are trying hard not to get greasy.

"What'll it be, guys?" she chirps, eyes twinkling. She can't decide which prince to concentrate on. Old Honorable is definitely the better looking, but it's the eager companion who's trumpeting his own zealous, undisguised lust toward a very receptive Kitty. And Kitty will take whatever she can get.

Sometimes I feel sorry for Kitty, but I get sick of her sometimes, too, and today is one of those days. She knows six is my booth, and even though we cover for each other when things get busy, I'm not particularly tied up right now, as she can plainly see. So I march on over there with my damp dishcloth in my hand, and I give her a good stiff tap on the shoulder.

Kitty winces and moves aside, and I step up to do my thing. The companion of The Honorable Charles twists in unashamed interest to watch Kitty twitch her hips in the direction of the kitchen, and I now know why these two dudes are in here. Call me a quick study.

The companion is a small, tidy guy with tight, curly brown hair and bright puppy eyes that have fastened onto my face now, since Kitty's has disappeared into the plastic silverware bins. "Just coffee," he says happily. The Honorable Smithson nods in pained agreement.

Oh, I know. Ordering coffee is *such* a chore.

The eager companion is giving me the once over. Jee-zum! Why would he do that? He must be desperate. I twist my dirty dishrag around the chipped polish on my nails, to hide them from sight, and I stalk off to get the coffee.

I pass a table full of kids - junior high boys who come in now and then when they've scraped up enough allowance to share an order of fries. "Hey, goonies," I say to them.

"Lucky, come here." They call me over with excited gestures to show me a trick they've learned to do with coffee creamers. Red, my favorite of the lot, hides a creamer in his fist just below his eye, picks up a fork and suddenly stabs. "Ow, my eye!" he shrieks as thick, white creamer drips down his hand and onto the tabletop.

I love it and groan and retch for them as I walk by.

I can just tell Sir Charles Smithson is going to hate our brew - especially our cups - and I select one with a big yellowed chip out of the rim, just for him. It's a test, Sister, to see how he reacts. I shouldn't, but just for good measure, I press my lips to the edge before bringing it to him. It makes a nice red "Poison Potion" lipstick mark, which I smear just enough, right there where he'll be wanting to drink. I experience a moment of guilt, Sister, yes, I do. I cannot think what possesses me sometimes, but you know it's not going to hurt him. I mean, I don't have cooties.

Besides, what he says and what he does could color his entire future. He doesn't know that yet, of course.

He stares at the cup, and the look on his face is so full of disgust that I wonder if he's thinking about complaining to Fred. But he surprises me. He doesn't say anything, just puts the cup aside and sits there waiting. His buddy drinks up, talking animatedly about the golf game, *his* golf game, darting sly looks at Kitty, who's now hovering over a pair of soft, wrinkled, little women a few tables down. Smithson's companion can't stop bragging, louder and louder, about how he expertly pitched up within inches for a tap-in bird on the seventeenth. Oh, he was a regular Jordan Spieth today. His voice sure is big. I'm hoping Kitty is getting it all, so we don't have to hear an encore.

Old Honorable looks bored to death, and a little sick, too. Can you blame him?

I've delivered the coffee and I'm about to turn back to the kitchen, when I spot the slosh of skillet grease on the floor. I couldn't have planned this better if I'd stayed up all night plotting. Of course I hesitate, Sister. I know what I'm about to do is wrong, but I'm sorry to say that I bury that flicker of guilt. I step forward confidently, swoosh my foot out before me, grab onto the metal coat rack, and go flying into the lap of The Honorable Charles Fitzham Smithson the Second. The coat rack clatters around me.

It's a perfect landing. My eggy apron rubs up against his Calloway golf shirt, and I smile a coy apology. He jumps up from the booth, latching onto my arms and looking more pained than any rich guy ever has a right to look. He doesn't shriek and brush me off like he might a cockroach, and I take this as a real good sign.

With his help, I stand up, but it isn't hard to get my legs to buckle under me. Smithson doesn't have much choice but to stand there holding me up with two unwilling fingers. Kitty glares at me and stalks off to take care of some folks across the room, and I gaze into The Honorable's wonderful blue eyes. He gazes at my dishrag, which is now plastered to his shirt front. He peels it off with a grimace.

"Lucky!" Fred yells from behind the row of soup tureens.

"What!" I scream back. We do this periodically at Chez Fred's. The customers expect us to act like grubs. We oblige.

"Whassa problem?" Fred says, all excited. He comes out from behind the lentil vegetarian and rights the coat rack. "Whassa trouble?"

"Well," I say slowly, with a sultry smile at Smithson, "it looks as if I won't be finishing out the day, Fred. I think I've sprained my ankle."

The companion has bounced up from the booth and is wringing his paper napkin into a tight wad. "Can you walk?" he says. He is greatly concerned.

"I'm not sure." I smile bravely. Sir Charles is still looking perturbed, and I don't trust him to come through for me, but the friend seems like a mellow kind of guy, so I turn my charm on him. "It's paining me fierce," I say. "I oughtta go home. Only problem, I don't have a car, and I don't think I should walk on this. Any chance you could drop me?"

"Of course we will," says Chuck's buddy with quick enthusiasm. "Where do you live?"

It isn't far. I tell him, and he gives me a warm smile, always happy to help a damsel in distress. Kitty is giving me killing looks over the soft ice cream machine.

5

Smithson tosses some bills and change on the table, and Fred says, "Yeah, but, hey . . . ," and I play my role of helpless victim, wincing in pain to add a little drama to the part. We leave Fred sputtering behind us, and Kitty glowering, and everybody else staring, while Charles and the friend help me out the door to the road, where the greatest little BMW convertible I have ever seen is parked. Just for fun, I collapse again before we get in. Friendly has already gone around to the driver's seat, which leaves His Royalty to take care of me.

He's not a happy camper. He reaches down and lifts me up, and a lesser person would wilt at the look on his face.

I'm not kidding when I say he picks me up. Literally. He hates it, but he does it.

He shoves me into the back seat, trying to hide his aversion, and slams me in. I'm ecstatic. I know, Sister, that this is wrong of me, but I've been waiting for this chance for years. Now that it's here, I'm carrying it as far as it'll take me.

Did I mention that Sir Charles Fitzham Smithson the Second stole my castle nineteen hateful years ago? Yes, every girl's dream, a real castle, complete with turrets and towers and leaking pipes. There may even be a treasure hidden there, and I aim to find out. Mainly, I aim to get my castle back.

He thinks I'm just a clumsy waitress with a rotten attitude. He's about to find out that I'm also a pest with a short fuse - and a long memory.

◇◇◇

It's such a neat ride. I've never ridden in a BMW before, and I adore every minute of it. The breeze blows my hair back, and I look out at the passing scenery with my nose tilted up in a happy snoot. Call it practicing for the future.

By now, of course, Charles Smithson's friend has introduced himself as Lionel Hawthorne, a card-carrying, bona-fide member of the local idle rich. He goes on and on about his many acres of wooded property, his boat, his new house, his car, his golf membership, and his several big wins at the casino, which make it all possible. He never asks who I might be, and I don't like to be indelicate, so I don't mention it. Mr. Smithson is silent and morose as we ride along.

"I suppose I'll lose my job over this," I say finally. It would be gentlemanly if they'd at least pretend some interest in my

6

collapsing financial future, but they don't. "Fred's not too keen on unexpected absences," I say. Lionel nods, and His Excellency looks straight through the front windshield. I keep trying. "Bills to pay, debts I owe. Fred doesn't pay that much in the first place; I really need to find something else. I don't know what I'll do now that I'm injured. What if he fires me?"

Finally, Lionel rises cheerfully to the bait. "But he can't fault you for a sprained ankle. It happened at work. For all he knows, you could file a complaint."

I sigh. "No, Fred knows I would never do that. I'm just afraid he'll throw me out if I miss too much time." This is such a huge whopper that I have trouble containing my grin, but neither of them is looking at me anyway.

"That's hardly fair," Lionel tries again. "You could sue-"

This Lionel could really screw up my progress here. I cut him off quickly. "I'm sure I'll be fine in no time, but I've probably lost my job now and it might be a little difficult searching for employment while I'm handicapped like this," I say. "It's a shame, too. I'm such a hard worker. Do either of you know of anything?"

Lionel glances at his buddy, but Smithson just stares straight ahead. It's as if he didn't even hear me. The bore's bore. Maybe this is going to be harder than I thought.

The ride is over all too soon. When Lionel Hawthorne pulls up outside the crummy house I live in and Sir Charles gets to doing that grimace-thing he's so good at, I get ready to hop out.

Then I remember I'm supposed to be injured, so I sit tight.

Lionel is around the car in a flash, opening doors, helping the little lady exit the car. Now this person is mannerly; I am truly impressed. He keeps up a happy chatter as he escorts me up the steps of my house. He's even discreet as he glances around to take in the three rusty mailboxes and the stained paint on the walls of my building's front hall. I can smell the hamburger and onions someone cooked for last night's dinner, and that little kid who lives above me is crying again. I always wonder why he's crying. I wish he'd stop.

Lionel doesn't make any comments, just looks politely past the wreckage of my environment and smiles benignly. Is that good breeding or what?

He leaves me there, and I thank him for the lift and glance out at Smithson, who is slouching in the car, rubbing one tired hand over his eyes. Impatient. Obnoxious. Doomed. I've given

7

him this opportunity to prove himself to me, and he has failed the test. You might think I should be more tolerant, Sister, but I've thrown myself into his lap and seen him respond as if I'm a slug on his watercress sandwich. He's all caught up in his own importance. Mr. Moneybags. Well, that won't last. If I didn't like him before, I despise him now, and it helps me stick to my guns.

The tiny paper square that I cut from last Tuesday's *Franklin County Express* is safely tucked away in my genuine imitation ostrich hide wallet. I still have time to rip his pompous ad into shreds to scatter into the dumpster parked permanently by my front door; I can dash the dreams I've been nurturing my whole life. Or I can turn Charles F. Smithson's life into a living hell; I can answer his Help Wanted classified.

I guarantee he'll be groveling before long. Don't forget; he has my castle. I ask you, Sister Mary Phyllis, haven't people, historically, gone to battle for far less? I'm not proud of myself, but I would be less than honest if I didn't say that I know now I'll be after him with both barrels. And I'll win. Oh, yes.

They don't call me Lucky for nothing.

# 2

THE DRIVEWAY TO THE CASTLE curls between a double row of high, straggly cedars which hide the building from view of the road beyond. I bet a lot of people driving by here don't even know there's a castle just a few hundred yards away. That's fine by me. I've never been big on sharing.

Chunks of driveway gravel are hard and sharp under my shoes, and as I walk toward my castle, I know I'm hoping to recapture the bright joy of the good old days.

It's weird to have a castle here in the Adirondacks. We North Country folk usually go in for log cabins, waterfront bungalows, and the occasional fake Swiss chalet. So my castle is unique, imposing, and very cool, and as I stand here looking up at this monument to my former life, I realize the castle has certainly seen better days.

It's small as castles go, but it's a real, live castle all right, with a circular driveway and three stories of gray granite, some of it crumbling now. There are funny side wings and a nicely rounded tower which is listing slightly to the left, plus a crooked turret which I happen to know has a little attic room. Tall, skinny windows pounce out here and there, with leaded mullions and old iron cranks you have to turn, sometimes with both hands, to get any air.

There are two terraces on the ground level, one in front and one in back; the one I can see is looking a little bedraggled. And, off the west side, there's a nice, slanty little balcony with a table you could use for luncheons if you didn't mind your plate and silverware sliding downhill and hitting the castle wall with a clatter.

Thick forest stretches away for miles in three directions. I remember my father warning me to stay out of those woods; you could be lost in there for days, he'd say. He didn't need to tell me twice. I spent my time on the lawns that still creep out on all sides of the castle, weedy and scratchy-looking. I can almost picture sweaty, rotund servants beating the dust from rugs or elegant ladies dancing out here in the moonlight in their gossamer gowns.

Not that I ever saw such things here. In my time, it was pretty much Dad and me sitting on webbed lawn chairs, letting the stiff, brown grass prick our toes, and Mother inside, lying down with a headache or admonishing Nancy about some chore left undone. Or Dad with his sawhorses set up on the side lawn, creating some crafty wooden bank or clock or sports team memento that he'd take to sell at whatever local craft fair he could find.

Not that he needed to do that. We had plenty of money, but the work amused him, and he loved interacting with the people. He sold those crafts for pennies and came home full of good cheer and ready to make more.

Right now, there's a dirty, fat-wheeled tricycle turned over on its side in the weeds and a dug-up dirt patch, where last year's brittle flower stalks poke hopefully into the air.

I wonder if the castle was always this decrepit or if Smithson has thoughtlessly gone to town destroying property that rightfully belongs to me. The place looks ugly as sin, cold, drafty, and dank. I can't wait to take over and cheer it up some.

But I loved it here as a kid. My father told stories that made me laugh, and Nancy played with me, and my world revolved around the two people who loved me best.

I'm on the terrace now, and I have to admit that I find the scarred, mammoth oak door before me just a mite intimidating. It's slightly ajar and about four inches thick, and those black hinges are as long as my arm. I square my shoulders, grasp the heavy iron ring centered before me, and bang it against the metal plate.

Some door knocker. I don't remember it, but it's even with my forehead, so I probably never noticed it as a kid. I wonder if anyone inside can actually hear the clang, so I look around, see the dimly lit doorbell button, and decide to push that, too.

The castle dates from 1860, and it isn't fair that my father was forced to give it up because of Charles Smithson Senior. Of course I've held a grudge, Sister! Anyone in my situation would.

I'm pondering this and other unfairnesses of life when this blonde-headed urchin with pudgy pink arms and a runny nose, maybe three or four years old, peers around the crack of the open door and then slithers onto the terrace. She throws her whole weight against the door, forcing it open. I step around her and enter what should rightfully be my castle. I'm wondering how she figures into the equation and am not at all happy with the answer I come up with.

It might pain me to evict a baby.

She hasn't said anything, just stares at me as I look around at the grand entrance hall to my former home, at the oversized foyer with its heavy stone walls and worn, cracked, black and white marble tile floor in a checkerboard pattern. The ceiling is way up there, and I have to admit: I, Lucky Wilta, feel small.

The sprightly scamp in her ruffled pinafore disappears and leaves me alone in the entryway, which I'm sure makes us both much happier. I take a deep breath and try to remember.

My most vivid memory of living in the castle is an incident that happened the day before we were forced out. I was heartsick and frightened, and would have been more so if I'd known the turns my pathetic life was about to take. On a table in this very foyer, there was a heavy glass star, a paperweight, I guess; neither table nor star is here now. The star was as large as my two hands put together, and I loved to heft it and run my fingers over the blunt points to feel the solidness of it. It was so thick that when I held it up to the light, objects on the other side would turn gray and hazy through the smooth glass.

I wanted to take that star with me when we left the castle.

My father said no. He said it had been left here by Clymna Borstrom, the first person to own the castle, that it belonged to the castle and wasn't mine. "You don't need to grab someone else's star, Lucilla," he said. "Find your own star. And then just make sure you keep it polished."

I knew vaguely what he meant, still do, but from that point on, I never seemed to have much of anything that resembled, in any fashion, a star. How could I keep it polished when I didn't know what or where it was?

Well, Sister, I tell myself that I'm about to claim my star. I just needed to come back home to do it.

But as I look around, I'm wondering why my memories seem so warm and wonderful. This does not feel like a warm and wonderful place.

The walls are stark stone - cold, creepy, and primitive. I can hear dripping in some far off corner, and there's not much light to cheer the place up.

I know, though, that other parts of the castle have been modernized, that wooden studs, plaster, and drywall give the rooms substance and a more modern feel. There are wires and pipes behind those walls, with real heat and real water running through. The castle was finished off in a happy-go-lucky fashion, with a variety of finishes, so none of the rooms match. When you open a door, you never know what you're going to get.

I know some of the rooms are decorated, cozied up with wallpaper and carved panels, painted woodwork and electric outlets. In some places, there are hardwood floors over the stone; there used to be rugs, furnishings, and lamps, and enough of those useless items people set around on tables to make some parts feel real homey.

I recollect feeling safe and warm here in the past.

But the front hall I'm standing in is all rock, drafty and empty and very, very big. I guess you could easily fit my whole furnished room and bath into this entryway if you were inclined to put rooms inside each other.

The last time I was in this room I was ten, and the first time Little Charles Smithson the Second was in this room, *he* was ten. We met that day, nineteen years ago, and the memory is still as clear as water. They came in; we went out. From that day on, I felt like a poor kid instead of a rich one, and I never stopped hating the smug little boy who told me to pick up my china doll off his floor or he'd flatten her with his Tonka bulldozer.

My father subsequently lost all his money, just got poorer and poorer until finally it was all gone. We moved from house to house, each one smaller than the one before. And the Smithsons just got richer.

I believe people's financial status has a lot to do with the way they see themselves.

Me? I see myself as someday being rich and snotty. Money talks, loud, and I aim to have me some.

Yes, Sister Mary Phyllis, I know it sounds materialistic and shallow. But see it from my point of view. The castle - and everything in it - is rightly mine!

Until our fateful meeting at Chez Fred's last week, I hadn't seen Sir Charles since our childhood tiff in this checkerboard foyer, but my disgust with him had grown and blossomed over the years. Oh, I'd seen his picture in the newspaper, never for accomplishing anything valuable like curing cancer or exploring Mars, just for rich people things. You know, horse things, boat things. Apparently, he has no purposeful way to occupy his time. With all that money, at least he could fund a mental institution or sponsor a clinic for retired rag sorters, or maybe a home for wayward waitresses. But not this prince.

I admit I'm feeling a little superior, and maybe that's wrong of me, but at least I'm not drifting through life completely without a goal. I have a goal: to get my castle back. To be a genuine certified snob.

◇◇◇

I wander around the foyer, trying to decide if I recognize any of the furnishings. Everything looks so much worse than I remember. On one wall, there's a clump of faded sepia photographs in frames, prune-faced people glaring archly, someone's rather important-looking, well-brushed hound, a cluster of men posed stiffly on the staircase I'm standing near. Some things haven't changed much. Same pitted floor, same Adirondack tapestry hanging on the far wall, although it's bigger in the photo. It looks pretty frayed on one side now, and I figure someone cut off a couple feet to even up the scraggly edges.

I glance around and my eye catches a printed sheet of paper framed in pale wood and tacked up on the other side of the room. I amble over to have a look.

*Live with honor*, it says, *refrain from lion.*
*The mane thing is to cease your sighin'.*
*If my orthography leaves you scowling,*
*Imagine my secretary weeping and howling.*

It's signed Lewie Forsythe, and I know he once owned the castle, but I have no idea what he was getting at with this poem. The castle foyer is like that, though. A weird, unmatching décor that sure doesn't make me feel welcomed or appreciated.

I'm concerned whether this pretentious Sir Charles is taking good care of my inheritance, and I look back at the pictures again to see what else has changed over the years. The nasty-looking guy at the front of the photo group is grasping the newel post of the banister, his hand closing over a lion's head about six inches around. The lion's beady eyes stare straight ahead; its ferocious wooden mouth is open, baring sharp, dripping fangs. Its mane is flying - jagged wooden points that could prick your fingers.

I glance back at Lewie Forsythe's poem on the other wall and make the connection. He may have been inspired by that very carving.

It isn't there now, though. The railing ends in just a rough wooden knob. But the photo jogs my memory, and I remember how scared I used to be of that lion's head. So scared my mother would urge me to touch it and then laugh at my quivering lip. My father would take me gently from her and carry me up to bed; by the time we reached the landing, we'd be smiling over shared secrets and whispering about the next day's plans.

Well, the lion's head must have broken off at some point and been tossed into the Smithson dumpster. Fine with me. Occasionally, change is for the best.

I glance around the foyer and shiver. I spot an odd-shaped, cut-glass bowl that looks familiar and a big, cracked Chinese vase that I think I used to hide in. On the side wall, there's one of those antique mirrors that stretches from the floor up twelve feet or so, and I creep over to see how I look for my interview. I turn my head this way and that, squinting a little to soften my own sharp features.

Okay. Here I am in this ornately carved, maybe even priceless - if it weren't for the crack down the center - mirror, and, to my great disappointment, I look the same as always. Long, straight, dull brown hair. Lusterless would be a good word. And I'm too tall and too thin, which makes all my features look the wrong size. I have a sharp, straight nose and angular cheekbones, nondescript brown eyes, and a smile way too wide.

I need to smile a lot less; I'm always reminding myself of this.

I also have a pointy chin that looks too small for my face. And ears that are flat, yes, but not tiny and delicate the way I'd like.

I do have a good complexion, though. Peaches and cream. Smooth as velvet. Sleek as a hairless rat.

All my life, people have looked me over, up and down and sideways, and then after a long, thoughtful, searching pause, shrugged and pronounced how lovely my complexion is.

I wonder why one of Fred's early bird regulars hasn't snatched me away by now.

It's a nice mirror though. And I'm examining the chipped gilt frame of that mirror, *my* mirror, when my new friend Mr. Charles Smithson enters from a far arched doorway.

Now this guy is good-looking. I've always known that from the newspapers, but his face was so sad and, yes, disgusted when

14

he came to Chez Fred's to not drink coffee that I'm surprised now to see how really fabulous-looking he is. He's smiling and walking toward me with his hand extended, and his blue eyes are twinkling a merry welcome. Wow. He's *really* looking forward to this interview!

He stops suddenly, his eyes hide behind themselves, and his mouth falls into a disappointed grimace. Obviously, he's spotted an earwig on the draperies behind me.

"It's you," he says.

"The same," I grin. Then I remember about not smiling, and pull a frown that almost matches his own.

He sighs. "Sit down, please." He gestures to a couple of chairs in front of a yawning black fireplace, and I take the one that's almost hidden behind a big, dead potted fern.

"This needs water," I suggest. A rough brown frond is tickling my nose, and I wiggle it, my nose I mean, to try to keep from sneezing. Finally, I just break off a handful of dead fronds to get a better view of the Greek god sitting opposite me.

Like before, he's dressed impeccably, this time in tan pants and a crisp navy blue jacket. I really like his tie, which has whimsical little sailboats all over it. Not many men could get away wearing a dorky tie like that. It's perfect on him.

Those blue eyes are clear and gorgeous, and his blonde hair is cut just right - not too long, not too short, just a hint of an unruly, boyish wave in the front. He must have some barber.

I like his nose, which is nice and straight, and I like his teeth, which are just slightly crooked, and I like his ears, which are a lot cuter than mine. Sir Charles Fitzham Smithson the Second looks just the way I've always wanted to look. But more manly, of course.

Not for the first time in my life, I wonder what pressing business God was attending to when it came my turn to get features.

"God, there's a girl here who says she needs features."

"Don't bother me, my child. Just tell her to select from the scrap heap."

"But, God, there is nothing left in the scrap heap."

"Then have her look under that rock over there."

I sigh. The Honorable Charles Fitzham Smithson the Second sighs, too, and sits staring at me, crumpled in his chair. Is he going to tell me how lovely my complexion is?

I find myself wondering what to do with the pieces of dead

fern I am holding. I look around for a wastebasket or maybe one of those elegant cuspidor things, but there's nothing, so I drop them to the floor. For a moment, we both sit staring at fern fronds.

"You're Lucilla Wilta?" he finally asks. It sounds like this huge effort, as if he had to reach way down into his innermost soul to pull up those three little words.

I grin. "Always was, always will be, forever and ever, Amen." Then I go back to frowning.

He sighs again and looks around, wondering if there might be a different Lucilla Wilta hiding behind that big urn over there or maybe lying perfectly flat, stifling a giggle, under the Oriental carpet. To his complete chagrin, there's only me, and he looks back at me and shifts uncomfortably in his chair.

"Lucky," I tell him.

"What?"

"Lucky."

"I know, I heard you. What is?"

"My name. No one calls me Lucilla. I'm just Lucky."

"Oh." He sounds incredibly sad, like this is really bad news.

"Well," I decide to help him along. "Thanks for answering my letter answering your ad. It's great to be here, and, as you know, I have perfect qualifications for the job. I've been cooking at Chez Fred's for years . . . ."

"Your letter was deceptive," he says. "I wouldn't call Fred's a gourmet kitchen."

I wave that away. "Chez Fred's," I correct him.

"The sign out front just says Fred's," he points out.

"Ah," I answer, "but those in the know . . . ."

"Anyway . . . ." He tries to pull us back on track.

"Good wholesome food served there," I say. "You look as if you could use some." He does, too. If he weren't quite so thin, he'd be perfect. Maybe I'll make that one of my projects - to fatten up The Honorable Mr. Smithson. "Anyway," I continue, "I can cook. And I can clean anything, use lots of spit and polish. This place'll sparkle." I glance around. Sparkle might be an exaggeration.

"Miss Wilta, I have to admit, I'm a little at a loss."

"I can see that," I say, misunderstanding on purpose, as I peer at the dust bunnies and cobwebs surrounding us. "What happened? Cleaning staff all quit on the same day?"

"No, there wasn't a staff," he says stiffly. "Just a woman who

16

came in to help me, Mrs. Frocks. She left suddenly. She's getting older, and my daughters . . . ." He looks profoundly sad as he looks me over. "She's not coming back."

There was a wife, though. I'm sure of this. I remember seeing their idyllic wedding portrait in the newspaper. His Honorable Self and a cute little blonde thing who presumably is the mother of the wee lass who opened the door for me. Where is she then? I'm guessing she's not around, thus his melancholy demeanor.

"Big place for one man to manage alone," I say with a nod. "Unless your wife . . . ."

"No," he says. "No wife."

Hmm. An interesting puzzle that I will have lots of time to figure out.

"Was that tiny being who let me in your daughter?"

His eyes brighten. "Yes, Pansy. She's four."

"Lovely," I say enthusiastically. I don't mean it however. Good God. Pansy.

"That's part of the job, too. To look after my daughters during the day."

I was afraid of this. The word was definitely plural, and I do some fast calculating. Cooking I can handle. Cleaning I can avoid. But wiping noses? Potty-training? Hearing whiny, high-pitched voices talk about pee? I hadn't counted on kiddies, and with my own mother as role model, I don't have a clue how to manage them. The learning curve will be not only long, but steep. As far as I'm concerned, the pay has just doubled.

My own experience of mothers is limited. They are people who promise a trip to town for ice cream after dinner, then do a quick U-turn when you forget to push in your chair or neglect to place your napkin on your lap. They are people who create difficult rules for every occasion, but never tell you not to run in the upstairs hallway, then snatch away your Barbies when they catch you running.

They are tired and hypocritical and sometimes mean, annoyed all the time and not much interested in you or your thoughts.

Motherhood, I am convinced, must be a terrible, exhausting thing. And I know I'm not cut out for it.

"Your ad says housekeeper," I remind him.

"Yes, but child care, too," he says. "Pansy is four. Violet is three." How quaint. A flower garden of little girls. Can three year olds walk? Can they talk? Can they eat anything besides mashed bananas? I feel like I've landed in Munchkinland. Since he's staring at me, I decide I should look enthusiastic. I brighten myself up.

He sighs yet again. "Look, Miss Wilta, why don't I tell you about the responsibilities of the position and introduce you to the girls. Then I'll be in touch with you in a few days about my decision."

"Gotcha." I grin. Then I wipe it away as he begins to tell me all the things he'll expect me to do. Cooking, cleaning, nursemaiding. Marketing and laundry. Raking and some gardening if I choose to, which I don't, and balancing a household budget, which I don't want to do either. He'll hire other people to work with me if I want. And if I could fit in some minor maintenance projects, that would be great. I could do a little painting, maybe put up some new curtains . . . .

What he really wants is a person to take over his life for him. This guy doesn't want a housekeeper, he wants a troop of slaves.

He hasn't mentioned digging wells or erecting cell towers, and I consider making the suggestion. I find myself wondering what he'll be doing all day while I work myself into an early grave.

Either he's hopelessly stupid or incredibly lazy. The third option is that he's fabulously rich, which seems unlikely, given the decrepit state of the castle. However, when he mentions the salary he intends to pay, I decide the fabulously rich option must be right. I'll get more in six weeks than I make at Chez Fred's in half a year, and that includes tips.

I can handle that. I'm no dummy. I guess I can learn how to do kids.

"There's no internet here," he tells me. "And no cell service. Just so you know. There's a land line, of course, with a couple of extensions, and mail is delivered right to the foot of the driveway. Would that be a problem for you?" I hate to say it but his eyes look almost hopeful. I dash that hope when I tell him I'm okay with that.

He takes me through a massive, scarred double door and into what looks like a big playroom. I don't remember playing in here; I think it may have been a reception room nineteen years ago, or maybe a parlor. Something we never used anyway, but I think I recognize the tattered curtains hanging over the wide double windows. The walls are rough rock, and it seems to me there were some velvet sofas, threadbare even then, but there's no sign of them today. Now it's full of Fisher Price furniture and little pink appliances pushed up against the stones, cunning child-size tables and chairs, shelves of puzzles, games, books, and dolls. Dozens of dolls.

Violet and Pansy are sitting on a miniature wicker sofa, each feeding a life-size plastic doll with a realistic-looking plastic bottle. The girls look alike except for the color of their dresses. One is yellow, the other lavender. Two tiny bodies, two pale faces surrounded by thick, pale hair. Two pink mouths twisted in suspicious reserve. Together, they tilt back their dolls' heads, letting fake formula dribble down fake throats. It all looks incongruous against the dark dampness of the rock walls.

"Hiya, kids," I say.

The mouths clamp tighter.

One little nose is running. "Pansy," her father says, and he pulls out a moist white handkerchief and wipes her snot lovingly away. I could regurgitate. But I don't. I think they can sense my ambivalence anyway because both girls stare at me, silent and unsmiling. Smithson gives me a bleak look.

"Girls," he says finally. "This is Miss Wilta." There is no mistaking the sorrow in his voice. "Why don't you come and say hello."

Together, his daughters jump up from the wicker couch and run to him, clinging to his legs, one on the left leg, one on the right. He keeps urging them to talk to me, but they refuse, burying their faces in his trousers. Pansy wipes her nose on her father's pants, and I watch, fascinated, as he tries unsuccessfully to remove first one girl, then the other.

"They don't go to school yet," he's explaining. "So I need someone who can keep them out of mischief all day long."

"And do all that other stuff besides?" I ask.

"Violet, stop," he says weakly. She climbs farther up his left leg and wraps both skinny legs around him. He pushes her gently down and says, "Well, other people can be hired to help, too." Violet, hanging on tight, has now hooked one muscular little ankle around a chair rung. Every time her father tries to move, the chair drags, too. I watch, spellbound. Finally, he decides we've all had enough and firmly extricates both children. The chair clatters sideways. He escorts me back through the arched doorway, and the tots follow.

"I have to have someone here by Wednesday," he says. "I need to be away for a while after that, so you'll hear from me by

19

then."

Both girls have crept up behind him and are hiding behind his knees, staring at me. By this time, I'm not really listening, and I've also pretty much forgotten which kid is which. They're both little, blonde, and aggravating, and except that Pansy is about two inches taller and has fatter arms and a runny nose, they look the same to me. Identical gnats. Interchangeable children.

I'm trying to remember a trick I learned from Miss Mavette's Study Skills class in junior high school. Making up a word game to recall information. A mnemonic device, mnemonic with a silent 'm.'

"Okay," she would tell us, smiling her big, lipsticky smile. "My Very Elegant Mother Just Served Us Nine Pimentos."

We'd all repeat that, then Miss Mavette would clap in hearty delight and say it again. It was the planets, see. In order, too. Mars or Mercury - that was 'My;' 'Very' was Venus; 'Elegant' was Earth; and on and on until 'Pimento' was Pluto. You get the idea.

The problem was I could never remember whether My was Mars and Mother was Mercury, or the other way around. And did Mother Serve the Pimentos, Slice them, Stew them, or Sanitize them?

Maybe she knitted the Pimentos into a Sock. Or Pickled them in Scotch.

It probably doesn't matter since Pluto was stripped of its planetary status anyway. So apparently everything we learn in school is up for rebuttal. You can see why school was never my strong point. Not because I'm inherently dumb, but because I just didn't care. Why learn a bunch a stuff that's just going to change?

Anorthosite rock. Now there's something that stays the same for about a billion years.

But, glancing again at these two messy-headed urchins playing peek-a-boo behind their father's legs, I figure one of these do-it-yourself devices is worth a try.

The one in the purple dress is Violet; on this I'd stake my Chez Fred's five per cent employee discount. So I think to myself that P (Purple) = V (Violet), and since her arms are Skinny, also S. The other one, Pansy, has Fatter arms and a Yellow dress, so P = F = Y.

So far, so good. P = V = S and P = F = Y. I start memorizing this, then take another look at the kids. It occurs to me that, by my calculations, they're both named Pansy, and I'm not sure why. If P = S (Skinny), how can P = F (Fat)? I have to back up some, and I'm doing that, standing there trying to identify the real Pansy and figure out whatever happened to Violet, when I realize Sir Charles Fitzham Smithson has been rambling on, and I've lost the thread.

One of his daughters looks up at him tearfully. "How many days 'til you go back away?" she asks in a wobbly little voice.

"A few, sweetheart," he says apologetically. "I'll be here for a few more days." He looks guilty as sin.

Her lower lip begins to tremble, and soon the tears begin. Daughter two, Violet maybe, takes one look; she had almost forgotten to cry on cue, but now she blats out nice and loud, a good, hearty sound. They both cling to him, sobbing away, and poor old Smithson looks slightly embarrassed. This guy is some effective parent. I almost feel sorry for him, but stop myself.

The castle, I think. He owes you big time.

"Say good-bye to Miss Wilta," begs Mr. Ineffectual. They ignore him. He's scraping Pilot/Vansy off himself again and blotting at Vansy/Pilot with his already damp hankie. They don't say good-bye, of course, and neither does he, just stands there wishing Mrs. Frocks could have hung on to see the babies safely into holy matrimony.

I chuck each kid gently on a wee, scrawny shoulder, which sets them to howling even more pitifully. Jeepers. It was meant to be friendly. "Great to've metcha," I say.

"You realize, though," His Eminence calls after me, "I do have a few other people to interview, several other interested applicants."

"Natch," I respond, and I let myself out the way I came in.

Who does he think he's kidding? No one in her right mind would make a conscious choice to take over that household. You'd have to be nuts. Or have an ulterior motive.

Already, my mind is reviewing all the things I'm going to insist on in my contract. I chuckle to myself as I skip on down the pretentious winding driveway. Several other people, yeah, right.

I check his rural delivery mailbox as I pass through the gate and thank my lucky stars we're in the primitive, backwoods Adirondack Park, where cell service and internet access are available, but not to everyone, at least not yet.

Yes, the mail has arrived. You're not going to like this, Sister, but I might as well come clean. Deftly I pocket three more letters that look like they could be answers to his ad. Of course I struggle internally for a second or two. I know it's wrong, but I'll check each one when I get home. If it's something else, a personal letter maybe, or a bill in disguise, I'll reseal it and re-deliver it, just like the ones I picked up yesterday and the day before. I'm honest, Sister. I'm not really stealing his mail. Well, I'm only stealing certain things.

Chances are, no one else would accept his outrageous terms anyway, but I have to ensure that.

The job has to be mine.

I want the sunny days of yore again; I want my castle.

No one is going to cheat me out of this.

# 3

I LOOK AROUND at the dingy green walls of my rented room. For one person, an unfussy person, it's not bad. Noisy sometimes, with kids crying overhead, and not your *HGTV* type of layout, but big enough to stretch out in, a little stove and refrigerator in the corner, my own bathroom. I've been making it home for the last three years, since I returned to Duck Vly, a tiny burg deep in the heart of the Adirondack Park, and the rent is cheaper than cheap. But my days here are numbered, and I heave a big, satisfied sigh over that. I'm looking forward to living in my castle again.

I dump Sir Charles Fitzham Smithson the Second's mail on my table and peer around in my cupboards for something to eat. A can of soup will do tonight. I heat it up and crumble in some crackers, and then eat right out of the saucepan. Won't be doing *that* much longer. Won't it be great? An unlimited grocery budget, fancy appliances, people to cook for. I like to cook, and I'm good at it. Smithson is likely to be pleasantly surprised.

Just as I suspected, the three letters are answers to his puffed-up newspaper ad, three perfectly qualified housekeepers who would certainly fit the bill better than I will. But let them find their own castles. Squelching a flicker of guilt, I tear the letters into tiny shreds and burn them in a bowl over my eating table, stirring the ashes with a little water and then dumping it all in the garbage.

So much for the competition.

My victory is so close I can almost taste it, and I feel like celebrating a little. I pop a Bud Light, and from the little strongbox in the corner, I pull my father's diary. It's an elegant thing, covered in red leather and monogrammed with his initials: *L. T.* for Luke Todd. He could afford such things before the Smithsons stole into our home and disrupted our happy lives.

*We leave today*, he writes. *Charles Smithson's belongings are strewn over the foyer and steps. I'm still getting used to the idea that he won the castle, and I wish we'd drunk a little less. I hope good things await me in Ohio.*

Sir Mr. Smithson the First, the father of the Honorable Charles, may have inherited a fancy title, but he was nothing more than a drunken gambler. I wonder if Charles has ever faced this fact. He must feel some guilt over the despicable way his father won the castle from mine. A drunken card game, a rash wager, and suddenly we were forced to move. My mother took sick shortly after when her kidneys began to fail. It was an illness that lingered for years and ushered in a long run of bad luck.

So, no, good things did not await my father in Ohio.

I have to admit, though, Daddy did a nice job caring for Mother until she died. Fooling her, actually. She was the upwardly mobile type, always reaching for those glittering stars just a tad out of reach on the social scale. I think she'd have died sooner if she'd known how fast we were going through Daddy's money. When she got sick, he spared no expense - round the clock nursing, all the necessary medical treatments, a live-in companion to keep her entertained.

Insurance didn't cover half of it, and Daddy and I watched in silence as the family fortunes drained slowly away - a succession of ratty homes, a car that hardly ran. Darned socks and threadbare sweaters. And a mother who could think of nothing but herself.

I've tried to convince myself that it was her illness that made her grouchy and selfish. But Mother was like that from the moment I first laid eyes on her.

And she thought we were loaded to the end.

If that had been true, I never would have settled for that bum, Nick Wilta. Even though my father tried to dissuade me from marrying Nick, he knew I'd do whatever I wanted to. So he indulged me, then he gave in and died and left me living with a thirty thousand dollar inheritance and a good-for-nothing bum.

Where that money came from I have never known; he had frittered his own away on Mother's so-called needs. But it was just like Daddy to find it for me. It's just a crying shame I had to share it with that worm, Nick Wilta.

Nick Wilta, now there was a piece of work. I married him because, I admit it, I'm an idiot. Daddy knew it wouldn't last, but, you couldn't tell Lucilla Todd anything.

For a while, I was Nick's obedient slave. Then I came to my senses and rebelled. We spent four years in a flat in Akron hurling ketchup bottles at each other and screaming our heads off for the amusement of the whole damn - sorry, Sister - neighborhood.

He finally packed up and went his merry way with a chick who works in a shoelace plant in Cleveland. Casual shoelaces, formal shoelaces, canvas, cotton, nylon, and jute shoelaces. The best shoelaces in the world. She should know. If she has any sense, she has strangled Nick with one by now.

I'm only sorry my father didn't live long enough for me to tell him how right he was.

Of course, that was years ago. And I'm glad to be back in the great state of New York. I miss my father, and any day now, I'm gonna notice how much I miss Nick Wilta. We're annulled, which, as you know, Sister, means we were never really married, at least in spirit. Like I need some piece of paper to tell me that.

I don't plan to repeat *that* mistake in this life. I shall never marry again.

And if I do, my engagement will be long and thoughtful, with plenty of time to seek your excellent guidance, Sister Mary Phyllis, and to see a good priest for advice, and to thoroughly digest the guy's most horrendous faults.

And he'll have to be rich.

I do miss my father, though. I'm still very sad that he died so young and left me to my own devices. But, heck, I'll survive; I always have. And I'm determined not to repeat my father's mistake and die in ignominious poverty.

I open Dad's diary to my favorite page. It opens there automatically; I read this page a lot.

*The castle walls drip with age and dampness. I hear the scurrying of mice and the shrill tones of a woman's voice,* he writes.

I don't recall the dampness - somehow I never saw it - but I know what woman he's talking about. Daddy's not kidding about my mother.

*Who would ever have guessed about the secret room,* he writes, *Strangely, I was led there by mice.*

Happily, mice don't worry me; I'm comfortable with mice.

Daddy continues, *And what a treasure - Diamonds of a thousand brilliant colors! My little Lucilla will stumble on that room one day - and the treasure hidden there, glittering like stars, but not as far from reach. Those diamonds! She can thank old Marsuvius Borstrom. There's the shrill command again, and coming closer. Time to find my way back to the secret room.*

*The quiet awaits me. All that's hidden there beckons.*

I've been reading that passage for years now, ever since my father died and left me his diary and pitiful bank statements and a few other pieces of useless junk that I treasure in spite of themselves. Besides his journal, the one decent thing he left me was that thirty thousand dollar wedding gift, and it's good he did or Nick and I would have starved that first year.

Marsuvius Borstrom is the chap who built the castle in the first place. By my calculations, he hid his treasure somewhere in the castle; my father found it - but at the time didn't need it - and now it's up to me to be smart enough to figure out where it is. I've cudgeled my brains speculating where there might be a secret room and how vast the treasure might be. It thrills me to know that in a few more days I'll be at liberty to explore the castle for myself.

I'm positive the elder Smithson never found the treasure. For one thing, he was much too stupid. He only won the castle by pure dumb luck. Could Charles, his son, be any smarter? Not likely. He sure hasn't figured out how to outwit his sniveling daughters. Besides, I have the diary. I'll know enough to look for the treasure; Smithson wouldn't even think of beginning.

Darkness has fallen, and I'm content as I snuggle into my familiar, lumpy bed with my library copy of *Moby Dick*. I'm loving this book, and I remind myself to recommend it to Hank before I leave Fred's for good. It's hard to concentrate, though; I can't stop thinking of my great new adventure.

Living in the castle. That's one of the perks I'm going to insist on. Enough time has been wasted over the years. My search must begin in earnest. My goal is double: to search out the treasure that's going to make me filthy rich. And to move back into my childhood home, to take back the castle that is rightfully mine.

◇◇◇

He offers me the job by dropping a note in my mailbox, since I don't even own a computer and, at the castle, the internet is only a hopeful dream. I know in my heart, however, it's to spare himself the terrible angst of having to deal with me yet again over the telephone, or, worse yet, in person. He tells me that Fred's reference was "outstanding." Fred never was a good judge of character.

He goes on for a while pretending it was a difficult decision, but says we'll give it a try, we'll see how it works, we'll reserve judgment on anything permanent, blah, blah, blah. All this in a nicely scripted note in a surprisingly firm handwriting.

He's not playing fair, and I'm not fooled.

I want him to grovel in person, so I do the logical thing and call the castle. At the last possible minute I do this, on Tuesday, since he needs me there by Wednesday. It won't hurt him to wait. This partnership is going to be on my terms, or no terms. And you know I won't settle for no terms.

He answers after seven or eight rings, and I can hear Pansy/Violet shrieking in the background.

"Yeah," I say, "put me on with The Honorable Sir Charles Fitzham Smithson the Second."

The voice at the other end exhales audibly. I recognize the trademark. "This is he."

"It's Lucky!"

There's a pause, but he doesn't say, "What is?" like I think he might. In this terrifically subdued voice, he says, "Miss Wilta."

"Forever and ever, Amen," I respond gaily.

"Have you decided to accept the position?" he asks.

Now you and I both know that I will, and we also know that he probably doesn't have any other prospects, but I decide I'll have a little fun with him before I let him hire me. Forgive me, Sister, I don't know what comes over me sometimes. I am working on this flaw.

"Well," I say, "I'm not sure. Was that your final salary offer?"

There's another pause. I can still hear Violet/Pansy screaming her head off, and then he says, "Would you excuse me?" The screaming goes off into the distance and eventually disappears. A minute later he's back, a little out of breath. "I'm sorry," he says. "What were you saying?"

"What did you do? Lock her in a closet?"

"No, of course not. She's out on the terrace."

It's a beautiful, blue-sky day, but the vision of Vansy out on that cold stone terrace while lightning strikes all around her is so appealing that I say incredulously, "In this weather? There's an electrical storm brewing. You knew that, didn't you?"

His voice becomes alert. "That's not true, is it?" I don't answer, and he hesitates. "Just a minute." Eventually, the screaming returns, softly at first, then doubled in intensity. "Now Violet's crying, too," he says, his voice getting loud. If I didn't hate him so much, I might feel sorry for him.

"Miss Wilta, are you coming to work for me?" he says stiffly, trying not to yell above his children, but needing to be heard. It's a trick - to remain cool and unruffled when inside you know you're only frantic Chuckie Smithson trying to con someone into taking your miserable offspring off your hands.

"Are you?" he repeats. He's giving in, shouting over the din of his daughters. "Because if you are, I need you as soon as possible."

"Well," I shout back, "we need to negotiate salary."

"Miss Wilta!" he hollers. "I already told you the salary!"

"Not enough!" I shriek. I'm not sure if he can hear me. Pansy and Violet have set up such a loud howling that I certainly have to work to hear him.

"Not enough?" he's yelling. I don't know how he does it; he sounds refined, even when he's shouting, and I'm pretty sure he isn't used to putting on this kind of a performance. Me, on the other hand, I holler at Kitty all the time, and on into the kitchen to let Fred know when your typical diner emergency occurs. Like the time we had a run of mealy bugs in all the pancake flour. Polka-dotted pancakes. We called them Circus Cakes and served them with a fun side of Jell-O.

Anyway, he's screeching at me over the phone lines about how it's a generous offer, more than I could hope to make anywhere else. I'm weighing all this and knowing, of course, that I'd take the job at a fraction of the pay, when suddenly there's an ear-splitting shriek right in my eardrum, and I go dizzy for a minute.

"Miss Wilta?" he's hollering. "Are you there?" He's apologizing all over the place and reprimanding Violet for grabbing the telephone from Daddy, and I can't believe it when he starts jabbering numbers at me. A new salary figure, double what he quoted me yesterday. Triple.

"Okay," I agree, pressing my advantage. "Now let's talk about benefits."

There's a huge commotion on the other end, and I can hear both girls crying and carrying on and Chuck Smithson trying to soothe them and admonish them all at the same time. They just keep howling.

"Miss Wilta? Miss Wilta?" He's back on the line.

"Lucky, please."

"Miss Wilta . . . ." It almost sounds as if he might start crying, too. "Can you come now? If you can, please come *now*. I have to *leave . . . .*"

"Well, I do have some pressing business," I say thoughtfully. "I might be able to break away the day after tomorrow . . . ." It's all wasted. Vansy and Pilot are drowning me out even before I speak.

"Please," he gasps, and the line goes dead.

I toss my cell phone aside and sit there in my ugly green room relishing the quiet. Then I throw a few things into my worn duffel bag, figuring I can return for the rest of my junk later. I call a cab, and I know it's going to cost a fortune, but, hey, it's a symbol of my new upscale lifestyle. I have the driver make just one quick stop before I give him directions to the castle.

I search the drugstore racks for a few minutes before I find it. *Dr. Harvard's Definitive Baby and Child Care Manual for the Uninitiated.* It's been a best seller for years, and I never thought I'd read it. Or need it.

The time has come. I'm on my way.

I'm going home.

# 4

THANK GOD YOU'RE HERE," he says. He grabs me by one arm and yanks me through the castle door. He looks a tad disheveled, and I can hear wild, childish noises beyond the closed foyer doors. He flings my overnight bag into a corner and starts to hustle me toward the children.

I have arrived.

"Don't we have papers to sign first?" I ask archly. "We still gotta discuss vacation days, sick leave, family leave, medical insurance, retirement, stock options . . . ."

He stops short and looks at me. "Stock options?"

"Stock options," I repeat. "Don't you offer them? I'm not going a step further until I'm sure you're not hiding what's due me." What's one more insanity? He groans and pulls me along.

I dig my heels in. Literally. "I mean it, Your Honor. These issues got to be settled." I snatch up my duffel and glance at the door as if I'm about to leave. I purse my lips and wait. Sister, I apologize, I know it's cruel, but, really, it's so funny to watch him shudder.

"Miss Wilta." His teeth are clenched. "All that can come later."

The screeching beyond has turned to hysterical sobbing. Smithson rushes away. I follow.

Pansy or Violet, whichever, is standing alone in the middle of a room I don't remember. Her little hands are clenched at her sides and her head is thrown back, eyes screwed tight shut, while she screams consistently and well. "Violet," The Honorable says. His voice is patient, but cracking some. "Violet, stop it." She ignores him.

He looks at me, bewildered and ashamed. "I'm not very good with the girls," he says. "Sometimes they mind me, but - Violet, please stop that!" he shouts. She doesn't. "When they know I'm leaving, they go crazy." Violet is still standing motionless, shrieking her little lungs out. "Can you do something?" he yells at me over the din. "Can you talk to her?"

Can I do something? Yep.

Can I *talk* to her? Get real, Charlie.

I'm pretty sure no mere conversation is going to stop this ruckus. I'm also pretty sure he's not that sincere in wanting to see my methods, so I look at him to be certain, a questioning look, and he stares back, helpless, embarrassed, begging.

Okay, then.

I walk briskly to the screaming Violet; her mouth is a perfect pink 'o' with a huge noise coming out. With one swift motion, I swing my duffel bag in a smooth arc and let it land, plop, on the floor beside me. It makes it big muffled thwack as it hits the floor. There's nothing in the bag but clothes, a couple books, a toothbrush and sage advice from Dr. Harvard, but the sound is loud, sudden, and satisfying. Violet pauses mid-scream and clamps her mouth shut. Her eyes bug out as she stares at me, then, the look on her face daring me to interfere, she lets loose with a shriek that puts her previous ones to shame. There's not a tear on her face, the little phony.

I flex all my muscles, ball my hands into tight fists, open my eyes wide and hunker down, leaning over and into her. Then, in as loud a voice as I can muster, I bellow, "Knock it off!" The sound reverberates in the suddenly silent room. "*Off . . . off . . . off . . .*" I suck in a breath and realize that Violet is completely still and absolutely silent, staring at me in awe. It worked.

No, it didn't. She yelps again, staring at me, but it's a short, pitiful effort; she's trying it out. I fill the void again, "I SAID, KNOCK IT OFF!"

I catch a glimpse of her father, grimacing and holding his head. "Miss Wilta!" he shouts over the din.

Violet's lower lip is quivering, and she's glancing at her father to gauge his reaction. I have the feeling she's considering crying in earnest.

Okay, so I screwed up. So what else is new? I always screw up.

Smithson gathers her into his arms, gives me a disapproving look, and carries her across the room to the door. She buries her yellow head in his shoulder as he pats her back with frantic, small pats.

Three year olds can walk, talk, *and* manipulate their fathers, I discover.

At the door, he turns back to me and musters a dignified tone. "Miss Wilta," he says evenly, "that's the last time you will shout at my children."

"Fine!" I shout. "I'll never shout at them."

"Or hit them," he continues. "Never hit them. No spanking, no hitting." He pauses. "You wouldn't, would you?"

I'm incensed. "Hit them? Of course I'd never hit them." What does he take me for? Some monster who beats innocent children? Who plays callous psychological games and chortles smugly at the confused looks on little girls' faces? I squelch the memories of my mother trying to creep into my brain.

"I would never do that," I say righteously. Then, just for fun, I add, "Well, probably not." At his chagrined expression, I add, "Jest joken widja."

He stalks off. Violet is burrowing into his shoulder, one suspicious eye fixed on me.

"Well, it worked, didn't it?" I holler after him. "Kind of?"

I return to the castle foyer. I don't know where Smithson has taken his daughter, but good etiquette requires that I wait for him. The exercise has taken its toll on me, so I lean on the rough knob of the banister and gaze at the old photos and portraits on the far wall. Old Forsythes or Rugginses, or maybe even Smithsons, former residents of the castle, pose unsmiling on the dark, creepy staircase. A glittering James Lowland, according to the brass plate below his jowly face. An ancestral Ruggins in a pretentious cutaway coat, extending a lorgnette and jeering out from the familiar far corner. The same tapestry of Adirondack flora and fauna forms a backdrop in several of the portraits. And all around are the shadowy walls, slippery and cold.

Suddenly it's eerily quiet in the castle, so quiet I can hear the tiny trickle of water down the stone walls. Horrible, damp place.

Is this really *my* castle? Land of my carefree childhood romps?

I have a feeling I've already botched my chance of success at this job. Well, why did he ask me to control her if he didn't mean it? How can he stand all that crying all the time?

I wander out of the foyer into a narrow corridor that's begging to be explored. Is this polite? Of course not. But I seem to have misplaced my Emily Post, and I wouldn't give a torn toenail even if I hadn't. The musty corridor is lined with heavy dark doors, crackled with age and all shut tight. I decide I might as well look around a bit.

If His Grace intends to toss me out after all, this could be my one and only chance to hunt for the elusive secret room and its fabulous treasure.

Lucky Wilta's favorite motto: Go for it.

I do.

◇◇◇

The castle was built by Marsuvius Borstrom in 1860 as a shrine to his beloved Clymna. Where these people got their names I don't know. But he built it for her - turret, tower, dank wet walls and all - as a monument to their love. Marsuvius moved his darling in, furnished the castle with all good things - and promptly lost it to his larger love, gambling. Marsuvius moved his darling out, a move that may actually have pleased her since she was, by that time, dying of tuberculosis. He turned the castle over to the dubious winner of the prize, a man named James Lowland.

One evening, not two years later, Lowland started a drunken brawl, which he lost, signing over the deed to one Harold Ruggins.

After Mr. Ruggins' inhabitancy, the history becomes a bit muddied until, years later, the name Robert Forsythe appears. His son Lewie managed to keep the castle and actually moved his family in for a number of years. But when he met up with my father, the irrepressible Luke Todd, Lewie was overcome with spirituous liquids and lost his mind temporarily one night. Thus, the castle changed hands again.

Its history is long and melodramatic. And since the Borstroms, Lowlands, Rugginses, and Forsythes are no longer around to fight for rights to the castle, it falls to me. Better a Todd should take possession than that it should languish in the hands of a Smithson.

Of course, my name is Wilta now, and this is probably the only valuable thing Nick Wilta ever gave me. C. F. Smithson the Second has no idea that he and I go back aways.

The corridor I'm exploring smells of mildew. Every door along the narrow passageway is closed, but I strike up enough nerve to open one and recognize a small pantry. Dusty, chipped crystal lines up neatly behind glass panels. Nothing spooky or mysterious here, so I decide to try my luck again, and I peek into the laundry room, newly outfitted with ultra-modern washer and dryer, a folding table, and a plastic tray of detergents and fabric softeners. An ironing board leans in the corner, and a few of

33

Smithson's shirts hang ready to be pressed. It all looks peculiar against the hard granite walls.

I turn a corner to find a tall, cramped bathroom with brand new fixtures. A thin window stretches from floor to ceiling, giving a fair amount of natural light. I steal a glance into the room next door and stop.

I recognize this room, an ugly, cavernous formal dining room. I know I ate meals in here as a child; I'd recognize that hideous wallpaper anywhere. This room hasn't changed much in nineteen years. The same complicated chandelier, the same tall windows and long, worn table. I recognize the tureens and statuary jumbled into the glass-fronted cupboards and some of the artwork, although I know the paintings on the far wall weren't here before.

The sounds of Mr. Smithson and his charge have long ago vanished, and I'm wondering if he might be looking for me or at least wondering where I've got to. I decide I'd better head back toward the front of the house. I get my bearings in the corridor and start back past all those closed oak doors. This is when I become aware of a figure scurrying toward me.

It isn't Charles. This guy's build is too slight, and his approach is much too eager. It isn't until he's practically before my face that I'm able to make out the friendly and unabashedly surprised features of Lionel Hawthorne.

"Well! Hello!" he greets me, and he instantly takes my arm. He's small and wiry, with an engaging smile and little white teeth like a row of sugar pearl August cob corn. I'm sure he has no idea what on earth I'm doing here, so I set about explaining.

"Capital!" he exclaims. It's one of those words rich people feel inclined to use when some little thing is pleasant.

"Yes, it just didn't work out at Fred's," I confide. "I'm so glad Mr. Smithson offered me this position. I'd be out on the street otherwise." It's not strictly true, Sister, but it *could* have been true. I need both men to believe it's true.

Lionel's face becomes sad, and he mumbles some sympathetic words. I know he's not sincere, but then, am I? For his millions, I could easily overlook a few faults. I decide to become interested in Lionel Hawthorne. There's something kind of cute about his elfish ways.

"How is your ankle?" he's asking me, and I tell him I'm surviving nicely. He's quite gallant as we walk back to the entry hall, and he pats my arm affectionately as I remember to limp along. He seems almost surprised to find The Honorable Charles Smithson there, in his own foyer, waiting for me.

"Where were you?" Smithson demands as we enter the room. He sounds petulant and spoiled. "I needed your help getting Violet settled."

"Getting acclimated," I say.

"Both girls are in bed for naps," he tells me. "Violet's already asleep."

The little darling must have worn herself out with her performance, and the father figure looks exhausted. "Lionel, go home," he says. "Miss Wilta and I have business matters to discuss."

Lionel doesn't seem the least perturbed by Smithson's brusque manner. He has feelings of steel. He turns to me, politeness a costume on him, draped prettily. "Miss Wilta?"

"Lucky."

"Lucky?"

"That's my name, Lucky. Always was, always will be, forever and ever, Amen." I grin at him.

"Charming," Lionel says, smiling. He takes my hand and gingerly kisses my fingers. I gotta admit, no guy has ever treated me this way before. I feel goosebumps come up on my arms. "Will you be living here, Lucky?" he asks with a sneaky glance at Smithson.

"Go home, Lionel," that person repeats. There's a tinge of annoyance in his voice, and his lips are puckered.

Lionel laughs. His tiny white teeth are merry. "Well, g'night," he says. "If it's okay with Mr. Smithson," he glances at his buddy Charles, "I'll stop by to pay my respects to you tomorrow." He laughs charmingly, and I succumb. He takes my hand and gives a little squeeze.

"Shore, why not," I like Lionel more and more, but does he think I can't see that he's laying it on a little thick? Well, maybe thick is good. About time some guy treated Lucilla Todd Wilta and her flawless complexion as they deserve.

Lionel moves away from me, and Smithson follows him, holding the door open. Lionel turns to him, amused. I know I'm not supposed to hear them, but I catch a few words. ". . . bet she won't last a month," Lionel says. He stands there grinning like a fool at Charles F. Smithson, but his host just holds the door, staring down Lionel Hawthorne until Lionel finally laughs loudly and jaunts out the door, crosses the terrace, and skips down the stone steps. I watch his retreating back as he leaves the castle.

Smithson looks back at me and clamps the door shut, a final, decisive sound. "Sit down, Miss Wilta," he says.

Here it comes. I've either blown my chance by waxing angry with the flower, or he's seen the light and plans to bluster at her a bit himself, as she so soundly deserves, once she wakes up. I sit down, and so does he.

I wait for the verdict.

"Miss Wilta," he begins, "I can't accept what you did in there."

"I shouldn'a."

"I'm surprised you would succumb to the child's level that way. You need to set a better example. Your letters of reference were quite good." They should be, I'm thinking; I wrote them myself, except for Fred's. Good old Fred. Smithson is still talking. ". . . had time to check them, although I have to admit that at times I'm not sure how to deal with the girls either. I don't seem to have a knack . . . ."

The time seems right, and while he's yammering on, I root around in my duffel bag and come up with Dr. Harvard's book. I hand it to him, and he takes it with the usual sideways scowl. He flips through a few of the pages, then lays the book on a small table between us. "You'll have to live here," he says finally. "They'll need you when they wake up in the morning and at nighttime, too."

"Just don't get any brassy ideas," I say demurely. He's too polite to laugh.

He glances at Dr. Harvard thoughtfully and says, "My girls . . ." Then he stops. Mr. Mysterious. "They need some kind of an influence."

"I'll say."

"I have to be blunt, Miss Wilta. You definitely are not ideal for this position." He looks stuck, dejected, as if he'd rather do almost anything than employ me.

"So hire one of your other applicants," I suggest innocently.

He nods. "Yes, if it doesn't work out with you, I could still do that." If it weren't pathetic, it might be hilarious. Sir Charles Fitzham Stupid the Second, still clinging to the illusion that he has a choice in this.

"So where do I sign?" I ask.

He reluctantly touches the cover of the book. "Maybe together we can learn," he mutters. He doesn't sound convinced.

I'm not either. "Just," he says, "I need to know you won't ever hit them."

"'Kay," I say agreeably. "No hitting."

He sighs. "And no slapping. No more shouting them down like you did in there. No . . ." He looks at me in earnest. "You know, be gentle with them. I require that you cultivate gentleness."

"Shore thing," I say agreeably, "gentleness in all things."

We settle all the details and agree to try it out for one year, which seems a tad long for a trial run, but, hey, the guy is obviously overwhelmed and needs me. We add the caveat that he can fire me if it's not working out, and he consents to pay me far more than I'm worth, including all kinds of crazy perks I bet he never would have thought of without me. He's desperate, a man defeated.

Charles F. Smithson signs on the dotted line, and so does Lucilla T. Wilta, and then he shows me to the room that's going to be mine, a big, chilly space with heavy burgundy drapes and scarred furniture. The shabby wallpaper sports floppy golden leaves tumbling through garden gates.

"Is this okay?" he asks me. "You can move to another room later if you want to."

"This'll do," I tell him. My new space is three times as big as the room I've been living in.

When he leaves me there, I can't help noticing how tired he looks, how sad. A fleeting thought races through my mind: Where is his better half? Why isn't she here to help bear the load? Yes, Sister Mary Phyllis, of course I feel a sting of conscience at taking advantage of a man when he's down. But I can't afford not to.

I'm Lucky Wilta. This is my castle, my treasure. I'm here to grab my star and hold on tight. Sad, depressed, defeated, or whatever else he may be, no mere man is going to stand in my way.

# 5

THE THING THAT WAKES ME UP is an insistent pounding, with a few intermittent shrieks that die away into soft moans. My first thought is that old Marsuvius Borstrom is clawing around in the secret room, trying to get out. My second is that Pansy and Violet are tearing the house down stone by stone. I yank the pillow over my head and burrow further under the blankets. The room he gave me is elegant, I suppose, but, like the rest of the castle, it's chilly and dark. I know it's May, but the castle doesn't seem to. And with that hellish screech floating up from below, why would anyone budge an inch?

So I scrunch in, shivering, even in my flannels, and note the first stabbing pangs of a headache. My first purchase with my outrageous new salary is going to be a big bottle of Excedrin-extra-strength. My second will be the fuzziest and hottest electric blanket I can find. They name them these days; they come in colors like claret, mist, and Nile. Me, I'll choose champagne, in keeping with my new image.

I can't get back to sleep with that infernal banging, and, anyway, it occurs to me that last night I signed away my right to ignore it. So I stumble out of bed and pull on my day-off finery, worn jeans and a big, tattered sweatshirt - today it's a Chicago Cubs shirt. Right, they never win. I've always been a sucker for the underdog.

There's a blowing rain outside, and it's pelting against my windows. I examine the rusty old latches and decide they should hold, at least until I take ownership and can make some changes.

"Knock off that racket," I snarl as I enter the kitchen, where Violet and Pansy are perched like identical idiot trolls on two tall stools. They have identical cereal bowls in front of them and are dribbling identical milk rivers down their identical soft, round chins.

Revolting.

"We're not doing it," one of them says. And I realize that they're not. The pounding continues, a bleak, doomed noise, and

38

what sounded like the shriek of children I now identify as the rhythmic whine of the old furnace.

The Honorable Smithson enters the kitchen, his hands greasy, streaks of grime across his face. He's tracking filthy water across the floor, and the bottoms of his sweats are damp above low rubber boots.

"Is the dike holding?" I yell above the din.

He has absolutely no sense of humor. "I was in the cellar," he says. "I think it will stop now. It's the furnace," he adds. No kidding, Sherlock.

"It's May," I say. "Why don't you just turn it off?"

He stares at me briefly, then motions to Thing One, who is running her cereal spoon over her sister's head and through her hair, both of them laughing like chimps. "Pansy's had this cold all winter," he says. "I hate to turn the heat off yet."

"Does it do that every day?"

"Pretty much." He leaves the room and returns minutes later, cleaned up a bit and looking like a fairy-tale prince, in spite of the sweatpants. He's wearing that hurt expression that defines his personality. He's unapproachable, and I sit silently on my own shaky stool, glumly eating cold cereal, listening to the furnace spend itself in a few last gasps. Hard rain beats against the tall kitchen windows.

"Miss Wilta," he says finally.

"Lucky."

He ignores me. "You have to be up when the girls get up. That's usually around six. They can't be wandering around the castle alone in the mornings."

"Make them sleep later," I offer. "We could lace their nighttime bottles with sedative. I've heard that arsenic-"

He glares at me. "You will need to get up earlier. Five-thirty. There's an alarm clock in your room."

Hmmm, is this in my contract? Well, it's no big deal to me. Chez Fred's opened at six, and I was almost always the first one there. "Shore thing," I say.

Smithson is rummaging in cupboards, locating a cereal bowl and spoon, and he grimaces as he digs into stale cornflakes. He's leaning against the kitchen counter, and his eyes avoid both his daughters and his hotshot new housekeeper. Didn't he say he was leaving today on some business trip or other? I wonder what he does anyway. Whatever it is, I wish he'd get going so I can begin living my fine new life, starting with a phone call to Fred and ending with whipping the Little Princesses into shape.

The noises from the cellar have pretty much ceased now; there's only an occasional bubbling burp to remind us that the heating system in the castle just might be breathing its last.

I decide to make that my first priority when he's gone. I can't believe he goes down there and dirties those graceful hands when he could just call a plumber. Looks he has. Brains he seems a little short on.

"Is this the day you're going away, Daddy?" asks Biffy, unless it's her evil twin Barfy, slobbering the last of her cereal down the front of her pajamas. The milk soaks in, a saturated spot. I shiver with the cold.

"Yes, sweetheart, I am," he says sadly. "Miss Wilta," his voice catches, "will be here to take care of you." Just mind Miss Lizzie Borden, he might as well have said. And if you run with all your might, you can probably flee her ax.

"Lucky," I remind him.

"What?"

"My name. Just Lucky."

"Miss Wilta," he tells them sternly.

"Lucky," I say again.

He looks at me, and our eyes lock. I stare at the space between his eyes, just above that gorgeous nose. It's an old trick I've used a million times before. As usual, it works. He looks away first, and I grin at the girls. "Lucky," I tell them. "Call me that. I'm just Lucky."

Pansy, or maybe it's Violet, smiles a little shyly and repeats "Lucky."

"That's a dumb name," says Violet, or Pansy. "Why is that your name?"

"I'm a lucky person," I tell her. "Always have been." Smithson is looking at me suspiciously. A plain-looking waitress with no taste and no future considers herself lucky? If he only knew. I keep talking to the girls. "If you do just what I tell you and listen carefully to everything I say, you'll be lucky, too. I can arrange it. If you don't, well . . . ." The implied threat hangs in the air.

They're interested, even if they're not completely convinced. Smithson himself seems a mite curious, too. A shame he can't stick around and see what magic tricks I plan to use on his kids.

He wanders away and doesn't reappear until I have the cereal dishes washed and put away and am whisking the girls back upstairs to get dressed.

When he meets us on the stairs, he's dressed quite nattily in a light brown suit. His tie is positively prancing with little ponies. Dork. Dork. Dork. Myself, I feel like Cinderella long before the ball.

"I'll be away three days," he tells me. "It can't be avoided." He's all business. "I'm trusting you to look after the girls with patience and authority." His mouth says he's trusting me, but his eyes say he's not. His voice falters. "I'll call tonight to make sure they're . . . to make sure everything's going well. And Lionel will be stopping. I've left his number by the phone. Here's where you can reach me if you have any emergency . . . ."

"I'm not planning to slam them with a cookpot, if that's what you're afraid of," I tell him. "I said I wouldn't and I won't. No slapping, no jabbing, no pinching, no nothing."

He doesn't answer, but picks up his daughters together and hugs them hard.

Not a wise move. Pansy starts in first, a low, wailing cry, then Violet elaborates on the theme and lets loose with a good strong soprano. Smithson looks as if he's about to start in, too. Where the devil is he going? Clearly, he'd rather stay right here with the little hothouse flowers.

I peel the girls off His Honorable Self, and they bite and scratch me in thanks. Smithson walks out the door into the rain, his shoulders hunched. Not a happy man.

The kids continue to shriek and blubber as I yank them up the staircase. What the heck. I can see their point. This is a mad, miserable household. And I'm stuck in it, earning my millions. So I give out with a few lusty wails myself, louder and even more resonant than theirs. They both stop and look at me sideways. Then I hear what I think is almost a giggle, and they each give out with a huge, cheerful squawk.

Whooping and yelping, determined to outdo each other, the three of us begin our three days of intensive introductory activities. Primal Scream Therapy. Aerobic Mud Wrestling. Slopping Septic Water On The Foyer Floor. They think they can make me wish I'd never met them?

Guess again, ladies. I'm Lucky Wilta.

In me, you have met your match.

◇◇◇

"Whassa matter?" says Fred, anguish oozing from every greasy pore. "You needa raise? You need more money? I still don't understand this, Lucky."

I'm opening and slamming cupboard doors in the kitchen, Smithson's land phone crammed between my neck and my ear, while I try not to get tangled in the long, twisty cord. I'm searching for a dishtowel that might not smell like someone's old feet.

"Nope. Got lotsa money coming, Fred. That's why I'm outta there."

"But, Lucky," his voice comes back, mournful, begging, "your favorite customers. Quiet George, he's asking for you. And Ancient Ella don't like the way Kitty does eggs. Mack with the Beans in his hat, he keeps saying, 'Where's Lucky?' and I keep telling him 'Hang on, she'll be in.' I think Mack wants to use your mug, Lucky. You better come back."

"Sorry Fred," I say. "I'll drop by for a visit one of these days."

Here we are. A nice flat stack of old frayed towels. I hold one to my nose. Phew.

"Come on back," he repeats. "I'll give you a nice raise."

"Keep my mug safe," I tell him. "And whack that toaster oven hard if it gives you any guff."

"Keep your mug safe," he mutters. "It'll be right here on the shelf for you."

I dump the whole pile of towels on the floor, scarfing the top one to wipe up the juice that's puddling over the countertop and stuffing another around a leaky windowsill. Maybe I'll wash them all later.

Living in the castle, I am finding, is not all roses. The whole place is unbelievably damp, and the noisy old furnace doesn't throw enough heat to melt a Popsicle. Windows leak and floors squeak. The parlor floor is always wet and I conclude that there's no cellar beneath that part of the castle. Stagnant water seeps in from underneath, making the cracked grout oozy. Maybe it doesn't matter much, especially since there's no furniture in there. I suppose whatever was there has rotted by now and is sitting on a dump somewhere.

I discover that all the towels in my bathroom are threadbare. Not to mention mustard yellow. God, what a color. And the hot shower I looked forward to is, at best, a lukewarm drizzle.

Things are not exactly as I expected.

42

Pansy mentions that water is running down the wall of her bedroom, and, when I investigate, I discover that the roof over the balcony is attached at such a peculiar angle that rain water has no choice but to trickle inside. Maybe that's why that whole section of the castle always feels clammy. I'd swear the stones are sagging. Can rocks do that?

"Pansy," I ask, "how long have you been sleeping in this room?" I'm fingering the squashy wallpaper above her bed. No wonder her nose is always running.

"Not very long. Mrs. Frocks said I could have it because of the mice."

"Were there mice in your other room?"

"In the closet. They were hatching."

Violet pipes up. "They ran across Pansy's bed one night. She screamed and screamed."

"I'll just bet she did," I agree. "So she put you in here instead." Pansy nods solemnly. "But it's wet, Pansy. You can't stay here." Doesn't her father realize how unhealthy this room is? Why doesn't the imbecile move her? I ask her, in those words.

"I never told him about the water," she says. "I never think of it when he's here."

"What's an imbecile?" asks Violet.

"It means daddy," I tell her. "So he doesn't even know you're sleeping in a river whenever it rains?"

"No."

It looks to me as if His Majesty needs to spend a little more time keeping the home fires burning.

We spend a few hours lugging Pansy's things to the empty room across the hall from Violet's. It's drier here and closer to my room, too. No, it isn't that I crave to be near her, but if I'm going to do this job, I might as well do it right.

While I make Pansy's new bed and toss her clothes and toys into drawers and a big, creaky closet, the girls slide, laughing shrilly, up and down the slippery end of the corridor where the runner runs out. I yell at them at first, and then watch for a minute. The more they race, the shinier the bare wood gets, and finally I take off my shoes and test my socks on the surface. I'm a better slider than they are, and they ask for some pointers, which I gladly give. Violet gets a sliver in her foot and yelps with pain while I yank it out, but she's a trouper. She's back in the thick of things in no time.

I call a halt to the game when a fragile painted bowl on a table topples over and smashes to the floor. Both girls look guilty and scared.

"Good thing that's not valuable," I say, and I dump the fragments into a wastebasket. Well, it's not. At least, not anymore.

Bob Cobb, the only plumber in town, is summoned from his shop, and he meanders up wearing a blue shirt that proudly proclaims *BOB*. He's drenched with rain, but happily spends some time harrumphing around by the furnace. He has thinning hair and a high forehead, and his face tends toward frowning. "Mr. Smithson had me here to look at this, oh, maybe three weeks ago," Bob tells me somberly. "I tightened the blower motor mounts. Not much else I can do, unless you want to replace the whole system. You Mrs. Smithson?"

"No," I say, "I'm Lucky."

Bob looks at me curiously. "Well," he shrugs, "I guess you'd know him better than I do. Me, I don't understand him. 'No, Bob,' he tells me. Just 'no.' Meaning, I suppose, he's too cheap to replace the system. I wouldn't either, an old place like this. Wouldn't be worth the trouble, no."

"Can't you just get rid of the noise?"

Bob looks briefly hopeful. "I could adjust the drive belts," he says. "If they're too loose or tight, they might cause a squeaking. Or I could replace them. See if he wants that." He closes his eyes in deep thought. "Not this week, though. Maybe next week. That'll be a hundred ten."

"What'll be a hundred ten?" I ask him.

"The fee."

Is this moron serious? "Send a bill," I tell him.

Planet and Visey are sprawled along the seventy-five thousand foot dining room table with an array of broken crayon bits spread before them. A nice wholesome activity for little girls, except that they're drawing on the chipped mahogany finish of the table, no paper in sight. I watch for a minute, admiring their artwork, and then find some sheets of paper to slip under their hands.

"Very good, girls," I tell them. "You behaved very nicely while the plumber was here."

"Bob comes all the time," Vansy says. "Daddy says he eats money for breakfast."

44

"He has six children," says Pilot, sniffling. "They eat money, too. Lucky, have you ever seen a person eat money?"

"Once in a while, I eat it myself," I say. "Raw. Or sometimes with horseradish." I wipe at her nose with a hunk of toilet paper I've been carrying around for that very purpose. "When I'm in the mood."

Their eyes go round. "Are you in the mood right now?"

"No." I peer at their drawings, little sunny flower gardens with blue flowers and pink stems, houses with curved roofs and clearly identifiable bricks. Not bad for a three and four year old. Actually, I don't know anything about art myself, but I would bet these two kids are better than average. "Who taught you guys to draw like that?" I ask.

"Nobody. Mrs. Frocks didn't like Pansy's pictures," Violet volunteers.

"How come?"

"Pansy made a tree yellow, and Mrs. Frocks said it was supposed to be green."

"Well, I liked it yellow," Pansy insists. "And I made my apples blue."

"Were they rotten?"

"No. They were beautiful."

"Look, Lucky," Violet says. With her stubby finger, she's making lines in the dust on the table top, two fairly straight ones that meet at the bottom. "It's a V. That's my letter."

"Not bad," I say. "Can you make an I? That's your second letter." I show her, and she copies it. Pansy wants to write her name, too, and gets a good start with PAN. I show her an S, but even though thick dust is flying about from her efforts, her S is just a crazy squiggle. I move her down a few seats to a dustier spot at the table, and leave her there to practice making S's.

I grab a piece of paper and a crayon and start to doodle. "All right," I say to Violet, "see if you can guess what I'm drawing." I make a few labored strokes. My picture looks like a kindergartner drew it.

Pansy is back, looking over my shoulder. She watches me intently, then laughs suddenly. "It's Daddy," she cries. "I can tell by his tie." I'm pleased. My little horses must have looked more like horses than I thought.

Violet laughs, too. "That's an Emily tie."

"What's an Emily tie?" I ask.

"That one is. And the other one with the ducks. And the one

with the watermelons."

"Who's Emily?" I ask.

"A lady."

As contrasted to Lucky Wilta, who's no such fine thing.

◇◇◇

While they take naps, lulled to sleep by the rain, I scrub the crayon off the table. I might as well clean it up so I can host extravagant dinners one day. Then I spend an hour getting my bearings in the musty halls of my vast castle.

As a child, I had strict rules, and much of the castle was off limits to me, but I'm feeling pretty confident as I meander the hallways and peek through doorways. Whenever I find a familiar room, I feel a surge of happiness at what I've regained. I've missed my castle, and I long to have it back.

Bedrooms, sitting rooms, a dusty library filled with worn books - as I wander through, it all comes back to me. I studied and played here as a child; I walked and ran these corridors and whistled happily, waiting impatiently for Nancy, my chunky cousin, when she had trouble keeping up with me. Nancy was twelve years older, but she lived with us, helped my mother, played with me, gave my days some substance. By Nancy, I was admonished and lectured, hugged and kissed, punished for my fractious ways, and praised on those rare occasions when I managed to act like a young lady. Through it all, I was comfortable and secure. This was home.

I feel convinced, strolling now through this second-floor hallway, that one of these doors leads to what was once my bedroom. And I'm right.

I know it when I see it because of the Palladian window surrounding the alcove that held my bed. The glass is dusty and stained with years of rough weather. Even now, the rain is beating on the window and dribbling gently into one cracked corner. I try to recall if that leak was there nineteen years ago. It couldn't have been, could it?

The shape of the window is the same, high and arched, and the shelves my father built for me are still there, cluttered now with a lot of squashy cardboard boxes. They look sadly out of place, and, curious, I look inside a few; I can't help it. But there's nothing there except a lot of color travel brochures. Must be the Smithsons traveled a lot, or thought about it.

46

When this was my room, those shelves held toys and games and books, and a row of little glass bottles that I called my collection - my mother's empty perfume bottles mostly, filled with colored water. Nancy used to fill them for me. I'd dictate the color, she'd mix in a drop or two of vegetable dye, and we'd place it on the uppermost shelf. When the sun streamed in the window behind, sometimes I'd get colored prisms, brilliant and magical, and I liked that.

Cheap entertainment for an easy-to-please kid.

My old bed is gone. It's just as well. If it were still here, I might ask for this room, or at least for the bed, and there's no use in getting sentimental. My dresser is gone, too, and the upholstered boudoir chair I used to throw my clothes on.

My cast-off sweaters, jeans, and shirts would always reappear, clean and pressed, on hangers and in drawers, and it never occurred to me to wonder how.

Good old dependable Nancy.

I close the door softly behind me as I return to the corridor. I like seeing my room again, but the past is the past, and I'm ready to move on. I have a job to do, and while the whiny Smithson Sisters are sleeping, I have to take advantage. I leave Lucilla Todd's childhood bedroom behind and spend some time searching for Luke Todd's secret room, *my* secret room.

I've retraced my steps to the back of the house, where solid oak doors line up down a long hall. Prince Charles must love closed doors. Me, I decide to fling them open. There's no fresh air up here, and not much light. Opening up a little can only be an improvement.

I wander along the corridor, trying doors, opening those that give. I peek into unused, half-empty bedrooms, sitting rooms cloaked in dust, and quaint old-fashioned bathrooms that drip. Here and there, a startled mouse leaps and flits away. Some of the doorknobs stick, and I'm not sure whether they're locked or just stubborn. I don't see any reason to break down doors yet, so I ignore them.

*Who would ever have guessed about the secret room,* my father wrote in his journal. *Strangely, I was led there by mice.* It's not much help. If I followed every mouse I spotted, I'd be bumping into myself coming back.

I owe it to Fred that mice don't shake me. The first time I saw one in the syrup vat at Chez Fred's, I had the health department number half dialed before Fred calmed the receiver out of my hand and explained gently that mice are a natural part of diner life. Not to worry, he told me. They run fast and don't usually want your company either. It's a simple thing to ladle their carcasses out of vats and crocks. And they don't eat that much when they do tear into a bag of bagels.

It's possible to co-exist.

*And what a treasure,* Daddy wrote. *Diamonds of a thousand brilliant colors! My little Lucilla will stumble on that room one day - and the treasure hidden there, glittering like stars . . . . Time to find my way back to the secret room. The quiet awaits me. . . .*

I come to a circular set of stone steps at the end of a hallway, familiar and enticing. It's so dark here that I squint, looking up and ahead, and stumble into the bottom riser. I cry out in pain, knowing I've made a nice purple spot on my ankle that will certainly turn sickly green and yellow in a few days. I remind myself to slap a bag of frozen peas on it later, and as I lift my head I almost think I see a movement. Something.

I look around, rubbing my injured ankle, but all is still. I must have imagined it. Or it might have been a mouse. There are certainly a few of those around.

I have a decision to make, and three distinct choices, and my mind is too full to be worrying about mice or goblins in the corridor. I can make a gentle left or a sharp right, or I can go up the shadowy stone steps. The left, I find, is just an empty servant's room with an attached bathroom, and the right leads to another hallway with more closed doors.

I opt for the circular staircase.

The steps are worn in the middle by a hundred years of treading feet, and my shoes scuff against them as I climb. I make two rotations on the tight circle, and as I round the second turn, I look behind me. I am completely out of sight of the hallway below. I remember climbing these steps as a child and relive a frizzle of anticipation at what awaits me. At the top there's a door, and I try it hopefully.

It's locked.

This locked door disappoints me more than all the others I've encountered, and I have an irrational urge to break the lock or force the door. I realize how silly this would be. When Smithson returns, I'll simply ask him to open it. Something in my childhood is calling me back to that door.

What does it look like now? I wish I could see.

I leave the locked door and retrace my route - down the worn stone steps, around two turns - and I'm back in the upstairs corridor, Pansy's and Violet's open doors in view. I peek in on the girls, stopping to smooth a fluffy pink blanket over Violet's shoulders. Both of them are still sleeping deeply, so I wander back to the hallway. Which direction might be most likely to hide my coveted treasure room?

How would I know?

My father should have drawn me a map, made it clearer how I'm to find Marsuvius Borstrom's stash, the diamonds Daddy obviously wanted me to have.

Well, he didn't draw a map. But he raised a wily, shrewd, cunning daughter, and I have all the time in the world. Or until Smithson evicts me.

I keep searching.

I haven't come up with a concrete plan of action, so I simply explore aimlessly. I try a brass knob. It gives, and I find myself in a dark furnished bedroom. I flick the light switch, but nothing happens, so I yank the draperies aside. That doesn't help much either, since it's a dark, gloomy day, but I can make out dark, sinister wallpaper. The rain pounds against the window and rattles the broken casings. I back away.

A quick look behind a massive walnut bed draped in threadbare blue velvet and a tall highboy filled with ancient clothing shows me there are no secret doors in this room. Cobwebs, yes, and fluffy balls of dust, but except for the bed and the highboy, the furniture in here is too spindly to hide a door.

I can't help wondering whose room this was. Someone once slept in this heavy, depressing bed. Someone once wore these wisps of old clothing. The cloudy cut-glass decanters and bottles on the dresser once held fragrances and powders that someone loved. The tarnished silver hairbrush was picked up, maybe thoughtfully, maybe sadly, by long-dead hands.

I back out of the room, shivering a little with the cold, or something else, happy to emerge into the comparative brightness of the corridor. I latch the door firmly behind me.

A sudden fist forms in my chest. Something just moved around the far corner of the hallway, a flash, out of sight now. I'm sure of it. I head in that direction, stealing quietly down the hall.

"Hello?" I call. There's no answer, just the dripping of the rain on the eaves outside.

"Who's here?" I yell. I creep around the corner and glance at a splintered chair; the heavy draperies beside it twist softly. I grab them roughly - nothing but air behind.

"Hi," says a soft voice behind me, and I nearly jump out of my skin. I whirl around and there stands Lionel Hawthorne, smiling a crooked little smile. "Sorry if I startled you," he says.

"For God's sake," I mutter. "Lionel. What are you doing here?"

He grins a little sheepishly. "Nothing, really," he says. "I just came to see how you're doing."

"I'm doing fine," I say shortly. I'm standing there, still trying to catch my breath. How did he get in here anyway? I'm relieved it was just Lionel, though. I worried it might be ghosts or intruders or . . . I don't know what I thought. Well, if there ever *is* an intruder in the castle, or a ghost or even a mouse, he'll have Lucky Wilta to contend with.

"Mind if I get some liquid refreshments?" Lionel asks. "I'll bring you something, too."

"Sure, that'd be fine. Whatever," I say vaguely. Lionel turns around and heads down the hallway and toward the stairs, then hollers back to me, "Stay right there."

Not likely. I must leave no stone unturned.

Stubborn and determined, I work the next doorknob. The door is either jammed or locked. It won't budge, and, with so many other doors to try, there seems little point in wrestling with it.

Soon Lionel reappears, and, I must admit, traveling the spooky corridors with cute little Lionel Hawthorne and an ice cold Corona with lime does make the job a little more pleasant. Lionel has some very nice qualities- he makes me laugh and he seems to like to have fun- and I vow to try to get to know him, since he seems to be part of my new existence.

He doesn't stay long, though, and soon I'm on my own again.

I explore four or five more rooms, taking in the high ceilings, painted, carved, or plastered, and the smooth paneled walls or formidable flocked wallpapers in their faded colors and patterns. Certain rooms have been updated and decorated for more recent use; electricity hums freely. Others seem tomblike, unused, as if Marsuvius Borstrom never got around to furnishing them, and no one else has ever bothered either.

In some rooms, I find the dressers arranged with hair receivers, combs and boxes, spotted hand mirrors, cloudy perfume bottles, and small cracked pots. In others, the furniture is barren; dresser tops are flat, dusty landscapes.

It's strange I haven't seen a single picture of Mrs. Smithson, the blonde beauty I recall from the newspaper. Wouldn't you think he'd have one around somewhere, mixed in with all the grit and grime?

I'm contemplating this and other mysteries of Borstrom's castle, when I come to the end of the main corridor. There's a door that seems stuck or locked at first, but soon gives under my persistent grip. I open the door a crack, and it squeals noisily. I listen for Pansy and Violet. They don't stir, so I force it further.

At first, it appears to be just another bedroom, even more somber than those that came before, but as I urge the door open, I can see dim steps fanning up and away from me, steps piled with things that couldn't belong to anyone but Smithson - a plastic dish drainer, a couple of cardboard cartons, a golf club, two ugly plastic Easter baskets with the green foil grass still clinging to them.

Obviously these are the tower stairs. My heart gives a little thrill. "The perfect place for diamonds," I mutter under my breath, and I'm not sure if it's excitement or fear that makes me want to hear my own voice, a test to be sure I'm real.

Now that I've found the tower stairs, it occurs to me that I could start at the top of the castle and explore my way down. After all, I know there's a turret room, and wouldn't that be a likely spot for a mysterious hidden treasure? "It must be here," I say to myself. It makes sense that a secret room might be tucked away behind musty trunks and discarded furniture.

I open the door wider, ignore the drafty chill, and tramp up the hard stone steps. From the collection of items piled at the bottom, it's clear that His Royal Laziness makes trips to the tower as seldom as possible.

At the top of the stairs, there's a small room, round and empty, the only room of the tower - nothing mysterious there - and then the door that opens into the attic proper. That door glides open with surprising ease, and my eyes are stabbed with unexpected flecks of glittering light.

Two small windows nearby let in just enough light to catch the sparkle and glitz of the Christmas ornaments still hanging on the fully decorated fake tree before me.

51

I can't help laughing. Charles F. Smithson the Second is not only profoundly lazy, but unimaginative as well. Cheap glass ornaments - red, gold, green, and blue - are fastened with hooks to the phony evergreen boughs and tangled with loops of cheap lights. Plastic candy canes and hard, cracked gingerbread cookies are suspended on dusty strings.

I feel slightly superior as I examine this pathetic excuse for a Christmas tree. Even Lucky Wilta has better taste. Who chose these ornaments? Was it some servant? The pompous and egotistical Sir Charles? Maybe his spoiled and sullen offspring?

My mother and father and I once went out to cut our own tree in the woods behind the castle. I was all of six or seven then, and every spruce in the forest looked beautiful to me.

"This one, Daddy," I remember saying, and he would lift the saw he carried and circle the tree, looking for the best place to begin sawing.

"Wait, Luke," my mother would say. She'd inspect the tree long and hard, examining the snowy branches coolly with her gloved hands. "No, let's keep looking," she'd say. "Let's go a little further."

"It looks good to me, Victoria," my father would say, winking at me.

"No, no it doesn't."

So we would trudge on through the acreage until finally I'd stop from exhaustion rather than enthusiasm. But it was hard to admit I'd been defeated by my small, weak legs, so I'd glance up at a tree nearby, find it green and sturdy, and say, "This one, then. Let's cut this one."

And we'd stop again, Daddy would nod and circle silently around the tree with his saw, and then Mother would proclaim that one, too, unfit for the Todd family's castle.

We'd trudge on. Eventually, when my hands and feet had all but frozen and the frigid air rasped painfully in my throat with every breath, my mother approved a tree.

That year we had a perfect Christmas tree in a big red pail on the black and white checkered foyer floor. It seemed as tall as the distant ceiling and wide enough to spread from wall to wall in the large alcove near the staircase. Mother hung it with tinted glass angels and fragile painted soldiers and snowmen, and draped droopy gold velvet ribbons on the outermost branches.

I would stand and gaze at it until Nancy trudged into the foyer and led me away to bed or homework. And on Christmas morning, among the carriages and puzzles, the LEGO sets and books and Barbie dolls, there was a china doll dressed in stylish black and white, a glossier reflection of the pitted foyer floor.

That, it occurs to me, was the same doll young Charles Smithson threatened to crush with his toy truck the day he moved into my castle.

The air in the attic is close and stale, and the rain is pounding in staccato beats on the roof. I shiver. The trunk of Smithson's cheap, ugly Christmas tree is a thin pole painted green. Its sparse branches are prickly and stiff. Green toilet brushes glued to a mop handle.

I reach out to touch one of the dime store ornaments and the globe falls away at my touch, fragmenting into brittle blue pieces at my feet, reflecting back an exaggerated impostor with big, curious eyes.

Our tree was beautiful; this one is a sham. The castle, when I lived in it, seemed a fairyland of wealth and happiness made that way by Nancy and my father. What is it now? A pile of crooked stone and mildewed walls, where two little girls scream for attention and fly into panic when their incapable father goes off for a private jaunt.

I vow to make this year's Christmas an event to remember.

I think we were out for three hours that day searching for Victoria Todd's perfect holiday tree.

The next year, I remember, I refused to go with them. They didn't mind. They went by themselves and brought home a majestic blue spruce to die for.

It became our yearly tradition. Mother and Dad would spend four or five hours running down the perfect Christmas tree, chop it down, and drag it home. Mother would decorate it, and my job was to stand there admiring it, getting lost in its lights and fragrance. Then, my father's turn again. He'd smile indulgently and encourage me to feel the wrapped presents underneath that Mother had strictly forbidden me to touch.

Worked for me.

# 6

WE'RE GOING TO INVITE the sun into this house," I tell the girls the next morning at breakfast. Today we're eating in the dining room, and the sun is misting through towering windows that are hazy with grit. Mrs. Frocks may have been a self-proclaimed art critic, but I can't say I admire her house cleaning. Maybe I won't look so bad by comparison.

The attic was a sad disappointment, but I reassure myself that there are still murky corners up there, old trunks, a few delectable nooks and crannies. It will be worth another look some day.

I deposit my breakfast dishes in the kitchen sink and make the girls do the same, then I slowly pace the perimeter of the dining room. They follow at a respectful distance.

The mahogany table, of course, is the centerpiece of the room, and it stretches much, much longer than we will ever need it. Various formal chairs line the walls, some with arms, some without, mostly damaged, most upholstered in a faded green and gold brocade fabric. I slap the seat of one and hear the rotten threads snap. Dust flies up. Violet coughs. Pansy sniffles.

There's a dingy brick fireplace at one end of the room, chalky with age, and above it two rather incongruous paintings. I know they weren't here when I lived here; I would have remembered them. One is a blue and white landscape of the New England coast, lighthouse, waves breaking, rocky shore. I like the cleanness of it. The other is a sand dune, big golden reeds reaching out of the bulging sand, the ocean and a ship beyond, the sun a bright haze. I like that one, too.

"Where did these paintings come from?" I ask Pansy, who has crept up beside me.

"No place."

They're framed in new wood, and they obviously don't go in the room, but they're the most appealing things here.

The wallpaper's olive green trellises are wrapped with splatty yellow and red flowers. The woodwork is cracked with age. And all around the room, on side tables and mantel, on window ledges and the high plate rail and jammed behind the glass doors of the cupboards, are doo-dads, assorted cracked bottles and jars and dishes and glasses. It's a raggedy collection. When any old Borstrom or Lowland or Ruggins or Forsythe or Todd or Smithson wasn't sure what to do with some weird collectible, he must have stuck it in here. The result is bizarre, a jarring mix of colors, styles, and periods. All of it dirty. Most of it broken.

Even Lucky Wilta can tell this is an ugly room.

But not for long.

I open one of the creaky casement windows and yell out, "Yoo hoo! Mr. Sun! You're invited into the castle!"

Pansy and Violet love it. They laugh and climb up on chairs and start hollering, too. "Come on in! You're invited for lunch, Mr. Sun!"

With some dubious help from them, I start taking down the heavy curtains that must have been hanging here for a hundred years. The tattered fabric falls apart in our hands. We drag the shredded remnants to a closet and stuff them in with the tarnished silver. Already the dining room looks brighter, and with my entourage in tow behind me, I head for the kitchen to fetch whatever assortment of cleaning agents Mrs. Frocks has left behind.

We shrink the table by removing a few leaves, which I carry to an empty upstairs bedroom, and we remove all of the odd dishes and chipped goblets lining the walls, washing our favorites until they sparkle and hiding the rest in a cupboard. We wash the windows, polish all the furniture, and vacuum the worn rug, and we dust the dark old paintings and the two newer ones and reposition some of them to better advantage.

We add a tattered white lace tablecloth and some ivory candles, and we stand back to admire our progress.

By lunchtime, the dining room sparkles, and we actually enjoy eating soup and sandwiches in there.

"Lucky," Pansy asks me as I ladle out seconds of chicken noodle soup. "Have we been good?"

"Reasonably."

"Then are we going to be lucky like you?"

Now that's cute. I had almost forgotten I said that. "You betchum."

"Then will Daddy be back pretty soon?"

"Daddy's an imbecile," says Violet sincerely.

"Will he?" Pansy asks again, and her eyes are wistful and completely trusting. Something stirs inside of me. I can't explain it, a little melting, a looking closer.

He will. Of this I can at least be sure, and I tell her positively that her daddy will be back in two days. She smiles happily and puts her little arms around my neck. Violet decides to get in on the act and climbs up, too. "What the hell," I say softly, and hug them both back, furiously.

◇◇◇

We have all kinds of visitors that afternoon, most of them obviously sent to check up on me.

Amuse yourself at the expense of Chuck Smithson's incompetent new maid. Be amazed at the spectacle of the offensive waitress-turned-nanny. Recoil in disgust at her substandard language, her earthy tawdriness, her total lack of savoir-faire. And it's all free, folks.

Step right up.

Lionel drops by, as promised, and kisses my hand again, and calls me French names that I can't translate. I know what he's doing. He's calling me a musk ox, or maybe a yucca moth larva, and I'm eating it up, every bit.

We show him our sunny dining room, with its bright, polished furniture and its leaded glass windows that sparkle as high as we can reach. We can't do much about the wallpaper - yet. But the rest looks darn good. Lionel is debonair and says all the right things, admiring our hard work, then leads the girls and me out to the back of the estate and organizes a game of Simon Says.

"Simon Says take two baby steps!" Lionel roars at Pansy and Violet.

The three of us mince forward over the grass, giggling.

"Simon Says twirl like this!" Lionel flings out his arms and twirls. We do the same.

"Leap in the air!" he yells, and they both do. "You're out!" he screeches, and everyone collapses on the lawn in giggles. He kisses my hand again before he leaves and says something else in French. Unless it's not. I think he has asked me to marry him, but I can't be sure.

Kitty drives up in her beat-up yellow Volkswagen and parks in the semicircle outside the castle's front door. "My Gawd,

Lucky!" she hoots, as she stumbles out of the car. "What the blazes are you doing here? How did you luck into this? Fred is absolutely the pits about it!" Her eyes are gunshots, slamming all over the house front, taking in the heavy door on its iron hinges, the filthy windows, the big gray rocks holding everything crookedly in place.

I give her the quick tour, and Pansy and Violet follow in my wake. They're a little in awe of Kitty with her brassy blonde hair and long, showy legs encased in their skinny jeans. Hard to believe she couldn't think of a better way to spend her afternoon off than gathering the goods on me.

"Fred's gonna kill you," she tells me, giggling. "He says he regrets the letter of referendum and you should get back quick. He says it's a game you're playing to get more money."

"No game," I tell her. "I'm set for life. We signed a contract."

"For life?" Her eyes are large and, oh, she so wants to believe me.

"For one year. But I'll make enough to be set for life." And to pay a team of high-priced lawyers to get me back my castle.

"Well, where is he?" Kitty is peering around, looking for The Honorable Sir Gorgeous Charles F. Smithson Two.

"Gone for a while," I say vaguely. "You just missed his friend, though. Lionel Hawthorne."

"Oh." Her mouth is a melancholy red ring. We've drifted out to the overgrown, mostly dead gardens in back, and Kitty is shielding her eyes from the sun, looking up at the round tower and uneven roofline. "I love this house," she says, and I want to correct her. It's a castle, stupid. It's *my* castle. "I love everything about it," she continues. She would. "The cute angles and the way it's all spooky and sinister looking."

Kitty Nellahopkiss has always been easily impressed. Any person of taste can see that the castle is a singularly ugly building and that Marsuvius Borstrom must have been just like Kitty, a man who'd choose pickles over caviar, who'd take a hayride over a Caribbean cruise. A vulgar oaf followed by a long line of vulgar oafs.

Except, of course, my father.

Okay, so the castle isn't exactly as I remembered. So what. I'm here for a purpose. A prize.

Those sparkling diamonds just waiting for me to get my hands on them.

I can't wait to get rid of Kitty. In the wretched world of Chez

Fred's, she's invisible, a showy dumb blonde. Here, though, her presence feels out of place. She loves the castle. What a twerp. And as her glance boomerangs around the property, up and down the castle walls, over the shaggy hedges and across the weedy lawns, I'm pretty sure it's Lionel Hawthorne she's really searching for.

I usher Kitty back to her rusty car and am still grimacing at her gray, smoky exhaust trail, when another vehicle pulls into the circular drive. It's a shiny black Mercedes, and even though it's not exactly new, it is exactly mint. A willowy, black-haired woman is at the wheel, and as she steps out, Vansy and Pilot creep to my sides and each take one workworn hand.

"Miss Wilta?" the lilting, cheerful voice begins. "My name is Emily Cheseworthy, of the Cheseworthy-Tafts. I'm a special friend of Charles'." She examines my face, my lank brown hair, my thin-as-a-twig figure in its limp, moist clothing. She smiles in earnest. I clearly have the okay to go right on living in Chuckie F.'s house. No threat here, ma'am.

She extends her right hand to me. I play it up big, wipe my sweating palm on my jeans, and then grab her hand, pumping it up and down like crazy. Talk about gracious. She doesn't even flinch, just allows me to wrangle her hand like that until I finally let it fall like a dead fish. I have to admit, she's a cool one.

"Charles told me I'd find you here with the girls," she gushes. Her voice gushes. Her face gushes. Her red, red lips and black eyes, and peachy complexion all gush. "Charles asked me to stop, just to see how you were getting along," she sings.

"They're not dead yet," I tell her.

She looks surprised. "Well, no," she says thoughtfully. She looks me over once again. "From his description, I pictured someone much older," she finally says, then she turns to the children beside me. "Are you little ones behaving yourselves?" she asks.

They nod.

"Kiss," she tells them with a simpering smile, and she bends down, offering her cheek. This is when I notice the ring on her left hand. It's not a diamond, although she wears it on her engagement finger. It's a big green stone, probably a real emerald, and I am now wondering if Secretive Charles is engaged to this woman.

Pansy steps forward and kisses her obediently. Violet does the same, on tiptoe, putting her hand on Emily Cheseworthy's immaculate shoulder. "Be careful of my blouse, Pansy dear," Emily says, standing up and smiling achingly at the wrong child. Violet steps back, chastised.

"I brought you something." She reaches into the back seat of her Mercedes, emerging with three boxes. Two of them contain dolls, big ones wearing ruffly dresses and vacant smiles. She hands the third box to me. "It's for Charles. To let him know I was thinking of him." I take the flat parcel and watch Emily Cheseworthy of the Cheseworthy-Tafts climb elegantly back into her vehicle. She looks at me sadly. "It's such a shame Mrs. Frocks left," she says. Then she shakes off her gloom and pastes a brave, anxious smile on her face. "Well, we'll all have to try our best, I guess." She sighs, regretting the unhappy injustice of it all, and drives off.

There we stand, watching her go, Violet, Pansy, and yours truly, Lucky Wilta. I clutch the package in my hand, feeling like some perversion of *American Gothic*. I feel as if I should have a pitchfork. Right about now, I could put it to good use.

"She always brings us a doll," says Pansy resignedly.

"We have a lot of dolls," sighs Violet.

"You didn't even say thank you," I tell them. "Little ingrates."

"We never do."

"It's nice that she brought your father something," I say. I'm turning the box over in my hands, wondering if it's what I think it is.

As if she can read my mind, Pansy says, "It's a tie. They always are."

"Are we going to see what it looks like?" Violet asks.

"That would be ill-bred, you rube," I tell her. "You don't open other people's presents."

They both look up in surprise. "We always do. Daddy says we can."

So I hand over the tie box, they rip it open, and we all giggle at the silk tie sprinkled with dancing blue flowers. I peek inside to read the label: *Charvet Place Vendome*. Lah-de-dah. But I bet she got it on e-bay. Anyway, it will look stunning for some very special occasion.

We re-enter the house, and Violet tosses the tie onto a chair. They skid the dolls into a corner, where they land in an expensive plastic heap. "Can we have corn curls for supper?" Pansy asks.

"Shore nuff," I answer. And we sit down to a pretty decent meal of corn curls, Cracker Jack, and ice cream sandwiches. I flip open a few cans of cream soda and glance around the table with satisfaction. Most of the major food groups seem to be covered, something Dr. Harvard can't stress strongly enough. We eat by candlelight on the beautifully polished dining room table.

Emily Cheseworthy of the Cheseworthy-Tafts ain't the only one around here with class.

◇◇◇

On the third day, I teach the girls some rowdy drinking songs I learned in college. Oh, yes, Sister, I went to college. Two years, and my parents had to borrow every penny to send me, too. I decided not to graduate the night I went out partying instead of studying for my Abnormal Psych. final. I was so close, too. But I just couldn't study for that final exam. All the case histories in the textbook reminded me spookily of myself, and the more I read, the worse I felt.

Who needed that? I found a few good friends, and, together, we hit every bar in my college town. The exam was a forfeit. And my degree was the sad, inculpable casualty.

Of course I feel guilty about the loan they took out. I've paid it back, though. Why do you think I lived in a cheap, one room flat for three years?

The songs are rousing and noisy, and they cheer us all up after the disappointment over the dolls and tie and the general dreariness that overtook us after Emily's visit.

We decide to go for a drive in the car Smithson has left for me, but we bypass Duck Vly, which has only a car repair place, a drug store, one church and Bob Cobb's establishment. Instead we go into Tupper Lake where the choices are grander and the streets look alive. We buy thick, fluffy towels, ivory and mint green, and my electric blanket and some cold medicine for Pansy, and we stop at a toy store to get clay for the girls. Dr. Harvard says clay is very good for kids.

On our return trip, we spot Bob Cobb loitering outside his shop, looking dejected, as if he might be hungering for some money to eat. We stop and invite him up sometime next week to replace the drive belts on the furnace and fix a leaky faucet in one of the bathrooms. He cheers up considerably. It does my heart good to know Bob won't starve.

Back home, I help the girls make green clay muffins and yellow clay meat, and we set them on the kitchen windowsill

60

wondering if they'll ever harden. I do a little more fruitless exploring while Pansy and Violet nap, and I decide that this could work out to be a very viable schedule for me. Breakfast, pal around with the girls, lunch, sing some sailor songs together, search for the secret room while they nap, entertain visitors, goof off with the girls, supper, bed. My basic choice seems to be what to do when the girls are awake. I could use that time for cleaning and cooking or spend those hours acting like a four year old. I'm not even embarrassed that it's such an easy decision.

Right now they're sleeping, and I'm prowling around on the second floor again. I hunted for a flashlight to brighten all those dark, dusty corners. I couldn't find one, but never would I let so small a disappointment stop me from my rounds. Kitty called my residing here a game, and maybe she's right, although neither she nor Fred could possibly guess my real motives. Anyway, if it's a game, I intend to emerge the winner.

I've discovered a very peculiar square door cut into one wall. It doesn't touch the floor or ceiling, but seems suspended at window height. It opens with a rusty creak, and, as I peer into darkness, I realize I'm looking at a ramshackle shelf suspended in all four corners by frayed rope twined around big rusty pulleys. The only thing on the shelf is an old yellow crockery cup.

I poke my head in to look up and, without meaning to, rest my hands on the slivery shelf.

And that's when the catch gives and the pulleys twirl wildly. I snatch my head back just in time and watch, with my heart pounding, as the shelf crashes rapidly down two floors. I can see light at the bottom and realize the dumbwaiter must have blasted through the kitchen and crash-landed in the cellar.

It startles me and frightens Pansy and Violet, too, supposedly asleep in their rooms. In minutes, I'm backtracking through their corridor, drawn by Pansy's scared whimpering. I grab her up and we go into Violet's room. She's sitting upright in bed with her bedspread taut over her head, and it takes a minute for me to persuade her that, yes, the castle is still standing.

Finally, she believes me enough to emerge, shaking, from under her covers, and I take them both to the kitchen, where we make a big saucepan of cocoa with marshmallows and share our excited views of the mishap. It helps.

When we feel calmer, we examine the dumbwaiter together, the three of us, checking out its sad remains in the cellar and investigating the hole in the wall several floors up and the little door, still intact, in the kitchen.

"It's too bad it broke," says Violet sadly. "We could have rided on it."

"No, you couldn't have," I say. "It wouldn't be safe. It's not meant for little girls, just for dishes and grime and gunk and things." I fetch some duct tape and seal up the doors, taping boards over the opening on the second floor. The displays are not beautiful, but certainly fitting for the Smithson estate.

We decide to take our supper into the woods, and we pack all our favorite foods. I'm partial to packaged, creme-filled cupcakes, so we toss those in, along with Pansy and Violet's personal favorites, salty cheez tidbits and pretzel sticks. Juice, of course, to drink, and a few grapes because, after all, we want to be healthy. We agree to wear our oldest clothes so we can do some serious romping in the mud, and I spray the girls and myself with plenty of bug spray.

The woods are pretty, and there's still lots of sunlight left. The black flies seem to be taking a little break this evening, and I only have to swat away a few. Things have dried off nicely since the downpour that welcomed me to my new home, and it's nice to drink in big gulping mouthfuls of fresh, cool air after being closed up in that musty castle all the time. It strikes me funny. I've waited all these years to get my castle back, and now that it's within my reach, I realize I don't even like it much.

But, Sister, forgive me for saying that I'm not letting Chuck off the hook that easily. He owes me big.

I wonder who this Emily Cheseworthy is. Cool as a catfish, that one. Maybe not horribly smart and not too imaginative. Terrible taste in ties. I don't think she likes Pansy and Violet much either. Not that I do. Well, a little. Seems like Smithson could choose someone a bit warmer to be his Significant Other, although she is beautiful. At least they'll look good together in the tabloids, even if they're miserable.

I decide they must be engaged, since he doesn't have a picture of his wife - his former wife - on display anywhere. I wonder where she is, what happened to her. He seems unhappy and it could be because she's gone, but, then, how well do I know him? If he's like other husbands I've known, like the insufferable Nick Wilta for instance, Mrs. Smithson probably flew the coop trying to beat him at his own game. Maybe she detested The Honorable Charles Fitzham Smithson the Second as much as I do, once she realized what a prize she picked. Maybe she hated living in the castle. Maybe she couldn't stand all the screaming.

Maybe the dumbwaiter fell on her head, and Charlie skulked her into a makeshift grave in the back yard.

Maybe she's decomposing in the secret room.

Or maybe she's sunbathing nude on the French Riviera right this minute, surrounded by beautiful men. Good for her. It's where I'd be, too, if life was anything like fair.

◇◇◇

The picnic is over, but I'm feeling too lazy to gather up our garbage and make the journey back to the sad, drippy castle. I'm lying on the ground trying to catch a few winks, and Pansy is running in circles around me, snuffing like an elephant. At least that's what she says she's supposed to be. Violet decides to join us as a cat and keeps meowing in this screechy, irritating way. How can people stand little girls?

"Violet, that's too annoying. Be something else," I tell her.

"I don't wanna be something else. Just a kitty." She puffs up her chest and braces herself with clamped shut eyes. "MEOWWW!"

It's impossible to rest with all this racket. I get up, frustrated, and grab Violet by the shoulders of her sweatshirt. I pick her up and dangle her, and her eyes grow suddenly huge. The meowing stops. "Now, what did I tell you about minding me? Do you want to be lucky or not?"

"Do." Tears are forming.

"Then quit being a cat," I say, meaning it.

Pansy is watching, fascinated, her eyes wide and wondering. "If she doesn't stop, will you make Daddy stay away?"

Violet, hanging in undignified remorse, is looking at me carefully, her face all screwed up, her mouth ready to let loose with a big, fat meow. She would like to rebel, but isn't quite sure. She glances at me, thinking it over, reading the situation. "Daddy is an imbecile," she whispers. A big, brave statement, and her voice hardly wavers.

Pansy is looking at me suspiciously, waiting for my reaction. Violet, dangling gently under my grip, puffs her chest out, and I know she's getting ready to screech out a big, bad meow. She reminds me so much of myself as a tot, and I know I better fix this rebellious side of her in a hurry. I plunge.

I strengthen my hold on Violet's shoulders and push my face

close in to hers. Her mouth closes in a hurry. Her little feet sway in the air. "If you continue to be a cat, Violet," I say quietly, "you may never see your father again."

My mother said stuff like that to me all the time. I spent hours in my room afraid my bad behavior would have horrid consequences, worrying over my father's demise, sure that Nancy would be forbidden to play with me, that I'd be going without supper, that my toys would be confiscated or I'd be locked in my room. My mother's threats were effective and my response was always to scurry off to contemplate my sins and vow to mend my ways.

But Pansy and Violet's reaction is a little different.

It's too much for Pansy. She begins to cry, a small, weak sound at first, then bigger, gulping sobs. "Don't meow anymore, Violet," she says. "Please don't."

Violet's mouth has drawn down into a frown; tears are forming. Soon she starts in, too, her high-pitched cries echoing through the woods, worse than any fake cat howling. This is the first time they've done this since Smithson took his leave, and I'm wishing, as I frequently do, that I could gather back the stupid words I've said. Apparently, emulating my mother is the wrong way to discipline the girls.

Well, one more flub for Lucky Wilta.

"Violet," I yell, setting her down, "very good. Thank you. You stopped meowing. Daddy will definitely be here tomorrow." They both keep crying. "Violet! Knock it off! Do you hear me? You were good! Daddy's coming home tomorrow! Pansy, stop it!"

Pansy's nose is running in great, slimy strands, and Violet is lying on the ground now, crying into pine needles that are sticking all over her shirt and pants and face, and in her tangled hair. "Come on, you guys," I yell. I'm desperate. "Quit it right now, or Daddy really won't come home!" They bawl louder. I threaten and cajole, make absurd promises and insane threats. It's no good. They won't stop. I ignore all the junk from our picnic, just leave it lying about on the forest floor, and I pick up the two sobbing children and start back for the castle. They cry all the way home.

I change their clothes for them and put them in their beds, and leave them to cry themselves to sleep. The happy atmosphere of the past two days is gone, shot, kaput, and my arms ache from carrying them.

I lock up the castle, trudge back to my room, and set my new electric blanket on seven. I bring a cup of tea to bed and grab a novel from the bookshelf in my room. I can hear the hiccuping of Pansy's last sobs even after Violet has fallen into a fitful sleep. I turn off my light and yank my blanket over my head, trying to drown out Pansy's crying. Trying to drown out my own worthlessness.

Even my fingers in my ears don't do any good.

Nothing helps.

I'm a rotten housekeeper and a wretched nanny. He never should have hired me. I know it. He knows it. They know it. All of yesterday's wardens who popped in so cheerfully all day long know it. The miracle is that I haven't destroyed them both by now. It's what everyone expects of me, and I know, deep down, that they're right.

I feel horrible.

I click my bedside light back on.

What's this? This is not the way my adventure is supposed to progress! Maybe a little vigorous exploring will ease my guilt.

I start in the foyer, checking thoroughly behind the tattered tapestry. Nothing. I tap carefully on the walls, listening for a tell-tale change in the sound. Nothing.

I shove chairs away from walls, lift tables, peer behind draperies and pictures. I branch out to other areas, measuring distances and exploring closets. I gaze at ceilings and stand in stairways, trying to measure with my eye the distance between first-story ceilings and second-story floors.

And I come to the conclusion that my father's secret room is exactly that - a secret. Slowly, I pad back upstairs. Finally, Pansy and Violet are sleeping deeply. Pansy has thrown the covers off and I replace them gently, then stand back looking down at her tiny face, at her long lashes brushing her cheeks.

I hardly mean to, and if I had given it a second's thought, I wouldn't have, but something unfamiliar comes over me. I bend over Pansy and plant a soft little kiss on her hair. She doesn't stir. It makes me feel so good that I return to Violet's room and kiss her, too.

Back in my own room, I pick up my novel again. I feel a little better now, but the longer I'm here, the surer I become: I have set myself a nearly impossible task.

# 7

WHILE THE GIRLS color quietly, I strip everything from the smallest living room and clean it with a vengeance. I need to do this because a) It's freezing in the castle and the work warms me, and b) I'm not used to feeling guilty and the work helps me forget.

I've already apologized to Pansy and Violet for last night's cruel threat. I can't find out from Dr. Harvard whether you should ever apologize to spoiled, disobedient children, but I do, and it makes me feel a little better, even if they don't seem changed. I've also discovered that the good doctor absolutely forbids hitting, pinching, slapping . . . . Not that I have done those things, but somehow Smithson knew that even though I didn't. So I pray, Sister, for the patience not to succumb to that kind of rash behavior. Rearing children is harder than I thought.

I'm shoving a shabby sofa against the far wall to face the television and yanking gobs of cobwebs and a few dismayed spiders away from the newly-exposed baseboards. The cobwebs are sticking to my fingers, and one worried spider is racing up my arm.

I swish away the spider and feel superior to Mrs. Frocks. It's obvious she never cleaned back here.

The other living rooms are too big to be comfortable. We only need one, and this is it. It has a fireplace, bookshelves, three tall windows, and a faded red Oriental rug. All the necessities. I figure I'll do a Major Furniture Switch and move in acceptable pieces from the other rooms. We'll make this our relaxing gathering place. It will look cozy, even if we do have to wear six sweaters.

And I'll never have to clean the other rooms.

"How many hours now?" Pansy asks again.

I'm trying hard to cultivate patience. "Three," I tell her.

"Is that more than you said before?" asks Violet.

"No, before I said four. Now it's only three. He'll be here in three hours." I pause a minute, thinking. "The amount of time between finishing breakfast and eating lunch."

"We already ate lunch," says Violet.

"We could eat again," says Pansy.

I go into one of the other living rooms and start checking out the furniture, deciding which pieces we could live with without gagging. A little hand slips into mine. I look down to see Pansy at my side, looking up at me with sad, hopeful eyes. "Can I help you?" she asks.

Sister Mary Phyllis, it must be some instinct, some primate mothering thing that's been lying dormant in me all these years. You know I'm serious when I say I don't mean to bend down and hug her, but I do it, Sister. I even kiss the top of her curly head. That's twice now. And it isn't even written in my contract. "Yes, my baby Mexican bean beetle," I tell her gently, "I would love it if you'd help me."

She's an enthusiastic helper, and soon Violet hears the commotion and laughter and comes in, too. We exchange some chairs and small tables, and decide that a tall, heavy highboy must go, and a more delicate piece must replace it. But we can't lift some of the bigger monstrosities, so we decide we'll get their daddy to help us with those when he gets home.

We take down the dusty draperies and the girls drag them upstairs and, squealing with laughter, fling them behind one of the closed doors. They slam them in there good, and then come tripping down again, all smiles.

Kids forget injustices very fast.

Lionel shows up again, and we get him to help us move the heavy furniture. He's pretty good-natured about it, calls me all kinds of endearing names, and collapses on one of the more comfortable sofas after we've finished. I get him a beer from the kitchen and figure I might as well have one myself. We've earned it. We're covered in dust, and my hands feel grimy, but the beer tastes great. Guinness Extra Stout. Imported.

Natch.

The girls are running around in the music room; it seems almost empty now, since we've reorganized and pushed some hideous tables and chests up along one wall. Smithson's desk is still in there; I know better than to touch that, since it's cluttered with stacks of books with little sticky notes in cute, vibrant colors pasted on some of the pages. Books like *Money Dynamics* and *Planning Your Financial Future* and *Building Financial Independence*. But they're not all boring. Some have catchy titles like *Portfolio Management* and *Classic Money Investments*. It's good to see that Mr. Sensitivity has such a varied and fascinating taste in reading.

There's an out-of-tune piano near his forbidden desk that gives out with a shrill chord every time Pansy or Violet crashes into it. They've discovered they can hear their voices echo in there and are doing what they do best, making a lot of noise.

I've warned them to stay away from the desk; I can only hope they comply.

"Two hundred acres, mostly woods," Lionel is telling me over the fracas in the other room. "And two houses. A lot of these big old homes have two houses. The main house and the smaller guest quarters or garden house. I razed the main house and built new. And it's on the lake, of course." He peers around. "I'm surprised Charles doesn't want to trade this in for something on the water. Living in the middle of the woods like this, it's kind of weird."

"It's very private," I mumble.

"Yeah, cut off," he says. "No internet, no cell service. How can you stand it?"

I shrug and begin to answer, but he isn't listening. He's back to his favorite subject. "A brand new log cabin. My great car. There's not much I don't have, Lucky."

I'm beginning to lose interest in all this, but I nod appreciatively.

"And nothing to do but soak it all up, figure out new ways to spend money." Lionel laughs proudly and slurps from his bottle of beer. "Could I have another one of these?" he asks.

"Fer sher. I'll get it." His first damp empty is wearing away the polished surface of the coffee table I've hauled in here. I don't much care. This is supposed to be a comfortable room, a room we can enjoy. And Lionel is definitely enjoying himself.

When I return with two more bottles, I find him slouched almost full length on the sofa, and I nudge him to sit up straighter and make room. He moves a little, not much, and then pulls me down next to him and gives me an endearing little grin.

"I never would have gotten into college," he tells me, "if the old lady hadn't pulled some strings. I was having too good a time to do anything like work. Out on the boat every weekend, parties that lasted for days." He chortles happily, gulps beer, and rubs his hand along my back. I move away from him, but he leans his wiry little body closer and starts telling me about his good old college days, about ordering stacks of loaded pizzas sent to some poor geeky freshman's dorm room, about rigging an amplified sound system into his ceiling so it rocked the whole dorm awake at three a.m. About swiping the college president's car for a joke, leaving it stripped five miles out of town.

One of Lionel's hands is strangling his beer bottle convulsively, while the other is tracing soft patterns on the back of my neck. I'm not sure I like it and I'm wondering if I should make him quit it. I don't; I sit there drinking beer, trying to decide how much I actually like Lionel.

"I'll take you out on the boat one day, Lucky," he's telling me. "I bought it a few years ago from a guy. You'll love it. Wind, water, sun. Until you've spent a weekend on Mandi's Kiss, you haven't lived."

Mandi's Kiss? A *weekend*? He's got to be kidding. "Sounds great, Lionel," I say, and he kisses the back of my neck with moist lips. I squirm away.

I can feel the two beers, and, after my third, I wouldn't exactly say I'm looking forward to Lionel's next moves, but I'm resigned to the fact that he seems quite smitten with me. He has great hands, very sensitive and kind of small, and he's playing with my fingers while I laze back peering at the serious, concentrating faces of two or three Lionels.

Not that three beers is a lot for me; I figure it must be the high quality of the brew, but anyway, I start laughing, thinking how funny Lionel looks with two noses.

His hand is stroking my hair now, and he's mumbling something about all his accumulated money and his latest winnings at the Saratoga track, when suddenly he whispers in my ear, "You cute thing." I kid you not. "You cute thing," he whispers, and I figure the beer has really gotten to him. "You're not cut out for baby-sitting and kitchen duty. What can Charles be thinking of?"

Well, I agree. I mean, we all know I never really believed in this work in the first place. And in light of yesterday's fiasco in the woods, it would be silly to pretend I'm a grand success. "You're so right," I say.

"Once you find the diamonds you'll be out of here, I'm sure," he says.

My throat constricts. A black mist descends on me, and I sit up stiffly, shoving Lionel off me and staring at him. He lands in a heap on the floor and grins up at me.

69

"Isn't that right, Lucky?" He picks himself up and resumes his spot on the couch. He leans back, sprawling, like he owns the place.

"What are you talking about, Lionel?" I have never sobered up so rapidly.

"I'm talking about the diamonds you've been searching for. You don't plan to stay after you find them, do you?"

How does he know? How can he possibly know the secret I have hoarded for nineteen careful years?

"Did you find anything in the tower room?" he asks.

"Lionel, I don't know what you're talking about."

"Yes, you do." He smiles at me and he sounds affectionate. And all of his faces look, yes, sincere. How I wish I hadn't had three beers. I tell myself to think carefully about every word that tumbles from my mouth. Did he find my father's journal? Impossible. I keep it in my room, buried and under lock and key. Did I tell him? I'm certain I didn't tell him.

"I heard you, Lucky. And I've seen you. You're searching for diamonds. That's why you're here, right?"

"No way," I say unsteadily. I start to get up from the couch.

He beckons me back, smiling a crooked smile. "Come on, Lucky," he cajoles. "Don't be mean."

Reluctantly, I settle in again. An image flits to mind - the fluttering draperies in the upstairs hall, the feeling of a movement just behind me in the corridor. Well, I know it was Lionel, and he thought he was funny sneaking up on me like that. He returned from the kitchen that afternoon with a couple of frosty beers, materializing next to me and whispering, "Boo," in my ear.

He didn't stay long that day, just long enough to guzzle one of Charles Smithson's brewskis and leave me to attempt to ferret out some of the castle's secrets. And to overhear me, apparently.

He likes to make a grand appearance, and now, when I look at his pleading face and eyes full of unabashed curiosity, I almost have to laugh.

He shrugs it off. "If you didn't want anyone to know," he says, "you shouldn't have been talking to yourself."

Good advice, which I will follow from this day forward. If I can remember.

"Lionel, you don't understand," I say. "It isn't what you think."

He's leaning forward, all ears, excited to get it straight.

70

"I can't talk about it right now," I whine. An understatement if there ever was one. If he gets me going, I'm likely to spill my guts to him like some overemotional female bubble. I need time to figure out what to tell him. "Ask me later," I say.

And if he were any kind of a gentleman, that's exactly what he would do. But of course he presses. He softly turns my face to his. His bleary eyes go crystal clear for a moment; I can practically see diamonds gleaming in them, and he squints straight into my eyes and says with great sympathy, "Tell me now, Lucky. I'll help you. I'd love to help you look for diamonds. Come on. You know you want to."

And horribly, I *do* want to.

My head is beginning to throb, and I'm aware of feeling every ounce of those three beers. "I can't tell you," I say. It comes out a wail.

He removes his gentle fingers from my face, and his puppy eyes droop, either from disappointment or the beer, I'm not sure which. It makes me feel kind of bad, in a way. Isn't he, after all, asking to be my trusted friend? I could sure use one of those.

Right. The friend of my arch enemy Charles F. Smithson Two. Not the perfect choice for confiding my secret quest.

I turn to Lionel, trying hard to plaster a sincere expression on my face. "Really," I say. "You're wrong."

"All right," he says agreeably, and relief floods me. "They're your diamonds. I was just offering to help." He gazes at my face for a moment, still hopeful, and then his voice softens. "I won't tell Charles, if that's what you're worried about."

A crash from the music room makes me jump suddenly, and I use it as an excuse to leap away from Lionel and race to the rescue of the wee ones down the hall.

"What are you guys doing in here?" I demand.

Pansy looks up from the floor where she's lying gazing up at the ceiling. A broken picture frame and dented canvas lie next to her. Violet stands idly by, the picture of innocence. "Nothing," they say together. Then they look at each other and laugh.

"Well, see that you aren't," I say. I'm not particularly steady on my feet, and it occurs to me that someone in charge of two preschoolers probably isn't supposed to be drinking in the middle of the day. I wonder vaguely if Dr. Harvard has opinions on that. I stuff the canvas and splintered frame behind a drapery and step carefully back to Lionel, where he's still lounging on the sofa.

I plop down next to him. "Tell me more about your college days," I urge him. Anything to escape the topic of my diamonds.

He complies easily and launches into a story about tying a mule to the campus fountain, then discourses on the pros and cons of various brands of beer. He has a lot of opinions and seems to have tried every brand there is. I giggle to encourage him, and he starts laughing, sliding his sneaky arm around me again. I'm feeling a lot more relaxed, as if a major catastrophe has been averted, or at least postponed, so I don't cringe away.

And that's when The Lord and Master lets himself in the front door with his key.

We don't even notice him at first. Pansy and Violet have resumed colliding and yelping in the music room, and Lionel and I are lounging on the sofa together, yucking it up, comparing college stories and failures, and reviewing the pluses of having big bucks while we gurgle Charles Smithson's Guinness.

I look up to see two Smithsons and decide they look out of place. Their navy blue suits are impeccable, their hair is combed, they look clean and neat, businesslike, and, now that I look closely, maybe a little anxious. Actually, they look the picture of worried control. They don't fit into the scene at all.

"Did everything go all right?" they ask, and as I blink, the two Smithsons stagger together into one. I'm not sure if he's talking to Lionel or me, but it doesn't matter because he's looking around the room, taking in the sunlight pouring through the sparkling windows, the different furniture arrangement, the wet rings our beer bottles are making on the priceless antique table, and the two of us sprawling congenially on his worn out velvet sofa.

He exhales audibly, something almost like a sigh, and then leaves us and heads in the general direction of his rambunctious children. "Daddy! Daddy!" they whoop, and I can almost picture him gathering them into his arms and hugging them both at once while they mess him all up.

Familial bliss.

"Later then," says Lionel with a cheeky grin, and he gets up from the sofa and lets himself out of the castle, whistling his way over the terrace and down the driveway.

I lunge up from the sofa and stagger off for a scrub bucket and a good, stiff cup of coffee.

◇◇◇

72

"Miss Wilta, why are the living room draperies in my bedroom?"

I look up, confused, from the fireplace hearth I'm scrubbing. It's amazing how the serious, overbearing presence of Charles F. Smithson can sober up even the most happily tipsy housekeeper.

Lionel, that flirting rascal, has left to get ready for a real date, leaving me to mull over what to tell him when later finally comes and how to explain myself to Smithson. The girls are in bed, taking much needed naps. The Honorable Mister Smithson has taken charge of that himself; I think he missed them.

"What do you mean?" I ask.

He's still wearing the meticulous navy blue suit, and I can see gold cufflinks gleaming at his wrists. "I mean that the draperies that are supposed to be hanging here in the living room are heaped on my bedroom floor," he says. "Why?"

Clarity dawns. "Your daughters put them there," I tell him.

"Did my daughters also climb up and unhinge all of the drapery pins, and move all this furniture around?"

"Don't be sarcastic," I tell him. "I did most of that. Pansy and Violet only helped. Lionel, too. Your pal Emily started to pitch in, but right off she broke a nail. Pity, wunnit."

He ignores that last. He's looking around, frowning. "Why?"

"We need more light in here. We need to stop living with stuffy, ugly things. *You* need to stop living with stuffy, ugly things."

He's still checking it all out, but he doesn't say whether he likes the change or whether he doesn't. What a simpering, impossible man.

"Miss Wilta," he says.

"Lucky."

"I can't call you that," he says, irritated.

"Why not? Everyone does."

"It just . . . . It's not dignified."

"*I'm* not dignified, Your Honorableness." Seems like I might not need to tell him that. I wonder how many times he found Mrs. Frocks bordering on intoxicated in the arms of his best friend, Casanova. I go back to scrubbing stone. Strands of my hair are falling out of the tight, unlovely bun I've yanked my hair into. I blow them back away from my face.

"Only because you choose not to be," he says.

"Just call me Lucky," I mutter, scouring.

"No."

What's this? A battle of wills? May the best guy win? Fine. I sit back on my haunches for a minute. "Look, Sir," I sneer, "I prefer Lucky for a reason." And even while I'm saying it, I realize it's one of the very few honest things I've told him. "My name is Lucilla Wilta, and I feel like limp lettuce. I'd rather just be Lucky, if that's okay with you."

Neither of us says anything for a minute. I plunge my hand into the metal suds bucket and bring out my wet, soapy sponge. I'm totally, completely, furiously sober.

"The girls don't seem any the worse for being with you," he says finally. Is this supposed to be some kind of compliment? They should stuff this guy and display him at Ripley's Believe It or Not. I swirl soapy patterns on the hard gray stones. I come across a crusty piece of dirt and scrape with a vengeance. "Thank you for keeping them safe," he says.

"No prob, Your Richness." I don't glance up, just keep swishing and attacking the floor.

He says nothing, and, personally, I have nothing more to say to him, either. The silence stretches so long and hangs so heavy that I think he must have sneaked out of the room. I glance up, startled to see his eyes fixed on me.

"Lucilla?" he says. Oh, I see. First name basis now.

"What, Charlie?"

"I'd prefer you not get too thick with Lionel Hawthorne."

"Why not? Any friend of yours is a friend of mine. Perfect or im."

"You don't know him as well as I do."

"I know him well enough. I know he has a sense of humor, and he likes to have fun. And he doesn't sigh over nothing every minute."

"I do not sigh." He says this with great indignation, pulling himself up to his full height.

"Okay," I say agreeably. I mean, I'm not the one who started this fight.

There's another big, long pause, and then he says, "You're too free and easy with Lionel. I think you should be more particular."

I stare at him. "What the everlasting brimstone are you talking about, Your Eminence? I don't remember signing any contract that said you could pick my friends, too." He's treating me as if I'm his third daughter. What a pompous, ignorant . . . . Angrily, I thunk the sponge into the pail of dirty water, and he jumps back, avoiding the spray that splashes out and dots the floor.

He's quietly annoyed for a moment and then he says, "Why do you do that to your hair?"

I glance up. "Do what?"

"That bun . . . thing." He gestures vaguely in the direction of his own head. "It isn't attractive, you know. You look like a washerwoman." He turns and heads for the kitchen.

"I *am* a washerwoman!" I call after him.

Tell me not to drink on the job, and demand that I hop to a bit more eagerly with Violet and Pansy. But *don't* choose my friends, and, for God's sake . . . my *hairstyle?* Perhaps he'd like me to curl and curry myself before his royal arrival.

I find an old stain and rub it furiously.

◇◇◇

Now that his mysterious three-day trip is over, we settle into a fairly routine schedule. His Insufferable Wealthiness goes off each morning after breakfast, leaving me to cook, clean, wipe noses, and, of course, pursue my quest for True Happiness, i.e. the diamonds of Marsuvius Borstrom.

I am trying to muster up enough nerve to ask about the locked door at the top of the circular stairs, but I make the cowardly decision not to worry about it. Somehow I suspect his response would be less than friendly.

I have no idea where he goes or what he does all day, and he never offers that information. It's driving me crazy. Not that he owes me any explanation. After all, who am I? Just the person who's bringing up the kiddies.

I try to pick up clues, but my sleuthing doesn't get me very far. When he leaves in the mornings, he sometimes wears a suit, three pieces, expensive, with one of his adorably gauche ties. I figure on those days he's going door to door selling dental appliances or vegetable seeds. Or making the rounds with Miss Emily.

But more often he wears a pair of jeans, an old shirt, sometimes two old shirts, one over the other, boots which return muddy if it's a wet day, and some kind of jacket if it's cool. He usually takes his car, driving out to the highway and disappearing in what passes for an Adirondack urban throng. But now and then he pulls a fast one and strides off into the woods behind the house. And I can never predict which it will be. There's no point in trying to outguess him. I can't.

He has left a phone number, of course. Can't take a chance on one of the girls kicking the bucket and him being uninformed. But he tells me to call only for near-death experiences. The occasional accidental poisoning I should handle myself.

He's unapproachable. And it's making me nuts.

Dinner, if he's there, is often a quiet, unhappy affair. Oh, I don't mean for the girls. They're neither quiet nor unhappy. In fact, their constant, high-pitched chatter often sends me purposefully to the medicine cabinet for something a little stronger than aspirin.

With them, he's talkative and animated. "What did you do today? A squirrel? Really? How big? And it was where? And you said what? Gosh!"

With me it's "Pass the bread, please," and "The butcher would give you a better cut of meat if you'd tell him who it's for."

He eats as if food is going out of style, and I know he likes my cooking, diner style, disparaging remarks about the butcher notwithstanding. One day, Pansy even tells me he once volunteered to her that they were lucky Mrs. Frocks wasn't cooking for them anymore.

Not that he'd ever tell me that.

When he doesn't return in time for dinner at night, I spend a lot of time warming food that would have tasted better the first time around, but he doesn't complain. Hell, I'm the one who should be complaining. I can't see any reason to do everything twice.

He must be spending his evenings somewhere, too; I wish I knew where. He leaves without an explanation, and I never know when to expect him back. Once in a while, I know he plays golf. My big clue is that I see him toss his clubs into his car, or that Lionel stops for him and he tosses his clubs into Lionel's car. Call me gifted.

Occasionally, when the mood strikes him, he spends an evening with his children. With their little soprano voices and sturdy, game-loving bodies, they wear him out. That could be why these family events are few and far between.

There's no particular rhyme or reason to his movements, at least none that I can see, and when I finally summon the courage to ask him where he goes and what he does, he ignores me.

So one day when I know Pansy and Violet are immersed in a

puzzle, I sneak out and follow him into the woods. He walks fast, and it's all I can do to keep him in view while I skulk around trees and bushes and hide behind rocks.

It doesn't work.

I get careless and crunch a stick too close behind him. He stops suddenly, stiffens, and turns around.

And there I am, guilt like a mask across my face. I smile sickly and give a little wave. He is not amused.

Slowly he walks toward me, and the closer he gets, the more clearly I can see the anger in his eyes.

"How dare you leave my children alone," he says quietly.

"They're fine," I start. "I was only-"

"I hired you for a reason, Miss Wilta. Go back at once."

"I will," I say, nodding vigorously. "But, really, they're not in any danger. They're just-"

"Don't you ever follow me like this again," he says. His blue eyes are hard and cold. I see a barely disguised rage there, but another emotion, too. Fear. Why would he be afraid?

"If you do this again," he continues, "you'll be finding other employment. Immediately."

I feel my face flush with shame. I, Lucky Wilta, have just been threatened with termination from the one job that has the power to change my life. Old Borstrom's diamonds flash before my eyes, then turn to liquid drops that fall to the ground and soak in.

Why does it bother him so much that I followed him? Why was I stupid enough to do it? Why do I even care where he goes?

Before he can say more, I turn and flee, running back through the woods, across the lawn, and into the house. I'm out of breath and damp with sweat. The girls are lying quietly on the floor fitting puzzle pieces into odd-shaped spaces. Violet is chewing on one, and I yank it roughly from her mouth. She yelps and twists away from me.

My cheeks burn with the memory of his words. I know I'll never risk following him again.

Fine with me. It saves me more time for exploring and makes me more determined than ever to find those diamonds and dump them in a brash, selfish pile - just beyond the reach of his remorseful, itching fingers.

# 8

BOB COBB STOPS BY and replaces the drive belt on the furnace. "Itza old hot air furnace," he tells me. "Kinda makeshift, yep. It was put in after the building went up. Done by guess and by golly, I guess."

"Will the clanking stop now?" I say.

"Can't make no guarantees, no," says Bob. "That'll be a hundred twenty."

"What will?"

"The bill."

"Send it."

When it arrives, I hand it to Smithson and he hands it back. "Pay him," he says.

"Bob thinks you should have the whole system replaced," I tell him.

"No, I should have Bob replaced," he says without smiling.

"Why do you hire him then?"

"There's no one else, except his crew. They're all just like him." He glances around our bleak environment. "What a waste, pouring money into this place."

One evening, His Holy Moneybags is looking around the kitchen at the shelves that are still dusty and the cupboards that could use a good scrubbing and a coat of paint. The kitchen access to the dumbwaiter shaft has been closed off and permanently sealed, but the rough boards he nailed over it are just as unsightly as my taping job. It looks ramshackle and crude, and his gaze takes it in the way he takes in most of the messes in the castle. He's hinting around that I might want to do some decorating in here, and I'm giving him my blank look.

"Don't women usually like that sort of thing?" he says. "Picking out fabric and putting ruffles on things?"

I can't tell if he's serious or just testing to see how loud I can scream, so I make the wise decision not to respond. I glare at him instead. "Well, you could at least do something with these cabinets, Miss Wilta," he continues. "In your spare time, I mean.

Couldn't you?"

Spare time? Has he glanced into his New and Improved Living Room lately? Or his Now Uncluttered Library? Has he noticed that there are no longer orange mushrooms growing behind the toilet in the bathroom by the back door? Or that I sewed, actually *sewed* a pair of curtains for that freaky, odd-shaped window over the clothes dryer? Has it occurred to him that his children are not only alive, but actually approaching happy?

What does he think I've been doing since I moved in?

"You're an idiot," I say, and I yank out two chairs that are pushed up near the kitchen wall, resting on spread newspapers. The green paint is still tacky on them, and I shove them under his hands, so he can experience firsthand the fruits of Lucky Wilta's free time.

"Oh," he says a little contritely, examining the trace of green on his hands, "I guess I didn't notice these."

"No, and a lot of other things."

"Well, that's fine," he says enthusiastically. "We have some green chairs now. But these cabinets . . . ."

And he urges me again to hire some people to help me. Finally, I resolve to do so.

I advertise and end up interviewing an absolutely beautiful man to help paint and repair and do small maintenance jobs. His name is Seymour.

Seymour works out fine for just about one week. That's when Bitsy, our new maid, comes into our lives. Seymour takes one look at Bitsy, and Bitsy looks back, and next thing you know they're both gone. We never see them again, but they later forward an address and request their wages, which I dutifully send. As I look around, I can't find one single thing that looks improved since they were here.

I don't bother to tell The Smithson that I have no intention of hiring any more people. As much as I thought I'd enjoy coming upon Seymour and his flexing muscles unexpectedly, I didn't. He seemed to spend too much time watching furtively for me, suddenly looking busy if I appeared, and it put a real crimp in my search for the secret room.

Bad enough that Lionel Hawthorne materializes in hallways and at windows, questioning me about my stalkings. So far, I've put him off with a breezy joke or two, but it does cramp my style a bit.

In fact, it cramps my style a lot. The whole point in moving to the castle was to pounce on my hoard and chuck Chuck out, my way lit by glittering diamonds as I haul him to the door.

So I prioritize the chores and do only what's absolutely necessary. And sometimes not even that.

Everything else slides.

After a while, Capitulation Smithson stops suggesting more hired help and turns a blind eye to all the tasks that never get done. We lapse into a dull routine. Every day he drifts off to the blanket factory or wherever, and I stay here with his girls, scrubbing the occasional bathtub and pressing wrinkly tablecloths, playing blindman's buff and London Bridge, and dragging Violet and Pansy into town to spend money wildly at every store I pass. When he's around, he doesn't have too much to say to me. He goes about his business. I go about mine. I start a nice little bank account for myself from my hefty paychecks. I scurry hopefully through gloomy hallways, playing my castle game, scratching my head in confusion when no secret room materializes, and I hum while I make fried fish or beef stew or baked ham for supper.

Our quiet, grimy life is getting to be a habit.

◇◇◇

The clanging furnace usually entertains us for the first half hour after Smithson turns up the heat in the morning. Bob Cobb pokes around, comes up truly stumped, and sings his favorite refrain: Out with the old, in with the new. Smithson sends him away and does his usual Bah, Humbug routine, disappearing into the nether reaches of the castle. I can hear him thumping for studs, following ductwork, climbing around inside cellar walls, pounding, tapping, banging.

He emerges covered with dust and cobwebs, and announces that there are animals living in the heat ducts.

"Animals?" says Violet, with wide, impressed eyes.

I smile softly at her. "Yes, my darling, giraffes."

"There must be holes in the ducts," her father says. "I might have to let Bob replace those sections. I hate to do that. This place is hardly worth it."

Hey, this is *my* castle he's talking about, and it is so worth it. Sort of.

"Miss Wilta, you'd better call Bob again and get him up here

80

to work on it."

Bob arrives several days later, wearing his favorite blue *BOB* work shirt. "We could tear out this whole system, put in a new one, as long as we're at it, yep," he suggests.

Smithson vetoes, and the next day a work crew arrives to begin the process of replacing only the broken, inhabited sections. As I watch them tramp through, I read their shirts: *EARL*, of course. And *JIM* and *HANK* and *WESLEY*. Wesley?

I mop the kitchen floor languidly while they clang tools together and shout greetings through the ductwork; then work begins in earnest as they begin to rip through ceilings and crash through walls.

"Lucky," Pansy asks, concerned, "why are those men ruining our house?"

"Those are Bob's friends," I explain. "Bob said they could."

Pansy nods in understanding.

"Lady?" the worker with *EARL* on his shirt calls to me. "You wanna move this wash away from here?"

I scurry to the laundry room and pick up the pile of jeans and stray socks and underwear and towels. I toss everything into a couple of baskets, and drag them into the pantry next door.

I can hear guys in the pantry ceiling, and I look up in time to see a drill explode through, its ear-splitting scream slicing the air. A chunk of plaster falls at my feet; a few more mingle with Pansy and Violet's socks and their father's dress shirts.

I heave the laundry out of there and shove it under the kitchen table.

"I hope they repair all this," Smithson says glumly. He's looking up and around, sad, like it's his best friend who's disillusioned him by wrecking his home, stone by stone.

"This is some place," mutters *JIM* as he drags by with an enormous alien killing tool with metal spikes. He's scuffing up rocks, glancing around, squinting.

"Maybe once," *EARL* responds, and they both chuckle like hyenas.

My hackles go up. Who are these bird brains who think they can come in and do all this damage and then insult my castle, too? I grab the mop and start sloshing violently at *EARL*'s muddy footprints. He gives me a surprised look and jumps into the hall. I follow close behind, slopping the mop into his frantic heels.

"Lady, watch it," says *EARL*. He's looking at me as if maybe I'm insane, and his feet keep jumping while I prod and thrust with the mop. "Ma'am!" he shouts.

I stop poking him, and, instead, lean on the mop provocatively. "Yes?" I say sweetly, and I gaze into *EARL*'s confused eyes.

That's when I realize that *EARL* is gazing not at me, but past me, and I turn my head to see Sir Charles Fitzham Smithson the Second standing there. His look is not friendly.

"Miss Wilta, please don't torment the plumbers," he says, and even while his eyes look pained, I'm positive I see a twitch, just a breath of one, at the corner of his unsmiling mouth.

By now *EARL* has made his getaway, so I hoist the mop over my shoulder to head back to the kitchen. Muddy water drips tiny pools onto the floor. "He slammed your castle," I explain.

"But that's no reason to-"

"Yes, Your Wimpiness," I sigh and toss the wet, dirty mop into a closet.

◇◇◇

Things are in full swing with *BOB* and The Plumbers when there's a feeble little pounding on our massive front door. The only reason I hear it is because I happen to be standing right there screaming at *WESLEY* not to swing his pipe wrench into the window three inches from his left arm.

"Settle down, lady," he says to me, like maybe I'm the one with a brain the size of a shriveled pea. The wrench goes through the window, and shattered glass rains down on the checkerboard floor.

"Huh," says *WESLEY* in weak surprise.

I fling open the front door and glare down at a rumpled little man in a charcoal gray suit, staggering under the double weight of a worn briefcase and a leather computer bag. He smiles tentatively up at me and inquires as to whether Mr. Smithson might be at home. Wordlessly, I open the door wider and let him lurch in over the broken glass.

"Keith, great you could come," Smithson says eagerly, approaching with great strides, shaking the little guy's hand and relieving him of one of his bags. "What happened to the window, Lucilla?"

"It broke," I say through clenched teeth.

The Keith person follows Smithson on through the house, hopping over piles of plaster, glass, and old wall.

It's intriguing, of course, and since my charges are safely swinging in the back yard and I've been waiting all these weeks to find out what kind of business Chuckles runs off to each day, naturally, I follow. Along the way, I duck into a pantry and grab up a few dust cloths and some furniture polish. I've learned it's important to camouflage one's eavesdropping.

"It doesn't matter about the internet," Keith is saying, as I follow them into the music room. "I downloaded a few things to show you. We can go over those first."

Smithson nods vigorously, apparently quite enthused about this visit.

They settle themselves in two cracked leather chairs near Smithson's desk, and I walk briskly to the piano, tsk tsking under my breath. "My, how grimy this keyboard gets," I mutter, and I spray a little polish on one of my cloths and begin to rub.

It's very quiet in the room, and I finally look up, hating to give in but realizing visits are not usually so completely silent. The Keith person and my Estimable Boss are both looking at me. They have Keith's laptop open and ready, a stack of folders and some loose, clipped papers before them, but those things are apparently less interesting than watching the household antics of yours truly.

"Miss Wilta," Chuck says calmly. "Mr. Gregoire and I would like coffee. Would you make some, please?"

What a pain.

"Of course," I tell him, and I stuff my greasy dust cloth into my jeans pocket.

It's not fun in the kitchen. I swipe at the layer of silt on the countertop, measure the coffee and get the water started, and then glance at the vents on top of the coffee maker. This will never do. Plaster and dirt are falling out of the ceiling in various places. Muttering expletives, I fetch an umbrella from the back hall, snap it open, and prop it over the coffee pot. A few bits of plaster sift down and skitter off the umbrella.

I'm finding this whole situation very irritating, especially since *JIM* has apparently come to the very incorrect conclusion that the coffee is for him and his pals. Well, it's not, and I resolve to bring the whole pot back to the music room with me. I dig out three cups and saucers, gather a few spoons, and pour milk into a cute little pitcher with daisies on it. I find a sugar bowl, too, and then shovel out some of the brownies I made last night, arranging them on a plate. I even stick a lacy paper doily underneath. We'll see if Charlie Smithson has the nerve to force me out again. Like some servant.

I bring my tray of goodies back into the music room and find an empty space on a side table. Chuck eyes the pretty display and the third cup and saucer, then glances up suspiciously. "Thank you, Miss Wilta."

The Keith guy shuffles some papers, taps his pencil on the desktop and says, "So that means ratios may be computed and interpreted from two perspectives, time-series analysis and cross-sectional analysis."

The Honorable Charles F. Smithson looks blank. I pour myself a cup of coffee, snag a brownie, and smile engagingly. Chuckie II scowls at me. I yank out my dust cloth and tiptoe my sloshing cup to the other side of the room. I'm a quiet little mouse, a fly on the wall. I make good brownies; I chomp happily.

"Are you with me?" the Keith person asks.

"I'm not sure," Chuck answers.

Keith loosens his tie and pushes his glasses up onto the bridge of his very sincere nose. He speaks slowly, looking carefully into Smithson's eyes. "If you compile ratios for a number of years that's time-series."

Chuck nods.

"And if you compare them for several firms within the same industry at any given time, that's cross-sectional."

Chuck nods again, looking kind of authoritative. "Yes, that makes sense."

The Keith person pushes back in his chair and breathes out. "Okay, good. So once you know your current ratio, you'll have the extent to which your liabilities are covered. Now, if we take a look at your shares for these Blue Chips . . . ." He peers at Smithson, who has turned slightly in his chair and is peering at me. I resume dusting energetically.

"Why do I have the feeling you're not following this?" Keith asks.

Smithson corrects him quickly, whirling his attention back to the papers before him. "Oh, I am. It's just . . . Excuse me, please." He stalks over to me where I'm polishing the same brass lamp I've been going over for the last five minutes. "Miss Wilta," he says, "are you aware that that chemical you're using will destroy the finish on this lamp?"

I pull my cloth back as if it's burning. "Yes, just finishing up here," I say briskly.

"Go and check on my daughters." His eyes are icy. I nod agreeably and leave the room in great haste.

His daughters, of course, are fine, taking turns dumping sand on each other's heads and screeching joyfully. They obviously don't need me, and I'm determined not to be outwitted so easily, so I meander around to the front of the castle. The music room window is open, so I mosey over there, trying to hide in the shadows of the cedars, crunching as little as possible on the dead twigs and leaves under my feet. I can hear the murmur of men's voices and catch occasional words like fluctuations and beta coefficients. I have the disappointing feeling that even if I could understand what they're saying, I wouldn't understand, if you know what I mean. But I can't give up. Mysterious Charles has shut me out for too long, and I have the right to know where the money he pays me comes from. For all I know, he could be a drug dealer or a common thief, and I do have Pansy and Violet to think of, too. I steal a little closer to the open window and crouch silently in the underbrush.

Their voices are clearer now, and I hear Keith Gregoire say, "Of course, you have to consider government relations and labor conditions, too. I don't think you'll have too much trouble if you-"

I never get to hear the rest because Smithson's face suddenly appears and the window slams down, hard. I jump and fall backward into the leaves of some kind of prickly flowering shrub growing up against the castle, and I scratch my arm on a dead stick protruding from the knobby trunk of the bush. My arm is bleeding, and I swipe at it with some leaves.

I do have a good view in the window, though, lying here in the dirt. Keith is standing up now, smiling, his wrinkled gray suit clinging to him like a loving caress. He extends his hand and Smithson takes it. They shake in a friendly way and wander away from the window. When I hear the front door open a few minutes later, I make one more valiant attempt to learn the truth, unsavory as it might be, about poor Pansy and Violet's father. Crouching on all fours, darting from bush to bush, I spider my way quickly toward the porch and crouch behind a tangle of forsythia.

"Well," Keith is saying, "just keep one thing in mind. You do want your assets to exceed your liabilities." Keith's eyes are *twinkling* - I'm not kidding - and they both laugh appreciatively. Two businessmen enjoying the understated humor of their profession, whatever that might be.

Keith turns down the circular driveway, and just as I'm about to uncurl myself from my sharp, twiggy environment, he leans out his car window and calls back to the castle, "Charles? You might want to watch out for that drip we talked about. I have my doubts." He smiles. Chuck chuckles and nods.

Keith drives off. Smithson gives a wave and goes back inside.

If that last was directed at me, I've decided to be big and ignore it. In fact, I aim to rise above this whole demeaning situation. Drip indeed. How dare they. I always knew The Honorable Sir Charles Smithson the Second was a conniving thief with no finesse, and now I have the scratches and bruises to prove it. And my arm hurts, too.

I tunnel my way out of the shrubbery, limp indoors, and fetch the tray with the coffee things. I near the kitchen just in time to see *HANK* and *JIM* coming toward me. "Did I hear there was coffee to be had?" *HANK* asks me. His mouth is twisted in a lop-sided grin that he probably thinks is devil-may-care. I think it's nauseating.

"Please help yourselves," I mutter through gritted teeth. I hobble to the kitchen cupboards and ignore the humiliated tears that are flooding my eyes as I set out more cups.

As I help Pansy bury an earwig she's found dead in the grass, I glance up to see the whole crew through the kitchen window, *HANK* and JIM, *WESLEY*, *EARL*, and *BOB*, chuckling in delight as they pour steaming coffee into their cups and share a laugh over the fun they're having dismantling my castle.

◇◇◇

The castle is getting colder and colder now that the heat is completely off. Yes, summer is nearly here, but it's been a chilly, damp spring, and today is a chilly, damp spring day. I've made the girls wear sweatshirts, socks, and shoes, and I decide to join them in the yard, where they're shooing at black flies and playing in the wet grass. They race for the swing set and I follow.

I'm feeling a little calmer now, and have decided to bury my animosity and give C.F.S. another chance to treat me with the respect I deserve. The Keith person and his insulting superiority are long gone, so why hold a grudge? I've made a fresh pot of coffee and whipped up some blueberry muffins for the gang, planting everything on the dilapidated picnic table Chaz uses to decorate his lawn.

I'm trying, Sister. You have to give me that much. I'm trying.

*WESLEY* wanders by, hooks a clean mug, pours coffee, and gives me a little salute.

I decide to ignore the hacking drone of *EARL*'s power tools and the occasional startled shriek of a plumber interrupting what I'm determined might still be a decent day.

Violet is chortling with joy as I push her higher and higher on the swing, and Pansy is climbing up a knotted rope and hollering, "I'm the moon! I'm the stars!" I see their father approaching from the castle, carrying something. His mouth seems to be moving, but since the moist air is filled with the sounds of drills whining, rocks crashing, and men whistling and shouting, who can hear him?

"It's Daddy!" Violet screams, and she jumps off the swing, falling on hard dirt. She finds her feet and races toward him, and soon Pansy gives up her celestial identities to become Pansy again, and she runs to him, too.

He's down on their level, keeping them at arm's distance, saying something and allowing them to peer into his gloved hands. Show And Tell With Professor Charles. I wonder what he has.

He has mice. Four tiny, pink, wormy, hairless creatures in a box, squirming and wiggling with tightly closed eyes.

"They're so cute," Pansy breathes. She's hopping excitedly from one foot to the other. She sticks out a finger to touch them, and her father pulls back.

"No, honey. You can't touch the mice. There might be germs."

"Can we keep them, Lucky?" asks Violet, looking at me sincerely. "We can keep them in my room. I'll water them every day."

"You don't water mice," Pansy corrects her, "do you, Dad?"

"But can I keep them?" Violet wants to know.

The look on Smithson's face shows me that he hadn't foreseen this turn of events. Hasn't he read Dr. Harvard yet? Doesn't he think he should? He gives me a bewildered look, and I shrug. The girls are still hopping, planning, and exclaiming. This is gonna be a tough one for the Prince of Leniency.

Well, it's not my call. I leave the three of them there on the grass, deciding the future of four naked, wet mice. Blecchh.

I have better things to do.

*Diamonds of a thousand brilliant colors! My little Lucilla will stumble on that room one day - and the treasure hidden there . . . .* As long as the walls are full of holes, what better time to do some serious snooping.

I poke around joists and rafters and scan a 1927 newspaper that some Lowland or Ruggins stuffed in as insulation. I dig between loosened stones and even pry a few right out of the walls. I come across ancient lath criss-crossed over wall spaces big enough to plaster in a small child. Now, there's a thought . . . .

I cut my hands, scuff my knuckles, and learn more than I ever wanted to know about the 1927 flight of The Spirit of St. Louis, but I do not find a secret room.

I emerge frustrated and even more moody than before, wondering why my diamonds elude me this way.

Maybe I was too hasty in rejecting Lionel's help.

And where has Lionel been lately, anyway? I might actually welcome his assistance in exploring these dusty new areas or in watching the girls while I search vigorously. He could be reading the riot act to *JIM* and helping us keep the castle intact. He promised not to tell Charles his suspicions about my diamonds, and I want to believe him. But I don't need the brain of a Keith Gregoire to tell me: Lionel doesn't visit when chaos rules; he only comes around when things are calm and easy. A fair-weather lothario, a fickle mirage of a buddy.

Still, I miss him - a little. He's fun and a little goofy, a nice contrast to stuffy old Smithson. Plus, he thinks I'm cute. At least he says he does. Not that I can believe anything he says.

His Lordship interrupts my reverie by stamping into the kitchen, sans mice, and impatiently following Bob Cobb down the cellar stairs. "No, Bob," Chuck keeps saying. "I don't want to put any more money into it. It's not worth it."

"Is *this* worth it?" Bob rejoins, making a grand gesture that includes the pandemonium all around.

They argue a bit going down, and bang some pipes together for good measure, then Smithson comes back up wearily. Bob follows, still harrumphing, his waxy brows knitted in serious thought. He wanders away to find *EARL*.

"Where are the mice?" I ask. I'm eyeing Smithson's shirt pocket, looking for movement.

"We took them into the woods. The girls were surprisingly agreeable."

"Into the woods? And you assume they won't be back?"

"They'll probably die, don't you suppose?"

"That's harsh, My Knight."

"Miss Wilta . . . ." His voice trails away as *JIM* and *WESLEY* stomp in, gouging the floor as they pass through, dragging plaster chunks and dirt behind them. *JIM* carries a section of old cast iron radiator, bumping it on the floor with every step. Slices of stone and grout fly up, spraying the air.

"Maybe you could be careful with that?" Smithson says.

"Sorry." *JIM* changes his grip on the radiator, complains that it's heavy, and scrapes it along the wallpaper. Smithson peels the neat curl of wallpaper from the wall and stands looking down at it in his hands.

"It's harsh," I repeat. "You know they'll die, yet you left them there. What kind of father are you?"

His eyes widen. "I left the mice, not my children, Lucilla." A loud reverberating clang reaches us from the next room, followed by a deep yelp of pain. Smithson starts, looks toward the pantry, and then shrugs. "Hank was about to drown them in a pail of water. They would have died one way or the other."

"What did you tell the girls?"

He answers me straight on, and he doesn't even smile. "That they'd be adopted by some father or mother mouse."

I consider. And I don't smile either. "Well, maybe they will be then."

Smithson makes a noise in his throat, more a snort than a laugh. "Yes, maybe," he says. He looks down at the chipped floor and fingers the new holes in the wall, then drops the wallpaper, sighs, and goes off to play hide 'n' seek with *HANK* and *BOB* in the heat ducts.

# 9

THE CASTLE ECHOES QUIETLY. No more drills. No more saws. No more hammers pounding or sheet metal bending. *BOB* and *EARL* and *JIM* and *HANK* and, yes, even *WESLEY* have gone. The silence is so vast that I can hear giddy squirrels chattering outside the broken windows. Leaves whisper. The sun streams in, warm and wonderful.

The castle is in chaos.

Dirt, debris, plaster, and stone. Odd nails, bits of wood, and chunks of frozen solder. Dust everywhere, white and gray. Scraps of wallpaper and metal. Chips of rock, glass shards glistening in pools of sunlight, holes in ceilings and walls. Sawdust. Filth.

The squirrels, mice, and bats that lived in our home have been dispossessed, abandoned in the woods like furry little Hansels who will never find their way back. And those are the lucky ones, the ones who escaped *HANK* and his murderous bucket.

I'm sweeping the kitchen, and my back aches. I'm tired of cleaning up after two little girls and their recalcitrant father. Why must I do it for five grown men in embroidered shirts?

Smithson has just turned the heat back on, a test. We shouldn't need it now that the nights are warmer. But we need to know, are on pins and needles to know. Will it make a difference? Was the terrible price of this unholy mess worth it?

The girls and I have been putting their winter things away in cartons, and they're having fun trying on last summer's favorite sunsuits and discovering how big they've grown.

"Look at this one on me," Violet says. She parades in wearing tight blue shorts and a midriff top with jellybeans on the front.

"Last year's?" I ask. She nods. "My, how you've grown."

She smiles. It was exactly what she wanted to hear. She scoots away happily.

Smithson comes up the cellar stairs, wiping at the sweat on his forehead. "It's hot down there," he says. "I won't leave it on long, just enough to see-" He never gets to finish. His words are drowned out by the insistent, angry clattering of pipes. A long, loud moan reverberates through the kitchen, then a shrieking whine. Something crashes, and a metallic buzz stabs the air, dying away to a dull, throbbing pounding.

Sir Charles stares at me and I at him. I don't dare speak for fear I'll laugh.

"But they replaced all those sections," he says at last. His nostrils flare slightly. I can tell he's trying hard to remain dignified under adversity. "Get Bob up here for me," he says brusquely, and turns on his heel to leave the room.

Bob is hopeful. His shiny forehead wrinkles into segments as he nods agreeably to everything Charles says. He's sure that rebuilding the motor will melt our troubles away, and, yes, he can take it with him this very day. He removes it, hauls it up the cellar steps and out to his truck, and smiles serenely as he drives off. We watch through the window. Gusts of exhaust flit cheerily behind Bob's tailpipe.

"He says he'll put new bearings in," Smithson confides sadly. "I wonder if it will make any difference."

"At least his children will eat this week."

The Honorable Chuck's face is lined with that familiar pained expression.

"Cheer up," I say. "It's summer. You won't need to give it another thought until October." He doesn't answer.

"Come on, Mr. Smithson, wipe those blues away," I say merrily. "Think of pleasant things. Don't be moody, bleak and broody." I snap my fingers twice, tapping into the rhythm of my words.

Oh, almost forgot. His Supreme Godliness doesn't stoop to smiling.

"Chill, Chuck," I say helpfully. "Lighten up. It's just a furnace, after all. Things could be worse." I have other pet phrases I could dig up, too, to jolly him out of his depression. I feel kind of bad for him. He's just standing there, gazing sadly out the window.

I try just one more. "Why be so glum, chum?"

Finally, he looks at me, stares for a moment, and then says bluntly, "Certain people always have that effect on me."

I think he means Bob.

But I'm not positive.

I whistle on up to Pansy's room and heave the carton of her little wool things into the hallway. She's tossed them in there at my instruction, ready to be saved until next year. Her cold weather jackets and hats lie in a heap in the back of her closet; they'll remain there safely until fall. She and Violet appear in the doorway, wearing identical gingham-checked sundresses, both a little tight and a lot wrinkled. "Can we wear these outside?" Pansy asks.

"Of course, my tiny citrus whitefly larvae."

They run off, squealing. I open the casement window in time to see them bouncing haphazardly out the back door. The air smells like good dirt. Summer has arrived.

◇◇◇

We're sitting in the music room one warm Sunday evening, while the sun turns the lawn outside a shiny gold. His Great Intellectuality is slouching over his cluttered desk and has donned reading glasses to pore over some folders, very important, official-looking folders with alphabetical, typed tabs on them, the kind busy, important people like to scurry around with. The glasses give him an intelligent, bookish air that's been sadly missing until now. I bet he fools a lot of people with those glasses.

Every now and then, he strikes a serious pose, as if Moses has asked him to step in briefly to accept, or maybe explain, the Ten Commandments. He adjusts his glasses, opens one of the thick, scary volumes on his desk, and reads carefully, glancing back at his folders and occasionally ticking something off with a pencil.

I'm sitting in a chair in the corner, duct taping my favorite slippers back together, and Pansy and Violet are sitting side by side on the piano bench, pounding on the keys of the heavy grand piano. They're singing together, two different songs, in wild, strainy anti-harmony. Every once in a while, their father covers his eyes with a hand and breathes deeply.

Finally he looks over at me. "Could you get them out of here?" he says evenly. Then he sees what I'm doing and says, "Are you taping those?" I glance down. The taping job is a little messy, and I wonder if I might be sacrificing style for comfort. Smithson has a pained look on his face. "Why don't you just buy new ones? My God, I pay you enough."

I quickly stuff the roll of tape into my pocket, don the slippers and stand up. I twist this way and that, getting the feel.

Just right. "Old habits die hard," I say to Smithson's frowning face. I take my charges to the other end of the house, and we engage in a fast-paced game of hide and seek.

"Holes in the walls are off limits," I say. "And no fair throwing plaster and rocks to create a diversion." We play for almost an hour, and when they start to get whiny, I toss them into the bathtub and then into bed for the night.

Chuckles is still reading documents and making the occasional penciled notation when I return to the music room. He looks up when I come in. His glasses slide down on his nose. "What was going on?" he asks, striving to sound calm. "I know they were having fun, but it was hard to concentrate with the noise."

"Nobody got hurt, and nothin' got broke," I say. "A good time was had by all."

He scowls and goes back to the facts before him.

I slide my hand over the piano keyboard, making just the slightest unmelodious sound. I remember this piano. I took lessons on it for a year or two before I was whisked away from the castle. Nancy always got a kick out of reminding me to put away my sheet music after practicing. It made her feel useful.

My eye travels to the wall cupboard on the far side of the room. I go over and stand before it for a minute. Nancy used to make a game out of opening this cupboard. It had a tricky catch, and in order to free it, she would murmur a magic formula and twist it hard to the right and down, then turn the top hinge very gently, and the cupboard would spring open. I follow her method, minus the magic words, and as I twist the hinge, I hear a tiny ping sound, and the door bounces open, hitting my arm.

The music is still there, old first and second level pieces. Songs I once knew how to play and a few that I never practiced because I didn't like them. I'm sorting through, reading titles to myself, when I become aware that Smithson the Second is watching me. I shuffle the music haphazardly and stuff it back into its niche.

"You can play," he says. "It won't bother me."

"Solly Chollie, no can do." I latch the cupboard, giving the bolt a little extra twist to keep it closed. Maybe someday, when he's down at the factory lacing footballs, I'll indulge. Pansy and Violet might love my music. I suspect Mr. High and Mighty wouldn't.

He's still staring at me, a puzzled look, so I say, "Will you be able to tear yourself away from your millions to spend some time with your children tomorrow? They were wondering."

He tosses the pencil down on the desktop and looks as if he's about to speak; his eyebrows knit together in annoyance. He finally picks up the pencil again and turns back to his papers.

"Not that's it's my beeswax," I say. "They're your kids. *I'm* not the one who stands at the front window watching hopefully for your return every night. *I'm* not the one who haunts the back door or sadly removes the extra plate . . . ."

"Miss Wilta." He has turned toward me now and removes the glasses with a quick gesture, agitated and angry. "I'm doing the best I can. Kindly stay out of things that aren't your business." He gathers up his papers and stalks out of the room. I hear him go up the stairs.

I wander over to his desk and take a look at the thick book he kept referring to as if it were God's own Bible. *Portfolio Management and Investment Theory.* Well, no wonder he was so fascinated. Investment theory sure would top my list, over keeping my kiddies happy.

◇◇◇

I make blueberry pancakes for breakfast, and I let the girls put ice cream on theirs. I've always believed ice cream and summer go together. Why wait for a fireworks display? I assume Chuck might have a problem with this, but do I care? If it's up to me to bring them up, then I'll do it my own way.

He doesn't even notice the ice cream, he's so busy picking the girls up and telling them how beautiful they both are, how proud he is of their exemplary behavior while the plumbers were here, how much he adores them both. I could gag.

"Is Bob finished rebuilding that motor?" he asks me.

"He brought it back yesterday. Can't you tell? It's so cozy and warm in here."

"It's summer, Lucilla." He heads down to the furnace to fool around for a while. What does he think? That Bob Cobb wouldn't leave things in perfect order? When he returns, he washes grease off his hands at the kitchen sink.

"It looks all right. I guess we'll know in the fall whether that will take care of the clanking every morning."

"You're not going to try it now?"

He doesn't answer, just opens the refrigerator and takes out a gallon of milk and slops a little into a mug of coffee.

"He left you this," I say, and hand him Bob's bill.

Charles glances at it briefly. "Bob is a crook," he says. "Pay him." And he sits at the table and looks at his food.

I was a little premature. I scooped ice cream on his pancakes, too, when he first appeared, and now it's a warm sloppy mess floating on his plate.

"Sorry," I say, whisking it away. "I'll make more." He sits at the table, a silent, unlikable thing, looking at the sticky walls and unfresh cabinets with a sour expression, while I pour and mix and ladle and serve, and this time I give him a choice about the ice cream.

"Is that what the girls had?" he asks.

"Calcium," I tell him. "All the latest findings support it."

"Sugar," he retorts. "All the quack dentists love it."

"So do you want ice cream or not?" I'm standing there with the scoop poised over his plate. The ice cream is getting soft in the carton.

"All right," he says. He's so immature.

By now, the girls have run upstairs to get dressed and not make their beds, and I lean against the kitchen counter watching their father eat.

"Do you realize," he asks me, "how rude it is to stand there watching me eat?"

"Pardon me," I say, and I sit across from him to watch him eat. A few minutes tick by. "I taught Violet how to blow her nose," I say after a while. He looks at me, but doesn't bother to answer. "Pansy, too," I continue. "It actually took Pansy longer. She kept sucking in instead of blowing out, and then she'd swallow it and-"

"Miss Wilta!"

"Oh, sorry," I say. I guess I was being undignified again.

He keeps eating, looking at me once in a while as if he's weighing the pros and cons of having me on the same planet. I believe the cons are winning. No contest.

"Miss Wilta," he says at last, "we're going to take the girls on a hike tomorrow."

"Who's this 'we'?"

"You and I."

"A hike? Not a good plan. I don't do hikes," I say.

"Well, you'll be doing this one."

"Like walking for miles and getting oozing blisters? Drinking

95

water that the forest animals use for a toilet, and getting bit up by black flies and mosquitoes? Carrying in heavy satchels and carrying out heavy satchels plus two tired, whining children?"

He's nodding agreeably.

I continue. "Getting sweaty? Getting rained on? Getting poison ivy? Wrecking your clothes? Having your legs ache? That kind of hike?"

He finishes the last of his ice cream. "Why not? The mountains are right in our back yard. And you were right about my daughters. They need to see more of me. We'll leave at eight in the morning."

"But what about your job?" I say desperately. "You have to go to work, right?"

He smiles crookedly. "I'll beg for the day off."

"Mr. Smithson," I try again. "They need to see more of you, not more of me. It might be a nice father/daughter event. And I could stay here and get a nice dinner ready . . . ." And search out those frustrating, annoying, elusive Borstrom diamonds, I'm thinking.

"Don't be ridiculous," he says. "I couldn't take them on a hike by myself. They don't mind me. They might fall off a cliff or something."

"Couldn't have that," I mutter.

"Get whatever you need to pack a lunch tomorrow," he says. He hops up from the table, leaving his dishes all over. "I won't be here for dinner." He darts out the back door, then he's back. "Lucilla," he says, and he almost sounds embarrassed. "These cupboards really look terrible. It makes the whole kitchen unappetizing. Couldn't you have them painted, or at least clean them?"

I'm not sure he's paying me enough.

# 10

HE COMES HOME LATE with a couple of those guides to the woods, one on plants, one on animals, and an array of hiking equipment that would put even Daniel Boone to shame. Daypacks, water bottles, compass . . . .

"What's all this, Chuck?" I ask him. "Is this your first hike ever?" I hope he knows what he's doing. I'd hate to spend the rest of my life wandering around lost in the Adirondack Park. I'd have to become one of those mountain hermits without any teeth and catch bugs for my supper. I'd construct a rude hut from twigs and bits of forest moss. And after I succumbed to the elements, they'd build a little shrine . . . . *Here lies Lucky Wilta, unlucky to the last* . . . .

I realize he's looking at me a little strangely, and I know my thoughts were on my face, easily readable to anyone with half a brain. Which would be him.

He pulls out a map, a flashlight, moleskin.

"What's moleskin for?" I ask.

"To prevent those blisters you were so worried about." He's shoveling raisins, nuts, chocolate chips, seeds, broken pieces of grain and chaff and hay into little Ziploc bags and sliding them closed. "Gorp," he says. He holds one up.

"What's it for?" asks Violet. She's wearing last year's summer pajamas, skintight, with bouncing blue rabbits all over them.

"Energy," he answers.

"Gorp. Gorp. Gorp," snorts Pansy. "Do we feed it to the animals? Gorp."

"To you," he says. She gives him a suspicious look. He turns to me. "We'll divide everything between the two packs and each carry half. We'll need jackets and the food, too. And insect repellent. And the water bottles will have to be filled." There's an excited gleam in his eyes that I've never seen before. Finally, something to excite Mr. Smithson.

The girls have a lot of trouble settling down in bed, and I have to keep going into their rooms to quiet them. It's getting to be a real pain in the neck, and I'm miffed. When they're cranky tomorrow, it will all fall back on me.

"Go to sleep, Violet," I say for the fourth time.

"I can't, Lucky. I'm too excited. Do you think Daddy will let me carry my own water bottle?"

"Probably. I'll ask him."

"Do you think he'll let me carry the flashlight?"

"Maybe."

"Do you think he'll . . . ."

I leave the room and go across the hall to her sister. "Go to sleep, Pansy."

"I want to carry the flashlight, Lucky. Will Daddy let me carry the flashlight?" I wish His Most Monstrous Stupidity would read Dr. Harvard's book, thoroughly, like I have. He would have known better than to come home with just one flashlight. I wonder briefly if there might be another one in the cellar. I couldn't find it myself, but that doesn't mean it doesn't exist.

"Lucky," Pansy says sleepily.

"What?"

"What's the name of the mountain again?"

"Esther Mountain."

"If I get tired hiking, will you carry me?"

"No, Daddy will."

"What if Violet gets tired, too?"

"He'll carry you both."

"What if *you* get tired, too, Lucky?"

"I'll grab a taxi."

Early in the morning, Lionel Hawthorne drops by on his way to the golf course and finds it a real hoot that Sir Charles the Second is spending the day playing Mister Dad. I invite him along and beg him to accept. I might enjoy this with Lionel's light-hearted company, and, to entice him, I even sidle up to him and suggest a wager - that he'll reach the summit faster than I will. Twenty bucks. I'm hoping he'll go for it; he loves a gamble, and I can guarantee he'll win. He thinks over my proposition; I can tell he's considering it carefully.

"Maybe for one of your diamonds," he whispers, smiling out of the side of his greedy mouth.

I glance back at Smithson, carrying packs and daughters out of the castle door. He must wonder what all the whispering is about. "Twenty dollars, take it or leave it," I hiss righteously.

Lionel laughs aloud, grins his little teeth at me, and zips his

BMW out the circular drive.

"Thirty?" I screech after him. "*Fifty?*" He gives me a cheery wave and leaves me standing in a cloud of exhaust. It's all I can do not to run after him and jump in.

We set off at eight o'clock, and the girls sing zanily all the way up the sunny road to Whiteface. Charles claims we can park there and then it's an easy hike to Esther's summit. He says that you have to go down first, then back up. This seems like wasted energy to me, and I tell him so.

"Fine," he says. "Let me turn around and take you all the way back down. I'll drop you at the trailhead at the base of the mountain and we'll take the shorter route and wait for you at the top."

Sometimes he's so sarcastic, and I don't have the patience right now. My head is pounding. I sneak a quick gulp out of my water bottle so I can swallow a couple of aspirin, but it doesn't help. The road is bumpy and rough from the winter's heaving, and my stomach is lurching painfully. Along certain sections, dead trees tumble crazily beside the road, fallen birch, spruce, beech, and pine looking almost red in the morning sunlight. In the distance, clumps of spruce trees look small and black under the hazy blue sky. It might be pretty if I didn't feel like heaving my breakfast.

By ten fifteen, we've reached a small parking area. The wind has picked up, and we decide we'll need to wear our jackets.

"But I don't need a jacket," says Violet. Her blonde hair blows wildly around her head.

"Put it on, honey," her father says. A polite request. Mr. Softly-softly.

"No, I'm hot."

I'm in no mood for this. "Violet," I say, "it isn't hot up here; it's freezing. Now put your jacket on."

"No, I don't want to." This is getting irritating. She's never this stubborn during our days at home. Well, not usually.

"Violet, if you don't put your jacket on, I'll make your father disappear over that ledge," I tell her. My eyes are menacing, and my voice is loud. Pansy watches, impressed, and hurriedly puts her own jacket on.

"Lucilla," says their father, "that kind of threat-"

"I mean it, Violet." I wish her father would keep out of this. Dr. Harvard may not condone it, but there are times when you simply have to threaten children. Like when you're feeling impatient and just want to get a stupid hike over with.

Violet decides not to take any chances. Her lip trembles, and she puts her jacket on, allows her father to zip it up, and gives me a reproachful look. Smithson looks at me disgustedly and takes Pansy's hand, and the two of them walk off. Well? He brought me along to make them mind, didn't he?

The wind is so fierce that I pull my hair back and fasten it with an elastic I brought along, then I jam my hands into my pockets. I'm wishing I had tossed in a warmer jacket, and I'm uncomfortable with the daypack digging into my shoulder blades at every step. Violet follows, independent to the last. No packs for the girls, of course. They carry nothing but their sunny dispositions, and often not even those.

We're lucky with the wind, though, since it will help to keep the bugs at bay.

We set out over the rocks, heading down into a valley and then back up again. The rocks are gray and mottled, and Violet bends down to examine the little bits of shiny quartz embedded in them. Here and there, a loose rock jiggles under her weight, and I have to help her keep her balance. My daypack sways annoyingly, and I work at keeping upright.

Pansy and her hiking buddy are far ahead of us.

The rocks have become sparser, and a dirt path follows the natural cleavage between two small cliffs. We have to grab onto trees and bushes for support at first, but soon this peters out, too, and we're walking on a lush path of pine needles and moss.

"Hurry up, Violet," I keep saying.

And she keeps answering, "I can't."

The pack I'm carrying is starting to feel heavy, and I'm thinking we might want to stop soon for lunch. I glance at my watch: ten thirty. I sigh and keep on walking.

Violet is scrambling around outside the path collecting something. Little beggar. "Violet," I say, "come here." Reluctantly, she does. "You shouldn't touch strange plants," I explain. "You might get a rash." I look at the fistfuls of green leaves she's clutching and those she has scattered on the ground. They look like three leaf clovers.

"What are they?" she asks me.

"We'll look it up," I tell her. A part of me snickers gleefully at this opportunity to rest. We sit down together on a boulder at the side of the path. I pull out the spanking new plant guide and thumb through the pictures, searching for one that resembles a three-leaf clover with heart-shaped leaves. "Does this look like it?" I ask Violet.

She agrees that it does.

"Sorrel," I read. "It says if you chew it, it tastes like lemon." I sniff it first and then put a small, cautious bit in my mouth and bite down. I can taste the lemon, a mild, sour hint, and I'm confident I've identified it correctly. "Try it, Violet," I say. And she does, putting a whole heaping fistful of little shamrocks into her mouth and chewing them up. "That's too much," I tell her. "Spit it out."

She grins at me, bits of green stuck to her teeth. "I can't," she says. "I already swallowed it."

This could be bad. What if I've let her overdose on something fatal? I start reading in earnest. Use in salads, it says. Create a cool drink. All right. It isn't harmful. Wait. I read further. Safe if eaten in moderate amounts.

"Violet, how many of those did you eat?"

"Three."

"Three?" Thank God.

"I mean thirty."

I groan. For all I know, it could be three hundred. And what if it isn't really sorrel at all? It could be anything. I decide the only thing to do is tell her father.

But first I have to find him.

I hoist my unruly pack over my shoulders and grab the hand of the little girl beside me, and together we trudge along the path, searching for the idiot who brought us to this stupid mountain in the first place.

"Do you feel all right, Violet?" I ask her as we hurry along. Can you tell this kid is a Smithson or what? Stuffing herself full of any old weed growing in the mountain dirt. Not too bright.

I can see Pansy and her father sitting on a dry log far ahead of us, talking quietly. The path is uneven and rocky and angles steeply down. Violet trips and gets her shoelace caught in some brambles. I yank her out and drag her along behind me, looking down all the while, just to keep from falling.

The leaves at the tops of the trees are doing a hectic dance, and every now and then a good noisy gust hits us and cools us down some.

By the time we reach Pansy and The Boss, Violet and I have removed our jackets, tying them around our waists. My legs are shaking when we finally stop; I'm not used to such a fast pace on a steep downhill. I sit down wearily on a mossy stump and Violet collapses on the ground.

"Get up, honey," says her father. "You're getting your jacket muddy." Violet ignores him.

"Can we go now?" says Pansy.

"Mr. Smithson," I say hesitantly, "do you know what these are?" I reveal my crushed handful of little shamrocks.

"I can find out," he says, and checks in the plant book, identifying it as sorrel. At least we agree. That's a good sign.

"Your daughter ate some."

"Violet! You ate this?" His voice is sharp and demanding, and her lip quivers.

"Lucky told me to."

He turns to me, abashed. "You told my daughter to eat strange plants growing in the woods?"

"No. Wrong," I say. "I told her she could *bite* it. It tastes like lemon. I did *not* tell her to eat it. I definitely did *not* say to swallow it."

"How much did she have?"

"I don't know," I mutter. "Maybe thirty of them. A good handful."

He's hardly listening, but has turned back to Violet, who is now sitting up in the mud. She wasn't scared before, but the frantic tone of his voice is making her lose control. "Do you feel sick, Violet?" he asks her. His hands are massaging her arms, rubbing hard and gripping tightly. He doesn't even know he's frightening her.

"I don't know." She starts to cry.

Pansy isn't sure what all the excitement's about, but, just to be sociable, she starts in, too.

"Will I die?" Violet bawls.

"Will *I* die?" sobs Pansy.

"No, no," I say with authority. "No one is dying. Sorrel won't hurt you. We are just going to open up the cookies we brought and wash away the taste of sorrel."

"But I didn't get any sorrel!" Pansy wails.

I look grimly at their father. "Aren't we."

He nods obediently and, at the same time, realizes he's been a little rough with Violet. He loosens his grip and hugs her gently. "You'll be fine, honey," he tells her.

"Hand me your pack," I say.

I fish around for the oatmeal cookies I made last night and

bring them out. Violet is now merely sniffling, but Pansy is hugging her father hard and whimpering about heaven.

"Pansy," I say quietly, "we can't have these cookies until everyone stops crying. Do you want to have a cookie or do you want to cry?"

"Cookie," she says tearfully. She's not really finished crying yet, and personally I would have waited for her to make a real choice, but Mr. Indulgence can't bear the suspense; he hands her a cookie anyway. Soon she's busy with that. Violet takes one, too, and picks all the raisins out, making a little pile on a nearby rock.

"Don't think you're going to eat those," her father says. I can tell he's irritated, but he's making his voice soft and soothing.

"I always save them for last," says Violet.

"I know," he says, "but you can't eat them after you put them on a rock like that."

Her face screws up, and I can see the emergence of a good, big tear squeezing out of one eye. She looks at me. Sorry, no. I'm not getting in the middle of this one. I bury my head in the plant book, making myself interested in downy phlox, which, by the way, grows not only in our own back yard, but also as far away as Wisconsin and Ontario.

"But, daddy, I always save my raisins," Violet is whining. "Ask Lucky; she'll tell you. And sometimes I don't save them in clean places, but she always lets me eat them."

He's looking from Violet to me, and I examine the full color picture of phlox. It's pretty, pink and lacy. Nice flower.

"Like where?" he asks, and I realize then that he's not asking Violet; he's asking me.

I close the book resignedly. "Under the bed," I tell him. "In her sock drawer." Just to name a couple. "Come on, Your Majesty, those raisins aren't going to hurt her."

Violet takes that as permission, scoops up the pile, along with a few bits of dirt and moss, and tosses them in, chewing happily. Smithson groans and stands up impatiently. "This was not a good idea," he mutters, "not a good idea at all."

Like maybe I didn't tell him that.

After a lecture about eating unknown plants, given by Smithson with unfriendly looks at me, we're on our way again. Brown mushrooms and soft green mosses dot the woods on either side of the trail. "Stay in our sight and don't touch anything!" Smithson calls to his daughters, and they scamper ahead and wait on a big rock, tossing pine needles into the air and pulling at the soft moss that covers the boulder. At least they aren't eating the mushrooms, and for this I give a little prayer of thanks.

"I can see why they like you," he says stiffly. "You give in to them a lot." This, from the Wimp King.

"I give in sometimes," I tell him. "It avoids a lot of garbage. I know them; I'm with them all the time."

"I'm with them," he says.

"So there's no problem."

He doesn't like that much, not that I blame him. But who does he think he's kidding? We walk next to each other, but a million miles apart. He talks first.

"They're throwing things at each other," he says dejectedly.

"Let them."

"Do you think what she ate will hurt her?" he asks me quietly.

"Didn't you read what it said?" I ask him. "You can make a drink out of it or put it in salads. How dangerous could it be?" In moderation, I'm thinking.

"It was irresponsible of you to let her do that."

"It was irresponsible of you to get so far ahead of her. She's your daughter."

"Lucilla, I trust you with my children," he says stiffly.

"Well, that's good to know," I say. "You've never let on before." He's so pompous I could spit. In fact, I do spit. My saliva mixes with the dirt on the trail and turns to a tiny muddy spot. I grind it with the toe of my sneaker. He doesn't react, just stalks ahead of me. He joins the girls and in a few minutes, I'm there, too.

Here, the path seems to verge in two directions, and after some debate, some heated debate, we decide to go with his choice and follow the left path. I know within minutes that this was a mistake. The undergrowth becomes more and more tangled the further we go. The path has all but disappeared. We can hardly get through the fallen trees and thick, spiky undergrowth.

He looks at me, superior, not giving an inch. "All right, go back. I miscalculated."

I grab Pansy's hand and pull her with me. Yes, Your Incompetence. Of course, Your Blundering Botchery.

Would it kill him to listen to me in the first place?

The forest is dense, and I can't turn around that easily. Going through once was hard enough. I have to go off the path, dragging poor Pansy along by the hand. I've lost sight of Charles and Violet, but I can hear them tramping around, and every now and then his concerned voice saying, "Still feel okay, Violet?" The spruce trees are so thick I can hardly see five feet ahead of me.

"This can't be right," I say.

Pansy looks up with wide eyes. "Are we lost?"

"No, we're fine. We just have to get back to the path." I'm finding it more and more difficult to get through the thick growth. "I can't get through here," I yell. "Where are you?"

"Go to your right," Charles hollers back. I try to do that, but exposed roots keep tripping me up and thick branches claw at my face and arms.

"Hang onto me, Pansy," I tell her. "Don't let go."

"I'm scared," she whimpers.

"Don't be. And don't start crying. If you try hard not to cry, I'll give you two cookies when we get back to the path."

She's a little trouper. All I hear are some little scared sniffles. I keep telling her how brave she is.

There must have been a storm in here at one time. Trees are blown down all around us, blocking what once might have been a path and cutting off our visibility completely. I try climbing on some of the leaning tree trunks, looking for Charles, but I can't see him.

"Hey!" I holler, and Pansy joins in with "Daddy?" We both listen, but we hear only the feathery rustling of wind in trees. She tries again, a shrill call, "Hey, Daddy, you imbecile!"

I'm getting an eerie feeling, and I force down panic. We've definitely lost the trail, and I'm wondering if we've lost Charles and Violet, too. "Mr. Smithson!" I cry. "Violet!"

At first there's no response, and I'm already trying to determine the best way to keep Pansy safe on Esther Mountain once dark falls. What do I have in my pack? Some food, the plant guide, a book of matches . . . . Suddenly I hear a faint call, "Lucilla?" and I shriek, "We're over here!"

The air is noisy with wind, but it must be blowing toward me because the words come through. "Don't move!" he shouts back. "Stay there and keep shouting!" So that's exactly what I do, and Pansy joins in.

They get to us eventually. Now all four of us are lost together, with just a prickly hedge of dead branches and thick trees separating us from them. A good feeling. All we need is Bear

Grylls. Instead we have Wrong Way Smithson. But I can hear him and see him, and it annoys me how relieved I feel. Pansy desperately wants to cling to her father, but the trees are dense, and the dead blowdown branches are so sharp that she can't get through them. She decides to cling to me instead and leeches onto me with her frantic, sweaty little hands.

I'm touched. We've bonded at last. Hear my heart sing.

"We lost the path," Charles yells. "Are you on it?"

"No, we can hardly move."

"Wait, this must be it. Here it is." He moves away from me.

"Wait! Don't go!" I cry.

His voice comes back clearer. "That wasn't it."

We shout all together and then hold very still, hoping some other hikers might hear us, but that doesn't work. Rustling leaves aren't much of a rescue party.

We make a lot of false starts in all directions, two of us climbing through brush to reach what we think might be a path, the other two staying put, connected by shouts and fake reassurances. We're constantly hampered by the clutter of twigs, fallen logs and dead branches, the slime of mud and slippery moss. And it isn't easy holding onto two frightened little girls through it all.

A broken branch stabs my back and twigs slap my face, scratching me.

And I can still hear Charles asking quietly every now and then, "Still okay, Violet?" Then he calls, "Lucilla, is the compass in your pack or mine?"

"Yours."

"All right, stay where you are."

I smile down at Pansy. "You have a smart father," I tell her. "Now we'll get out of here." And I pray that I'm right.

We do get out. We discover we were completely disoriented, all of us, and we have to backtrack, ducking under logs and slanting dead trees. We climb over thick, prickly limbs and hoist ourselves over fallen trunks covered with wet moss.

We are filthy, punctured, tired, and achy. But we make it.

Back to mud and earth and a clear, flat path.

We decide to follow the right hand trail.

"That was scary," says Pansy. "If we had to stay overnight, how would we sleep in there?"

"Very uncomfortably," says her father. "What time is it, Lucilla?"

At first, I think my watch must have stopped. "Eleven twenty," I say. Can that be? "Were we only lost for twenty minutes?"

"It sure seemed longer," Smithson says. He drops to the ground and brushes a hand over his dirty jacket. "Hand me your pack, will you, Lucilla? I want to get that gorp."

"Gorp," says Pansy. "Gorp, gorp."

We spend some time resting, pulling twigs from our hair and clothes, wiping mud from our jeans, exhilarating in the delicious, cool water from our bottles. Pansy, Violet, and Charles get two cookies each for being so courageous.

The latter is looking at me intently. "That's a bad scratch," he says.

I put my hand to my face. I can feel the raised welt, and my fingers come away with a trace of blood. "It's nothing," I say. "You oughtta see the tree."

By noon, we're on top of the mountain. We've followed the flat, rocky trail that winds up and around, and the wind is a screeching howl. A row of perfect spruce trees lines the trail, sheltered just below the summit, and Violet begs to bring one home.

"For Christmas," she says. "We could put it in a pot of water."

"Daddy could cut it down with his knife," I tell her. "Go ask him if he'll carry it down for you. If he really loves you, he will."

We sit and lie on the brilliant, sunny summit rocks, looking at the view, eating lunch. A few deer flies make a half-hearted attempt to swarm our heads, but we spritz on a little bug spray and they wander off to find a more receptive target.

A sudden violent wind ruffles our hair and clothes and cools our sweaty bodies. Mountains line up in layers of black, charcoal, gray, and powder blue, blending into the hazy, pale sky.

The girls are taking tidy round bites out of sandwiches, and their father is lying back with his jacket over his face, blocking out the sun. We've been up here for a while, and I can hear other hikers approaching from below.

"Okay, ladies," I tell the girls, "wake up your father and let's start back."

"I have to go to the bathroom," says Violet. "Bad."

"Your Lordship," I say, "look alive. Your daughter needs you."

He sits up. A wintry smile appears. "That's what I pay you for, Miss Wilta."

# 11

THE HIKE BACK seems more grueling than the climb to the summit was. First a long, long downhill, and then that steep uphill path over rocks to get back to the car. Before long, my knees feel as though they're about to buckle, and I'm stopping every five minutes to get my breath.

Smithson must feel guilty for making me come along; he surprises me by waiting while I rest. The girls scamper ahead and he yells for them to stop and wait.

"Take your time," he says to me. "The sun won't be going down for a couple of minutes."

I stare at him. Has Solemn Smithson actually made a joke? It's early afternoon, so he must have been kidding. I don't laugh, though. I just can't; I'm so tired and achy that it's hard to summon up the enthusiasm to respond. "Don't wait for me," I tell him. "Join the girls." Truthfully, I wish he would go ahead. I'm sprawled against a tree, knowing my water bottle is tucked into my pack, but too tired to get it out. It makes me nervous to have Chuckles sitting there on a fallen log, gazing at me.

He gets up from the log, comes to me and busies himself rooting around in my pack. My, a mind reader. He holds the water bottle out and I take a long, cool drink.

"Do you like living in the castle?" he asks me suddenly. Now this is truly a surprise. He's never shown any interest in whether I like or don't like much of anything that goes on around us. And, do I *like* it? Who would? A worried flicker touches me, and I think of Lionel Hawthorne prying into my business. It occurs to me that Lionel may have decided to share my treasure hunting with the Big Boss. I haven't exactly been forthcoming to either of them about my enterprise.

But his face looks so sincere that I banish that thought.

"Because sometimes you seem angry about being there," he says.

Angry? Me? Boy, is he ever way off on this one.

"Nope," I answer. "Happy as a clam, that's me. Gladdened,

blissful, and content."

He looks into the deep forest, the rocks and trees stretching away. There's a sad, serious look on his face that makes me wonder what he's thinking. I almost want to reach over and soothe him. I don't, however. He is Charles F. Smithson, and I am Lucky Todd Wilta; never the twain shall meet.

"Have you seen much of Lionel lately?" he asks now.

"Now and then, not a lot. Why?"

He shrugs. "You might want to take it easy with him, that's all."

"So you told me before."

"But you didn't listen."

"No, I rarely do."

He glances ahead to the rock on which Pansy and Violet had been sitting. He starts suddenly and grabs my arm. "Lucilla, where are the girls?" He has jumped up, and since he's gripping me like a vise grabbing a choice chunk of wood, I have no choice but to jump up, too.

I crane my neck, but I can't see them either.

His fingers are biting into my arm, and I place my hand over his. "They're fine," I say with a gentleness I hardly know I possess. Do I know this? Of course not, but it seems necessary to say it.

I expect him to run wildly up the path, screaming and shrieking for his beloved children, but his feet must be rooted to the spot. I feel his arm loosen a little and sense the tension draining out of him. When I look toward the path, I can see two little blondes cavorting in the dirt.

"They're okay," I repeat, and he nods. He hasn't released my arm yet, and I'm trying to figure out how to disengage myself gracefully. It feels strange to be grasped needfully in the deep, dense woods by Charles Fitzham Smithson the Second.

He calls to his girls, and they run back to join us.

"I don't want you to get so far ahead," he says. Then he looks away from them, glances into my eyes, and releases me. I can feel the burning where he touched me, and I can't put my finger on the uneasy feeling inside. Anxiety, maybe, or distress. Maybe sympathy. He takes Violet's hand firmly, and I take that as my cue and look expectantly at Pansy.

Pansy puts her hand in mine; our blowdown experience impressed her, so she sticks to me as if she's coated in super glue. Mr. Smithson and Violet stroll just ahead of us, hand in hand.

Pansy and I are both tired, but Violet and her father are traveling at such a nice, slow pace that it works out okay. They stop momentarily to sip from their water bottles, so we get to do that, too. Then they start up again, he walking leisurely, she skipping happily by his side.

Pansy and I plod tiredly.

We're a nice little foursome.

The tedium is starting to get to Pansy, though, and to liven things up some she glances at her sister's back, then looks up at me and says loudly, "I don't see why Violet gets to carry the flashlight."

Here we go.

"'Cause I'm littler," Violet says matter-of-factly, turning around to rub it in a bit.

"It isn't fair," Pansy whines.

Earlier, to appease her, I stuck the baggie of trail mix in her pocket. "You have the gorp," I remind her now. "That's just as good." I mean, does Pansy really think we're going to be needing a flashlight any time soon? What a silly thing to be jealous over.

"But I want the flashlight," she insists.

"Well, I want it, too," says Violet, "and I had it first."

"Listen, you two," I say. "I'm going to tell you a story about a real person who always wanted things she couldn't have. Are you listening?"

They are. Pansy's eyes are wide, and Violet's step has slowed a little so she can hear the tale, as well.

"There was once a woman who was very spoiled. She wanted everything her own way, and sometimes she was cruel and unkind to people in order to get it. When she became old and sick, even her own daughter was tired of her, and she asked her father why he bothered. Why did he wait on her hand and foot? Why did he cater to her every whim?"

"What's a whim?" asks Violet.

"A wish. He gave in to every wish she had."

"She was sick, though," Pansy says, "so that's okay."

"No," I insist, "it wasn't okay. She wanted things that weren't necessary or practical, and the daughter asked her father why he gave in to her."

"Well, what did he tell her?" Pansy wants to know.

"He did it because . . . because . . . ." I can't believe this, but I actually can't go on. I want to finish up by telling them to mend their contentious ways, but the story doesn't really end that way.

I put a hand on Violet's shoulder and yank the flashlight off her belt loop. "You've had a long enough turn, Violet. Here, Pansy."

"Hey!" Violet cries.

We've all stopped walking and Pansy is gloating as I hook the flashlight to her belt.

"Well how does the story end?" Violet asks. If she has to give up the prize, she at least wants to know the moral.

There is no moral. "I don't know," I say lamely.

Charles looks at me, but he doesn't ask, just soothes Violet's hurt feelings and strides ahead with her, leaving me in his dust.

Pansy is happy now and trotting along at a better pace, her hand in mine, and I'm trying to figure out why I even brought up my mother in the first place. It isn't as if I enjoy thinking about the good old days.

◇◇◇

When Pansy upsets the bees' nest, it takes a minute for me to figure out what the heck happened. Suddenly the air is thick with buzzing, Pansy is screaming her head off, and thoughts of my mother dissipate like ashes on the wind. I feel a quick sting on my arm and one on my hand, and I haul Pansy away from there and into the woods, far enough that the bees don't follow.

As near as I can figure out, the nest must have been hidden in the path somehow, under a stone or clinging to a stick. Pansy sure didn't mean to earn the angry attack of those bees. She was just walking along, clenched to me.

The stings on my arm and hand hurt, but I figure they'll be all right by tomorrow. It's when I take a good look at Pansy that my heart lurches into my throat. Her upper lip is three times its normal size, bloated all out of proportion to her face. How can a bee sting swell that way? Then it occurs to me: there must have been multiple stings. She's crying and saying that it hurts, and I don't wonder.

I gather her up in my arms, make a wide circle into the woods to avoid the darting bees, and hobble back to the trail.

This isn't particularly easy. My legs are aching already, and even though we're on fairly level ground right now, Pansy is not exactly a feather. Plus she's sobbing against my shoulder while the flashlight bangs on my ribs, making a nice series of bruises that I'll enjoy for days to come.

"Pansy, sshh," I tell her. "We're going to find Daddy right

now. He's just ahead of us. Be a good, brave girl. When we reach Daddy, you can have some cookies." The placebo for all hurts. We can't afford too many more calamities on this trip; I'm running out of cookies.

To say I race toward Charles would be a lie. I stumble toward Charles. I falter toward Charles. I bumble over the uneven path, not dropping Pansy, but not making any impressive progress either. That brief sympathetic feeling I had for him before is gone. What is this problem of his that he has to be so far ahead all the time?

I gather my energy, take a big breath, and plow on through the woods, keeping the goal in sight: Charlie Smithson, Olympic Hiker.

When I finally heave into his view, he stands up immediately, noticing that I'm carrying Pansy, that I seem to be trying to hurry.

"She stirred up a swarm of bees," I tell him. "Is she allergic?"

He looks horrified as he takes her from me. "I didn't know she was."

"She was probably stung more than once. That might explain all that swelling."

"Did we bring anything to put on that?" he asks. "Calamine or something?"

"I didn't pack anything like that," I say.

"We'd better get to a hospital." He lurches off with Pansy in his arms, and I take Violet's hand to follow. The pace is quick, and I can hardly manage to stay on my feet. Obviously, Smithson gets ahead of me again, but I just can't go any faster. I can see him up ahead, slowing down a little, too. He puts Pansy down on the ground and gets down on her level, talking to her and touching her face.

"Go ahead, Violet," I say. "Catch up with them." She runs on ahead. He sees her coming and waits for her.

We've reached the last half mile, going uphill over huge, ungainly boulders toward the parking lot. I'm completely out of breath, and the stings on my arm and hand are still hurting. The rocks ahead of me might as well be skyscrapers. I can't fathom how I'm going to make it across them.

My legs are throbbing from the running and hiking, and my arm and hand are burning from the bee stings. My ribs hurt from the rhythmic banging of the flashlight, my face smarts from the scratch I got in the blowdown, and my shoulders ache from the steady pressure of the pack on my back. All of me is begging for a hot bath and some soothing ointment to mend all my injuries. A nice, cold Saranac Pale Ale would hit the spot, too. Or even a Bud. Black Crown, of course.

The expanse of rock ahead of me is manmade. It's an enormous retaining wall holding up the highway far above. I glance up to see toy cars zooming by over my head. I need to get up there.

I bend my leg to reach heroically up the first boulder, and heave myself onto it, lying there. Okay, one down, seven thousand to go. Well, I can't just lie here. I get up and jerk my body to the next rock. That one wasn't so bad. Two down . . . .

For every rock I spill myself over, wincing in pain, the Smithson Acrobatic Team dodges briskly over two or three. Obviously, I'm losing ground fast, and while I'm not exactly proud of this, I'm too tired, hurting, and out of breath to care.

"Come on, Lucky," yells Violet. Her mouthful of sorrel doesn't seem to have affected her much. She's prancing eagerly over the tumbled rocks.

"Go on," I yell to her. "I'm fine. I'll be there soon."

They go ahead a little further, and Smithson glances back at me. I'm limping along, the woman who told one daughter to eat sorrel and allowed the other to probe a bee colony. Hired help. I bet he's thrilled he brought me along. I see him sit the two little girls on a big rock, safely together, and talk to them for a minute. Then he starts back toward me.

"Go on ahead," I shout. "I'll catch up." Liar.

I'm stuck on a boulder, and ahead of me is a big black crevice that I'm afraid I'll fall into if I try to jump. I have to do it, though.

I can't. I need to regain my strength, and I'm gasping for breath.

Charles has reached the rock beyond me, the deep black hole between us. He steadies himself and extends his hand. His feet are planted securely, and I know I could make it easily with his help.

Still, I hesitate. Do I want to be indebted to this man? This Charles Smithson whose pretentious name sounds like a snake that can't get going? Paint the cabinets, Lucilla. Pack a lunch, Lucilla. Raise my children, Lucilla. Do this. Don't do that. Everything must be done my way. My way.

"Give me your hand, Lucilla," he says. "I'll help you."

Pansy and Violet are getting itchy on their far boulder, and he glances back at them briefly. "Settle down over there," he yells, and by some miracle, they do.

"Find some medical help," I tell him. "I'll hitch a ride to the nearest bus station or something. Go."

"No, don't be silly. I think Pansy's okay. The swelling has already gone down some." He reaches for me again, and I don't see that I have any choice. "Take my hand, Lucilla." Not angry or impatient, just coaxing. "Come on, take it." I grab his hand, which is strong and capable, just as I knew it would be.

Insufferable.

He yells to his kids to sit still again and helps me over another rock. We stand face to face, inches apart on a mammoth boulder. The sunlight is glinting in his hair, making him look even blonder than usual. He really does have nice hair.

He swallows once, looks at me frankly, and says, "How did it end?"

"The story?"

He nods.

"My father told me that he owed her, that he would give her anything he could, everything, because she gave him me." I feel like bawling even as I say it. On certain days, I miss my father more than ever; I don't know why this is one of those days. "He said you should always value what you do have instead of worrying about what you can't have. You should keep your own star polished, never mind wishing you had someone else's."

There's no response, and more surprisingly, not a hint of a question on his face.

He helps me over a few more big rocks, and when things even out a little more, he goes on ahead to his antsy daughters. I climb the rest of the way alone.

◇◇◇

The car looks just like the Taj Mahal, and I collapse against it gratefully. We drink lavishly from the cooler of water and juices stowed in the trunk and then examine Pansy's mouth. Smithson is right. The swelling has improved, and so have her spirits. "It feelth funny," she says, and it makes Violet laugh.

Off in the distance, we can see the blue-gray summit of Esther Mountain nestled between two taller peaks. It's picturesque and pastoral, peaceful and pristine. No. It's putrid, pathetic, and profane.

114

"Pansy, do you feel okay?" her father asks. "How about you, Violet?"

They both nod. They're too busy eating celery sticks and pretzels and apple slices and slobbering juice on their clothes to answer.

And you, Lucilla? He doesn't say this, but I ask it to myself, and I gripe to myself that no, I don't feel okay. I ache everywhere, and I resented this hike, and I'll snivel all the way home if I feel like it.

When we reach the little town of Hunting Fork, we spot a sign announcing a small health clinic and pull gratefully into the tiny parking area. We are welcomed warmly by an assortment of loafing nurses and PA's. Since we are apparently the only patients there, we are smothered with attention and assured that sorrel shouldn't hurt Violet. Pansy seems to be improving nicely, and they give us a tube of salve for her lips. They pronounce, like magic, that she should be fine.

"Let me put something on that scratch, too," a nurse says to me, and I hesitate briefly. How much is this going to set me back? Then I remember that Charles Smithson II will be picking up the tab, so I let her go to town. She cleans the scratch and smoothes on a cool ointment, and then she attends to my bee stings. Just for a moment, I sit relaxed, letting someone else take care of me.

I could get used to this.

As we return to the car, everyone cheers us off. Clearly, they don't get much business in Hunting Fork.

◇◇◇

It isn't until two o'clock in the morning that the offensive side effect of sorrel overdose is made clear to me.

Violet comes into my room and stands by my bedside, jerking the covers in the moonlight. "Lucky," she says, "get up. I'm sick."

I turn to face her, slowly and painfully, like an arthritic granny. "Sick? Did you upchuck?"

"What?"

"You know, heave, spew, ralph." She's looking at me quizzically. This is a well-bred three year old. I try again. "Vomit?"

"No, come and see."

115

My arm is throbbing, and my hand stings, and my back aches, and my face is swollen. And my legs are still shaking with the relief of being off that mountain. But I manage to stumble to the floor and then to her room, where I cling to the doorframe of her bathroom. I can smell long before I can see. And dutiful Violet wakes me up all night long, every twenty-five minutes, each time a new bout of diarrhea hits her.

And I, also dutiful, drag into her cute pink bathroom every single time, to take my obligatory peek, flush the toilet, wash our hands, and assure her she'll be fine.

Pansy comes in to find out what's going on, so I smear more ointment on her lip and treat my own stings with a little as well.

After a while, all three of us just collapse in Violet's bed. I sleep with one eye open until the next alarm. Each time, Pansy accompanies us to the bathroom, nodding sagely. She doesn't want to miss out.

I tumble back into Violet's bed and shove away Pansy's foot where she's kicking me in the gut. I gaze at the faces of two sleepy tots, at their small, firm noses and pretty, tangled hair.

If these are my stars, I believe I'm disappointed. I heave a burdened sigh and close my eyes, anticipating Violet's next distress signal.

Sir Charles Fitzham Smithson the Second is, of course, sleeping like a baby in his own room three doors down. "Wouldn't you like me to get Daddy?" I yawn at Violet, somewhere between the four o'clock and four-twenty performances.

"No, I want you," she says.

"Me, too," says Pansy.

"That's great," I say.

He's definitely not paying me enough.

# 12

WHEN LIONEL SEES ME the next day, he does a double-take and backs up to see if he has the right castle. It's mildly amusing, and I grin to let him know that all the scratches and bruises don't faze me.

"You look like hell," he says.

So what else is new?

"Hiking doesn't agree with me," I tell him. "I tried to tell The Maharaja that, but since he knows absolutely everything, he didn't bother to listen."

"What happened?" Lionel is helping himself to a beer from the refrigerator.

"Isn't it a little early for that?" I ask him. It's ten twenty-seven a.m. by the kitchen clock, and I'm no prude, but beer at this time of day sounds just plain repulsive.

"Never too early," says Lionel, "never too late." He opens the bottle and takes a good swig, then places it on the countertop. "You poor thing," he says, touching the scabby scratch on my face. "You look like you could use some cheering up." And he puts his arms around me and kisses me, just like that. It's a kiss that pretty near singes my eyebrows, and he's right; it cheers me up considerably. I carry it around with me that whole day.

A few days later, Smithson comes in through the kitchen door, boots muddy as usual, and tracks over to the sink, squelching brown footprints on the damp, dull floor.

"Your Honor," I say, exasperated. I'm just putting the mop into the closet, and I haul it back out again and slosh over the dirty puddles he just created.

"Don't call me that," he mumbles into a glass of water.

I look at him, surprised. He's never objected before. "I just mopped this. You messed it up."

He looks down at the dirty swirls on the cracked linoleum. "Sorry."

"Forgaven."

"Why do you do that, Miss Wilta?"

"Do what?"

"Use bad grammar. Make a point of being less than you are. Call me all those ridiculous names."

"Ridiculous names, Yore Dukey?"

"If you got it from the newspapers, you should know they do it to make a big sensation out of nothing."

"Nothing?" I say. "You call hitting the bullseye in an axe-throwing contest nothing?"

"That was five embarrassing years ago. I have since retired from axe-throwing."

"A noble gesture, Your Eminence."

"Just call me by my name, would you, Lucilla?"

I salute him. "As you wish, Your Royal Monarch."

He sits down heavily on one of the kitchen stools. Mud on the rungs. No prob. Lucky Wilta loves to wipe down other people's dirt, and she's an expert. I hunker over to the closet and heave out a cleaning rag with a loud, exasperated sigh.

"Miss Wilta," he says, "we have to work together for the sake of my daughters. They respond well to you, and I appreciate that, but you have to meet me halfway. I'm trying to make it as painless as possible for both of us."

"All right, all right." And I call him Mr. Smithson - for the rest of that day and whenever else I remember.

◇◇◇

I'm in the upstairs hallway. I don't know where Charles hid the flashlight he bought for our hike, but I'm grasping a derelict one that I found in a kitchen cupboard. This one lights only if and when it feels like it, so it's not much use. I'm counting doors and peering into dingy rooms to count windows, hoping to discover an odd measurement that might hide a secret panel. Some of the doorknobs are still stuck, or locked, and it frustrates me that I can't get into those rooms. And the door at the top of the winding staircase is still on my mind, too. How will I ever find the secret room with so many locks and bolts?

Well, I know the answer: Very Stealthily.

I wander casually to the cellar, pass walls of rock, a couple of empty wine casks, and numerous cold storage squares, and root around until I find Smithson's toolbox. I have the oversized box balanced in one arm, and I'm rummaging for a screwdriver with my other hand. I don't hear Mr. Smithson come up behind me, but he scares the living daylights out of me when he says quietly, "What are you looking for?"

I scream, and about forty tools - screwdrivers, chisels, hammers, pliers - and a packet of long, deadly-looking nails go flying up and then rain down all over the damp cement floor. The commotion saves me from answering for a moment. I can't very well admit I'm about to pry loose his locked doors. After all, he doesn't even know this is rightfully, morally, ethically, everything but legally, *my* castle.

"Looking for?" I repeat dumbly.

"Maybe I can help you find it." His eyes are fixed on mine; he's innocently waiting for a sensible answer. He bends to help me pick up the mess and says again, "What were you looking for?"

"Well," I start, "there are a lot of rooms here that I haven't had a chance to clean yet. I think some of the doors are stuck. From age, or the settling of the castle . . . ."

"And so you were planning . . . ?"

"To maybe oil the doorknobs." He isn't buying it. "Or maybe to, uh . . . unscrew the locks," I mumble. I feel like a cad.

He replaces the last of the tools in the toolbox, tosses in the loose nails that are within sight, and shoves the whole thing into a corner. He stands up and dusts off his palms on his jeans. "Couldn't you have asked me for the keys?" he asks. He doesn't sound terribly angry, but definitely not amused either. Maybe puzzled.

"I didn't know if you'd let me use them." I decide to meet his eyes, and I know I must look a little belligerent.

"You can use them," he says, "any time. There aren't any secrets here, Lucilla. You can go anywhere you want to." His eyes are probing, and I'm convinced he must have spotted me lurking behind old draperies or darting into shadows as he rounded dusty corners traveling through the corridors of his home. I feel as if I should explain more.

But how? What do I say? The truth is, Sir, that I'm trying to steal your inheritance and make off with a pile of diamonds that you don't even know you own. Well, I can't say *that*, so I decide not to talk, just let him escort me back upstairs. I leave my flashlight behind; I know he would draw unsavory conclusions if he saw me pick it up.

"When I was growing up here," he tells me, "I used to wonder about all the rooms, too. I was only ten when we moved in, and I

119

was positive there must be secret passageways and hidden towers, if I could only find them."

"It's that kind of a house," I say lamely. "But I only wanted to clean-"

"There was a cupboard in the music room that I could never open," he continues. "I used to work at it and work at it. I finally had to ask my father to show me the trick. It turned out it was a kind of safe - not the kind of latch you can figure out easily. It annoyed me that I couldn't work it out on my own and even more that there was nothing in it but sheet music. Pretty disappointing for a young boy."

I can feel my stomach tightening; my mouth tastes like sand.

Smithson glances at me. "Once you know about the hinge, it's easy, but until someone shows you . . . ." His words trail off.

I laugh lightly. "Oh, the girls showed me one day." It's not true. I don't even know if the girls realize about that cupboard. I wait for him to pounce. Aha! Lucky Wilta caught in a bold-faced lie!

But he doesn't respond, and I clamp my mouth shut.

He makes it so easy to hate him.

He keeps the keys in a leather case in his bedroom dresser drawer. I could have found them if I had gone prying around in his personal belongings, but I do have some standards. He hands them to me, a thick iron ring with dozens of keys on it, and shuts the door behind us when we leave.

"Just put them back when you're satisfied," he says.

Ha! I'll be satisfied when I'm rich and can claim this joint. When I can throw him out to starve on a garbage heap. When I can run diamonds through my fingers like so much water.

But for now, one of these keys fits the door at the top of the winding staircase, and my heart is pounding at the thought of finally opening it. The rest of the bedrooms, with their glittering piles of gems and baubles, will have to wait.

I ignore a hallway full of intriguing locked doors to ascend the worn circular steps. I thought Charles had remained downstairs, but now, too late, as I stand before the mysterious door, I realize that he's coming up right behind me. I fumble the keys in my hand. Which one? There's no choice but to proceed by trial and error. I try two keys, and neither works. My hands are so agitated that I have trouble gripping the third. Again, I'm aware of the anticipation that I felt weeks ago when I stood here. I wish Charles The Magnanimous would stop spying on me, but

I'm not about to give up graciously and go away. Something warm and safe awaited me in this room long ago; I need to recapture that feeling.

I grope with the keys, trying to turn one of them right side over in my shaking hand, and I end up dropping the whole ring to the floor. It makes a huge, clattering noise.

"It's funny, Miss Wilta," says Mr. Smithson, appearing at my side, "you bypassed all the other doors on this floor; some haven't been opened in years. Is there something special about this one?" He has retrieved the key ring and is looking at me strangely.

How can I answer him? He doesn't know I'm one of the infamous Todds that his father cheated out of hearth and home. He couldn't possibly remember the bulldozer/doll incident when we were ten. I'm sure he never even knew my name. To him, I'm just Lucky Wilta, a strange, empty-headed creature who manages to keep his girls alive from day to day, a witch who somehow opened a secret cupboard.

"I'd like to see it," I say truthfully. "I just have a feeling about it. I want to know what's here."

"I'm afraid you'll be disappointed," he says, and he unlocks the door.

The room is small, but familiar. The little table is still there against the wall with my miniature china tea set on it. I recognize it instantly, and everything comes flooding back. The sunlight streaming in the single window. The child-sized furniture. The blue and yellow wallpapered walls.

Nancy, my Nancy, would occasionally play up here with me. It was our special retreat after homework was finished, and she would dress me in the lacy costumes in that trunk, and sip my pretend tea out of those fragile, small cups. I was Guinevere here, and Juliet, and Cleopatra. And I was Lucilla Todd, too young to know how unpretty I would grow to be and too innocent to know my life was a fragile thing about to be broken.

The cracked mirror still hangs next to the trunk, and I catch a glimpse of myself, a plain, unlovely person, and Mr. Smithson, my nemesis. I long to go to the trunk, to open it and feel the finery again in my hands.

"You can go in," he says quietly. "I'm afraid there's not much here."

Just my past, my childhood. A happiness that got lost somehow. No biggie.

"Thank you," I say. "I don't need to go in." I turn from the room; my heart is aching too much to continue, and I can't explain my feelings. Nostalgia, strong and sweet, at the sight of my pale cups and saucers. Anguish that anyone could wrench innocence away from a child. Despair that this handsome stranger next to me is indirectly responsible for the pitiful thing my life has become.

I go quickly back down the worn steps, quickly so he won't see my feelings on my homely face or the start of tears in my eyes.

"Lucilla?" he calls, but I'm gone, back down the corridor and into the safety of my own locked room. I can just make out the words. "Lucilla? Are you all right?"

You betchum.

# 13

I LIKE THIS ROOM, that's all," I'm telling Lionel. Smithson has given me the key to my special room at the top of the stairs. Just unclipped it from the ring and handed it to me one morning over breakfast. He didn't say why and I didn't ask, but that's where Lionel has found me today. I'm annoyed that I have to explain myself to him; when did Charles the Second ever say Lionel could have free run of the castle anyway?

He's balancing on one of my little chairs, and has swept away my powder blue tea set, piling the little teapot, cups, and saucers on the floor under the window, safely out of the way where we won't step on them. He's replaced them with an icy six pack of Saranac, and the soggy cardboard carrier is frothing a damp rectangle on my little wooden table. I'm wishing Lionel and his six pack would go away.

"You're a child at heart," he says, taking a long swig.

"And you drink too much," I say bluntly. He does, too. I hardly ever see him without his hand around a bottle or a glass of something. And I'm not talking about pink lemonade.

I've found a thick, woolly, black and orange shawl in the top of the steamer trunk, and I'm wearing it over my New York Giants tee shirt. I tilt my head in the mirror, examining my new look. Red, blue, black, orange. I look sensational - maybe a little Spanish.

Lionel is sipping at his third beer. For a little guy, he can really put them away. One of the empties has rolled off the table and into a corner, leaving a trail of tiny wet drops and gathering up the fine layer of dust that coats the wooden floor.

"Querida mía," he says, "you look exquisite." He comes up behind me and puts one hand on my shoulder, looking into the reflective glass at both of us - me, the tall one with the garish outfit - him, the small one with the lecherous grin. With his other hand, he presses the wet bottle on my neck until I wiggle away.

He laughs. "Afraid?"

"Of you?" I say. "Not likely. You're a dope."

I adjust the scarf, knotting it and letting it droop provocatively over one shoulder.

Lionel laughs again. "Found your treasure yet?" he asks.

"Don't be ridiculous, Lionel. I'm not hunting for treasure." Okay, it's a fib. I look almost every day, and I feel as if I've exhausted all the places that are accessible to me. My room. The girls' rooms. All the downstairs rooms we use every day and all the extras that Sir Chuckie leaves unlocked. I still don't feel right helping myself to the keys he keeps in his room, but I take them now and then and unlock a door or two, feeling guilty all the while. Somehow Charles must understand about the guilt; it must be why he gave me the key to the room I like best.

The truth is I'm getting sick of acting the part of sneaky housekeeper. It's my castle, and I want it back. And I'm tired of tiptoeing around, tapping and probing, when I'm supposed to be cooking, cleaning, washing, and ironing. I may be a lot of things, but a shiftless employee has never been one of them. Well, not much anyway.

"Lucky," Lionel says to me, "it would be so much easier for you if you'd just trust me."

"That's not what I hear from Charles F. Smithson."

His eyebrows arch. "He said that?"

I shrug. How do I know which of these morons I can depend on. Lionel obviously knows what I've been up to, and he clearly hasn't spilled his suspicions to The Lord of the Manor. But how can I entrust him with the secret that directs my life?

He stands up and drains his beer bottle, then picks up the remaining three in their cardboard holder. "Are the girls asleep?" he asks me. "Let's do some treasure hunting right now. I could be a big help to you, Lucky."

A big help. Right. This immature Romeo is not exactly the type you like to entrust with your heaviest confidence, but I don't know how to get rid of him. And besides, he amuses me.

"I'll take these down and get the keys," he says.

"What keys?"

Lionel just laughs and picks up his bottles.

"Here," I say, yanking the fuzzy empty out of the corner of the room. "Take this, too." He disappears out the door and down the steps, and I have my special room to myself again.

I don't like sharing it. It would be too easy to start rambling about Nancy and our afternoons here, and I know I can't do that. I shrug the shawl off my shoulder and fold it into the trunk with the other old clothes. Someday, I'll go through the whole collection.

The discolored wet rings on the smooth, golden, child-sized tabletop annoy me, and it irritates me that I care. What's my problem? Either I like Lionel or I don't, and I'd better decide one way or the other.

The guy is funny and irrepressible, and it's good to know I could actually have a friend in this cold, sad place. The guy is also a gambler and a careless slob who can tap dance his way around any topic.

I glance around for a cloth of some kind and finally end up swabbing at the rings with the hem of my shirt. It doesn't help much. I pick up the miniature porcelain cups and saucers and arrange them on the table top, then center the little teapot, the sugar bowl, the creamer. They're thin and fragile, and I marvel that I never broke any pieces when I played here as a child. I close the lid of the steamer trunk and look around. Except for Lionel's beer rings, everything looks right. It's important to me to leave it just so.

I can hear Lionel returning as I lock the door. He pokes his head around the curve in the stairs, smiling at me with bright teeth and glistening eyes. "Come on, sweetheart," he says, and he reaches for my hand. In his other hand, he holds the heavy key ring, thick with the keys that will open up new doors to me, maybe get me my treasure, maybe make me richer than I've ever dreamed. So, he has known all along where Smithson keeps them.

"You got those from his room," I say.

"Sure, he won't mind. Come on."

I stare at him for a long moment, hating to give in. "I need your word," I say to him finally, "that this will stay just between us."

"Let's put it this way," he says. "I can go running to him this very night. Or you and I can enjoy the hunt together, and he'll never hear anything about it from me."

"And what are you getting from this?"

"Getting? Just the fun of helping you. It's your treasure, whatever happens."

"There probably isn't even a treasure," I say lamely.

"But you believe there is, or you wouldn't be looking. It's diamonds you hope to find, right?"

"Maybe," I mutter.

"Nice. Care to tell me why you're so convinced?"

"No," I say. He throws back his head and laughs. "And, Lionel," I add, "if we do find anything-"

"They're yours," he repeats. Then he glances at me, wondering, "But why are they yours, Lucky? If they're in someone else's castle?"

I swallow and think back to that sneaky Smithson Senior winning the castle from my father in an underhanded card game. I know it was nefarious, dishonest. It had to be. I do own the castle. I do own the diamonds.

I can't tell Lionel why I'm so convinced, so I just shrug.

"Well," he says. "I'll just take that on your say-so. I'll help you, and all the rocks we find will belong to you." Then his eyes glint. "Except for the smallest one."

Now this beats all. I am not giving Lionel Hawthorne my smallest diamond, no matter what he may be thinking. "Why would I do that?" I ask him.

"Oh, come on, Lucky. It's just one little diamond." He laughs and pulls my hand closer to him. "How about this then?" he says, "Because otherwise I go to Charles."

What a skunk. It's times like this that I don't like Lionel much at all. "Fine," I say abruptly. I tell him that, but I'm already thinking that when it comes right down to it, no way is Lionel getting one of my diamonds. I put my hand out. "Give me the keys."

He hands them over, bursting with enthusiasm.

Together, like two criminals, the lowest of the low, Lionel and I pad quietly down the circular stone steps and down the hallway.

"The girls should be good for another hour, shouldn't they?" he says, radiant with pure, untarnished greed.

I grit my teeth and accept my newfound partner in crime.

We wreak havoc for a good hour or so, and when Pansy awakens and shouts for me, Lionel accepts the interruption graciously and leaves us to go get dandied up for his big night out. He has a lot of them; every night is a big one to Lionel. I gather up the girls and take them downstairs and get them to tenderize a flank steak by beating it to death with mallets.

I'm still poor, I'm still homely, and now I'm conniving against Saint Charles the Moral with a guy I don't even trust.

Can I sink much lower?

I'm impressed and a tad disconcerted that Lionel Hawthorne has memorized the schedule the girls and I follow. Their own father never has a clue whether they might be awake or asleep when he pops in at odd times during the day, but Lionel knows. He also seems to know, often, what I'm about to do before I do it - when I'm likely to start lunch, when the girls and I are heading into town for a Creamsicle, when I've just settled into a chaise longue and am about to drift off in the hot sunshine with a worn paperback novel from Smithson's library. Or when I'm setting off to probe into uncharted territory, delighting in my castle game, searching for Borstrom's mysterious hoard.

That's when Lionel's sixth sense tells him to materialize, and he appears suddenly, eager to get in on the action. It's a gift, and one that I don't particularly mind. I like coming across his loopy smile and lazy enthusiasm. He gives my days purpose; he makes me laugh.

When we search together, Lionel's eyes sparkle, and I'm never sure if it's the excitement of the hunt or the alcohol he has inevitably consumed. Either way, he's a spirited accomplice, and, as door after door reveals no secret and no treasure, it begins to look as if I'll never have to share my treasure with him after all.

We're walking toward the east wing, the spacious suite of rooms Marsuvius Borstrom claimed as his own master chamber. I haven't done much exploring here yet. I peeked into some of the rooms quickly one day, after I finally fitted the right keys to the locks, but this whole end of the castle is dark and unappealing. The rooms are removed from the ones we use, and since this is the furthest corridor from our bedrooms, I always worry that I won't hear the girls if they need me. My Mary Poppinsesque devotion to the children aside, it's shameful how easily Lionel persuades me that they will survive even if they awaken to find I've cut and run.

Sister, I hate to admit it, but finding my treasure means more to me than being there to wipe Pansy's runny nose.

We approach the master suite quietly. It's somber, bleak, and dismal, and I wonder that Borstrom's beloved Clymna ever agreed to stay here at all. I'm happy I have my flashlight in my hand, even though it throws a dim light at best.

The wiring in this part of the castle is almost nonexistent, and if the modern miracle of electricity ever reached this far, it's sadly defunct now. There's a gray granite fireplace in the bedroom, and a worn parquet floor, and paneling that's black with age and grime. Through an arched doorway, a dressing room is draped in soiled green velvet, and a single window looks out on the east side of the estate, where a criss-cross of overgrown gardens gives way to the encroaching evergreen forest. A balcony juts from that window, and off the balcony is a sheer forty-foot drop to the slate terrace below. Just looking over the edge makes me dizzy.

Coils of dust dance along the baseboards and cobwebs hang thick on the drapes. Borstrom's private bedroom probably hasn't been used since the original master lived here, and it's easy to see why. It's dark and spooky, with just one small window high over the bed.

This, of course, is the thing that gives us hope. It's the only source of light in the room, and it's the reason Lionel insists we explore here. And Lionel has a point: Why would a man build his own master bedroom without windows - unless he were hiding something?

Lionel is exploring the fireplace, aiming the flashlight around, hoping to find a loose stone that might masquerade as the button to a movable panel. He sets the flashlight on a dresser top so his bony hands can grasp the coarse edges of rock and dig into crumbling mortar. As his nimble fingers make their way around the edges, dust puffs sift down, making tiny piles along the baseboard. The bit of light that filters in through that one high window gives the whole room a warped, queer atmosphere, and I find myself squinting involuntarily.

I don't like this room.

While Lionel is pawing at the fireplace mantel, I make a slow circuit of the grubby paneling that surrounds the heavy bed. There are so many carved curlicues - angels with bowed lips, clusters of grapes and pears, spiny leaves - that I'm positive one of them must be something more. I'm practically holding my breath as I slide my hand gently over the carvings.

"Anything there?" Lionel calls softly from his side of the room. He has stopped clawing at the granite, and is sitting on the tattered bed, watching me.

"Can't tell," I say. "I can't see very well."

He comes toward me, his eyes bright, and hands me the flashlight. I have to admit, he's thrown himself into my project with gusto. He joins me in going over the smooth wooden vines and tendrils, the fruits, the carved ribbons, as I direct the murky beam. Carefully, we touch and push, scraping away dirt and grime.

We spend close to an hour, and finally, guilty and annoyed at the fact of two little girls and the apparent absence of a secret panel, I chuck it all and go back to Pansy's and Violet's rooms, just to be sure they're still sleeping.

They aren't. I know that even before I reach their corridor. Violet is wide awake, yelling her head off for me, and Pansy is whimpering under her covers, begging her noisy sister to cut it out.

"All right, I'm here," I say. Okay, so my tone isn't exactly loving. "Be quiet and get up, and I'll show you something cool." They must see the dirt and cobwebs in my hair and the smudges on my clothes. Whatever I'm doing, it looks like fun. The crying stops and they jump from their beds, run into the hallway, and each take one hand.

Lionel is sitting in a dejected heap on the floor of the Borstrom master suite. "It's no use," he says when we enter. "I've come to the conclusion that these are just carvings. Every single one of them."

A grubby cupid grins insolently out at me from the wall; a fat pear seems to be sniggering. Pansy edges closer to me. "I don't like it here," she says.

"Haven't you ever been in here?" I ask her. "It's just one of the extra bedrooms in the castle." I loosen my hand from hers and rub my eyes, trying to become reaccustomed to the gloomy light. Pansy is right. The rest of the castle, in comparison, is a bright Disneyland of birdsong and lollipops. She squints around suspiciously and finds my hand again.

Violet adjusts better. She's wandering around the room, touching things and looking under furniture. "It's too dark in here," she finally proclaims. "Somebody forgot to put the windows in."

Lionel laughs. "Doesn't it make you wonder what he was hiding?"

Violet looks up, interested. "Is there something hidden in here?"

"No," I tell her shortly. I give Lionel a warning look. "Let's go downstairs and you girls can help me make supper." Pansy doesn't have to be asked twice; she's clinging to me like a little weed. But Violet is off again, pulling on drifty curtains and crawling under an ancient Queen Anne secretary.

"You'll be filthy, Violet," I tell her. "Come out of there." I lean against the side of the desk and reach under to pull her out. And that's when I realize the floor is quivering.

I yelp and jump away, and manage to pull Violet from underneath the desk just moments before the section of floor she was crawling on disappears.

Lionel is by my side in seconds, and Pansy's eyes are as big as saucers. A neat rectangle of parquet flooring has lowered several inches and slid neatly underneath the existing floor. The legs of the secretary straddle the darkness in the four corners, and as I look more closely, I can see that they're secured with bolts.

The rumbling movement takes only seconds. The four of us stare. Half hidden from view is a delicious, enticing, black, yawning hole.

# 14

MY HEART IS RACING, and I'm almost unable to gasp out words. "We found it, Lionel. This is it." I glance at him and see victory on his face as he looks back.

"Found what?" Violet asks. She's shrinking back, probably thinking how close she came to plummeting into that unknown void.

I gather my wits about me. "Found a little secret space," I say brightly. "All castles have them." I'm steering both girls toward the bedroom door. "And after supper, we'll come back up with Daddy, and let him go in and have a look around. Maybe he'll even let you look, too."

And by then I'll have confiscated my haul.

Lionel is looking after me like a crazy man, half ready to jump into the black pit. He's aiming the milky flashlight beam toward the hole, urging me with his eyes to quit prattling and get back there. And I want to. But how can I with Violet and Pansy ready to run to their father with this most exciting news?

If there are diamonds . . . .

"We'll come back after supper," I tell the girls again. "Come on, Lionel."

He stands there staring at me.

The flashlight sputters and winks off, then on again.

"Lionel, please."

Violet has had time to recover from her brush with death and starts whining, "But I want to see now. There might be something in there. A treasure chest, maybe, or a secret staircase, like in books."

Pansy catches on. "Treasure?"

Nineteen years I've lived in cheap, uncomfortable rooms, put up with that maggot Nick Wilta and his lying, cheating arrogance, sweated behind Fred's stewpots. Nineteen years of struggling and scrimping, plotting and planning. And now that it's here, now that my treasure is finally within my anxious, waiting grasp, I have an audience. And not only an audience, but a couple of blabbermouths who will run right to Sir Charles Fitzham Smithson the Second and deposit my diamonds, my future, my past and my present, tarnished and unholy as they are, right in his most uncaring and unworthy lap.

No!

"We're not looking right now!" I say with finality. "I'm in charge here, and we're not looking until later." My eyes are stinging with frustration. Nothing is turning out the way I wanted it to.

But Lionel's eyes have softened. That brilliance has toned down some, and he seems to understand my predicament. He flicks off the sputtering flashlight and takes Violet's unwilling hand. She fights him, so he picks her up, and I pick up Pansy, and the four of us start out of Marsuvius Borstrom's horrible, wonderful, black bedroom.

If the footsteps in the hallway had belonged to the ghost of old Borstrom himself, I could have handled it. If the Headless Horseman had suddenly materialized, rearing back on his terrible black stallion, I'd have managed to adapt. But when Charles F. Smithson the Second appears right then, right there in the corridor, it's all I can do not to howl in rage and frustration.

"What's going on?" he says cheerfully. "Why is everybody up here?"

And Violet jumps from Lionel's arms and runs to her father, shrieking, "A treasure, Daddy! There's a treasure in that room! But Lucky won't let us look until after supper!"

He gives me a look of surprise, picks up Violet, and then says to her, "Show me."

We troop back into the cheerless master chamber, and no one is more cheerless than I. I can almost hear old Marsuvius Borstrom, hiding there in the flaking ceiling, looking down on me and chuckling wickedly.

Smithson has Violet by one hand, and she's dancing around excitedly, trying to peer into the hole while her father makes one of those half-hearted Smithson attempts at control. He grabs the flashlight, which immediately flickers out, and kneels by the squared off hole. He tosses the flashlight aside and pokes his head under the secretary, peering into the dark like an excited boy. Joe Hardy and the Secret Spot.

"Want me to get the other flashlight?" Lionel asks. He knows where the other flashlight is? And yet he has let me go on searching for diamonds with nothing but this cheap, wretched imitation to guide me.

Smithson nods with enthusiasm, and Lionel jogs deliriously off to the cellar.

What is the problem with these men? Acting so irrational over the thought of a hidden treasure.

Pansy is still clinging to me, unsure. She's willing to wait until after dinner to explore the opening in the floor, but her father insists happily that there's no time like the present.

*Now* he chooses to wax enthusiastic.

"How did you find this?" he's asking. "What were you doing in here anyway?"

"I was thinking about cleaning . . . ." My voice trails off. What's the use of pretending with this man? He knows *WESLEY*'s heaps of old plaster still sit undisturbed in the damp corners of the parlor. He knows I change the bed sheets by turning them upside down every other week. He knows I dust the crystal in the china cabinet by turning my hairdryer on high and aiming. Sure, occasionally I actually scrub something that really needs it, but why would I suddenly clean up here?

"I was the one that found it," Violet says proudly. "I was crawling under there, and the floor disappeared."

He's examining the sides of the opening, feeling in the dark for a switch or lever of some kind. "The floor just slid under itself," he says, "but I wonder what triggered it."

"You didn't know this was here?" I ask casually. My heart is beating faster. I *have* to get into that hole first.

"No," he says. "My parents kept this room locked, probably because of that balcony. When I inherited, I guess I looked in here once or twice, but I never knew enough to look for this." He smiles lovingly back at Pansy, trying to charm her. "Our very own secret passageway, Pansy! Isn't that fun?"

She doesn't seem to think so. She buries her face in my knees.

I've regained a little of my usual savoir faire, and I figure I might as well be as natural as possible. He's asked how we happened to find the opening, so I offer an explanation. "I leaned against the secretary over here, trying to make Violet come out." I show him the recessed panel on the side of the desk. It isn't long before we find the little raised bubble in the wood.

"There must be something connecting the desk to the floor," says Smithson. "Are there pulleys or something? We should explore inside before we try to close it up, just in case we can't

133

get it open again." Mr. Practicality. The Answer to All Our Prayers. How I wish he hadn't found us up here.

Lionel is back, and I take the slick, black LED flashlight from him and start to maneuver under the secretary to climb into the hole. Tarantulas? Who cares. Rats? Let me at 'em. I'm after diamonds, and no one, especially The Honorable Charles F. Smithson, is going to beat me to them.

"Lucilla, wait," says that person, and there's such a note of authority in his voice that I actually stop. "Don't go in there. We have no idea what's down there." He pulls me gently aside, takes the flashlight, and edges himself toward the hole, lying on his stomach, playing the flashlight around the edges.

"No, if it's anything bad, I should be the one to go," I say bravely. "Your daughters couldn't get along without you." I slither under the desk again, grab the flashlight back, and shine it on old wooden lath strips and dusty walls. I knuckle one shoulder forward and swing myself around, trying to hoist one leg over the edge.

"Lucilla." He puts a hand on my shoulder, gently, but oh, he means it. We're lying there side by side in this cramped space underneath a musty piece of furniture, and I'm about as contorted as a human being can get. I'm itching to get into that hole, and he's just as determined to keep me out of it.

"Mr. Smithson," I start through clenched teeth.

"Miss Wilta," he answers. His hand is still very firmly on my shoulder, digging through the sleeve of my shirt, and he's keeping me from moving, just with that. Who would ever guess how strong this wimp really is?

"Mr. Smithson," I start again, gritting my teeth in earnest. "I am going in here, and I am going first. Violet and I found the hole, not you."

He looks at me strangely. Then, still lying full length on the floor and gripping my shirt with one hand, he moves forward lightly, thrusts his head into the side of the hole, pries my fingers off the flashlight, and shoots the beam around inside. "All right," he says amiably, satisfied. He releases my shirt.

I didn't realize I was still straining away from him, and when he lets go, my head clunks up and hits the underside of the secretary. "Oof," I say, and I pull my head back down sharply, so that my chin slams into the floor. "Ouch."

I can hear Pansy give a little squeal of distress and Lionel laughing.

"Are you hurt?" Smithson asks. His voice oozes gentlemanly concern.

Honestly, I could do without the Knight in Shining Armor Routine.

Of course, we can see by now that it's perfectly safe for me to hurl my entire body into the hole if I want to. Smithson is illuminating the space with great interest. It obviously doesn't go anywhere and there's certainly no danger. The hole is only a couple of feet long and not much deeper than that. The walls are wood slats that almost touch, with the fraction of space between strips stuffed with finely shredded paper. It's definitely not a secret room; I guess you could call it a secret space.

But that doesn't mean there's no treasure here. For the space is not quite empty.

Mr. Smithson's flashlight has come to rest on a small canvas-wrapped parcel lying in one corner of the opening, coated with powdery dirt. How long has this intriguing little grapefruit-sized package been here? Could it possibly be . . . ?

I can hardly wait to get my hands on that canvas and rip away the covering to expose my beautiful, brilliant cache of diamonds.

I can hardly stand it that all these obnoxious people are gathered to witness the discovery of my precious prize.

"Pick it up, Lucilla," Charles says to me softly. His face is angled under the bottom of the secretary, and I can't see it behind the flashlight he's holding. He just looks like an anonymous intruder.

Which is pretty much what he is.

"We might as well unwrap it," he says.

I'm crouched in the hole already, so I reach out and place my hand around the sack. It's fairly light and a little lumpy. I can hardly breathe.

"Open it," Violet is saying. Her featureless face has joined her father's. Her voice is subdued, awestruck. "It might be a treasure, Lucky."

I climb out of the hole in time to see her father smile at her indulgently, and, right there in plain view of everybody, I unwrap the parcel.

◇◇◇

It's wood, a lump of wood carved into the shape of

135

something, with a hollowed out center. I have to turn it over in my hand to make out what it is, and then I stand there surrounded by Lionel Hawthorne and his brilliant, expectant eyes and Charles Smithson and his bright, inquisitive ones, and Violet with her frankly curious ones and Pansy with her slightly scared ones. And we're all staring at the animal features and bulging eyes carved into this piece of wood. It looks familiar to me, and I'm pretty sure why, but I can't very well tell him that.

"Have you seen this before?" I say, looking at Mr. Smithson. "Do you know what it is?" I hand it to him carefully, and he takes it, turning it over in his hands and examining the leonine face, the mouth open in a silent roar, the sharp, wildly carved mane.

Recognition splashes over his face, and he says, "In the picture, Lucilla. That photograph that hangs in the foyer. Remember? There's a lion on the newel post. It was there when I first moved here, then it disappeared. This has to be the same one." He turns it over, showing me the round hole carved out inside the lion's head. "I bet this fits right over that knob at the bottom of the banister."

"What's a newel post? What's a banister?" Pansy is asking, finally coming alive. Leaving her cares behind.

Big deal. Someone removed the lion's head and hid it in Marsuvius Borstrom's hiding place. A cute prank. They're all talking at once about it, wondering why and how and whether or not it will really fit.

Me, I've lost interest, and I'm wondering if this opening has any more secrets to share with me. Looking at the size and shape of the hole, it occurs to me that the top shelves in the library below might very well be phonies.

I was in a house like that once, where the owner had a passion for old books, but no room for a library. So he cut the real leather bindings from hundreds of books and glued them onto boards, then arranged them all over his walls with little splints of stained wood in between to look like shelves. It looked real, and it saved on a lot of reading time.

Smithson is showing the wooden lion's head to Pansy and Violet, explaining his theory about it, and making plans to try fitting it there tonight, but Lionel has crept into the pit, and, quietly, I join him there. He's fingering the shredded paper stuffed into the thin gaps between the wood strips. "I have a Swiss Army knife, Lucky," he says quietly. "I'm just going to scrape between the lath to see if there's anything there."

Good old greedy Lionel. Of course there must be more to this pit than meets the eye. I start to respond, then I realize that Curious Charles has poked his head under again, and is listening eagerly to every word we're saying.

"Not tonight, though," I agree nonchalantly. "Let's go down and start dinner."

"I have a knife, too," Smithson says enthusiastically. "Let's do it now." Leave it to the men of the great Adirondacks to carry pint-sized weapons in their pockets. They never know when they might have to fight off a bear or coyote.

Smithson entrusts Pansy with the wooden head and pulls out a pocket knife. Then he climbs in, too. We're a cozy threesome: Larry, Curly, and Moe. All bent over, squatting in old dust, digging with pocket knives or, in the case of yours truly, with our eager fingers, examining clumps of paper filler. One hopeful. One merely curious. One resentful.

That would be me.

Smithson starts poking the shredded paper. It falls in small, silty lumps to the bottom of the space. "Isn't this fun, Pansy?" he says, still trying to convince her. "Just like a real adventure, finding a hidden treasure right in our own house." She's clinging to Violet now, and both of them are looking tentative, maybe wondering if the floor beneath them is about to start quaking.

Yes, loads of fun. A real family affair.

I'm watching carefully, waiting for a glistening diamond to fall, kerplunk, at my feet. And if one does? Then Chuckie Smithson will celebrate the added inheritance he'll pass on to his daughters. Why can't he be content with that nice old lion's head? It's such a great family keepsake.

The scraping goes quickly while Pansy and Violet squat at the top of the hole, clutching their treasure, watching the proceedings with great interest. As the Brothers Grimm dig, I watch them pull out the paper packed between the laths, rapidly covering the floor of the space with wads of dense filler. Even as I sift through, looking for suspicious lumps and stones, it's pretty obvious that there are no diamonds here.

Lots of powdery dust. A few bugs that crawl up my arm. Dark, cold, disappointment. But also a great relief, mingled with a little bit of guilt, that, as it turns out, I don't have to share at all.

◇◇◇

We troop downstairs, surprised to hear the insistent banging on the huge front door. Lionel opens it to the bright, annoyed features of the beautiful Emily Cheseworthy. She stalks in, her hair a seductive black cloud, her eyes snapping fire, and goes directly to Smithson, who is busy fitting the hollowed out lion's head neatly over the rough wooden ball on the bottom newel post. It fits, of course. There's a little 'plip' as it clicks into place.

"Perfect," he says with satisfaction.

"Well, I'm glad you're so happy," Emily says. She has by now taken in the whole group of us standing there, and it's with some little effort that she manages to squelch her irritation. The cool, refined look I saw before replaces the hot anger, and she says to Mr. Smithson, "Where have you been, Charles? You're filthy. "

He turns to her suddenly, as if he has just remembered her. "Oh, Emily, I'm sorry. We were up in the east wing. The most amazing thing-"

He doesn't get to tell her the most amazing thing, at least not right then, because she interrupts him. "You said to come at five. Well, it's twenty after."

"I know, I know. I really forgot. You see-"

She sweeps past him and arranges herself in a chair, the same chair I sat in for my faux interview, as a matter of fact. I can't help noticing that she dresses up that chair a lot more decoratively than I did. Even the dead ferns perk up some. She doesn't respond to him, just looks pointedly at her silver watch.

Charles looks contrite. "I'll be down right away, and we'll leave," he says. He bends to kiss her lightly on the cheek, and she melts a little and gives him a simpering smile.

"Where you going?" Lionel asks her. He's found a cloth somewhere, probably a cleaning rag I left displayed on some table or other, and he's polishing the wood of the lion's head. It's beginning to glow. Wrapped and stashed away all those years, it hasn't accumulated its fair share of dirt and grime like everything else in the castle. Actually, it's the best looking thing in the whole foyer.

Except, of course, for Emily.

She tells him their plans for dinner at a popular new place that's almost forty miles away. Drinks first at the golf club, then dinner, then who knows? That's the way she puts it. Who knows? Well, I'm hoping that Chuckles does, because I trust Unworthy Emily of the Cheesy-Tafts about as much as I trust Lionel to swear off the applejack for the rest of his life.

Lionel explains about the lion's head, and she half listens.

His Excellency returns in minutes, and we all stand around admiring The King of The Foyer. Not Charles, the carving. Well, all but Emily. She lounges in the chair, pretending to be very patient. Lionel acts proud of his thorough cleaning job, like some little kid who's never dusted anything before, and everyone talks at once about the newest addition to this cold, glum room.

I glance across the foyer at Lewie Forsythe's framed poem and wander over to steal a peek. No one is paying any attention to me as I skim the words. *Mane*, it says, and *Lion*, and *Secretary*. If the foyer weren't so full of people, I would slap myself silly at my stupidity. Duh. I should have realized Forsythe was playing a game and daring someone to find the lion's head.

"Who do you suppose removed it?" Lionel is asking.

"It must have been my father," says Charles. His father? Then I recall him saying the lion was there when the Smithsons moved in, and Charles has been living here since that day. But Lewie Forsythe lived here long before that, even before I did. So did Forsythe remove the head or did Smithson? This is not making sense to me.

"But why?" Charles continues. "Why would he hide it up there?" He's checking all his pockets, looking for something, a million dollar bill probably, so he can treat Miss Emily in the way to which I would like to become accustomed. Finally, he finds his wallet and searches through it quickly, looks satisfied, and puts it away again.

"A secret compartment. That was fun!" Violet says.

Pansy hangs back and I feel her hand creep into mine. Her frightened eyes haven't left the wide, staring eyes of the wooden lion, gazing back at her, gleaming.

Her father notices and picks her up, carrying her to the banister. "It's just a little statue," he tells her. "It isn't real." Pansy stares down at the wide open, roaring mouth, and clings a little tighter to her father.

Emily is watching with mild interest. "What is she afraid of?" she says. "It's a piece of wood."

To you, Emily. But not to Pansy. Not to me. It's a nightmare, a monster, a frightening horror that will haunt Pansy in her infant sleep. It's all the goblins that her mind can invent, given credence, living right here in her own castle. It's a demon.

"Children are so difficult to understand," Emily says to Lionel. Lionel, since he is one and should know, nods in agreement.

"Like this, sweetie. See?" Charles is saying, patting the lion's head. "It can't hurt you, Pansy. It was carved on purpose to look scary." His touch lingers on the wild mane, and he does not disappear in a poof of smoke.

Pansy hesitates at first and I see her scared glance travel to Emily, then she makes a sudden decision and sticks out her hand to pat the lion's stiff wooden mane. Smithson smiles at her indulgently, devoted and proud.

"Can I name it Marian?" Pansy asks softly.

"Marian? Why Marian?"

"The girl in the book Lucky read us was named Marian. I like that name."

Violet has been out of the picture for too long. "I found it," she interjects bluntly, "and I think it's a boy."

"Violet," Smithson begins, and I have a feeling we're about to engage in another battle. In this corner, the obstinate Preschooler. In this corner, her dull-witted, simple-minded Father. Place your bets.

Surprisingly, it's Lionel who steps in. "It *is* a boy," he says with finality. "Only males have a mane like this." Pansy looks crushed, but Lionel continues. "But isn't Marion a man's name, too?"

Violet is impressed. "It is?"

So the ferocious monster who has retaken his throne on the first floor newel post is christened Marion. Pansy has named him. The power lifts her.

Lionel and I tramp into the kitchen, looking for food, and, to my surprise, Smithson follows. "I remember it vaguely," he says. "I wish I had asked my father about it then."

Probably best that he didn't. It must be that Little Chuckie was your basic wimpy kid and maybe had a few nightmares of his own about Marion, so his father removed the carving and tossed it into a handy secret space in a room no one ever used.

"Well, he's back where he belongs now," says The Royal Master heartily. "Lucilla, have you started anything for the girls' dinner?"

This has to be for Emily's sake. She has followed us into the kitchen, and I see her looking around with a grimace on that lovely face. What is he trying to prove to her? That he didn't hire a complete fool after all? That he cares what and when his children eat? He never has before.

Obviously, *she* doesn't. She hasn't even greeted them yet.

"Their dinner? How could I?" To my surprise, it comes out nasty. "You know I was upstairs with the girls. I'm not Super Nanny, after all."

He doesn't answer, but gives me a bewildered look. I squash the tiny bubble of guilt that flickers ever so briefly inside me. Yes, I'm disgusted with myself, Sister. I shouldn't care what *she* thinks, and I shouldn't take out my feelings of inferiority on Smithson.

Emily, at this moment, is picking up a row of china salt and pepper shakers, one at a time, reading the marks underneath, examining the symbols and trade names. I can see her emerald ring sparkling in the kitchen light as she turns the shakers this way, then that. Pansy and Violet are dancing around the kitchen squealing, "Pizza, Pizza, Pizza," and Lionel has his head stuck in the refrigerator.

And that's when, I swear it, I see Emily Cheseworthy of the Cheseworthy-Tafts deftly drop one of Charles Smithson's tiny porcelain salt shakers into the leather handbag slung over her shoulder. She pats her bag and picks up another salt shaker, grimaces at the mark, and places it back on the shelf.

I stare at that handbag, and she turns easily toward me, her eyes forcing mine to meet them. "It must be such a treat for you to be here, Miss Wilta," she says. "Charles tells me he rescued you from a diner."

Smithson has picked Pansy up, and she curls her pink arms around his neck. "Not rescued, Emily-" he begins.

"Pizza, daddy," Pansy interrupts him. She has her grubby little hands pressed to either side of his face, forcing him to give all his attention to her. "Can we?" It's a foregone conclusion. Whatever Pansy wants, Pansy shall most assuredly have.

I'm still staring at Emily Cheseworthy. Did I really see what I thought I saw? Does Charles know? Does he care? With effort, I pull my eyes away and start ruffling through some fast food flyers to find the number of the pizza parlor. A thief? The Honorable Sir Charles Fitzham Smithson the Second has himself tangled up with a thief!

What do I do with this knowledge?

I make a decision right then and there. I do nothing.

After Emily and Charles have gone, Lionel orders pizza, and the four of us sprawl happily in front of the television. Let them have their fancy restaurant, their club, their fabulous good looks, their salt and pepper shakers, and their piles of money. This is good enough for me.

Marion becomes a part of the household. His bulbous, cruel eyes stare me down with my every ascent of the castle stairs. His wide open mouth, teeth practically dripping with saliva, or maybe blood, roars an unfriendly greeting at every visitor who enters through our front door.

Smithson jokes about it, even brags about it, and reminds Violet every chance he gets how clever she was to find it. And he decrees that, for safety's sake, Marsuvius Borstrom's bedroom will, from this day forward, remain securely locked.

Well, that's fine, Sister, and I'm sure you'll appreciate my attitude. I'm finished in there, anyway. Chuck may enjoy his feline skull and assume he's exposed all the castle's secrets. But as for me, I intend to keep looking, thanks.

# 15

NO, VANSY!" I yell, "You look like a chipmunk!" It sets her off into gales of happy laughter. "Watch the way Pilot is doing it." Violet gives a big leap over the rolled up blanket on the floor, and Pansy snorts loudly. "Yes, that's it!" I cry. "Now watch me." I curl myself into a clumsy ball and then spring, flailing my arms and legs and leaping high and clear of the blanket. "FWAA!" I howl, landing on a stack of soft quilts. The girls jump up behind me, tackling me, yelling, "Fwaa! Fwaa!"

The big ornate mirror on the opposite wall is reflecting the sunlight, and the spark catches my eye. I glance to the mirror, and my Fwaa dies in mid-throat. Mr. Smithson is leaning in the doorway, watching us. Spying. I thought he had a golf game this afternoon, and I'm wondering how long he's been here. I feel like an idiot.

Well, his opinion means less than nothing to me. Big Deal. Big Shock. So Lucky Wilta is undignified.

"That's enough, girls," I say. "Put the blankets away. We'll be flying squirrels again some other day."

"No," whines Pansy, "we were just getting started."

"I said put them away," I say stiffly. Her lip puckers, and I wonder if she's about to cry, but she doesn't. They drag the blankets out of the room and I hear them stuffing them into the hall closet, making disgruntled noises.

He's not in the mirror anymore, but I'm through playing. The fun has gone out of the game for me.

The girls go off with their father, and I sit thinking for a while, but I don't like my thoughts. So I wander to the window and gaze out at the dry, brittle summer lawns. They could use a watering, but no one bothers. I catch my reflection in the mirror and go to it and stand looking for a time. I run my fingers through my disheveled hair and straighten my shirt which is twisted from being a flying squirrel. I wish I were pretty and witty and that I were rich. And I wish I had class. There are many things I wish, and it's a lucky thing that I'm not left standing in front of that mirror indefinitely, or my list would grow rather unwieldy, and quite ridiculous.

Old Kill-Joy has come up behind me, and he stands there looking at me in the glass. Serious, as usual. Only his daughters can pierce that melancholy facade. It sure would be nice if he'd smile spontaneously once in a while, or, heaven forbid, laugh. Maybe his face would crack and shatter. Then I'd get stuck sweeping up the pieces . . . .

"Miss Wilta," he says, "I need to talk to you."

"Sorry, sir, I have to tuck them in for naps." I dart to the left.

He lays one restraining hand on my arm. "I just did that. They were worn out; they're already asleep. Would you come with me?" He gestures to the outside door.

"Leave the house? But Dr. Harvard clearly says children should not be left sleeping alone in the house." I look up at him. "I'm shocked you would suggest it."

"We'll be in sight of the house. I opened their windows; we'll hear them."

I shrug. "Yer the boss."

We walk around to the woods behind the castle. In the quiet, the dry grass and pine needles crinkle under our feet. I wish Kitty could see me strolling casually beside Adonis. Not that our conversation is scintillating; there isn't any. Well, he'll speak when he's ready. If he thinks I'm going to beg him, he's off target.

Suddenly his pace becomes brisk, as if he has made a decision, and he walks toward an old stone bench and hesitates, then sits down.

I stand before him waiting. "Lucilla," he says finally, "I need your help with something." His mouth twists into something closer to a grimace than a smile. "You know, of course, that Emily and I have been engaged for a while."

I didn't know, but I had surmised. I stay silent.

"Emily has some things to sort out, but we're thinking of moving the date up."

Moving the date up? I didn't even know there *was* a date.

"I'll need your help," he says. Good grief. What is he planning to ask me? To cater the event? Plant flowers and decorate the terraces? Help Emily select her bridal trousseau? Maybe she wants me to be her maid of honor.

"I need to get rid of the castle," he says, and my heart stops. My first thought is that he's offering it to me, a happy idea. My second is that I'd be stuck with this pile of doom and gloom.

"I just hope I can find a buyer," he adds. My third thought collides with the others, and I feel my world shift.

"Really?" I whimper. My voice is weak, I can feel it. I'm hoping I don't faint right here in the pricker bushes. Sell my castle? I thought I had a full year to work out the details of my coup, to find my treasure, to uncover documents, see lawyers. And now I find I have only a few months, maybe only a few weeks. I have only until Emily decides it's time.

"Emily doesn't like it," he continues, "and we don't need it. It's getting harder and harder to maintain it." He actually smiles a little and glances at me. "Well, you know that, I guess." He sighs again, a good, familiar sound. "Do you realize how much money I pour into this atrocity year after year?" He looks up at the moss taking over the decaying roof and the tower strangled in dead vines. "I'm trapped by an aggravating property I don't even want. I don't know what my father was thinking. He thought he was leaving me such a great legacy . . . ."

Emily Cheseworthy. My brain is stuck on that one thought. How ridiculous for him to plan on marrying that insipid clay goddess. Yes, of course, I've known all along, but to actually hear him say it . . . . "Are you sure you love her, Mr. Smithson?" I can't believe those words tumble out of my mouth. I really am undignified.

"Sure," he says easily, "we're fond of each other; we've known each other for years. And she's . . . nice to the girls. Pansy and Violet like her."

"No, they don't; they're barely polite to her."

His eyes avoid mine. "Well then, they'll learn to like her. She's a perfectly nice person." He gets up and starts stalking around in the woods behind the castle, a little agitated now, and I suspect I caused that. I'm listening for shrill, wakening voices, calling us back. No such luck. Just the light wind rustling the leaves. I follow him.

"Well, if you want my advice-" I begin.

"I don't, Lucilla. I don't want your advice at all, but I need your help. I want you to make this as smooth for Violet and Pansy as you can. Explain it to them. Make them understand how good it will be for all of us." His tone is hopeful.

I squash that right away. "How can I," I say, "when I don't understand that myself?" Smithson is an even bigger fool than I thought. Emily as his daughters' mother? How many fussy dolls does he think they need? Has he taken a good look past that perfectly chiseled face and expertly casual hairdo? Or maybe this is just a plot for more ties.

"There's nothing to understand," he's saying impatiently. "Just get them accepting the idea of moving to a new home; that shouldn't be hard. We'll probably build something on the lake, waterfront with a nice beach . . . . And help prepare them for the idea of a new mother. I know you can do it." He glances across at me. "For someone who convinced them to try liver for lunch, this should be easy."

Well, I am rather proud that I got both girls to eat liver. Once.

And, yes, I decide not to say aloud, living with Emily Cheseworthy would be on a par with that.

◇◇◇

He's pacing faster now, chewing his lip over whatever thought has taken hold of him, and I can hardly keep up with him. I can't believe what I say next, Sister, but I told you I'd come clean about everything, so I might as well admit it. I'm a little winded from all the vigorous pacing, but I draw in a big breath and ask him, point blank. "Mr. Smithson, the girls never mention their mother. Where *is* she?"

He glances at me, surprised, and stops walking. I know I'm impudent, but the time has come, and I want to know. "Did she leave?" I continue. "Did she die? They never say anything about her."

"They don't remember her. They were babies when she died."

"She's dead then."

"Yes, I thought you knew that."

"How did it happen?" I stop. I'm sure he's about to tell me this is definitely not my business.

He hesitates and looks at my face and then says, almost belligerently, "She died in Italy. We wanted to get away. It was hard with two babies, always crying."

I think back to my first visit to the castle, to Violet filling the castle corridors with her lusty, piercing cries. I can just imagine both girls letting loose as babies. "I'll bet it was," I say.

His hands are clenching into tight fists, and I'm not even sure if he knows he's doing that.

"Well," he says, "neither of us was really ready for that responsibility. I guess it was stupid to leave them, but at the time . . . ." He pauses and listens briefly. There's no sound from the castle. All we can hear is the wind pulling the tops of the trees. "The girls were difficult, Lucilla. Colicky, cranky. I wasn't around a lot and my wife was resentful. We had a very capable woman to stay with the girls, and I thought the trip might help." His voice gets lower. "It sounds so much worse when I tell it."

Is he kidding? I'd have left, too.

"Anyway," he thrusts his hands into his pants pockets. "My wife kept talking about Italy, a villa on the ocean. She made all the arrangements. All I had to do was go along with it. It was three years ago."

"Violet's only-"

"I said they were babies. It hasn't been terribly easy."

"But how did she die?"

Something happens to his face then. A crumpling, a hurt, whipped look.

"Never mind," I say. I hold up a hand like a traffic cop to stop whatever words he might say. "Don't tell me." Never let it be said that Lucky Wilta lacks sensitivity. Anyway, for all I know, he murdered her, and do I really want to know that?

"It's all right," he says. "You're with them every day. You really ought to know. She drowned. It was a boating accident." We're walking again, and even Lucky Wilta doesn't have the nerve to demand more information. I never knew he had a tragic past, and, as much as he irritates me, I can't help feeling a little sorry, too.

When my father died, it was all I could do to drag myself out of bed in the mornings, the hurt was so deep and so aching. If anyone can sympathize with Charles Smithson's tale of woe, it's sensitive old me.

"I imagine the girls will be waking up soon," I say finally. It's not really true; they're good for another half hour at least, but he'd never know that, and I'm suddenly anxious to get away from Mr. Morose by my side. Our conversation is dredging up all kinds of depressing memories I'd prefer to leave buried.

He surprises me by saying quietly, "It was an awful time, Lucilla. I came back home alone to two little baby girls. I didn't have the faintest idea what to do for them, so I didn't do anything." He's not really talking to me, so I don't answer. "Basically," he says, and his voice is a noiseless word, the beating of tiny insect wings in the still air, "I stayed away from the castle and abandoned my children."

"Well, you didn't just leave them alone, did you?"

"With Mrs. Frocks."

He walks in silence until I finally say, "They don't feel abandoned. You weren't so terrible."

He shrugs, not buying it.

"Are you sure you want to disrupt their lives again?" I say it before I think. But Emily Chesworthy. God! I would never sacrifice my children to the likes of her!

He shakes his head impatiently. "I don't have a choice. No matter what I do, their lives will change. I have to unload this castle, Lucilla. It's destroying me to live here."

A long stillness descends on us and I search for a way to keep up my end of the conversation. Sister, I know I could be more tactful, but I have yet to achieve the gift of sensitivity. Finally, I say, "Mr. Smithson, I never read about your wife's accident in the paper. Wasn't it reported?" I do feel a little uncomfortable harping on a rotten subject, but I reassure myself. Sometimes, they say, it does us good to blat out about our miseries.

And I figure having your wife drown ranks right up there.

He almost smiles. "Lucilla, are you trying to tell me that you remember every little news article that's ever appeared about people you didn't even know?"

If he only knew! "I might have noticed that, though," I say lamely.

"I kept everything but a small death notice out of the papers. People like to embellish the facts, so I didn't give them any." He strides ahead again, unsettled. "Anyway, all of this has no bearing on what I'm telling you. For the sake of my daughters, I need your help. I'd like to know I can count on it."

I'm almost running to keep up again. "But are you sure this is best for Pansy and Violet? Why are you doing it? Don't you think you should spend more time considering-"

He turns to me, exasperated and suddenly very closed. I almost collide into him. "Lucilla! Couldn't you just do as I ask without barraging me with questions and advice? You don't need to know everything."

I step back a little, surprised at his sudden change of tone.

"You simply need to carry out my wishes."

I correct him. "Orders."

"Fine. Orders. You work for me, remember?"

I try again. "I still don't understand why-"

"Just- please, start preparing Pansy and Violet for this. We'll be married as soon as Emily decides. As soon as possible."

"Is it something to do with money?" I ask. "Did Lionel bet you a million dollars that you wouldn't have the guts to do it?" Why else would any man marry Emily Cheseworthy? He doesn't respond. I lower my voice to a confidential tone. "Are you pregnant, Mr. Smithson?" I say it delicately, wishing I could make him laugh, but he doesn't. He just ignores me.

"I just hope to get this done soon." He doesn't sound as if he's hoping that. He sounds pained, worried, distraught. But then, he always sounds like that. His mouth is contorted, his eyes brooding, a picture of the joyous bridegroom.

"So I'll need your help, Lucilla." He's suddenly all business, as if he hasn't just bared his soul to yours truly. "People will be coming through to view the castle and I'll need to know it's being shown to its best advantage. I need to count on you for that."

"There is no best advantage to the castle," I mutter. "It has no good points, as it turns out."

I know he agrees with me, so I'm surprised when he looks at me sharply. "My wife loved the castle," he says.

"Then your wife had no taste." I know that was cruel, Sister Mary Phyllis. I know the man is grieving for his wife, and I shouldn't disparage her memory. I know this, but, really- she *loved* the castle?

He's getting irritated again; I can tell by the way his nostrils flare when he's making an effort not to explode. If I didn't despise him so much, I might find that kind of endearing.

"Anyway, I'm trying to line up some potential buyers. My attorneys are already working on that. This won't be a typical sale."

"No, I guess not," I say.

He's droning on and on about selling the castle, and I'm walking fast to keep up with him. Selling the castle, my foot. If he wants to marry Emily Lah-de-dah Cheseworthy, there's nothing I can do about it, but there won't be any money changing hands from the sale of the castle until Charles Fitzham Smithson hands over all he's stolen from me these past nineteen years.

I'm already thinking fast; I need to step up my search for the secret room.

Smithson has stopped walking and is eyeing the earth beneath us. Soggy, misshapen cupcake wrappers, candy boxes, and empty juice bottles litter the ground. He pokes at a frayed damp napkin with one foot. "Trespassers," he says glumly. "They love to use the woods, but don't bother to pick anything up."

He spots, tangled in a bush, a blown away plastic bag that looks very familiar to me. He retrieves it and starts gathering up the garbage.

"I'll do it," I say, and I take the bag from him gently.

He watches me gathering up trash and finally says, "That's not in your contract, Lucilla."

"No, but I'm the one who left it here. I brought Pansy and Violet here for a picnic. Then I made them cry, and I just forgot all this." I keep on stuffing litter into the damp bag, knowing he's watching me.

"A picnic?" he says quietly. Then, "I didn't even know about that. I haven't been much of a father."

"I'm no expert on little girls either," I say with a weak smile, remembering how my arms ached the night I carried them, sobbing, home from our ruined outing.

"My wife's people aren't very happy with the way I'm raising them," he says suddenly. I look up, startled. "That's where I was for three days when you first came. They love Pansy & Violet, but they specifically asked me not to bring them to visit, so they could lecture me freely about all my shortcomings. It happens every now and then. They summon; I go. They always mention that their lawyers just might be there, so I don't dare assume otherwise. They don't think I'm doing a good job either."

Either. He means me and the way I badger him constantly, ridiculing his efforts and making everything harder. I feel an unaccustomed spasm of remorse, and bury it.

"What do they not approve of?" I ask.

"Pretty much everything," he says vaguely. "In her will," he continues, "my mother left me everything- money, the castle, and her hope that I'd spend at least five more years living here. That was my father's idea. My parents were sure I'd grow to love it and hoped I'd pass it down eventually. For some reason, my father thought the world of this place."

Him, too? To each his own, I guess.

"I've tried. I brought my wife here, like we were living some fairy tale. But I just don't want to be here anymore. I need a fresh start."

"And you think Emily will give you that?"

He shrugs and then smiles, a rare and magnificent thing. "Emily knows me well. She knows exactly what I need and is willing to help me."

I can't help myself. I'm still reeling from the game plan he's concocted. "By marrying you?" I say. "That's usually for life, you know. You'd run out of conversation in the first six months." I can't keep the scorn out of my voice.

"I don't want to lose my daughters, Lucilla, and I'm terrified my in-laws might start something legal if I don't fix this soon. I'm not even sure they'd lose if it came to a court case. If I remarry, give the girls a real life with two parents and a normal home, I know they'll stop pressing." He pauses for a second, and then says, "I told them about you, that you're competent and that the girls are thriving, but it didn't matter. They want real stability; they want to see a family. And you don't know Emily. She may not be perfect, but she's a good person."

I have all the garbage now, and I clutch the bag as we walk, slower now, back through the woods.

"You'd marry her for their sake," I finally say.

"I'd do anything for their sake," he answers.

◇◇◇

Emily agrees to marry Charles as soon as the castle finds a buyer. She would rather start married life without that particular albatross around their necks. Charles seems relieved and pretends to be happy.

He tells the girls his exciting news himself, and I listen at the door. They don't shriek or clamor, just stand there not having a hint how their lives are about to be turned upside down. Pansy asks me later which bedroom is going to be Emily's, and I tell her it will most likely be her old one with the wet walls. She approves.

Charles spends most of his evenings with Emily, of course; I guess he always did. Or at home hunched over his desk, memorizing his computer screen or sticking Post-its onto pages of thick, dull books about his favorite topic: money.

Now, I've always liked money, too, not that I've had much in recent years. But this guy is ridiculous. During the day, when he's not around, I sometimes take a quick peek into one of his fat, new-smelling volumes, and find he has underlined, starred, and highlighted passages that say things like, *The cost of underwriting, that is, the difference between the price of the securities to the public and the proceeds to the firm, is illustrated in the prospectus given in Exhibit 4.7 in Appendix*

*Six.* Yes, you betchum. And what's more, eggs are a buck-twenty-nine on special this week at Food World.

When Lionel isn't busy on a hot date and Emily gives Chuck the evening off, the two men sometimes play golf, but The Big Boss's heart just isn't in it. Even the hole in one, Smithson's first, doesn't seem to be much of a thrill. Lionel talks it up big, excited, proud of his pal. The Righteous Sir Charles says, "Yes, I was pleased."

Emily stops by the castle more frequently now, looking over the furnishings to see if there's anything salvageable enough for the new house she and Mr. Smithson are having built. She brings gifts - flowers for the dining room, pale, waxy candles, a box of creamy chocolates that the girls and I scarf down in minutes. Dolls. Every now and then, she carries something out with her, a lamp, a silver tray, a set of antique brushes. I think I recognize a gilt-edged picture frame from old Marsuvius Borstrom's master suite. The painting has been removed, but the cupids frolicking in the corners look very familiar. She doesn't ask, and she acts pretty furtive, if you ask me, but what difference does it make? One day soon, this will all be hers anyway. She glides in and out of bedrooms, inventorying the shelves and drawers, taking stock of her new goods, her new possessions. Her haul.

She doesn't say much to me, just gives me a bright, practiced smile and makes an effort not to trip over Pansy and Violet as they race through the house.

I've never been scared of a good fight, and I'd try to put a stop to this farce, and lose my job in the bargain, if his goal were money or glory or even good, old-fashioned lust. But it isn't any of those things. For his two little girls, he'll sacrifice himself. How can anyone ask him to do less?

# 16

THERE'S A TIMID KNOCK on our front door early one Saturday afternoon, and as Keith Gregoire and his rumpled suit enter, I manage to give him a cold, unwelcoming look. I haven't forgotten that he called me a drip during his first visit, and I find it hard to demonstrate my usual flair for hostessing.

He and Smithson barricade themselves in the music room; I know because I try the door, and it isn't until two hours later that they emerge looking wiser and richer.

"Why did you treat him that way?" Smithson asks me as the door closes on Keith's sprinting heels.

"What way?"

"You were barely polite, Lucilla. Keith came here as a favor to me, all the way from Plattsburgh. It's a little embarrassing to have you treating him like some vagrant."

"I haven't forgotten, that's all," I sniff. I walk with dignity to the kitchen.

Chuck looks confused and follows me. "Forgotten what?"

"You know what," I say righteously. "What he said about me when he came before. When I was out in the bushes watching him leave."

Charles makes a frustrated move. "I don't know what you're talking about," he says. He sounds annoyed and exasperated. "Do *you*?" Then, under his breath, "In fact, do you ever?"

"Oh, come on, Chaz," I say. "I heard it. He called me a drip. He told you to watch out for me. He *warned* you against me."

Charles looks blank, and this annoys me, so now there are two of us standing there stiffly, feeling irritated.

"Watch out for the drip, remember, Mr. Smithson? Your friend didn't think anything of calling me names, yet you expect me to greet him with the red carpet treatment . . . ." I'm staring right into his eyes. Let him try to explain this away.

Suddenly his eyes are crinkling at the corners, and he's stifling a laugh. "Lucilla," he says, "come here." He leaves the room, shaking his head in what looks like great amusement. I throw down my dish towel and follow him from the kitchen.

He's toying with his computer, flicking buttons and pressing keys and fooling around with the mouse.

I stand back a good, safe distance. I've never touched this machine, and I know I never will. Far be it from me to accidentally explode the precious financial data he has hidden away behind that glossy black screen.

"All right, look," he says. He plugs in a thumb drive and clicks some buttons and a picture appears, a pile of money - bills and change in an appealing heap. I like the looks of it, but I wouldn't let *him* know that.

"So?"

He pulls me closer to the screen, so that I can read the words. *Dividend Reinvestment Plans, or Drips*, it says, *are programs offered to shareholders . . . .*

"Oh," I say.

"It's an investment program," Smithson tells me. "Keith downloaded the pages for me. He wasn't sure if the one I was considering would charge a fee if I decided to reinvest."

"Oh," I say again.

"That's all you have to say?" he demands. "*Oh?* No apology? No 'Gee, sorry, I guess I was wrong?' You insulted a friend of mine, Lucilla." He's leaning against his desk, arms crossed, smug, waiting for an apology that will never come.

I start back to the kitchen, feeling, like, you guessed it, Sister, a real drip.

"Lucilla!" he calls after me. "Don't you think you should say something? Anything?"

I stop, turning back. "Okay," I tell him. "I made a mistake. But even if he didn't call me a drip, he could have. It's been known to happen."

"Oh, come on." He dismisses my words.

"I've been called all kinds of things," I say. "A nitwit. A numskull. A lamebrain."

He's shaking his head, coming toward me, and he has sympathy written all over his face.

Not acceptable. His pity I ain't interested in. I hurry on, thrusting my chin out defiant. "But I'm not the only one, Mr. Smithson. In this household, there are at least two of us."

There. Got him.

I'm glaring recklessly, and he's staring back, scowling now. "I'm sorry to say it, Charles," I sneer, "but you know I'm right.

And marrying that dimwit Emily is a bigger blunder than misunderstanding some little . . ." I search for the right word, then finish scornfully, ". . . *financial advisor*." I stalk off.

Moments later, he slams the front door and disappears for the rest of the afternoon.

He really is obnoxious sometimes.

◇◇◇

When Emily stops by, he's still out, and she asks me to give him a message: They must go to Albany to choose a crystal pattern and would he please call her about this. I assure her I'll tell him and usher her out, glancing down at the tiny silver vase protruding from her handbag. Five minutes ago it stood on the marble-topped table hugging the front door. Maybe she'd like to strip off some of the better wallpapers, too, or snag a few roof tiles, and I consider making this offer.

I wander through the crowded pantries peering around me at the years of accumulated crystal behind glass. What could they want with more glassware?

Two greedy rich kids, settling in together to furnish yet another home. They actually make such an ideal couple.

I spend my time playing with Pansy and Violet, making an effort to talk with them about marriage and what it is and how it will affect them. I even force myself to say some nice things about Cheesy Emily of the Cheseworthy-Tafts.

The girls aren't fooled. They know boring when they see it. They don't like her, and they know darn well that I don't like her much either.

I have a constant sick feeling in the pit of my stomach.

And I search, I keep searching, for my father's secret room. Countless times, I almost give up. I tell myself that my father eventually took the diamonds from Marsuvius Borstrom's bedroom. Took the diamonds and lived it up big. High on the hog. Rolling in it.

Happily choking on a silver spoon.

But that can't be, and I know it. My father knew he was dying of cancer. He left me his diary, a definite message, and he knew I would read it, and besides, the space under the secretary is just a space, and my father described a room. I have to find it.

I've repressed my demure shyness over taking Smithson's keys, and now that I know where they are, I flit about the castle

155

unlocking everything, rooms he's never bothered to open before, rooms that look exactly as they must have fifty years ago.

Lionel and I discover a locked door in a corner of the attic, hidden in the shadows of a heavy wardrobe. And when none of the keys fit, we feel the same excitement that immersed us in Borstrom's old bedroom. Within seconds we agree to break it down, and Lionel does it easily, ramming it with a loose board he pulls from the floor. The wood splinters and the hinges give way, and I hold my breath when he finally pushes in the cracked, warped door to reveal - an empty closet.

Small, too. A cramped, narrow space lined with smooth cedar, and with nothing inside it. Nothing, unless you count the tidy little pile of mouse droppings in the middle of the floor. Well, what did I expect?

My throat tightens in familiar disappointment and frustration, and I brush rudely past Lionel and head back to the attic stairs.

He stops me with his strong arms and soothing voice and keeps repeating "Lucky, honey," trying to calm me, while he wonders if I've gone off the deep end.

And then we have that conversation that we've had a few times before. Why do I believe there's a treasure in the castle? How can I be so sure?

But, of course, I can't tell him, I will not tell him, and I yell at him to quit badgering me. He thrusts me away a little roughly, stung, and we go back downstairs. He leaves stiffly, without saying much of a good-bye.

It doesn't matter. I don't need Lionel, and I never wanted his help anyway. I just want to be left alone to do the thing I set out to do when I came here.

I've counted windows, from inside and out, I've scaled trellises to get a better view, I've haunted the attic, counted off square feet, tapped walls and passageways. I've broken into closets and hidden in shadows when Mr. Smithson comes home early and passes near me, wondering where I am and what I'm doing while his daughters sleep. Every foot of the castle is accounted for. Every inch. Every millimeter. There can be no secret room.

And then I go back to the diary. . . . *Diamonds of a thousand brilliant colors! . . . Time to find my way back to the secret room. The quiet awaits me. All that's hidden there beckons . . . .*

There *is* a secret room. There has to be.

156

Emily Cheseworthy takes to hanging around the castle some days, even when her affianced is clearly not here. Why? I can't imagine, unless it is my tasteful company. She follows me from room to room, watching me dust, and stands simpering by at a safe, clean distance as I bury a chortling Violet in the sandbox and leave her there for Pansy to unearth.

She starts conversations that begin, "When Charles and I are one," and they usually end there, too, since I tend to discover at that very moment that it's time to switch on the blender for a prune frappe or start up the clanky old vacuum cleaner.

When Charles and you are one, I'm thinking, you'll actually be four. And it wouldn't be a bad idea for you to learn the names of those identical moppets of his. It turns out they have distinct personalities and definite opinions. They are not, as it happens, interchangeable.

"Look, Emily," I tell her one day. "Violet is doing a puzzle, right? And Pansy is spilling juice. Are you with me?"

Emily is giving me a weird look from her sooty, dark eyes. She glances at the children and nods suspiciously.

"So," I continue, "V = P, and P = J, okay?"

She doesn't catch on. What a dumb broad.

She joins us for dinner one night, and I cook up a storm. We have several of Chez Fred's specie-alities - greasy, heavy, and pale - and I do it on purpose for Emily. I don't want her ever to eat with us again. The girls whine more than usual, Charles looks distracted, the meal drags on.

"You'll have lovely new bedrooms in the new house," Emily says. "Great big ones with pretty flowered wallpaper, pink for Pansy and yellow for Violet." She nods vaguely in what she hopes is the right order of children. "I'm going into New York to meet with the architects tomorrow." She's pushing her biscuits with sausage gravy around on her plate. Only her good breeding keeps her from gagging. I wonder idly if she's ever been to Chez Fred's. Maybe it's up to me to throw a bridal shower for her. I could rent out the back section that overlooks the highway, get Fred to tack down some new linoleum . . . .

"But we want a room together," Pansy whines. Her nose is dripping, and she runs her hand across her face, then wipes it on the white lace tablecloth. A little glob of mucus glistens prettily.

"Can Lucky live with us?" asks Violet. She's stirring at her food, forming little glutinous pools of cooling gravy, looking unenthusiastic.

"Lucky?" says Emily as she watches the path of Pansy's damp hand fumbling around in the basket of dinner rolls. Her voice is muted. Her eyes never leave the basket of rolls.

"Yessiree Bob," I say. "That's me. Lucky. Always was, always will be, forever and ever, Amen.

"Can I? I could be your cook."

Emily looks down at her plate and grimaces.

The Honorable Mister Smithson actually almost smiles. I'm sure I see the corners of his mouth flicker, and his eyebrows shoot up, just for a second while he leans over to pick up the glistening roll Pansy has dropped to the floor. Emily laughs brightly while she stealthily slides an exquisite silver jelly spoon under her napkin.

She might as well hire a Van Lines mover to back up to the front door and cart off all the junk she wants. We sure don't seem to care.

I clean up the dishes, dump the rolls, and take the girls up to bed. I hook a can of beer out of the refrigerator as I pass by, and Pansy gives Marion the lion an affectionate pat as we go through the foyer and on up the stairs. I'm looking forward to relaxing alone in my room. It's been a long evening.

She's trying. She's trying so hard to be civil to me and the girls. She's trying to become someone Charles Smithson might possibly fall in love with. She *is* a good person; she's doing this for him. And it's my job to make it easier for her, for all of them. But I just can't do it, not even for Pansy and Violet.

I admit that prolonging the niceties with Miss Emily does not make it to my top ten. Or ten million.

◇◇◇

Pansy and Violet require two stories each to get settled properly, and then they both come stealing into my room anyway. I'm just about to flip open my beer, and I feel a little put upon. "No fair," I say. "Youse guys is suppose to be sleeping."

"We couldn't," Violet says. "We felt lonely."

"Well, I don't wonder," I say grandly. "Whoever heard of two little sisters so close in age having separate chambers."

"Chambers?" says Pansy.

"In regular houses, they're only bedrooms, but in castles we call them chambers."

"I want a chamber in my new house," wails Violet.

"You can't," I say sadly. "It will only be a house."

Pansy has her head tipped sideways, thinking. "But we could have just one bedroom, couldn't we? And use the other one to keep our toys in."

"Yes, all your dolls," I tell her. "You tell Daddy that when you move out of the castle, you want one big room together, and an extra one besides for Emily's dolls." I pull back the tab on my Utica Club and take the first drink. It's icy cold and tastes good.

"But what about tonight?" asks Pansy. She's eyeing my big bed, waiting for an invitation.

"Go on. Get in," I say, and they both race to my bed and jump under the covers.

"You come, too," Pansy says. I prop myself there, still in my jeans and tee shirt, and drag down a few books from the shelf.

"Let's see," I say, checking over the titles. "These are not kids' books. These are X-rated."

Violet scowls. "What's that mean?"

"Pornographic," I say. "Salacious." They're looking at me with complete trust. "Let me run and get some from your chambers." I kiss them both on top of their heads, dump *Gulliver's Travels* and *Robinson Crusoe* to the floor, and go out into the hall, sipping.

Emily has left, but I can hear Lionel's laughing voice below as I step into the corridor. He's never very serious, and it's a marked contrast to Smithson's businesslike tones. Here we have two good friends, one who gibbers like a monkey all day long, one who would drop dead if he ever cracked a smile. Take your pick.

"She might do," Lionel is saying, and the mirth in his voice comes pouring out.

"Lionel, why do you do this over every woman who comes along?"

"I do precisely what I want to do!" Lionel responds gaily. "And I want to get Lucky tonight." He giggles cheerfully, highly amused at his own joke.

"I wish you wouldn't come here when you've been drinking," says Charles. "It's not good for the girls." I steal a guilty look at the beer can in my hand. Then I take a satisfying swallow.

"If you can get married, I can get married," says Lionel.

"Lionel, you know you're not interested in marrying her or anyone else," Charles says.

"Why shouldn't I?" Lionel rejoins. "She deserves diamonds much as the next person." His words are slurring a little, and I'm horrified to hear him mention diamonds. He *has* been drinking, and more than just a beer with dinner. If he says the wrong thing to Charles . . . . I hear a crash as he falls into something. "Sorry," he says, and then, "She may never get another chance. And the more I look at her, the better she looks."

"Oh, for God's sake, Lionel."

"She's not really *ugly*."

"Go home, Lionel," Smithson says. "Leave her alone." His tone is bored, as if he's been here a hundred times before.

"She'd consider herself Lucky," Lionel says, and he deteriorates into spasms of laughter.

"Go home," Smithson says again, and I hear him propelling his friend toward the door. "Sleep it off. Come back tomorrow."

"Aren't you going to go get her?" Lionel asks. "At least give her the chance to say yes or no."

"I'm saying no for her," Charles says. He sounds less bored now, more impatient.

I'm beginning to get provoked. One, Lionel's words are insulting and humiliating. Are they true? Of course. But it's plain bad manners for him to say them. Nobody, and I mean nobody, gets to laugh at Lucky Wilta. How can they? I always beat them to it by laughing at myself first.

Two, this dialogue has everything to do with me, and I don't like the way Bonnie Prince Charlie is acting for me, as if I'm incapable of handling a worm like Lionel Hawthorne. If there's one thing I am, it's independent and capable.

Yes, Sister, I know that's two things.

Smithson already has the front door open, and Lionel is half out of it, when I emerge at the top of the stairway, beer can clutched in my hand. "Hello, Lionel," I say evenly. "Did you want something?"

"To marry you," he shouts, and goes down the porch steps, snorting with laughter.

Mr. Smithson closes the door and looks at me, embarrassed and sympathetic. "Lucilla . . . ." he starts.

"No," I say loudly, ineffectually, and then I'm stalking down the stairs in my fury, shouting. I yank open the heavy front door and scream at the retreating figure lurching down the driveway. "No, Lionel! You cheap, crass, arrogant, mad-headed ape!" I continue on, throwing in a few good, juicy names that I hope

Pansy and Violet won't remember.

I slam the door hard, and, breathing heavily, stomp back up the stairs. I turn at the landing and roar one last insult down the stairs, the worst. "You're not good enough for me, Lionel!" My words hit the closed door and bounce back, and I'm so angry that I fling my beer can and watch it smash against the door. Beer sprays wildly, and the can thunks to the floor and rolls into a corner, still gurgling.

I turn to Charles with dignity. "See?" I say to him icily. "I am perfectly capable of saying it myself." I sweep back up the stairs furiously.

I hear a movement below me and then Charles' voice following me gently up the stairs. "Mad-headed ape?" he says.

"Shakespeare," I spit out. "I'm not as stupid as I look." My eyes feel like two hot coals, and I can hardly see straight, and it isn't until I'm in the upstairs hallway and making the turn for my room that I glance back.

The Honorable Charles Fitzham Smithson the Second is standing down there looking up at me. His arms are crossed over his chest, and his legs are a little apart, his feet planted firmly on the checkered marble floor. And, to my great dismay or my complete and utter relief, he's grinning. For the first time in all the time I've known him, he's grinning. At me.

I flee to my room.

# 17

IT'S ONE O'CLOCK in the afternoon, and His Holiness is home. I still haven't figured out why. He spent most of the morning hanging around the castle being a pest while I cleaned around him. If it isn't Miss Emily, it's Mister Charles.

I can't abide these aristocratic types.

He took Pansy and Violet into Tupper Lake to buy new shoes, a chore I expected to do, so that was a plus. They came home all excited about black patent leather buckle shoes that Daddy said they could wear even for play. The practical canvas sneakers still sit in the boxes, unpopular. And the floppy, wide-brimmed straw hats decorated with straw flowers and ribbons made them squeal for an hour. Good Old Daddy.

We're sitting down to lunch in the kitchen, and Pansy is arguing with her father about the relative good manners of wearing her new hat at the table. "But Lucky didn't say I couldn't, and I love it," Pansy explains patiently, tossing her head so that the streamers fly around and slap my arm as I dip the knife into the jelly jar.

"Take it off," he repeats, "before you get food on it."

"No, I don't have to," she says, and then she looks into his menacing eyes and quickly removes the hat.

"I'm good," Violet reminds us. "I didn't wear my hat. I just wore my shoes." She thrusts one shiny black foot up onto the table, wiggles it around to get comfortable, and knocks it into her bowl of vegetable soup. "Oops," she says. She removes her foot from the table and picks up the soup bowl. The suction from the spilled soup makes it stick, so that when it finally comes loose, it also comes fast, and Violet sloshes more over the sides and onto her shirt.

"Oops," she says again.

"Well, get a cloth," I tell her. "You know how to wipe up spills." She gets a dishcloth from the drawer and swirls it around on the wet table before she tosses it to the floor.

His Imbecilic Highness is watching all this without

comment, and I'm wondering if he doesn't notice or doesn't care that his little darlings are basically total slobs at the lunch table. He looks away from Violet pointedly and says to me, "The cabinets look good. I like the yellow."

"I picked it," says Pansy, and I give her an incredulous sneer.

"Pansy, you did not," I say. Little liar. "You wanted blue, remember?" Then I shake my head in mock dismay. "Trying to steal credit for my yellow paint."

"It's my yellow paint," she says. "This spot right here," and she runs over and points to the place I let her paint.

"Isn't that wonderful," her father says, meaning it.

Violet is tearing her jelly sandwich into bite-size pieces, smearing grape jelly on her fingers, then wiping them on her shirt. "Daddy," she says, "will you tell that story about Old King Charles?" Now she's pulling up the front of her shirt and licking the purple globs from the fabric.

Her father watches with distaste. "Violet, you know better than that," he says, then turns to me. "Doesn't she? Do they always eat like this at lunch?"

I shrug. "We gear up for dinner. We usually do lunch as the mood strikes. Knock it off, Violet. We have a guest."

Violet stops in mid-lick and gives me a quizzical look. "Who?"

"I'm not a guest," says her father. "Just go right ahead and be disgusting. Pretend I'm not even here."

"Will you tell it, Daddy?" Violet insists. "I like that story about Old King Charles."

"Me, too," says Pansy. "I like it, too." She has crawled out of her chair and is leaning all over Charles Fitzham Smithson the Second, her pudgy arms around his neck and her curly blonde hair tucked under his chin. He's trying to eat his soup while she mauls him, and a few drips from his spoon splash onto her head.

"Pansy, get off me," he tells her gently. "Come on, honey. I can't eat with you there."

"Besides, you have a carrot on your head," I say matter-of-factly.

She reaches up and finds the slippery cube of carrot, grasps it, drags it through her hair, and pops it into her mouth. "Tell the story," she urges her father.

He glances at me, decides I'm not worth considering, and says, "Well, maybe the short version. There once was a king," he starts.

"A mighty king," Violet corrects him.

"There once was a mighty king named Old King Charles who lived in this very castle, and he had a son named Prince Charles." Pansy looks up at him adoringly, and he smiles crookedly at me and shrugs his shoulders a little. "You might recognize some of the characters," he says.

Oh, yes, I'm sure I will. I can't wait to hear the rest.

"Stop talking to Lucky, Daddy, and tell the story."

"Okay. Anyway, the king had a son named Prince Charles, and when Charles grew up . . . ."

"Wait a minute." Pansy looks at him in disgust. "You forgot that whole part about how handsome and smart the prince was and how he threw an axe the best and won a prize."

I roll my eyes and get up from the table, clearing bowls half full of soup and smeared with jelly. I fish out a saturated paper napkin and toss it into the trash.

"That part's not important," he says. "So when the prince grew up, he fell in love with a beautiful princess and married her, and they became the King and Queen of the castle. And they had two daughters who were the fairest in the land . . . ."

"Wait a minute!" Pansy is really irritated this time. "You left out the whole part about the old king's royal death and the funeral procession that had four thousand horses."

There's a little silence while I clatter dishes into the sink and squirt soap on top.

"All right," the Lord of Embellishments continues patiently. "There were four thousand horses in the old king's royal funeral procession. And *then* Prince Charles grew up and became king, and *then* he . . . ."

"How old was he?" Violet asks.

"He was fourteen when the king died. You already know that, Violet."

"I thought maybe he grew."

"That's stupid," Pansy says. "The story has to stay the same every time."

Hans Christian Smithson ignores them, keeps right on hammering away at this handsome, brilliant, young King Charles and his beautiful, accomplished bride. "And then, tragedy struck," he says in a solemn voice.

"I know what it is," Violet says. She makes her voice match his, a sad but accepting melancholy. "The Queen was taken from them."

"Yes," says Mr. Smithson evenly, "but the new King and his daughters remained together in the castle, never to be separated, and they always remembered their beautiful mother the Queen and the old King who was their grandpa."

"And one became a scientist," Pansy says dreamily, "and the other became a famous singer, and one day two handsome princes came along and married them. And they all lived happily ever after."

"Yes," her father says, and then he adds thoughtfully, "But first the new King decided that his two fair daughters needed a new mother, so he found another beautiful princess . . . ."

Both girls are staring at him, and Pansy has uncurled herself from his neck. He ignores their disapproving looks.

"Another beautiful princess," he plods along, "named Princess Emily . . . ."

"That's not the way the story goes," Pansy says. "Put it back the way it was before."

"It's the same," her father insists, "except for this one improvement. And their lives became even happier and more exciting and more fun than they had ever been . . . ."

I look at the two little creatures sitting on either side of him, and I know they're not buying what he's selling. Violet has crossed her arms over her little chest and is looking at him with a suspicious frown. Pansy scrunches up next to him and says in a whisper, "Emily can be our new mother, but don't change the story anymore."

I'm rinsing dishes under a thin stream of water, trying to be quiet so I can hear how this is all going to turn out, and I feel kind of bad for him when this big, fat silence descends on the kitchen. He looks at me, and Pansy squnches up against him more tightly. "Okay, Dad?"

He kisses the top of her head. "Okay," he says quietly. "Next time I won't."

I excuse them from the table, and they grab up their hats and run outside. Mr. Smithson sits there for a few minutes with a dejected look on his face, until I feel as if I have to say something. "It might take a while," I say. "They'll be all right."

"I don't understand," he says. "It's not as though they miss their mother. What are they so worried about?"

I just shrug in answer. Well, if you don't know that, Charlie My Boy, then I can't help you.

It's quiet in the back yard now, but with Mr. Smithson home, I don't feel as if I have to rush to figure out where Pansy and Violet are. I've been rattling pots in the kitchen for the past hour, and I'm pretty proud of the dinner I'm getting ready for tonight. Why not? With Storyteller Smithson home for the day, my usual form of entertainment is out, and, besides, when he left the kitchen, he looked as though he could use a nice meal to lift him out of his doldrums.

Call me Rachael Ray, cute and bubbly.

Okay, call me Betty Crocker.

I have a turkey and asparagus casserole all prepared for later, and I've just put the finishing touches on a deep dish apple cranberry crumb pie. This is something I learned to make at Chez Fred's. Fred is known for his pies. I slide this one into the oven and set the ancient timer. Then I wander toward the front of the house to find the girls.

I can hear their father's voice long before I see them. "Come on, Pansy," he's saying, "just try."

"I can't," says Pansy.

"Yes you can," Smithson urges her. "Remember when you were so afraid of Marion? And now you pet him all the time."

"I love Marion," Pansy agrees.

"Then try this, too, honey." He's coaxing her. "You'll be able to do this, too. Remember how Miss Wilta taught you?"

There's no answer from Pansy, but I do hear Violet say, "That's not the right way, though."

"Yes it is," he insists. "Watch."

By this time I've reached the door to the foyer, and I stand there not quite believing what I see. An old olive green blanket from a spare bedroom is rolled up in a neat bundle in the middle of the floor. Pansy and Violet are shrinking together on the side wall, clearly doubting their father's sanity. And The Honorable Charles Fitzham Smithson the Second is leaping into the air, his teeth clenched tight, his eyes closed. His arms are stretched out at his sides, and his legs are sprawling. His foot gets tangled in the blanket, and he lands with a thud on the marble floor. Ouch.

And he calls me undignified.

"Aah," he says, rubbing his shins in pain. And then he looks sheepishly at his girls and mutters, "fwaa." They giggle.

"Not like that, Daddy," Violet says. "This is the way Lucky

showed us," and she executes a flying leap and a good loud "FWAA!" and lands on top of him. He leans over her and starts chewing her hair, and she screams cheerfully.

"Me, too," begs Pansy. "Eat my hair, too!" And she stumbles over the blanket and gets gobbled up by her father.

They haven't seen me yet, so I sneak away.

I pick up the shoe boxes and hats from the dining room table and go around and up the back stairs. I take the girls' purchases into their rooms and put them away, then walk down the hallway, wishing I might stumble upon a sudden clue to the secret room. I gaze up at the broken carved panels and down at the worn, discolored Persian runner under my feet. I peek behind urns and vases, glance at dark, oily paintings on the walls, and peer into open rooms. The corridor is cold, as usual, and it's so dark that I stumble into a low chest and give myself a nice aching bruise that I can show off for a week or two.

It's amazing that Chuckles has stayed here at all.

I'm at the end of the corridor and I have a choice to make. It's not difficult; I come here frequently now. The stone treads are shallow, and as I make the two turns, I leave the rest of the house behind me. I take out my key and unlock the door, pushing it open.

The one small window looks out on the south lawn, where the shiny blue metal swing set glints in the sun. Gloom hangs here in long hazy tendrils, but I see Nancy, her broad, cheerful face moving over the pale blue china teapot, speaking in her soft, subdued way. I sit down opposite her, fondling the delicate lines of my teacup, remembering. Her quiet voice, her round, scrubbed face, the way she always wore a misshapen sweater, pulled tight and buttoned once across her protruding stomach. I wonder whatever happened to Nancy, how she ended up. She went her own way and disappeared out of my life, like all people do. My parents, that hog Nick Wilta, my college comrades, even Fred.

Hey, I tell myself, at least I still have Kitty Nellahopkiss. She may be dumb, but she likes my castle.

And, for what it's worth, I have Lionel.

Time slows as I open the steamer trunk in the corner and pull out the ancient clothes. I hold up before me a pale yellow dress with layers of lace, and then a green riding suit that would never fit me now. A big straw hat with cascading red ribbons, a frilled bonnet of stiff linen. I try the hats on, one at a time, fingering the fragile, aging material. I pick up a gauzy veil and place it on my head, letting it stream down my back, and find a headdress of small ivory artificial flowers intertwined with pearls and lace. I fasten it over the veil and fluff out my hair, pulling the veil smoothly over my shoulders. Then I admire myself in the mirror.

Well, I'm no Emily Cheseworthy. I'm sure she'll have satin and Venice lace. Probably real out-of-season flowers, too, and a hundred bridesmaids all dressed alike in pale pink gowns . . . .

"I thought I'd find you here."

I start and turn abruptly, yanking the veil and flowers off my head, clutching them to my chest. My long hair goes flying in all directions, and Smithson says, "Sorry if I startled you. The oven timer rang. Do you want me to take the pie out?"

"No, I'll do it." I can feel myself blushing furiously. Why? What difference does it make if The Honorable Smithson thinks I'm some lovesick adolescent playing bride? After all, didn't I have my very own marriage proposal just last night? Okay, so the guy was out of his mind with alcohol. Beggars can't be choosers.

I toss the veil down carelessly and push past him.

Time to re-enter reality.

The casserole turns out even better than I expected, and even Pansy tries a little. She's notorious for hating little green bits of things, but she likes turkey, so she takes a chance. And the pie is magnificent.

Mr. Smithson doesn't say so, but he has two pieces and goes back for a third one later.

I reign supreme.

◇◇◇

"Lucilla," he's telling me over breakfast, "you have to watch your language with the girls. They're using profanity."

"The hell they are," I say. He doesn't laugh. It's not easy living with God. "Damn," I say, "I thought I was doing so much better." I brush a lock of my soft, newly blonde hair away from my face.

"It isn't something to joke about, Lucilla. This morning Violet swore at me when I told her to brush her teeth. And that song I heard Pansy singing . . . . Do you want them to grow up like . . . ." His voice kind of trails away.

"Like me. You betchum. Things could be worse." I remove

my plate from the table. I've made a superior breakfast today, French toast with ham and eggs, all stuff he likes. He's on seconds already and shoveling it in. Naturally, I get no thanks, just this latest criticism. I come back to the table and sit beside him again. "You haven't mentioned my makeover," I say. "It took me two hours to look like this."

He sighs, not a happy sound. "You know you look ridiculous."

"But no one could ever mistake me for a washerwoman, what?"

"You worry too much about your appearance, Lucilla," he says. "There's more to people than what they look like. Don't you think there's more to *me* than just what I look like?"

I give him a frank stare, an up and down once over, until he laughs and hides his face in his coffee cup.

What he looks like, of course, is gorgeous. And he's conceited enough to know it.

I twirl one ash blonde tendril around my finger and bat my heavily mascara'd eyes at him. He just stares. I can tell he's trying not to laugh again, and he's pretty successful. I have to admit, he has terrific self control. He looks away, finally, and says, "Lucilla, I found the strangest thing when I was up on the third floor a few days ago. One of the window casements has been battered apart."

"Really, Sir?" I stare at him with wide, innocent eyes.

"Yes. Someone obviously wanted to expose the little alcove next to the window. I can't imagine why. Can you?"

I shake my head, nonplused.

"He . . ." He looks at me pointedly, and picks up a forkful of eggs. Then he looks away again. "Or she . . . went about it very crudely. Even the floorboards are broken."

"No kidding," I say. "Do you think we should invest in a burglar alarm?" I try to make my face match his. Concerned, slightly distressed.

He doesn't even bother to answer, just swallows the eggs and drinks thoughtfully from his coffee cup. "It will be the devil to repair. Those old windows, you know."

"Maybe I could get someone up here this week to do it," I say.

He appears to consider this. "No, no," he says at last. "I don't think I want to incur that expense. Maybe you could just fit it in. Do it yourself. Just get a few boards, cover up the holes . . . ."

I swallow. Ouch. Extra work. I hadn't counted on that. "Shore," I say genially. "I could do that, I guess." Cheapskate.

"Meanwhile, keep the girls out of there, would you?" he says. "It would be a shame to have one of them wander in there and fall three floors."

"Right."

There's a little silence, and then he says quietly, "Lucilla? Would you like me to tell you which room it is? Wouldn't it be silly for you to look in all thirty of them for the broken casement?"

I laugh good-naturedly. "That's true. I guess you'd better tell me."

He does, and then repeats again his concern that someone would bash in one of his window frames and leave a mess of plaster and wood.

"I know," I say righteously, "And that I should have to clean it all up . . . ."

He just stares at me. Then, finally, he looks away, and I can see his shoulders relax. He's giving up. The enemy is retreating. "Is there any more of that ham?" he says finally.

"Coming right up," I say perkily, and I jump up and slide two perfectly browned slices from the pan to his plate. "More eggs?" I ask him. "More coffee?"

"No." His early morning manners could do with a little polish.

He eats silently, watching me watching him, cleans his plate, gets up from the table, and stretches. And then he says, "Lucilla, we're going to take the kids to Maine."

"Who's this we?" I go to the sink and dump some dish detergent in, then start frothing suds. I hope I don't ruin my nails. It took me twenty minutes to do them.

"Us. You and I."

He's really caught me by surprise this time. I turn and gape at him. "I'm not going to Maine with you! I have three days off coming up. And big plans, buddy. Very big plans. Take Emily."

"I can't take Emily, and you know that."

"Why not? Worried about her reputation?"

"She would be. She worries a lot about what people think."

"I love this. What about my reputation? Who will want me if I come back from Maine a tarnished thing?" I'm stirring soapsuds furiously. A few fly out and hit his shirtfront. He wipes them away.

"You'll have your own room, with a lock and a bolt. Believe me-"

"Oh, I believe you. Why can't Emily have her own bolt? I have days off coming to me. I have a window frame to fix."

"I need you, though. I need you there to help me keep track of the girls."

"This isn't in my contract, Buster." Who does Chuckie think he is to whisk me off to Maine without a say in the matter? "It's gonna cost you."

He sighs. "I'll pay you for those days."

"Darn tootin'."

He smiles a little. "I'll pay you double."

"Triple."

"Lucilla, you're not being reasonable." He stops. "You're never reasonable. You haven't been reasonable since this whole charade started."

I just look at him. My face is soft with Mineral Dew Conditioning Creme. My lips are red with my favorite Poison Potion lipstick. I have Midnight Madness on my eyelashes, Forest Fawn on my eyelids, and Petal Pink on my nails. My hair is Bombshell Blonde, although, like the rest of it, that will wash off in the shower.

If Emily Cheseworthy of the Cheseworthy-Tafts can look so alluring every single time she steps foot on our property, I guess I can manage it just this once.

I keep staring at Mr. Smithson, waiting for him to blink first. He doesn't.

I glare at that spot right between his eyes, and I know I'm gonna win this. Don't I always? Finally, he looks away. "All right," he says. "Triple."

"And all expenses paid."

"That goes without saying."

"And I need an answer," I say. "That's the last thing." I stare right at him, wondering how he can resist the beautiful new me. "Answer this, Yore Excellency. *Why* are we going there?"

"My girls have never seen the ocean," he says. "And I think every kid should jump in the waves now and then. And you told me yourself I should spend more time with them." He glances at me and swallows, pauses for a moment, and then decides to just tell me the real reason; it's easier. "To get away," he says.

"Yeah," I say, "I'm sick of her, too."

"I meant from . . . everything," he says. "The stress."

"Oh, yeah?" I sneer. "Well, I meant from Emily."

I wait for him to come dashing to the defense of his blushing bride. He doesn't.

"When do we leave?" I ask him. "I love Maine, sunsets on the ocean, sand between your toes."

He laughs, a nice sound. "I think you would have gone without the money . . . ."

I smile endearingly. Lucky - one. Smithson - zero.

He shakes his head. "I'll take care of these dishes, Lucilla," he says. "Why don't you go wash that stuff off your face. We'll leave as soon as you and the girls are packed."

"Today? Right now?"

He shrugs. "Why not?"

I dry my hands on a dish towel and toss it down on the countertop, and I dance on out of there. He's crazy if he thinks I'm going to destroy my nifty new look this early in the morning.

I yell to Violet and Pansy, grab up some bags, and throw in enough junk to sustain us for a few days. Fifteen minutes later, I'm waiting by the back door, looking ravishing and ready to go.

To get away, yeah. It's as if he read my mind.

# 18

I'VE BEEN TO MAINE two or three times before, as a kid. Back when we had cash, we would stay in hotels along the coast. Sometimes we had a view of the ocean, where we could watch the waves crash from our windowed balconies. I loved the frothy whitecaps that crept up the smooth sand and then gave up, sliding quietly back to sea under newer, more aggressive waves. I loved the expanse of white beach and the breezes that were never still.

But it's all different now. Standing here with Sir Charles Smithson the Second, all I see is a lot of water, and all I hear is a lot of noise. Maybe I've simply been away from it for too long, but, believe it or not, I feel irritated that I can't hear him over the thunderous ocean, and I'm longing for some peace and quiet, or even just the calm of his voice.

"It's dirty," I yell over the constant noise, pointing to the next big wave gusting ahead of us. If you really look, you can see tons of old debris in there, visible just as the wave reaches its highest crest and before the white foam folds over it.

"What?" he yells. I'm reminded of one of our initial conversations, screaming back and forth over the telephone lines.

"All that junk," I scream back. "Old leaves and dead fish and stuff. Filthy."

He nods. An old plastic bag has just rolled up next to us, and is jounced around a little by the next two waves. Then a big one comes in, and the bag is wrenched back out to sea.

There's a duck bobbing on the water a short way out, and I wonder if he's as sick of this constant noise and motion as I am.

Violet and Pansy are skipping around on the sand, making footprints and gathering up junk to build a sand castle. Violet has someone's old Styrofoam cup in her hand, and Pansy has discovered the torn plastic cover of a forgotten take-out salad. Whatever happened to seaweed and stones? These are twenty-first century kids, I remind myself, with modern preferences.

Prince Charles wanders off down the beach, and I watch him go, admiring his tan. It's good for him to be here. He seems more relaxed and more talkative than usual. He's fattening up nice, too. I may have to change to healthier recipes if he keeps it up; he may not compliment my cooking in words, but he does in actions. He looks good - broader than a few months ago, stronger. It's a pity. He needs a wife, and the girls need a mother. I could be interested if I didn't dislike him so.

He picks up a stone and hurls it way out into the waves. It disappears. He watches for a minute and then keeps walking, slowly, thoughtfully, and I turn back to the girls.

We build an enormous sand castle, Pansy, Violet, and I, and we use all the trash they've collected on the beach, as well as odd-shaped stones, shells, and bits of seaweed. Turrets and walks protrude from our castle, and we design a moat and run to the water's edge over and over to gather water to fill it. I look up and down the beach and wonder if these other people would be surprised to learn that we really do live in a castle, a *real* castle.

Smithson returns and joins us in the sand, helping to mold the highest tower, and positioning a little leaf flag so that it won't fall out. We run in the waves a little, and the girls collapse in the water and then screech from the cold.

Later, we're sitting on the sand well back from the water, where the crush of noise isn't quite so deafening. Pansy and Violet are at the water's edge, running backwards with great glee to avoid the meanest waves. "How much of the story about Old King Charles and Bonnie Prince Charlie was true?" I ask him.

"All of it, I guess," he says, "except nobody was royalty."

"You were fourteen when your father died?"

He nods. "It was a motorcycle accident. He was speeding." Some royal death, I'm thinking. Smithson continues. "We'd been in the castle four years. My mother and I stayed on. She died young, too, of pneumonia, just before I married. The infection was so bad she didn't respond to treatment." He smiles ruefully. "She probably caught it living in the castle."

"So she never knew her granddaughters at all."

He picks up a weathered stick of driftwood and examines the smoothly knotted surface. "No. It's too bad, too. She would have loved to spoil them. She sent me to college and figured I was all set to make a success of myself." His smile is tainted with self-deprecation. Charles F. Smithson the Two clearly does not feel like a big success.

"What did you study?" I ask idly.

"Business. It was boring."

"So, you work in business now?"

He's never told me. It seems like a logical next question, but all he does is bark a short laugh, "Hah!"

A gull has swooped down the beach and settles near us, investigating a cast-off sandwich wrapper left by the tide.

"Four thousand horses is a lot for a funeral procession in these parts," I say thoughtfully.

"A slight exaggeration," he says. "I made up that story a few months ago when Pansy was acting scared about the future. She was really clingy, kept worrying that I'd leave again."

"She doesn't seem worried now," I say. We both look toward the horizon. No worries there. Just a lot of chattering and giggling while they fill plastic buckets with sand and turn them out upside down on the water's edge, watching the green waves eat the edges.

There's a peculiar look on his face, satisfied, but maybe a little anxious, too. I recognize the look. It's one I saw on my own father's face when he watched me hook up with that animal Nick Wilta, a look that implies acceptance of the inevitable, but suspicion that the future might be less than ideal.

A look that men wear when the happiness of their beloved daughters is at stake.

"How's the new house coming?" I ask now.

He shrugs. "It's delayed again, I guess. Emily's having fun fighting with the contractors."

"You're convinced it's the right thing, aren't you."

He looks at me. "Yes, I know it is. Our parents were friends. My mother always liked Emily. I think she would have liked to see me marry her."

I harrumph something unintelligible.

He shrugs. "Maybe she was right, I don't know."

"I doubt that."

He stares at me. "Look, I know you think Emily's not ideal, and maybe she's not, but it will be a lot better than what they have right now."

It stings when he says that, and, I can't help it, I let my face show my feelings.

He's immediately contrite. "That's not what I meant, Lucilla. You're wonderful with them, but they need more than just a hired worker. They need someone who'll be there for the rest of

175

their lives . . . ."

I've regrouped, and I'm already sorry I let him see that quick pain that flashed over my face. "No prob, Yore Grace," I say lightly. "Don't worry about it. I'll just enter it into my memoirs under the chapter, *Stupid Things Said to Me by Ignorant People.*"

"Well, I'm certainly one of those," he says. He gets up and goes to the water's edge to admire the messy sand sculptures taking shape there.

◇◇◇

Later we drive up the coast and look at the white boats against blue sky, the red roofs and golden sun. Weathered ropes knotted around thick wooden posts keep boats anchored, and hundreds of lobster traps sit piled on a wharf, a beehive of criss-crossed wooden slats. The colors are brilliant and clear, a palette of primary hues. Some of it is so picturesque that tears sting my eyes.

"Daddy, Lucky is crying," says Violet in the back seat.

"No I'm not, silly," I reassure her. But she urges her father to hand me his handkerchief anyway, which he does. I'm a little embarrassed, so I make a big show out of blowing my nose. I get a good loud honk going, and it makes the girls laugh. I hand the handkerchief back to Mr. Smithson. He shakes his head, bewildered, and takes the hankie, where most of my alluring new make-up now reposes. He grimaces and tosses it to the floor of the back seat.

We have to eat out every night, which I love. And he takes us to good places, places I never would have known enough to choose. We eat lobster and clam chowder, and steak and fish, and every night we go back to our fancy motel and I lock myself in and bolt the door, and take long, leisurely showers to wash the salt from me. Pansy comes in later, and she sleeps in the big double bed next to mine. But I find her snuggled in with me every morning.

We walk barefoot on the beach in the evenings, when the waves seem more tame and the tide is out. Pansy and Violet run ahead a little and get excited over and over again about pretty shells and stones, and hunks of seaweed that have floated up. "Daddy!" squeals Pansy, "Look at this shell. It's beautiful and has a hole in it."

He admires it, and she runs off.

Violet has found a dead fish, and as we approach, her father tells her not to touch it.

"Why? I like it," she says. "I want to pet it."

"It could make you sick," he explains. "There could be bacteria, germs-"

She interrupts him lovingly. "Daddy, you're an imbecile." She smiles at him, then skips off down the beach.

We stroll in silence until finally I say, "Wow, good vocabulary. I wonder where she picked that up."

Her father smiles crookedly. Not at me, just at the world in general. "I wonder," he says. The sun is sinking behind us, throwing long shadows on the beach. He stops suddenly and scoops up a handful of sand, letting it sift through his fingers. "I'd love to never go back," he says.

"It beats Esther Mountain."

"That's true." He's strolling slowly again, hands in the pockets of his shorts, and smiles at me briefly. His eyes look clear and unworried. I like that look. I'd like to see more of it. "We should do more things like that hike," he says thoughtfully. I stifle a groan, but he catches it and grins at me. "We should," he insists. "The girls need it, don't you think? Every outing couldn't be as disastrous as that one."

"I guess that's up to you and Emily," I say lightly. I try to picture Emily hauling herself up Esther Mountain. "You should do Esther again with Emily," I say. "She'd probably enjoy it a lot."

He's not even listening. "More picnics, more adventures. We should go to the Wild Center."

"I dunno," I say. "I'm not sure they need lessons in wild . . . ."

"They'd like that I think. We should take them into the woods in December and cut our own Christmas tree."

"No," I say adamantly. "No Christmas trees."

He looks at me in surprise. "You don't like Christmas trees?"

"No, I don't like cutting them."

"But that's fun, Lucilla. It's wholesome. It's American. Kids love to help cut down the family Christmas tree."

"No, they don't," I insist. "I helped my parents one year. Just take my word for it, it's not fun."

"Where did you do that?" he asks. "Where did you grow up?"

Lying to him has become more and more distasteful to me as the weeks go by, and I feel as if I'm squirming under layers of soggy wool instead of walking on this beautiful summer beach.

"Forget it," I say. "I don't feel like reliving the past."

He looks at me, wondering, but he doesn't insist. "Well, it could be fun," he says. "We have a lot of beautiful trees behind the castle. And there are other things, too. There are museums to visit and parks and lots of lakes not too far from home."

"What do you do there?" I ask him suddenly.

He peers at me, hedging. "What do you mean?"

"You know. What do you do at home? Work at the Dollar Store? Fly an airplane? Design libraries? What?"

"I have a portfolio that I look after," he says. What does that mean? That he does nothing all day? "Well," he says, "I don't actually look after it. I hire someone to do that. I'm looking for a new person right now, as a matter of fact." I must look confused. "Money, Lucilla. I make money by investing money."

"And Keith is the person you're hiring?"

"Keith?" He smiles. "No, Keith is just a friend. He was doing me a favor those days he came over." Yes, the day Smithson nearly slammed my face in the music room window. The day I treated Our Friend Keith like an intruder from the wrong side of the tracks. I can feel myself blushing and decide maybe I don't want to hash over my relationship with Keith Gregoire after all.

I look up to find Smithson smiling down at me. He's remembering, too. Ho ho. Funny Lucky Wilta.

"But what do you *do*?" I say doggedly. "When you leave the castle and don't come home for hours, where do you go? How do you get your shoes muddy?"

He laughs lightly. "I don't go anywhere. I don't do much of anything."

"Come on, Yore Grace," I say, "You do. You must."

"Not a darn thing," he says. "I'm useless, like a boy, with no purpose." He smiles a little. "Except to bring up my children. At least I've figured that out."

Mr. Mysterious. Okay, I try another question, as long as I have his full attention. "Mr. Smithson," I start, and he smiles at me suddenly.

"Charles."

This surprises me. His given name has slipped out now and then, but I've always assumed that hearing it from my lips was torment to him. Why else would I use it?

"You want me to call you that?" I ask him.

"Why not? Everyone does, except the girls."

"You're my employer."

He laughs, a rich, mirthful thing. "Lucilla, you call me every corruption of my name that exists. You've even made up a few. And Lord only knows how you refer to me under your breath, when I'm not paying attention. You and Lionel."

Me and Lionel? Hardly an item, I'm thinking. I'm not sure I want C. F. Smithson linking our names that way.

"Still, that's different," I say finally. "I can call you the Most Reverend and Honorable, the Most Highly Exalted, the Most Estimable-"

"Lucilla."

". . . and all that because it's a joke. But not just . . . ."

He doesn't make me finish. "I checked once to see if there was a title," he says. "I couldn't find any proof of it. My father thought his grandfather might have been knighted in England, but I don't think it's true."

"It seems like there'd be documents or some kind of proof," I offer helpfully.

He nods. "It's all just part of the hazy past. A fun joke, just like you said."

"Lionel wouldn't think it was a joke if he had a title."

"No, Lionel wouldn't."

It's interesting that he's not impressed by his own possible title. Myself, I'm more like Lionel, and I don't burst with pride to say this. If I thought I might have a title, I'd want people to know it, even use it. I guess I'd brag. Well, must be that Charles F. Smithson the Second is more humble than I am. If I liked him better, I might admire that.

I can see the girls just ahead, bending down to admire pebbles and shells. Now and then they find one appealing enough to keep; their fists are bulging.

"What was your wife like, Mr. Smithson?" Now that he's asked me to call him Charles, I can't get the name out. Go figure.

He thinks a minute. "My wife was . . . very pretty. Beautiful, in fact. Everyone considered us a perfect match." Yes, of course they did. "Her name was Rose."

Rose? Pansy? Violet? Do I see a pattern emerging here?

"How did you survive the boat accident in Italy?" I ask. I couldn't tell you why I'm asking this, Sister. I'm nosy. I deserve to have my mouth taped or be excommunicated. Why don't I just subscribe to *The National Enquirer* for all the latest gossip and leave this poor man alone? "Were you steering it, maybe? Were you the skipper?" Wouldn't that be awful? If he were to blame?

He's looking at me, deciding how to answer. Or maybe whether to answer. "I wasn't even on it," he says finally. He gazes across the gray ocean, watches a few weak waves hit the near shore. I only have to look at his face and it's easy to resolve not to ask any more hurtful questions. And then he turns to me.

"I guess I'd like to tell you about this." He says he'd like to, but his eyes say he'd rather do anything but. I'm not sure what to say, so I just walk alongside him, listening, matching my slow pace to his.

"She said she was going to the street market to shop," he says finally, "not to expect her for a few hours. I stayed at the villa, reading. I ordered theater tickets." His voice catches, but he goes on. "We never used them of course. It was a beautiful morning like the one we had today. She'd been gone almost three hours when they came to tell me." He looks at me, and a weak, sad smile flits over his mouth. "There was a man, too. We'd met him in Rome two years before and run into him twice in Boston. Quite a coincidence. He died, too. When the boat capsized, Rose was pulled under and drowned. Her friend was hit by a mast."

Pansy and Violet have run some distance up the beach, two little specks staying well back from the water's edge. "Charles," I say, "Let's catch up to the girls." All this talk about drowning is making me nervous. All this talk about a wife and her friend and her lies.

"They're so good, aren't they," he says. "You couldn't trust many kids their age to play on the beach without an adult hovering closer."

"I think we should hover," I tell him, and I start forward.

He puts a hand on my arm and looks into my face. "He was a doctor, Lucilla. That's a useful profession. My wife must have liked that; she was probably impressed."

"There are more important things than being useful."

"I wondered for a while if the girls were even mine," he says. Then he smiles slowly. "They are, though. You can tell, can't you, just by looking?"

I nod, not trusting myself to say anything.

"Come on," he says. "We should be with them." He starts up the beach, taking long strides. I follow, trying to keep up. "Did you love her?" I ask suddenly. I don't mean to; it just jumps out of my throat.

He stops to look at me, shocked. I stop, too. "Of course I did," he says. "I didn't even realize there was someone else until

180

that very day. It wasn't entirely her fault, you know. I could have taken better care of my marriage. I avoided coming home sometimes, with two cranky babies in the house." He stops and then repeats his answer. "Yes, I loved my wife. I wouldn't marry someone I didn't love." There's a pause, and then he says. "Back then, I wouldn't have. I have different needs now."

His different needs, as he so poignantly called them, are scampering up the beach toward us. Their hands are full of stones and bits of polished shell, and they're both jabbering at once. Yes, they look like him, and it relieves me to see that. How has he managed to keep them so basically happy and normal?

I can't help wondering, Sister, if life with Emily Cheseworthy Smithson will really make their lives any better.

◇◇◇

We eat dinner in one of those weathered lobster shacks along the water's edge, and the girls turn up their noses at most of the food. Charles has the bright idea of stopping for hamburgers later, and it seems to appease the natives. They're tucked into bed and sleeping peacefully when I'm surprised by a rap at the connecting door and open it to find Smithson standing there holding a bottle of chardonnay.

"Lose something?" I say tersely. Our unspoken agreement has been that once doors are closed and locked for the night, no one and nothing is important enough to pierce that barricade.

He shrugs, looking somewhat flustered. "I thought . . . . It's such a nice night, and with a balcony right outside the rooms . . . ." He stops, straightens himself up, and starts again. "I thought we could talk. About Pansy, specifically. She's not as afraid of things as she used to be. I wondered if there's some technique you're using . . . ."

Very weak. What is his real motive?

Who cares? A bottle of vino with Sir Charles Himself, under the Maine moonlight? Tsk, tsk. We'll have to hope this little escapade doesn't make it back to Duck Vly and the virtuous ears of Emily Cheseworthy of the Cheseworthy-Tafts.

Stop it, I tell myself. The poor man just wants to talk.

"Hang on," I say. "I'll get my plastic cup from the bathroom."

The balcony is the length of both rooms, with a concrete wall separating my half from his. Each side has a wicker sofa and one chair, a small table, and a pot of summer flowers. We have a

181

couple of choices here: I can go through his room and abandon Pansy, to sit on his balcony. Or he can abandon Violet and sit on mine. Or we can sit on opposite sides of the thick concrete wall and fling the bottle back and forth, hoping our night vision is amazing and accurate. Our fourth choice is to forget the girls altogether and take a romantic stroll along the beach, which would cause the dry heaves to well up in both of us, I'm sure.

We select choice A, and I leave my screened balcony door ajar, open the door between our rooms, and join him on his side. I'll be able to hear Pansy's slightest murmur.

"Give me your cup," he says as I come through to his balcony and plop myself down on the wicker sofa. I leave his glass door open and close the screen. Charles has turned the lights off so Violet won't be awakened. The sea is dark, with flickering lights all along the shore, and we can hear the surf crashing below. "Listen to that," he says. "What a great view, too. It's too bad we're leaving tomorrow."

"I'm not here for the view," I say. "I'm here strictly for the wine."

He laughs politely and pours me a cupful. It's smooth and mellow and I gulp it greedily. He raises one eyebrow, but pours again when I stick my glass in his face.

"I think it was good for the girls to come here," he says, sitting next to me.

"Sure, they seem to have survived rather nicely."

"No, I really think it was good for them. Fresh sea air, lots of sun. They loved digging in the sand," he says.

"Yeppers. Their sand castle was the pride of the beach."

He pours us each another glass and places the bottle on the concrete floor. The surf pounds below us, a lulling, rhythmic sound. "They seem more confident lately," he says. "Especially Pansy. I'm very happy about that, Lucilla. Have you noticed it, too?"

"Shore thing." I finish my third glass, and it suddenly occurs to me that I've had a lot of wine. Charles doesn't seem bothered, though; he just keeps talking about the girls, how they didn't like lobster, but did like the taffy we bought this afternoon. How they used to cry a lot, but now their delightful personalities are beginning to emerge.

"Is it something you learned from that book?" he's asking. "Maybe it's something you could teach me so that when I'm with them . . . ." He seems to be ignoring the fact that I am basically slack-limbed and open-mouthed from drinking too much chardonnay. There's not a thing in the world I could teach him right now, but I screw up my face in serious thought, hoping a logical statement will emerge from my mouth. None does, so I remain mute.

"We should have bought one of those woodchoppers," he's saying. I have no idea what he's talking about, but I am enjoying the lilting cadence of his voice. The sound is nice, a rumbling masculine baritone. "They would have liked having one out in the yard."

Suddenly, my eyesight catches the moon above again and I interrupt him. "Anorthosite," I say. "It's up there."

"What?"

"It's a rock. It's here, too, I mean in the Adirondacks."

"Oh." He sounds interested, maybe even impressed. On second thought, I think maybe that was plain old confusion I heard. I try a new subject.

"It's like *Star Wars*," I say reverently.

"What?" he says again. He turns his face to me.

"Two moons, like in *Star Wars*."

He glances at the moon and laughs. "*Star Wars* had two suns," he says.

"Well, we have two moons."

He laughs again. It's a really nice sound and I tell him so. "You should laugh more often," I say.

"I laugh plenty," he says.

"No, you don't."

"Sure I do. You just aren't always there to hear it."

I ponder this. If Smithson laughs in the woods and there's no one around to hear it, is he still a spoiled rich guy? The answer is probably yes, so I nod my head sagely.

He's looking at me again, and I have to admit, this is one good-looking bit of royalty. "Why aren't you down at the bar?" I ask him. "There must be plenty of women down there who'd like to meet someone like you."

"Are you forgetting Emily?" he asks stiffly.

Actually, the thought of her hasn't crossed my mind in a few hours. "Of course not," I lie, "but I bet you could do better."

He's quiet, so I pursue this brilliant line of conversation. "You aren't that bad looking," I say. "And you have a few nice qualities. You have all your own teeth, and you're good at puttering around with things. You fixed the toaster that time and the cabinet door in the panty. You also are a very good eater." This is clearly the wine talking. I don't even know if he has all his own teeth; I'm just assuming.

"Gosh, thanks, Miss Wilta," he says sarcastically.

"And you . . . ." I can't remember what I was going to say next, and suddenly I'm so tired that I can't hold my head up either. It drifts down onto his shoulder, and he starts with the unexpected pressure of it, then he looks at me for a long moment and shifts into the cushion of the sofa, making a cradle for my head. "Sorry," I murmur.

"That's okay." His voice is as soft as the moonlight above us, pale and creamy, and his shoulder is a nice pillow.

"How far away do you think it is?" I ask him.

"The moon? I don't know how far. Three days by spaceship."

"That's a long distance. We've been here three days. I'm glad we're here, not there."

"Yeah." He moves slightly again, and I can feel his arm around my back, his fingers on my other shoulder. I'm resting comfortably against him, trapping him, and I can actually feel his breathing, the rhythmic rise and fall of his chest, we're sitting that close. "Lucilla?"

"Mmm?"

"Maybe it's time to go in." His voice is hardly audible, husky and near to my ear. I lift up my head and gaze at his eyes. He does have such beautiful eyes. It occurs to me that Emily Cheseworthy is one very lucky socialite, and I wonder if Charles realizes that all the gain is on her side.

It's the same old story. Lucky Wilta sitting around thinking about all that she doesn't have, will never have. Under the moonlight, sipping wine with another woman's man. This is probably the best I'll ever get, and a deep, melancholy sigh somehow escapes me.

"Why the sigh?" he asks quietly. His voice is a soft breath, a whisper in the night.

Well, I can't very well tell him, but some impulse in me doesn't want to let him go just yet. My hand finds his face and I touch his cheek just so slightly. It feels a little bristly since he hasn't shaved since this morning, a rough surface that's smooth and warm underneath. He's gazing at me intently and I feel a big, deep breath ready to burst inside me as his face moves toward mine.

"Lucilla . . . ."

When the ceiling fixture suddenly sears hot yellow light over us, Charles springs sideways and I jump up, knocking over the wine bottle. A river of chardonnay gurgles over the balcony floor and he leaps for the bottle, righting it.

Whoa, whoa, whoa. What was I thinking? I almost felt myself opening up to some of the old longings - always a big mistake. I quickly straighten the seat cushions.

Violet stands there, rubbing sleepy eyes. "I'm thirsty," she says.

"I'll get you some water," her father answers. He trips all over himself escaping from the balcony, from me actually, and races into his room.

"I want soda," she says.

"Water," he says. He disappears into the bathroom, and while he's there, I flit through his room, passing Violet's rumpled bed, his own neatly made up one, his suitcase, Violet's clothes on a chair, the assorted gimcrackery of hotel life. I flee into my own room, thudding the door closed behind me. I lean against it, breathing hard.

Any trace of the mellow mood induced by the chardonnay is gone.

What nearly happened out there? Was he about to *kiss* me? That can't be; that can never be, and I try to breathe evenly, giving my heart a chance to plunge from my throat back down to my stomach, where it belongs, feeling something inside me that must be panic. A disaster narrowly averted; a catastrophe barely missed. I don't even like Charles Fitzham Smithson the Magnificent.

A sudden rap on the door startles me and my head cracks back against the door. A painful spasm circles my brain. I clear my throat, smooth my shirt, and open the door a crack.

"Lucilla," his voice is hoarse. "I'm so sorry-"

"Yep, no problem. Nothing to be sorry for."

"It wouldn't have-"

"Good night, Yore Excellency."

"Here's your glass. You might need it to brush your teeth, I guess." His hand inches through the crack in the door. I grab the glass from him.

"Thanks."

"Tomorrow, we'll just-"

"Seven o'clock, I'll be ready."

"Yes, okay. Good night."

"Right." I shut the door; my heart is hammering in my chest again. I lock the door and check it twice. Pansy is still asleep and I stand gazing down at her for a minute while I collect my thoughts and catch my breath.

Then I change my clothes and creep into bed and lie awake for an hour or two.

Sometimes things happen in the dark, I tell myself. You have to be careful or you're likely to wake up to stabbing sunlight and see that what you thought was real wasn't real at all. Charles Smithson is in my life for one reason and one reason only. He has my castle. My treasure.

I intend to get them back. Period.

And I shall never drink wine again.

And if I do, it won't be with C. F. Smithson sitting near enough to touch under a hot, milky, Maine moon.

Morning arrives and I almost wonder if I imagined the scene on the balcony. The girls chatter and sing all the way back to Duck Vly. Charles is no more and no less preoccupied than usual; he actually smiles at me once or twice as we ride along, which leads me to believe that at least he isn't blaming me for my alcohol-induced indiscretion.

We arrive at the castle and we examine the list of buyers the lawyers have produced. It's a short list - one name. I go back to my hunt for the figmentary secret room and the elusive diamonds, back to scrubbing floors and cooking meals and fussing with drawers that stick with the dampness. Back to dripping walls, broken plaster, and quick, energetic visits from Lionel Hawthorne.

Back to Emily.

Maine was a memorable interlude.

# 19

DAMN IT, LUCKY," Lionel is saying, "you know it only happened because I had a few drinks." We're in the attic, and the big ring of keys is hanging on a nail jutting from the wall. Lionel is sitting on a trunk drinking something cold out of a tall plastic tumbler. I can hear ice thudding against the sides of the glass. "You didn't have to go running off to Maine," he says.

"Oh, please," I say haughtily, "don't flatter yourself. My decisions have nothing to do with you." I'm in a foul mood, agitated and snappish. Men are stupid, all of them.

Lionel's humiliating proposal of marriage still rankles when I think of it, and I've decided to enjoy being mad at him. "And anyway, Lionel, drinking is no excuse."

"Well," he says easily, "I can't help what I do when I've had a few."

"Which is usually. And you should help it."

He leans back against the cobwebby wall, while I pick up splinters from a shattered closet door and toss them into a garbage bag. I've already thrown in the blue glass chips from the Christmas ornament I broke weeks ago, and I stand back to gaze at the fake tree and its tacky decorations. "This is an incredibly ugly Christmas tree, Lionel," I say.

He watches me sweep up chips of old wood. "It's the thought that counts."

"No, look at it. Did Charles buy it? It's so seedy looking. Did he choose these candy canes and horrid, awful cookies?"

"No, he'd have better taste. It was probably the delightful Mrs. Frocks."

"Was she delightful, Lionel?"

He laughs. "She was big and fat and critical."

"You're coarse."

"Just honest." He shrugs. "I'm short. You're no beauty. Mrs. Frocks was fat."

His words sting. Of course I'm no beauty, I've always known that. But what gives Lionel Hawthorne the right to be so blunt

187

about it? I turn back to the tree. Heaven forbid that Lionel should be offended by having to look at my hideous face, for pity's sake.

"I'm surprised he'd want to let someone else do that for his kids," I say finally. "Don't parents usually get all involved in Christmas? You know, anticipating the look of joy that lights up our sweet baby's face and all that?"

"Well," Lionel says thoughtfully. "I guess maybe it'll be like that this year. Last year, he wasn't exactly here."

I turn toward him, astonished. "Not here for Christmas? Where was he?"

Lionel leans forward, interested in the turn the conversation has taken. "Didn't he ever tell you about his wife? When she died, he went a little nuts, came home from Italy so grouchy the kids' baby-sitter quit. He was impossible. All the help he hired kept quitting. I stayed away myself for a good year and a half."

"Very supportive of you," I say.

He ignores me. "I couldn't stand seeing him struggle with those two impossible brats."

"Well, they're not really-"

"Finally, he'd had it." Lionel is forging head full throttle, enjoying his tale. "He hired Mrs. Frocks and went back to Europe for about eight months. So he wasn't here for Christmas, or Easter, for that matter. He wasn't around much until just before you came. Something happened then that changed his mind. He's really just getting to know his daughters now."

Something changed his mind, and I know exactly what it was: the interference of Rose's family, sick of their darling's daughters being shoved off on a housekeeper while Charles Smithson cavorted around Europe. Their threats must have frightened him, frightened him so much that he can't wait to get a wedding ring on Emily Cheseworthy's anxious little hand.

"That's why the castle's in such bad shape, too," Lionel is saying. "You can't neglect a building like this without having it take its toll."

"Well, a lot of what's wrong with the castle didn't just happen in the last three years," I scoff.

Lionel grins at me. "My, we're touchy. You don't have to sound so belligerent. I'm not saying he should have done anything differently. Anyway, Mrs. Frocks must have rigged up the tree."

I nod, agreeing, and tell myself not to jump to The Tragic Mr.

Smithson's defense anymore. It's not up to me to explain his undignified desertion of his children. Or to excuse the mess that his castle is in.

I mean my castle.

Lionel has drained his glass and set it on the floor. He leans back comfortably and looks at me. "How much has he told you about his wife?" he asks me.

"Not much," I say honestly.

"There was a scandal," he continues, and I can see his eyes glinting. He looks just as he does when we believe, for the umpteenth time, that we've hit treasure. "She was less than an ideal spouse." He waits to see if I might jump in and elaborate, if the two of us might get some chuckles over Charles' bad luck.

I don't answer. I've never liked Smithson much, but I'm sure not going to pry up all his old wounds and gloat over them with the likes of Lionel Hawthorne, his sad excuse for a best friend.

"They said at the time there was a question about the accident that killed her."

"A question?" I can't help asking, and I hate myself for encouraging him.

"Another man."

I turn away. "That's not our business, Lionel."

He's quiet for a minute, then I hear him come up beside me until his face is even with mine. He puts his arm casually across my shoulder and stares at me for a moment. "You've turned into a very loyal employee, Lucky." He says this seriously, no suggestion of the sarcastic tone he usually uses. "You know, I wondered at first what Charles could possibly have been thinking when he hired you. You didn't seem the right type at all. You didn't like the girls, you're not much of a housekeeper, and you were downright rude to him. I couldn't believe he had chosen you."

"Well, believe it," I say. His hands are creeping along my shoulders, and his face is drawing close to mine. Something turns over inside me, and I know he's going to kiss me. Not like his cheer-me-up kiss the day after the hike, but a real kiss, a meaningful, soul-searching kiss.

"But he did choose you," he says softly. "He saw something in you that I missed. But now I'm starting to realize."

His arms are around me, and he's aiming in, sincere and loving as all get-out. Is this what I want from Lionel Hawthorne? The little troll with the elfin face and a couple dozen women on the side? My pal with the blunt words and the full bubbling bottle attached permanently to his wrist? I think it through and decide that, sure, in spite of everything, I *like* Lionel. I like his amusing nature and his happy-go-lucky attitude. Of course he hurts me, but who doesn't? And how choosy can I actually be? I liked his kiss the day after the horrible hike, so, yes, I guess I wouldn't mind if Lionel wanted to kiss me again today.

I move in nearer to him, and I smile a little as I see him begin to close his eyes. And then I do a terrible thing, Sister.

I laugh.

Not a soft, embarrassed giggle. Not a shy schoolgirl trill that implies I'm just nervous about this big step. No. A big, hearty laugh, remembering the day he stole half of Pansy's doughnut, I *saw* him, and then he tried to convince both her and me that he knew nothing about it. Remembering the time he and Charles were moving a heavy sofa from one room to another, because I asked them to, and Kitty Nellahopkiss breezed in. Lionel dropped the sofa, crunching his own foot, but managed to limp all the way down the hall and out the front door, eagerly following Kitty into her beat up car.

A big, amused laugh. Not a With-you laugh, but an At-you laugh. And I can't stop.

Lionel Hawthorne is such a transparent little gremlin.

His arms drop, and he backs away, surprised. "Lucky?"

"I'm sorry," I say, still chuckling. "It's just that you're so short, and I'm no beauty . . . ."

He doesn't understand, and he isn't sure whether he should grin and bear it or get mad and stomp off. In the end, he picks up my broom and heads down the attic stairs ahead of me. Not mad, just wondering.

I let him go because I don't know what else to say to him. After a few minutes, I gather up the bag of wood and glass chips and old dust I've swept up, snag the ring of keys, and follow my pal Lionel down the attic stairs.

I go into Mr. Smithson's room and open up his top dresser drawer, taking out the familiar leather case and dropping the keys in, then closing everything up again.

His room is one of the better ones in the castle, not as dark and ugly as some, spacious without being overwhelming. I stand at the window for a minute and watch Lionel whistling down the driveway and hopping into his BMW. He seems to have survived my impolite rejection rather well, and I'm glad. I do like Lionel, just the way I like those little yellow butterflies that flit over the lawns on sunny days. Nice in passing, good to have around, but up close, they look pretty wormy. And I know I wouldn't want to kiss one.

I turn back to Mr. Smithson's room, seeing the familiar furnishings that I dust now and then, only when I feel like it. Lionel's right; I'm not a great housekeeper. But Pansy and Violet are growing on me, and I've been pretty good lately about not insulting their father.

The things on his dresser are different from those in other rooms in the castle. A plastic comb, a small cut-glass bottle full of some kind of cologne, a pile of loose change, a golf score card, some tees. I pick up the score card and read it: 78. I wonder if that's a good score and decide it must be; he got a hole in one once. And he plays often enough.

My hand strays to the bottle of cologne. It's unmarked. Someone, probably Emily, took the time to pour the amber liquid into this antique bottle. I open it and hold it under my nose. It has a nice scent, but I can't say it's familiar. I might have noticed if he ever wore it.

The coverlet on his bed is wrinkled where I dropped the garbage bag so I could put the keys away. I should try to stop doing things like putting trash bags on the beds. I put out my hand to smooth the bedspread, pull it up gently, and tuck it under his pillows, letting my hand linger there for just the briefest moment.

What must it have been like for him when his wife died? Is it any wonder he left his daughters and escaped to a place where he wouldn't have to answer nosy questions from thoughtless acquaintances?

Even his best friend can't resist gossiping about him.

I hear a car in the driveway and shake off the thoughts that are filling my head. From the window, I can see that it's Mr. Smithson in faded jeans and a white golf shirt, returning home early from the mysterious place he never talks about. He slams the car door behind him, and I turn back to pick up my sack of attic refuse. This coverlet that I have so carefully neatened, I remind myself, is *my* coverlet. This heavy mahogany dresser is my dresser, and these chairs in front of the crumbling fireplace are my chairs.

I don't approve of him or of anything he stands for. This is my castle. I'm a fool if I have to keep reminding myself of that.

# 20

IT ALL HINGES on this visit," he's saying distractedly. "These Garloffs are our only chance right now." He's dressed in a new slate gray suit I've never seen before with a weird, moose-laden tie under his collar. He's jamming his feet into expensive black shoes and searching out a paper in a briefcase.

"I wish they hadn't called right now, of all times," he mutters. He's off to meet with Rose's family. They've stepped up their legal wrangling and demanded he show up to have a little chat with their family attorney. He's bringing Emily, his trump card, and feels hopeful that this might settle things for good.

"Here, this is the number," he says. "Don't call it, though, unless you really need me. I don't want them to think things don't run smoothly here."

"I won't."

"I hope I have everything," he says.

"You do."

"Did you put in those papers from the safe?"

"They're in."

"When the Garloffs get here, make sure they know I had the furnace motor rebuilt. That's important." He looks around. "I wish we'd taken the time to fix things up better."

Pansy comes running in. "Are you leaving now?" she asks. Her little face is screwed up, and a big wet tear is dangling on one eyelash.

He picks her up and hugs her, then hands her to me. "Where's Violet?" he asks, and goes off in search of his other daughter.

"Why does Daddy have to go?" Pansy whines.

To keep you out of the clutches of your dead mother's family, I think of saying. I don't, though. "On a business trip," I tell her. "Don't cry, Pansy. I have all kinds of fun things planned for us." And when he gets back, Rose's family will be a bunch of relatives you merely visit now and then, and you'll be flung securely into the bewildered, improbable arms of Emily Cheseworthy of the

Cheseworthy-Tafts.

Tomorrow morning, the Realtor is bringing the Garloffs to view the castle. My castle. And he's going off, expecting me to make a grand showing. To make it easy for him to swipe away every dream I've nurtured for the past nineteen years.

And then where will I go? Emily and Charles and Pansy and Violet will move to a gorgeous new house on the lake to be a cozy little family. The Garloffs will move all their pretentious possessions into my castle. And Lucky Wilta will be down at Chez Fred's, begging Mack with the Beans in his hat to let her have her mug back.

No. It's not going to be like that.

Smithson is back, grabbing up his briefcase, kissing his daughters, yelling last minute instructions to me as he goes out the door. "I'll see you tomorrow night," he says. "Take care of them." And he's gone.

"Pansy, Violet," I gather the little girls into my arms and wipe away the tears trembling on their lashes. "Wait 'til you hear about the fun we're going to have while Daddy's gone. Remember how I said you must never, never draw on your bedroom walls or hang clothes from the light fixtures upstairs?"

They nod, willing to wipe their tears away at my promise of fun and games in the castle.

"Well, that's all different now." I brush aside a scurry of guilt. I have to. For my own survival, I have to.

◇◇◇

The Garloffs will be here any minute, and I have to keep reminding myself: this is my castle. I can't let them want it. Guilt is foreign to me. I squelch it down.

If only I had followed my instincts these last few months and allowed the dust to ripen just a little longer. I realize now that I was too willing to fix up, scrub, and make things more comfortable. But Kitty and some other Chez Fred's regulars have pitched right in to rehang frayed, musty curtains and plant broken knickknacks in strategic spots. If anyone can create cheesy, they can. And Violet and Pansy have been an enormous help. "Make messes!" I told them. "Leave stuff around! Spill things!" They complied, grinning and chortling, getting into the spirit of the thing almost immediately.

I coerced Bob Cobb into taking a good look at the furnace.

He played stupid at first, wrinkling up his glossy, worried forehead: "What do you mean you *want* it to make that noise? I just rebuilt the motor. It's not supposed to make that noise, no." But, hey, Bob has six kids to feed, and they all eat money. He caught on. It's a glorious sound.

I walk through the castle, listening to the furnace writhe, viewing everything with a critical eye. Dirt ground into the rugs, spills on the furniture and walls, dampness saturating the tacky upstairs wallpaper. I wince at bare bulbs throwing their garish light onto broken plaster and porcelain in one of the bathrooms; the light shades are hidden away in a cupboard.

It's going to take some effort to put this all back the way it was, which I will, of course. I want to discourage the Garloffs, not ruin Smithson's life.

Pansy, on duty in her room, is ready to let loose a carefully-collected jar of bugs in just about twenty minutes. She can't wait to pet them. And Violet is in the gloomy east wing bedrooms, smearing the corners with frogs' eggs. I'm just glad they're edible because she's likely to taste them.

If only it were raining. Pansy's old bedroom shows best in a solid drizzle.

But the sun is gleaming, and so is the white Cadillac pulling up outside the castle door. A distinguished-looking man with a monk's fringe of tangled gray hair emerges and holds the door for a perfectly round, jiggling dame who must be his wife. She's wearing a white wrap-around dress that looks like a Turkish towel. A gaudy copper moon dangling from a chain is half hidden in the cleavage between her mammoth breasts.

She turns and watches as the Realtor's car pulls up right behind theirs. I hope they notice that the castle doors stick and that the furniture on the porch is desperately in need of paint and repair. I hope they trip on the plaster chunks and crumbling rocks we resurrected from the pile in the woods, where WESLEY and JIM threw them when they pretended to clean up. I hope a big, cold drip from the aging walls falls right on Mr. Garloff's bald head.

"Mrs. Garloff?" I say, graciously extending my hand. "I hope your drive here was pleasant. Miss Bellthroop?"

The tall, skinny lady in the cheap dime store dress is Miss Bellthroop, the Realtor, and, as she looks around, I wish she were the prospective buyer. She hates the castle and doesn't bother to hide her disgust as she walks through.

194

The other woman, the rotund one with hair like a slick white cap, is Mrs. Garloff, and my heart sinks as she greets me. "Mrs. Smithson," she burbles happily, "how delightful. Well, this was definitely worth the trip."

"The Garloffs arrived last night," Miss Bellthroop adds. I know they're from some place downstate, one of those rich burgs near New York City. I can't imagine why they want to move here.

"Such a wonderful home," Mrs. Garloff chirps. The copper moon winks fleetingly, then disappears again into her size 3XX beach towel dress.

Miss Bellthroop is glancing past me, ignoring her clients, frowning at the mess around us. She purses her lips as if to keep a flood of nasty comments from spilling out.

Mrs. Garloff is still fluttering. "So magnificent, Mrs. Smithson. So classic."

"No, I'm just Lucky-" I begin, but she interrupts me.

"Indeed you are, dear. This is a magnificent home. Just awfully, *awfully* lovely. Isn't it, Ippy?" She turns to the dignified-looking chap beside her, but doesn't let him talk. "A real country estate, and so unique to find it in this area."

"Well, it's not waterfront," I say. "Most people would rather have waterfront. There are some real nice-"

"Bosh," says Mrs. Garloff, dismissing that thought. "Do show us in, Mrs. Smithson, and let us have a good go around."

"Yes, let's," says Miss Bellthroop grimly.

Mrs. Garloff has brought along an oversized magnifying glass, and she's mincing around the dining room, holding it up in front of platters and salt dishes, checking out baseboards and lighting fixtures.

"And the furnishings are included?" she asks.

"Yes, but most of them aren't much good, I'm afraid." I pick up a broken candlestick and brandish it before her eyes.

Miss Bellthroop is grimacing over the greasy, broken china on the sideboard, trying not to get her dress dirty against the walls. Mr. Garloff stands soldier-like in the middle of the room, taking everything in.

I try to draw Mrs. Garloff's attention to the stains on the wallpaper, the cracked windows, and the piles of damp debris in the leaky corners. As we wander through room after disgusting room, her husband nods politely, but Mrs. Garloff won't be put off. Squalor excites her. She takes my arm as if we are fast friends. "Now what does Mr. Smithson do, Mrs. Smithson?" she asks.

"Oh, portfolios, you know," I say vaguely.

"Ah, I do so admire men like your husband," she says, "and this picture frame."

"Excuse me for a minute," I say, and I race up the musty stairs to give Violet her cue. I catch a glimpse of Marion, his nasty wooden mouth open in a big, loud roar, and I see something glistening inside that frightening cavity. A June bug glares up at me from Marion's tongue, his hard, glossy back catching the sunlight.

Nice touch. I'll have to remember to congratulate the girls on that.

As I escort my guests up the damp stairs, I feel bewildered. This Mrs. Garloff is crazy about the castle and everything in it, and I have a feeling that, no matter how I try, it's not going to be easy to pry her away from her insane enthusiasm. Why, oh, why, did we have to snag an eccentric?

It's getting warmer and warmer in the castle, and I wonder if they've noticed. "I apologize for the noise," I say. "These old furnaces . . . ."

Mrs. Garloff waves my concern away. "Fixable. Very fixable." Apparently, she's never met Bob. Mr. Garloff nods and wipes at his perspiring brow with a pristine white handkerchief.

"Oops," I say, peering down at the step below me, "looks like more ants got in." I pick up a terrified ant, and spot a slug stretched out on the top step. "Watch that slug, Mrs. Garloff."

She ignores me and steps right on it, dragging slug guts down the upstairs hallway runner. Miss Bellthroop recoils. Mr. Garloff steps gingerly around the mess. I toss the ant aside and watch it scurry into a crack in the baseboard.

"Now this room, unfortunately-" I begin, opening the door to a rank, foul-smelling chamber.

"Charming, just awfully, *awfully* charming," she gushes.

I sigh. So much for Limburger cheese. I should sue the grocer.

"Well, really, my dear-" Mr. Garloff begins.

But she cuts him off. "No, no, Ippy. I really don't see anything a little loving care won't help."

I look to her husband encouragingly. Is he, too, blind, deaf, and dumber than a rock? He appears to have a few little reservations about the place, but he trudges on stoically.

This is ridiculous. Annoying. Hateful! I have wallowed in the gutter of Chez Fred's and fought my daily skirmishes with Kitty. I have survived Lionel Hawthorne's insincere and humiliating proposal of marriage. I have won the sweet affections of Pansy and Violet, weathered the superior looks of Miss Emily Cheseworthy, and even gained some small trust from Mr. Smithson himself. And I've finally, after years of waiting, found a way into my castle, my beloved, if forlorn, castle. I can't let this horrible, terrible, *awfully* posh woman steal it right out from under me!

"Please," I beg, "let me show you the rooms in the east wing."

But suddenly Mrs. Garloff is still. "A castle," she says softly. "A *cawstle*!" She shivers with delight. "With a vine-covered turret, and an ancient, screaming furnace, and lovely rock walls, and massive stone terraces. And it's right here in the Adirondack Park." She beams at me in ecstacy. "You have no idea how long we have been searching." She turns to Miss Bellthroop. "How many acres did you say it sits on?"

"S-" That's as far as Miss Bellthroop gets.

"Those are going to developers," I say wildly.

All three of them look at me, astonished.

I nod vigorously. "For condos. Nice new high-rises that will look down on the castle from all directions." I wave my hands gaily, taking in the thirty foot plunge to the scuffed foyer below us, the warped doors to our right and left, the view out the window of acres of forest about to be obliterated.

"Condos?" Mrs. Garloff leans back weakly against the unsteady banister, feels it give, and springs forward so as not to tumble backwards through the air.

I nod vehemently. "Condominiums. You know, like an affectionate team of big brothers keeping track."

"Well, er . . . ." says Mr. Garloff, still swiping with the handkerchief, which is now quite moist.

Miss Bellthroop suddenly voices her opinion. She gestures vaguely to the sheaf of papers in her hand. "This listing doesn't say anything about developers. The Garloffs and I were under the impression-"

I look at her disdainfully. "Well, you couldn't expect Mr. Smithson to say no to the kind of offer he received."

Wrong move. Mrs. Garloff is sidling in, even more interested than before, if that's possible. "Perhaps we could counter that offer."

Old Ippy gives her a shocked look. She smiles needfully at

him. "I must have it, Ippy," she says. Her eyes are wistful. "I know it will mean a move for us, and that there will be repairs and some decorating. But can you imagine the entertaining we can do here? I knew from the first moment that I must have it."

"You can't have it," I say.

"If it's a matter of money-" says Mrs. Garloff.

"You can't have it," I repeat louder. "It's not for sale anymore."

"This is outrageous," says Miss Bellthroop. "Wasting the time of people like the Garloffs."

But Mrs. Garloff's eyes have softened, and she takes my arm gently. "Ah," she says. "Your home, place of happy memories. My price will be fair, Mrs. Smithson." She squeezes my arm affectionately and starts to waddle me down the hallway. "I don't believe you would like to see condos here. Am I right? We can work out the details, and your castle will retain its historical dignity." She pats my arm reassuringly. "We shall be in touch. Do you have internet? No? A note, then."

"No," I sputter, "it's not that. It's just-"

"Hush, my dear," says Mrs. Garloff sympathetically. "Life is a constant game of flux and chance. I know it will be difficult to lose your home, but we will make it worth your while." Ippy emits a choked sound. "Oh, stop, Ippy," she says, waving away his discomfort. The moon wobbles crazily, peeking out from her ample chest. Mrs. Garloff toddles down the stairs and out the door, followed by her entourage. Miss Bellthroop shudders and wrinkles her nose as if she smells something bad, which she probably does. Mr. Garloff turns back to me, gives an aristocratic little nod of the head, wipes his forehead one last time, and says, "Yes, er, thank you."

The door thumps shut behind them. I watch in despair as both cars leave my driveway, *my* driveway.

Pansy and Violet come scrambling down the stairs. "How did we do?" they ask. They're chortling, giggling, covering their sweet pink mouths with stubby hands, loving the secret trick we're playing on their daddy. "Did you see the bug I fed Marion?" asks Violet, grinning, dancing delightedly, proud of her contribution.

I despise Mrs. Garloff for loving the castle, and I despise Miss Bellthroop for hating it.

And, for some reason, I even despise myself.

"Yes, I saw it," I say quietly. "You both did just wonderful." And I gather them into my arms and hug them. They don't even know that I, Lucky Wilta, am crying.

◇◇◇

Before Charles arrives home, I've undone most of the damage. The walls are still wet; I can't do much about that. But Bob has come and banged around in the furnace room for a while. He scratches his oily forehead, hands me the bill - one I will need to pay myself - and says, "Should be good as new, yep." For what that's worth.

Violet and Pansy have done a good job gathering up grasshoppers and moths, and the musty old drapes are stuffed back in the closets. Kitty helped me vacuum the dirty rugs and clean up spots and spills, and I suffered in silence her stupid chatter and endless questions. A couple of times, I almost screamed at her to go back to Chez Fred's and leave me with my weak, sad life, but, after all, she was doing me a favor, so I let her stay and help.

Why am I like that, Sister?

Things don't look too different from when His Most Trusting Eagerness left me in charge yesterday morning.

For dinner, I'm making almond-stuffed pork chops, a favorite of his, and I'm standing in the kitchen measuring and mixing ingredients, when he arrives home. I hear the front door of the castle close, that loud, resounding thud it always gives, and I try to squelch the sick, shaky feeling inside me.

Will he notice the new stains on the marble foyer floor or the broken picture frames piled in the pantry? Will he see the discolored spots on Marion's crazy mane or wonder why the dining room chandelier is hanging at a new weird angle?

He comes straight back to the kitchen and searches me out, a first. He hasn't even put down his briefcase yet, and he still wears his suit jacket and vest and a carefully knotted helicopter tie. "Look," he says to me. "This was outside the door. Did you know it was there?" He hands me a small folded note in a top quality envelope: Mr. Smithson and his lovely wife are invited to attend a private reception at the Trayson-Ruge Gallery, hosted by Mr. and Mrs. Gabriel Garloff, followed by a meeting to discuss the sale of the Smithson property . . . .

"Wow, that was fast," I say. I hand it back wordlessly and give him a sick smile. If I had known it was there, I would have confiscated it. Why wasn't I thinking?

"I've heard about this new art gallery," Smithson says. "I'm sure they want me to give a donation. It's kind of a nice idea, though, meeting with me socially and then tying up business. I just wonder about one thing," he says, following me into the pantry. "It's a little soon to be mentioning my lovely wife."

I shrug.

"Lucilla? Why do they think I have a lovely wife?"

I'm yanking lettuce, spinach, carrots, tomatoes out of the refrigerator. A nice big salad with dinner, I'm thinking. Roughage is so good for the system. Let's see, I know I have some croutons somewhere. I begin opening stained yellow cupboards, peering around.

"Lucilla."

Finally, I look at him. "I didn't say I was. They assumed I was, and I never had a chance to correct them."

"The whole time they were here?"

"There wasn't an opportunity," I mumble.

"So they think you're my wife?"

"Guess so."

He's silent for a minute. I can see his agitation rising. "And you never bothered to correct that." It's a statement, and one that needs no response. "Terrific," he continues. "So you had a pretty good time making fools of them, didn't you."

"I didn't make fools of anyone."

"Of course you did, Lucilla. Everything in life is a joke. Everything you touch is up for ridicule." He takes the note and refolds it, replacing it in its envelope. "I don't know how I'm going to explain this," he mutters. "Selling the castle is important to me. I thought you might take it seriously for the sake of the girls." He wanders out of the kitchen, going off to change his clothes, to locate his daughters.

I find the croutons.

Dinner is the pits. I feel as if I have to watch everything I say, so I say nothing. Now that I know how he sees me, all the fun has gone out of being Lucky Wilta. I'm just plain, unlovable Lucilla Todd Wilta, hired help, a loser, dishonest and tacky.

And I've hurt him, something that, to my surprise, makes me feel wretched.

Why wouldn't Nick Wilta start sneaking around with some bimbo? Why wouldn't Lionel Hawthorne chortle in drunken mockery seconds after his phony marriage proposal and remind me, in no uncertain terms, that I'm ugly as sin? Why wouldn't

Charles Smithson choose someone like Emily Cheseworthy, who will never, ever understand how to love his children?

My pork chop is sticking in my throat, and I have no taste for the rest of the meal staring up from my plate. I can hardly breathe because my stomach is churning so.

Violet is prattling on about our plans to build a tree house in the woods, a waste of time I thought of instead of mending the torn curtains in Pansy's bathroom.

Her father is barely listening, and when the meal ends, he sends both girls into the playroom to amuse themselves before bed. They argue, and Pansy looks as though she's thinking of crying, but those days are basically behind us. After some half-hearted whining, they race each other out of the dining room, arguing about the oversized coloring book with the bird pictures.

I start clearing dishes away. He follows me to the kitchen. "Why does everything look so dirty in here?" he asks. "This is new paint. It looked fine the other day."

"I brought in my bucket loader to dump mud down the walls," I tell him. "Just my idea of a good joke." I return to the dining room for another load.

"I'm sorry about before," he says. "I know you work hard. The girls love your sense of humor. Anyway, the Garloffs sound interested. Maybe it will work out all right."

Pork chop bones, pools of dressing, bits of scalloped potato, tomato fragments into the garbage, forks in the sink, soap on the dishes . . . .

"Lucilla." He has followed me to the sink and is standing behind me. I'm so damned unhappy I can't even talk. The last thing I want is to start crying in front of this man I have hated for almost two decades. He doesn't talk either until finally he says, "Things went pretty well with the lawyer."

Who cares? I just keep scraping plates.

"They seemed to like Emily, and I told them about putting the castle up for sale. They were pleased."

"Super," I say. "As long as they were happy."

"Well, it's best for the girls, isn't it?"

Why on earth is he asking *me*?

"Lucilla, did you try to sabotage this sale?" he says. "Violet said you told her it was okay to dump her cocoa on the rug in the playroom and stick marshmallows on the wall. You didn't say that, did you?"

I wipe the dishes and rinse them, making a neat little stack in the drainboard. I like old Borstrom's china. Heavy duty, with neat gold stripes around the rims. Mostly chipped and cracked, but good and solid. The kind of plates you'd like to throw against a wall to hear them smash.

"I don't understand why you would do that to me," he says.

I start on the crusty pork chop pan, scrubbing. My, my. What tough stains. Someday we'll upgrade the plumbing so we can get a dishwasher. Top dog. The kind with a Pot Scrubber setting.

"How am I supposed to bring a wife to a reception with the Garloffs, Lucilla?" he says, insistent. "I guess if I had a wife, I could manage, but I don't." He pauses, waiting for some kind of answer from me. I turn on the hot water, hard, and let it thunder into the sink. For a few moments, the chaos of rushing water is the only sound. I turn the tap off.

"Take Emily," I shrug. "It sounds like her kind of shindig."

"Yes, that would be fun to explain. To them and to her."

"Say your wife is sick," I tell him. "Indisposed. Confined. Diseased." I rinse the chop pan until it sparkles. "Mentally incapacitated."

He's standing there looking at me with an odd expression, and I have a terrible feeling I know how his mind is working.

"Or . . . you could come with me." It's soft, a whisper of a suggestion, tentative and unsure.

"That's a stupid idea."

"Well, not really." He hesitates. "It's a private reception. I bet there won't be more than a hundred people there. Over two hours away in Glens Falls, I'd be surprised if I know any of them. And you certainly wouldn't." Oof, sucker punch. "The Garloffs think you're my wife," he continues. "You could pull it off just for one evening, couldn't you?" Lunacy clearly runs rampant in the Smithson genes.

I don't answer. How can I?

"Lucilla, I need to sell this place. I'll do almost anything and take almost any amount, just to be rid of it. You know you could help me if you came. You could explain and undo whatever went on today. We'll smooth things over and do some friendly negotiating."

Some place in this kitchen, I have a plastic container just the right size to hold this leftover applesauce. I start hunting through cabinets that are noticeably grimier than they were yesterday. He's getting annoyed that I won't answer, and I can hear his voice getting sulky, that spoiled, rich kid voice I hate. "Besides, you owe it to me, don't you think?" he says. "I don't know what you did while they were here, but I'm willing to forget it. Just help me make it right again."

"You're crazy," I say finally.

"*I'm* crazy?" he says. "*I'm* crazy?" He walks away from me, a frustrated movement, and then says more calmly, "Lucilla, I am asking you to come with me. Not ordering, but asking."

"What about Emily?" I say. I turn and face him defiantly. "The jet set isn't that big, Charles. Word will get around."

He dismisses the thought with an impatient wave. "She'll never know."

I stare at him, not quite believing what I just heard.

"And it wouldn't matter anyway," he continues. "She's as anxious to sell the castle as I am. I could explain it to her if I have to."

He has clearly lost his mind.

"I can't do this," I tell him. "It's a terrible idea; it's dishonest." Look at Lucky Wilta, the epitome of forthright honesty. "And anyway, I think I've already done enough damage. You'll do better on your own."

He shrugs. "At least think about it," he says. "I'd like you to come. And I think it might work. Those people don't know us. Two minutes after it's over, none of them will remember us."

I don't answer.

"Lucilla?" He tries again. He gives one of the famous, deep-down, all-encompassing Smithson sighs and then says gently, "You'll be leaving the castle anyway, you know. If I marry Emily . . . ." He colors slightly and corrects himself. ". . . when I marry her, Lucilla, you won't be a part of things anymore."

"I know."

"There isn't any reason to try to hang on to the castle. If you used poor judgment when the Garloffs were here, why not do the right thing now? Help me."

I stare at him for a moment, then turn back to the task of wiping off the counters, wringing out the dishrag.

I hear him leave the room. He gets his jacket out of the pantry closet and walks out to the back storage room where he keeps his golf clubs. The back door closes gently.

Oh, what a tangled web we weave . . . .

I pick up one of old Borstrom's sturdy dinner plates and heft it. A good solid weight. I hurl it across the room, and it shatters against the wall with a satisfying smash. Some big hunks crash to the floor, and splinters rain down. I stand there for a moment looking at the scattered bits of broken china, wondering if Clymna Borstrom chose those plates with an eye to the future. Good and solid, almost unbreakable. But if you smash hard enough and lie well enough, you can wreck just about anything, I've found.

I'll pick up the pieces tomorrow. I have a job to do. I go off to see what my charges are doing.

# 21

THE LIBRARY," Lionel says.

"No," I tell him listlessly. "That doesn't make sense. We've already explored every wall, window, and shelf."

"Ah," he says smugly, "but not every book."

We're sitting on the front terrace in a summer haze of gold and green. The grass is scratchy in thick brown-green clumps, and the paint blistering on the old chairs and porch swing is hot to the touch. Lionel is lounging in a broken, rockerless wicker chair, and I'm sitting on the top step while Pansy does her version of somersaults in the coarse thatch. Violet's arms are around my neck, and I keep thinking she's asleep. Her eyes are half closed, but she blinks them awake. She won't give in.

"Explore the books?" I repeat. "How do you mean?"

Lionel shrugs, thinking. "A diary, maybe. An old journal. Maybe even blueprints for this place or some kind of description from the old days." There's a bottle of cold ale on the rickety table next to him, and he picks it up and takes a long swig.

I smile up at him. "Good thinking. I might as well exhaust all the possibilities before he sells this dump." I hoist Violet more sturdily in my arms and call to Pansy, enticing her with the promise of a Popsicle. She comes willingly, smelling sweetly of summer earth and dry grass.

"I bet he doesn't sell it," Lionel says, rising and stretching.

"Why would you say that? This Mrs. Garloff is very sure she wants it. There's no reason for him to hang onto it."

Lionel looks around him. A few rotten roof shingles lie on the ground; thin weeds poke through cracks in the terrace; a window pane is glued together with discolored caulking. "Just a hunch," he says. "How much?"

"What? You mean you really want to bet?"

"Sure." His eyes gleam and a tightness takes over his mouth. "One of your diamonds. That would give me two."

"That's foolish." I stand up and carry Violet into the castle. Pansy follows along, reminding me about the Popsicle. She chooses a red one and slurps happily as we trundle to the back of the castle and into the library. Violet's eyes are closed in earnest now, and I lay her on a musty settee and watch her curl up in a happy sleep. Pansy sits nearby dropping pink ice flecks on a chair cushion.

"Did he tell you what I did when the Garloffs came?" I ask Lionel. I can tell by his expression that he doesn't know. "He thinks I kind of wrecked the house, made it look dirtier than it really is . . . ."

"If that's possible."

I grimace. That was a low blow, even for Lionel.

"Did you?"

"Of course."

"Why?" he asks. "Ah, never mind. Your treasure hunt."

I shrug. "I don't have anywhere else to go, Lionel. It didn't work, though. The Garloffs want us to come to a reception they're giving. We're having a meeting afterward to close the deal."

Lionel's eyebrows go up a little. "They included the housekeeper in this?"

"Well, they thought I was his wife."

Lionel hoots happily. "You're something," he says. Notice he doesn't elaborate. "That ought to go over big with Emily."

"He doesn't think she'll ever hear about it."

"Charles said that?" I know, I know. My deceitfulness is contagious.

"Well, it's not my idea, Lionel."

"Why are you doing it?"

"Because he wants me to."

Lionel gives an amused howl, and I refrain from kicking his gut in. For days I've been practicing being a lady, in preparation for the big event. It'd be a shame to sprain my foot on something as low as the chortling idiot standing beside me.

"Things have changed in the Smithson household," he says lightly, then he pulls a bunch of old hardcover volumes from the lowest shelf and hands them to me. "Here, look through these. See if you find anything interesting."

What I have here is a collection of classic novels: *Madame Bovary, Ivanhoe, Tom Jones.* I'd like to collapse in a chair and begin reading, but I don't. I look inside the covers and find nothing, riffle the pages a little, then hold them upside down by the bindings, inviting any stray documents to fall out. Some loose pages flutter to the floor and brittle binding glue drops softly over them. Nothing else.

I cram the pages back in, replace the books on the shelf and take out the next handful.

Lionel is on the other side of the room following a similar routine. Once in a while he stops and reads something, harrumphs a little, then goes on. He doesn't bother with the books on the top two shelves of that wall, of course. They aren't real. They're clever false covers disguising the space under Marsuvius Borstrom's secretary.

"Too bad we don't have a gold bug," I tell Lionel.

"What?"

"A gold bug, like in the story."

Lionel stops what he's doing and looks at me. "What story?"

*The Gold Bug*," I say slowly. What is he, deaf? Stupid?

Lionel goes back to examining books. "Never heard of it."

"It doesn't matter," I say. "It was a false lead anyway."

He looks at me again. "What was?"

I groan at him. "Lionel, jeesh. The gold bug."

"What gold bug?"

"Poe's *Gold Bug*."

He looks bewildered. "Whose?"

"It's a story of Edgar Allan Poe's," I say slowly and carefully, to be sure he gets every single syllable. "It was his most popular story while he was alive. It's good. It's a puzzle."

"What is?"

*The Gold Bug*, Lionel."

Lionel shrugs. "Never heard of it." He returns to blowing dust off book jackets.

"What are you guys doing?" Pansy asks.

I smile at her, willing to engage in conversation with someone a little more literate than Lionel Hawthorne. "Oh, just exploring a little," I say. "You never know when you might find something interesting."

"Are there bugs in those books?" she asks. "Gold bugs?"

At least someone was listening. She tilts her head, staring up and at the book I'm holding.

"No," I reassure her.

"Then can I help?"

Why not? With her sticky hands, she pulls a book off a bottom shelf and copies me, letting it dangle there. "Nope, not this one," she says. She tosses it aside.

A few feet to my left, I've spotted a shelf of leather-bound

207

volumes that are bigger than the others, and I pull one down, wondering what they are. Photo albums, modern ones. My first reaction is to replace the book on the shelf. Who needs to look at pictures of the deceitful Rose or the Smithson children as babies? I've never been sentimental about old pictures, and I sure don't aim to start today. But the date inside the cover arrests me as I realize these pictures date to my own childhood, to the years when the castle belonged to my father.

I open the book and am immediately disappointed. Groups of adults I don't recognize, mostly. They stare at the camera in color Polaroid shots or from glossy Kodak paper. I can recognize the back gardens of the castle. They looked better then, with red, purple, and gold flowers enticing the eye. But the building looks the same - falling down around them. I never saw that when I lived here. I thought I was growing up in the Magic Kingdom.

I flip the page and look at a slightly out-of-focus shot of a tall woman with short, dark hair. Her features are sharp and her smile is sarcastic. It startles me for a moment. I've never seen this particular picture before, but I'd recognize that face anywhere. Don't I see it in my own mirror every morning? Carefully, I loosen the picture from the page and sneak a look at the back. No name, no date. But I don't need it. I'm pretty sure I'm looking at my own mother, a snapshot taken before we left the castle, before her illness, when she was in her prime.

"Lionel," I say casually, "I found some old picture albums." He comes over and glances down at my mother. Will he recognize me in her? I'm betting not. He'd have no reason to make any connection. "These must be old Forsythes and Todds," I say. "Do you think she's pretty?"

He laughs. "Pretty? Like my Airedale."

"Oh, come on," I say, "she's not that bad."

He looks again, takes a second to really examine her face. Her features are angular, like mine - long, straight nose, high cheekbones, wide, spaced-apart eyes - but on her the result is a superior look. A person you don't want to mess with. High and mighty.

On me, it all comes out plain.

"Oh, she's all right, I guess," he says. "Not pretty really, but there's something impressive. Aristocratic, I guess. Confident. In charge."

In charge. Yes, that's it. The kind of woman men would rush to open doors for or throw their coats in a puddle for. I wonder how many toilets she scrubbed when she lived in the castle. Not many. Nancy would most assuredly have had that task.

I close the album and return it to the shelf.

"Have you found anything that looks like a blueprint?" I ask Lionel. "Something that would head us in the right direction?" Pansy has stopped working her way down the bookshelves, and is now sitting on the floor examining an ancient picture book of Peter Rabbit. She's getting Peter sticky with Popsicle juice. Do I care?

"I don't see anything so far," Lionel says.

I've worked my way to a different section of the room and am gazing at the top four shelves, out of my reach. "Lionel, come over here and help me get these down," I say.

"Get them yourself," he says. "I'm busy over on this side." I give him a disgusted look. He's busy, yes, giggling like a schoolgirl over a stack of musty *Archie* comics.

"Lionel, please," I say, then I remember that Lucky Wilta has never had great success cajoling men into doing her bidding. I sigh and drag a chair over and blow years of accumulated dust from the top shelves. It's obvious no-one has touched these books in years, and I wipe my dirty hands on my shorts and start taking them down, one by one.

I'm on maybe the eighth or ninth volume, riffling through fragile pages, when something catches my eye. It's a slim sheet of folded paper, probably placed in here as a bookmark. I steal a glance at Lionel, who isn't the least bit interested in me or what I'm doing, then I peek surreptitiously at the slip of paper. It's a note written from someone named Margaret to Clymna, and I know that's Clymna Borstrom, the original occupant of the castle. There's no date but this note must be well over a hundred years old. I glance at Lionel again, then back at the letter.

I certainly want to devour it now, but I don't dare. I fold it into quarters and nonchalantly stuff it into my pocket, wondering who Margaret is.

We spend a good part of the afternoon in the library, and we do a pretty thorough job of examining the books for hidden clues. My scrap of notepaper is the only thing that turns up, however, at least the only thing I know of. For all I know, Lionel has stuffed his socks with diamonds as he pries them from the book bindings.

I can't help noticing how patient he is about helping me in my fruitless search, even coming up with avenues I wouldn't have thought of myself. I ask him why.

"Why not?" is his answer. "I don't have anything better to do. The real question, Lucky, is why do you? What makes you so sure there's a treasure in the castle?"

"Just a hunch," I shrug. But I know he doesn't believe me because he looks at me funny.

He glances at his watch and stretches, then stuffs a volume back into a shelf. "Gotta go," he says.

"Big date tonight, huh?"

He laughs. "They're all big, honey." He leaves his empty ale bottle on a table and scoots out the front door. Tonight he will wine and dine some woman he met last week at a bar or a club, and tomorrow afternoon he'll mosey over to give me the highlights.

Lionel Hawthorne is an amoral lothario.

But at least he makes me laugh.

I glance at Violet still sleeping on the settee, and at Pansy, who has tossed Peter Rabbit aside and discovered an encyclopedia of birds. I take note of the ale bottle and decide I don't care if the Garloffs have rings on their tables or if Emily Cheseworthy marries a library full of sticky old books.

I settle into a chair, pull the fragile note carefully from my pocket, and read it.

*My dear Clymna,* it says, *I am so pleased that you thought to send the paintings to me. They will remain safe here until you are ready for them. You are wise to have hidden your wedding gift away, as well; it would never do to have Suvie wager your jewels in a game, too.*

Clymna was married to Marsuvius Borstrom, and I decide he must be the "Suvie" mentioned in this note.

*Someone must speak to him. To lose your dear pony must be the last straw. Be assured that we will enjoy the pictures and keep them safe, and that they will be returned to you as soon as you call for them.*

*Your devoted friend,*

*Margaret*

It's a short note, something Clymna must have received and then stuck in this book, maybe to hide it from Marsuvius, and my heart is throbbing as I reread that third sentence. She hid her wedding gift from Suvie, and what did Suvie Borstrom give his wife to commemorate their wedding? *Jewels.* Jewels that are valuable enough that Clymna snatched them from his greedy, wagering hands and hid them somewhere in the castle.

So where are those glinting diamonds already?

Not here, apparently. I look around me at the mess we've made in the library, the books askew on the shelves, clumps of fallen dust and gritty paper bits knotted around the baseboards, the sticky Popsicle juice running down Peter Rabbit's spine. I yawn voluminously and pull that photo album down again to have another good long look at my superior, sophisticated-looking mother.

Mother? I ask, Where are Clymna's jewels? Did you ever find them? No sudden inspiration hits me. Mother is deafeningly silent.

I examine her hard, confident face. She gave me the gift of life itself, and it must have tired her out because I don't remember her doing much for me after that.

It was Nancy who seemed to take an interest in my existence, and I flip through the album, hoping for a glimpse of that wide, cheery face. I'm disappointed, though. There are no pictures of Nancy.

My parents took her in when I was four, Sister, when her own parents, my aunt and uncle, decided to divorce. Neither of them could handle - or they simply decided not to handle - the added stress of an ungainly adolescent daughter who was a constant disappointment - slow, lumbering, and unproductive. She wasn't a disappointment to us, however; my mother gave over all the household chores to her, and I had a built-in best friend. I wonder, though, how much fun that must have been for Nancy - companion to a cousin twelve years her junior, and household drudge in a cold, clammy castle. All in exchange for her room and board and, now that I think of it, a pretty hefty salary, which she never spent.

My mother wasn't particularly nice to Nancy, treated her more like a servant than a beloved niece, so it shouldn't have surprised me the night I overheard my parents arguing. It was a sticky August night, too hot to do much of anything, and I was crouched on the central staircase, hiding behind a curve in the steps, listening to their voices drifting up from below.

"They're becoming too tight," my mother was saying. "Nancy spoils her." I perked up my ears, realizing I was the topic under discussion.

"Oh, leave the girls alone," Dad retorted. "Living way out here like this, they're both cut off from friends. Let them enjoy each other's company."

"Enjoy each other?" my mother scoffed. "Nancy's twenty-one years old. It's time she moved out and found herself a job somewhere. I don't like the way Lucilla depends on her so much. "

My father sounded surprised. "You want her to leave? I thought you liked having her help around the castle."

"I could hire someone with a lot more energy than Nancy. Someone smarter."

I wanted to leap over the banister and come to Nancy's defense. It's true she wasn't brilliant, but she tried hard to please. She was kind and she loved me. I could feel pain gnawing my stomach. Send Nancy away? I was torn between listening to more or running to find Nancy, my friend, my *only* friend, to tell her this terrible news so we could plot a way to keep her here. I found myself running up the stairs, making my way to Nancy's room, and barging in on her.

She was sitting at her little desk listening to her radio and leafing through a magazine. "Nancy," I cried, "you have no idea what they are saying down there!" I spilled my guts, told her everything, and she sat by silently, her brow furrowed, handing me Kleenexes when my eyes leaked tears and my nose began to run. "What'll we do?" I whimpered.

Nancy asked me a few questions. Was I sure? Was I positive I had heard right? She looked thoughtful for a moment, and then she paid me an enormous compliment; after all, I was only a girl of ten. She confided in me.

"Lucilla," she said, "Jimmy was here again this afternoon, and, you know, he's been asking me to go away with him."

"Go away?" I wailed.

"I thought maybe I wouldn't, not yet. But maybe this is the right time." Her eyes were glistening, whether with thoughts of Jimmy or sadness over leaving me, I couldn't be sure.

"But where would you go?" I asked.

Nancy smiled and pulled her brown sweater a little tighter over her stomach. Nancy always wore that sweater, her protective shield, even on the hottest days. "Jimmy thinks maybe he can cook for a restaurant he heard about in Buffalo. His cousin works there, and he might try to get him in."

"I didn't know Jimmy could cook," I venture.

"He has experience," Nancy nodded, sure of herself. "He's been working at the Wendy's in Queensbury, you know."

I did know this. It was why we only saw Jimmy occasionally, when he had enough time off to make the two hour drive into the Adirondack Park to visit Nancy. They'd sit on the front terrace, or they'd play cards in the dining room. Sometimes they'd go to a movie. Or they'd get food at McDonald's and treat me sometimes. It was a tradition I wasn't willing to let go of.

"He'll be a chef," Nancy added with great dignity. "And I'll get a job, too." Her eyes gazed into the distance, and I could tell it was her future with Jimmy she was thinking of, not her disappointing past living in the castle with me.

The next morning, Nancy came to my room carrying a laundry basket full of my clean clothes. As she hung my shirts on hangers and folded shorts and tee shirts into drawers, she talked to me in a way she hadn't before, about goals and dreams and going after the things you want in life. Jimmy's name kept coming into it, too. I didn't understand it all, but it left me feeling worried in the pit of my stomach. Nancy sat on my bed, reached over and hugged me, and told me to be good. Then she left my room, the empty laundry basket under her arm like an awkward cage from which the bird has flown.

That was the last time I talked to Nancy alone, and pretty much the only heart-to-heart Nancy and I ever shared.

That night, as I huddled on the couch next to my father watching a favorite television sit-com, Nancy plodded in and stood there for a moment, probably gathering courage. Approaching my mother took a certain amount of courage, even for me. For Nancy, it must have been excruciating.

"Aunt Victoria?" she said. Her hands had wrung her shirt front into a sweaty ball, and she chewed the inside of her lip.

"What is it now, Nancy?"

"I made a decision, and I'd like to talk to you all."

My father flicked off the television, and I whined. We were right in the middle of *Get Smart* reruns, after all. But my whining was brief. I definitely wanted to hear what Nancy had to say.

And there it was, Nancy explaining her plan to us, telling us her bags were packed, that Jimmy was there, was waiting for her, that she was leaving.

We all just stared at her.

"He's going to be a chef, Nancy?" My father couldn't hide his surprise, and my mother didn't even bother to temper her amusement. "A *chef*? Nancy, does Jimmy think he can *cook*?"

Nancy chewed her lip more forcefully. "Yes," she whispered.

She looked down at her shirt and tried to smooth the wrinkles from it.

"Nancy," my mother said, rollicking with laughter, "what job do *you* propose to get in Buffalo?"

"Well, Aunt Victoria, I'm not sure, but I thought maybe I could be a teacher's aide, or maybe I'd see about getting in at the Post Office."

"You have to pass a test," said my mother jovially, "and they only take the top three scores." She dismissed Nancy with a wave of her arm. "Don't be silly, Nancy. You'll never make it."

"Or possibly write jingles for greeting cards," Nancy whispered desperately.

My mother was doubled over with mirth, gasping short, barking laughs.

That was when my father intervened. "Victoria, I don't think that's fair. I think Nancy's old enough to make up her own mind about things. If she wants to try these things, she should go ahead and do it."

Nancy's eyes brightened and she threw my father a grateful look. My mother stopped laughing abruptly and closed her eyes in displeasure, I looked back and forth between my parents, and Nancy walked out of the room. She looked taller somehow.

"Lucilla?" she called, just before she walked through our front door.

I jumped up and ran to her.

"You be good," she said to me. The same thing she'd said earlier that day. She leaned down and hugged me, and that was that.

I could hear the loud rumbling of Jimmy's car as they left the driveway.

Nancy was gone, and the next morning, my mother was tight-lipped and angry, making her own coffee and getting my breakfast. It was just a few months later that Smithson won the castle from my father and we were ousted.

I had met Jimmy a handful of times, but it had never occurred to me that Nancy would leave me high and dry for a scrawny boy with pimples and a bad haircut. In fact, she had never before confided her affection for him either, although I had my suspicions.

She had saved all her earnings, just squirreled them away until the day she left us, the day she escaped from the castle to spend her life with Jimmy.

I guess Nancy was smarter than any of us realized.

I never saw her again. Maybe she didn't know where to find me. Or maybe she never tried very hard. Maybe she was just too busy being suddenly free.

I've always wondered if Nancy's leaving was my fault. If I hadn't gone running to her, my mother might never have let her go at all, and she might have turned Jimmy down indefinitely. I might have had Nancy longer if I had just thought before I spoke.

It's a lesson I never seem to learn.

Photo albums depress me; they always have. And this trek down memory lane is no exception. I stare again, hard, at the face of my mother. Lionel didn't even see the resemblance. I wonder how much like her I really am.

Not much, I hope.

Victoria Todd. Aristocratic, confident, in charge. Those are Lionel's words. Notice no-one's ever said them about me.

# 22

I'M READY, and I'm nervous. The girls keep telling me I look beautiful, and I avoid mirrors so that I won't learn the truth. I shouldn't have let him bully me into this, but I did.

We are off to meet the Garloffs.

Part of me is terrified that the gauche, awkward Lucky Wilta will win out, that I'll be found out as a fraud. Another part of me is teetering with excitement, dressed in this beautiful dress, with my hair piled in a soft chignon. I've been practicing walking and sitting all day. I need to be graceful, engaging, witty, but not funny. It's such a fine line. I don't think I can do it.

I'm sure I can do it.

I just hope I don't throw up.

Charles is waiting below, and I know he will look killingly handsome. He told me once that I worry too much about my appearance. Yes, like right now, for instance.

I wish it were a quiet, intimate dinner for four, just the Garloffs and us. An opportunity to visit informally, donate a nice sum to the gallery coffers, negotiate some details, and somehow escape with our dignity intact.

But it's not. There will be other people there, and we will need to make them believe, for this one evening only, that I am something besides a diner dingbat in a brand new designer dress. I have been given this chance to prove myself a better class of person.

I am burdened by the questions of high society, things I may have known about once, thanks to my mother, and I have a two-hour drive to ask for answers. There will be hors d'oeuvres; not munchies, mind you, but hors d'oeuvres. And there will be drinks. And I must make an effort to consume them correctly. How does one hold a champagne glass? By the stem? By the bowl? And when you must hold both a plate and stemware, how do you eat anything? Do you place your lips on the edge of the plate and snuffle? I will ask Charles.

My earrings feel heavy, and my shoes feel like stilts, and I just know that my hair is going to flop down over my eyes halfway through the evening. Would it be permissible to remove earrings? Shoes? Take down my hair? I will ask Charles.

My biggest fear is that someone will scream, "Why, Lucilla Todd! Who'd ever have thought to see you here!"

I must handle all situations with grace and poise. I must speak slowly and with dignity, and I must not burp or sneeze. I must remember at all times who I am not. I'd like to tie a string around my finger to remind me, but it would clash with my dress.

I must meet with the Garloffs, and I must sit by while Charles answers their questions and sells my castle. My stomach is squeezing into little knots, and I know it has nothing to do with shoes or earrings or how to hold a glass.

Why do I insist on fighting for this ugly, beloved building?

"Lucky?" says Pansy. She has taken a brief break from jumping on my bed, and I take advantage of this to swab at her runny nose with a corner of the bedspread. My blankets are crooked and lumpy, and my pillows are on the floor. Just the way I like it.

"What?"

"Daddy is still waiting for you."

"I know, honey."

"When I don't come when Daddy calls, he hollers," she informs me. I bend down to give her a kiss, and Violet climbs on me. It feels good to have little girls messing me up. I stand up again, and I know I have to take a final check in the mirror. I hold my breath. Elegant, sophisticated, expensive. Not beautiful, but passable. I make an effort not to trip on the frayed edges of the upstairs runner, and I start down the stairs. He's standing by the front door looking at his watch, and he glances up as he hears me coming. He smiles a little, just right. It would be too much if he stared open-mouthed, overtaken by my sudden beauty.

I descend slowly, and I do not reach up to scratch the place where hairpins are stabbing my head, right above my left ear.

He comes to the bottom step to meet me and gives me his black tuxedoed arm. I slip my hand through, nice and kind of delicate. My hands are clean, my nails polished. He smiles down at me, and we're off.

The teen-ager who's watching Pansy and Violet stands smirking behind one of the dead ferns in the foyer, and I try to remember that I'm Mrs. Charles Fitzham Smithson the Second, not just some waitress with a lucky date. I smile at her graciously. Kinda superior, if she's smart enough to see that. Then I catch sight of us in that big hall mirror, and I gasp. The cracked glass is a little dingy with age, so that might explain why my features are softened, why my tallness has become statuesque instead of awkward. I can't stop looking, and Charles sees where I'm gazing, and looks, too. Then he laughs, right out loud. We look gorgeous.

Here we come. Lucky and Chuckie together. Antony and Cleopatra. Romeo and Juliet. Kermit and Miss Piggy. Out on the town. Posh. Ooh. It feels awfully, *awfully* right to me.

Together.

At last.

Us.

◇◇◇

People are clinking champagne flutes, so I clink mine. People are eating little raw things with toothpicks, so I do, too. I said I can cook, and I can. Meatloaf, stuffed chicken breast, and I make a mean lasagna. But not this stuff. These are foods that look like things. Carved foods. Shaped foods. Foods with fountains growing out of them. I try not to gawk as Charles leads me around. I mingle with the other guests. I eat sparingly, and I don't pick at my teeth.

I try to recall all the etiquette my mother tried so hard to drill into me. It's been a long time, and, truthfully, I made it my business to forget. But now, as I totter about on my extremely high heels, my mother's words come flooding back.

"Put the books back on your head, Lucilla. Shoulders back. Stomach in."

I elongate myself and, surprise, surprise, it makes walking on these things a little easier. Maybe mother knew a thing or two.

I wander around, aloof, putting on airs, and I don't - I definitely don't - stuff Swedish meatballs into my purse to take home to the girls.

I don't say much either, and, when I do, I watch my grammar. There are lots of opportunities to be sarcastic, but I let them pass me by. Instead, I listen to what other people are saying, and I notice that people immediately like my date. I try to figure out why this is, and I discover the reason. He listens instead of talking.

I find that a very novel idea, and I file it away for future use.

I drain my glass and then see that Chuck is giving me a slightly disapproving look. Guess the idea isn't to drink the champagne, just to display it. I murmur an apology and deftly slide the empty glass onto a table we're passing. I'm so cool that I don't even break stride.

We hook up with a little crowd of chuckling folks and stand there tittering along with them. Smithson is polite and pleasant, and he introduces us as just 'Charles and Lucilla.' That's me, a being with no last name, no past, and certainly no future.

Mrs. Garloff welcomes us, waddling over on midget's feet, talking a mile a minute. Her copper moon winks in and out of her black silk neckline, and I decide it must be some kind of a good luck charm. This lady can afford more than one necklace, after all. She drags me around, introducing me to people. She does use a last name for me, which worries me a little, but I determine to accept the insult with dignity and humility.

"Let me introduce Mrs. Smithson," she says, and a dumpy little woman with quick, shrewd eyes looks suddenly interested. I entertain a fleeting concern that Emily Cheseworthy of the Cheseworthy-Tafts might very well have a spy among the guests, but I decide that will be a problem for The Almighty Charles to deal with, not me.

Mrs. Garloff tells me a little about the opening of the art gallery, scheduled some weeks in the future. That opening will have many hundreds of guests. "Isn't it lovely that just we few could have this little sneak preview tonight?"

"Divine," I tell her.

She hopes Charles and I will be steady patrons. I burble an interested reply. She tells me that her husband is in readers, and I have no idea what that means, but I smile and say, "Oho!" Then she tells me that Miss Bellthroop, poor dear, will be unable to attend our little session later - a bad case of the grippe. But not to worry. The lawyer will handle everything. I hide the despair I feel and murmur regrets.

Charles has stepped aside to talk with a group of well-put-together men, and eventually I'm on my own. I take a sophisticated stance beside a table of munchies, I mean canapés, that look alive, wondering what I'm supposed to do with my hands. I look around and see that everyone has a glass of some kind in one hand and is using the other to delicately feather the air in conversation. So I pick up a glass of something from a tray that glides by, and walk around sipping it. Mmmm. This one is even better than my first. I'm thirsty, so I have to make an effort to pace myself. Just call me Lionel Hawthorne.

The walls, of course, are hung with paintings, and it's my duty to look at them since this soiree is in their honor. I feel smart that I'm able to come up with the label: Modern Art. The thing that clued me in was the big tasteful easel with its scripted poster proclaiming, "The Trayson-Ruge Gallery of Modern Art."

Right now, I'm standing before a picture of a very full, very yellow plastic mustard bottle that looks as though it's ready to burst. Little drops of mustard are spurting wildly from its rim. But there's a surprise for the unsuspecting viewer: Those droplets are *blue*. I peer closer to read the title: "Synthesis."

Aah. Of course.

I move on: A spotted horse drinking quietly at a purple stream. I kind of like this one, and when I tip my head slightly to the right, the horse's eye takes on a glinting, demonic glow. I tip back up slightly and the glow disappears. Tip down, it's back. Up, down, up, down. Gone, then back.

I become aware that the tuxedoed gentleman standing next to me has stopped admiring the painting and is watching me instead. I give him a rakish smile and glide away, sipping furiously. I glance back briefly to catch a glimpse of him tipping his shiny, bald head very definitely to the right.

I'm gazing longingly at a painting of fried eggs floating in air when a woman I've never seen before comes up beside me. "Jane Loyolla-Bridges," she says, extending her hand.

I take it gingerly. "I'm Luck-" I stop myself, but she has very keen hearing and has already figured out the rest.

"Lucky?" she repeats, grinning. "How cute! I once had a spaniel named Lucky!" She introduces me to a group of her friends, and finally someone asks what my real name is.

"Lucilla," I say, feathering the air.

"I like Lucky much better," says a thin, intense woman. "It describes your whole aura. I'd wager you're a Virgo, aren't you?"

"No, a Leo if I ever saw one," someone else says.

I don't have to answer any of this. They're happier arguing among themselves than ferreting out the truth. I wander away to examine a picture of something beige and lumpy. It looks suspiciously like the Thursday Night Special at Chez Fred's, something I've seen up close and personal every Thursday night for the last four years. I look away and spot Mr. Smithson across the room. He's peering out over the crowd with that troubled look he usually wears. Wondering, probably, if I've spilled caviar down the front of my gown or agreed to do a raucous rendition of *La Cucaracha* right here in the Grand Gallery. He sees me, and the worried look fades.

He comes striding over, takes my elbow, and ushers me to a corner. "You fit right in," he says quietly. "Eliza Doolittle at the ball." He takes my empty glass and hands me a tall stemmed glass of something pinkish and fizzy. I taste it and smile up at him. I wonder if he remembers it's my third. Or is it my fourth? "You can play any part, Lucilla," he says.

"I like this part," I tell him. "I've always wanted to be rich agai-" Oops. Maybe it's my fifth. I sip demurely.

"Rich *again*?" he asks.

I laugh the silky, cultured laugh I've been practicing all week. It's instead of an answer. He doesn't press.

I spend the evening pretending to be intelligent, gracious, and beautiful. So they treat me that way. Is that all it takes? You are what you pretend to be?

I say witty, sophisticated things, and I talk about important best sellers I've never read and arty movies I've never seen, having opinions that are popular and well-received. It's easy. I just repeat whatever someone else says, only in different words.

I discover that to be an art critic you only need to use an impressive word or two. "Its depth is truly suggestive of the period," I say. I gracefully indicate the picture nearest my hand. Several people nod in agreement.

"Leave it to Trayson-Ruge to make a statement that's not only profound but understated," I add.

A little, birdlike man glances at me with a bewildered look. "Trayson-Ruge?" he says. "You mean Renlatto."

"Ah. Renlatto," I agree. I stare at the painting in front of us and plunge in to fix my faux pas. "It's very centered, isn't it, very dynamic within the artist's scheme. Did you notice the boldly delicate organic angles, the way he uses the context of beauty? Quite impressive."

The little crowd around me looks at the picture, too, and someone says, "I see what you mean." The others peer more closely at the painting, figuring they must have missed the point their first time around.

I catch my date smirking at me once or twice. He knows darn well that I don't know what I'm talking about. He's amused and impressed, and I'm having a blast.

It's clear I'm a great success.

◊◊◊

I wish I could say that the Garloffs' lawyer is as easily bowled over as the rest of the mob. She's not. Her name is Miss Koons, and I have the feeling right from the first that she couldn't care less whether this meeting goes well or badly.

"Mr. and Mrs. Garloff are interested," she says lazily, spreading a sheaf of papers over the table, "but not committed."

"Of course," I say.

"Mr. Garloff has a few questions about the property that he'd like to ask you," she continues.

Charles nods sagely, and I say again, "Of course." A sick feeling is forming in the pit of my stomach.

"Well, yes," begins Mr. Garloff. "My wife, well, yes, my wife was quite taken-" Mrs. Garloff makes some happy squealing noises and he lets her finish. "Yes, quite taken, but, sir, the heating system?"

This is territory Charles knows. He nods enthusiastically. "The furnace motor is completely rebuilt. I just had that done."

Mr. Garloff removes thick spectacles and wipes them with a special tissue he brings from his breast pocket. "But, the . . . er . . . noise?"

"Noise?" Charles looks blank. "From the furnace? It's August." He looks in confusion at me. "Lucilla, did you have the furnace on?"

I mumble something incoherent.

"And, oh," Mr. Garloff bumbles along, "a few bad smells, we noticed, well, yes."

"Sometimes it's a little musty," Charles explains, and both Garloffs stare back.

"No, not the musty smells. The other smells," Mr. Garloff says. I do my best to look confused. Smithson doesn't even have to try.

"But they weren't that bad, Ippy!" Mrs. Garloff volunteers. "I thought it was just the holes and the rubble that concerned you. And the dampness upstairs."

"The architecture-" Ippy begins.

"-is charming," his wife finishes.

He looks at her. "And the high taxes."

"We expect that." She's beginning to look a little concerned, then crestfallen, as her husband suddenly has opinions about the damp corners, the crickets, the earwigs, the dirt. About the odd layout of the castle, the clanking furnace, the damage to the walls and ceilings, the dead squirrel in the dining room, and the horrendously high fuel bills.

"But Ippy," she says breathlessly, "it's a castle. A real Adirondack castle. Surely we can overlook a few little distinguishing marks . . . ."

"But it's full of holes," he tries again. "And all those insects and things." He looks at Charles amiably. "Maybe they live right in the foundation?"

"Insects?" Charles says bravely. "What insects? Flies? Spiders?"

"Bigger," says Ippy, and he and his better half don't even bother to explain.

"The girls had left the door open," I say, smiling apologetically. "All kinds of things will come in when the door's left open. Country living . . . ."

"There were pigeons in one of the bedrooms," Ippy says sadly.

"Removable," says his feisty wife.

Charles looks sick.

"They smelled, you know," Ippy continues. "It would be difficult to get rid of the odor. I'm sorry, my dear."

Charles can't even imagine how to respond. He looks at me, and I shrug helplessly.

"Looks like there's still some negotiating to be done here," says Miss Koons, the lawyer. "You people want the house, right?" Clearly she hasn't been listening.

"Oh, yes," beseeches Mrs. Garloff. "I know Mrs. Smithson would like to keep the castle safe from progress." She says 'progress' as if it's a dirty word. "We'll offer whatever the developers were offering."

At the same moment, Charles says, "Developers!" and Ippy says, "No." Ippy is louder, but Charles makes a valiant effort. "I can assure you that there are no plans to-"

"I'm sorry, Mr. Smithson." These are Mr. Garloff's final words.

Miss Koons looks back and forth between the buyers, one determined, the other heartsick, then at the castle's uncertain owners. Charles starts talking, explaining. Everything will be put right before they take ownership. If there were problems, he'll certainly see that they're fixed. He's sure all the little differences can be ironed out . . . .

Eventually his voice dies away, and he looks at me. I'm silent, just sitting there pulling a hangnail and watching a little drop of blood ooze up on my finger. He looks away and sits back, tired. I consider excusing myself to go find a bandage for my finger, or maybe a hangman's noose for my neck, but I can't bear to leave him alone with the wolves, so I press my other fingers over the torn spot in my skin and look at the tabletop.

Miss Koons gathers up her papers and snaps her briefcase shut with finality. "If the Garloffs decide to reconsider, someone will call you," she says. Mrs. Garloff is beginning to sniffle, and Ippy is consoling her. "It just wasn't the right one, my dear."

"How many castles do you think there are in the Adirondacks?" she snaps back at him. "Do you think they grow on trees, Ippy?"

Everyone stands up and shakes hands crazily. We all try to smile, all but Mrs. Garloff, and a few hearty platitudes fall flat upon the table. As Smithson and I escape, Mrs. Garloff calls after us, "I do hope this won't influence your decision to become patrons of the gallery." Her voice is tinged with hysteria.

My date and I walk stiffly out of the arts center and back to the car. And that's that. My castle is safe, at least for now. I never would have guessed I'd feel so miserable.

# 23

THE DRIVE HOME is the longest two hours I've ever spent. I can feel the silent tension in him, and I think of a hundred ways I could try to get myself out of this, but all of them make me feel cheap and shoddy. Well, it's his own stupid fault, after all. I only attended the idiotic event because he wanted me to.

I'm still trying to come up with a way to put things right between us when he pulls up to the front door of the castle and lets the car idle. I get out. He waits there while I pay the baby-sitter and get a run-down on the evening's highlights. Then he drives her home. We haven't exchanged one word.

There's no point in going up to bed. I will never be able to sleep if I don't talk to him, and I don't suppose I'll be around here much longer. Why wait until morning, when Cinderella turns back into a rat, or however it goes. I might as well do it as the good-looking, cosmopolitan, cultured new me.

I decide to put on a pot of coffee, hoping he'll be gracious enough to chew me out in a civilized manner. Half of me is hoping he'll avoid the kitchen and go right up the front stairs. The other half of me is pretty sure he won't.

The coffee is hot by the time I hear the front door open and close, and just to smooth things over a little, I've heated up some cinnamon muffins that I made for breakfast, the kind he likes, with sugar all over the top. I put them on a little plate on the kitchen table and pour the coffee when I hear him come in. Just in case.

He comes straight to the kitchen, and I don't understand the relief that floods through me. He has untied his bow tie and looks casual and elegant both at the same time. I wonder how he does that. He stands in the doorway for a moment, sees the coffee cups on the table, and makes the most generous gesture imaginable. He holds a chair for me, then sits down at the table opposite me and looks at me calmly. "Well, you had a successful evening," he says.

"I'm sorry you lost the sale," I say. And I really mean it. But some terrified part of me begins to babble. "I shouldn'a put mud on the velvet window seat," it says. "It was a dirty trick. A filthy trick. A muddy-"

"Lucilla, now is not the right time for jokes."

"No, I guess not." I clam up.

He decides to try the coffee. It's too hot, and he puts it away from him. "Why did you do it?" he asks. His voice is sad rather than angry, and that makes it worse. How can I tell him? I shrug and try to look innocent. He sighs and approaches from another direction.

"Maybe insects did just come in." His eyes are narrowed, staring far away. "Maybe I simply don't see the filth that the Garloffs saw because I'm so used to living in it." His slitted eyes glance at me to be sure I got that particular dig. "But pigeons, Lucilla?"

I grimace.

There's a big silence, and he pulls his coffee to him. "Tell me why the furnace was on."

"It seemed a little chilly in here . . . ."

"It's August."

I meet his eyes. "Bob's kids were starving, Charles. I had to do something."

He sips coffee silently, staring back at me. When he speaks, I can hear the dejection hiding under his calm words. "Stop joking, Lucilla. This isn't funny to me."

"I know," I say. It's barely audible.

"What did you do to make the upstairs wallpaper damp?"

My answer comes out in a whisper. "Your daughters and I . . . brought buckets of water to all the rooms. We soaked sponges and threw them . . . ."

He looks keenly disappointed. "Even my daughters?"

"It was a contest to see how high they could reach," I admit. "They loved it. Pansy won. She high-fived me."

He shifts a little in his chair, and, I'm not sure, but I think I see the corner of his mouth twitch very slightly. I feel a sudden flicker of hope.

He extinguishes it immediately. "Lucilla, who are you? What's going on?" He's looking at me hard, and I shrink under that gaze.

"I'm Lucky," I say softly. "Just like I told you, Lucky Wilta."

"And you'd like to be rich. Again. And you're terrified that I'll sell my home, which should mean nothing to you. And you fit in perfectly with a bunch of pretentious snobs."

I almost confess the whole thing right then; it would almost be a relief to have him know. But I don't. I take a cinnamon muffin and begin to pick at the sugar crystals, dropping them into a neat little pile on my plate. They catch the light from the overhead lamp and glisten provocatively.

A tiny pile of miniature sparkling diamonds.

"I've always wondered about that haughty look you get sometimes," he says. "Why don't you explain it to me."

"Haughty?" I say. "I never look haughty."

"Of course you do. Superior, righteous, sticking your nose in the air. Oh, you pair it up with bad grammar and a homespun attitude, but the whole picture doesn't work. It makes a person wonder about your background."

I say nothing. The ticking of the kitchen clock has grown suddenly loud and intrusive.

Charles leans back in his chair, serious. "What exactly is your background, Lucilla?"

"My background?"

"And how did you know about the music cupboard? That's another thing I've been wondering."

"The music cupboard?" I'm buying time. "I told you, Pansy-"

"No, Pansy didn't show you. The girls don't know anything about it. And Mrs. Frocks didn't tell them, because I never had any reason to show her."

"Then they must have watched you-"

"I never open that cupboard. Why would I? I don't play the piano." The look in his eyes is making me feel more and more ashamed. I need to be on top of this situation, and I'm not. I'm sinking slowly to the bottom of the slush pile. "You're quite an actress, Lucilla," he's saying now. "I especially enjoy the role of uneducated waitress."

"It's not a role, Charles. I am a waitress; I have been for years. And I'm a college drop out. A flunk out. And a light-hearted divorcée."

"You were married?"

And that's when I decide to spill my guts. "Yes, I was married," I tell him, "to the biggest jerk this side of the Mississippi, who cheated on me with some hot babe with no brains, but, oh, what a body. A Venus with arms."

There's sympathy on his face. Poor Lucky. Thrown over. Cause? Perfect Homeliness. Verdict? Guilty. Sentence? An empty life. Poor, pitiful Lucky.

Can't have that. I'm Lucky Wilta, inferior to no man. And I've been creating a character for nineteen years. Surely, I can keep her intact for a little while longer.

I can't. When I see the look on his face, I can't. The truth comes pouring out of me, and with it all the ridiculous hate that I've been nurturing and feeding. I do not hate this man sitting across the table from me, and I know that. It's the most horrendous kind of lie to say so. In fact . . . .

"My name was Lucilla Todd," I tell him. "I lived here."

◇◇◇

At another time, I might actually have enjoyed the shock that passes over his face. "Your father won this house from mine in a card game," I continue. "Nineteen years ago, you tried to run over my doll with your toy truck. We were ten."

It's very quiet for a couple of minutes. Charles sips his coffee and stares at me over the rim.

"We had everything when we lived here," I say. "We were wealthy, but then later . . . . everything fell apart after we moved out."

The silence that descends upon the kitchen is oppressive and ominous. I can't say any more, and for minutes which seem like hours, he doesn't speak either. He places his coffee cup on the table and looks down at it as if he's never seen it before. When he looks up, his face is composed.

"I thought the Todds moved away," he says finally. "My father used to say that they - that you - had left the area."

"We did," I manage to say. "We moved to Cincinnati, then I lived in Akron. My parents both died. I came back for a reason." He's waiting. I swallow the humiliation rising in me and tell him the truth. "I moved back after my marriage ended and eventually I got a job at Fred's. I read about you, and I watched, and I waited. I came here with a purpose, to get the castle back from you. I didn't care what it took."

There's a long silence. "So that's why the Garloffs . . . ."

"I didn't want you to sell it."

"And the little room upstairs . . . ."

"Was where I spent my happiest times." And I tell him about my cousin Nancy, my friend, who lived with us because she had nowhere else to live, and how we escaped from my mother and her vicious tongue in that room. About my tea set, and the pretending, and how beautiful I thought I looked in that cracked mirror.

I came here to find my star, I realize, to polish it to a fiery brilliance. I can't even say my star is dull and tarnished, with broken points and a sloppy, greasy feel. For I have no star. All this time spent, and I have nothing, just this terrible feeling of sadness, humiliation, and pain.

"And I don't suppose I just happened to hire you," Charles is saying. He's certainly smart enough to figure that much out.

I go ahead and tell him the rest, about filching his mail, enjoying watching him suffer. Ironically, I'm watching the same thing right now, and I am not enjoying it - not one little bit.

"Charles," I tell him, "I'm sorry I spoiled the sale of the castle. I'm sorry I stole all the other responses to your ad. I was wrong. I'm always wrong. But this was my father's house, my house, and it didn't seem fair that you had it, that you had everything, and I had nothing, and then that you could sell it right away from me." I'm looking down at my hands on the table, at the little bubble of blood that has dried now into a shiny blob. I can hear my voice getting scratchy with tears. "I waited all those years," I tell him.

Bless me, Sister, for I have sinned. This is my first confession in a very, very long time.

"My life seemed so horrible," I say to Charles, and it's almost a whisper. "I decided you were to blame." He's listening, accepting everything I say. Shame is new to me. I've never had the good sense to feel it before. "I spent all those years hating you for a thief," I say.

"Hating me, Lucilla?" He sounds puzzled, as if no woman in her right mind could hate him. He's right about that.

I shrug. "I didn't know you. I didn't know anything about you. But I'll make it up to you about the castle. I'll do all the right things now, so you can sell it. Just let me stay."

Begging.

Pleading.

Everything but Down On My Knees.

Charles is looking around the kitchen. "It's not going to be that easy to find another buyer for this place."

"I'll call the Garloffs and tell them what I did. Maybe they'll reconsider."

And for my penance . . . .

"No," he says, "let them find a different castle. They'd find out soon enough that this place is a curse. I'd feel guilty talking them into it."

"Someday," I tell him optimistically, "the right buyer will come along." My voice is hopeful, wildly eager. "And I'll do everything I can . . . ."

"That's not very likely," he says. "You'd have to be stupid to want to buy this place."

"You really don't love the castle, do you?" I say. And why would he? Why would anyone? "I wonder why your wife liked it."

He's gazing at me, and at first he doesn't answer. Then, "She liked the drama of it," he says quietly. "She thought it was some magical fairyland." He looks away, at the chipped light fixtures, the crooked hinges holding dirty cupboards in place.

That was the way I saw it, too, when I was a child. Maybe Rose had some growing up to do.

"Then why didn't you move after she died?" I ask.

"I don't know. It was easier not to. I was never here anyway." He meets my eyes. "So, this is Lucilla Todd." He thinks that over for a moment, and as usual I wish I were someone, anyone, else. He shifts in the chair again and rubs a hand over his forehead. "Tell me about the insects."

I take a breath. "We captured them in a jar. I told Pansy she could let them loose."

"Inside, of course."

"Upstairs. Mrs. Garloff squashed a slug. It's ground into the Persian runner in the hallway. She's a disgusting woman."

He surprises me by laughing suddenly, a quiet laugh, but maybe a forgiving one.

"She's ridiculously enthusiastic, I'll give you that much," he says. He tips back in his chair a little and grasps his coffee cup, searching my face, probably waiting for more confessions, more appalling revelations.

But what emerges is merely a gentle request, and it's from him. "Be on my side, couldn't you, Lucilla?" he says finally. There's not a hint of a smile on his beautiful face, but no anger either, none of the rage that I so richly deserve. "For once?"

"I am on your side," I tell him. "I am."

He pours more coffee into his cup and reaches for the sugar.

"Charles?" I ask him. My voice comes out quiet, a little nervous. "I've tried to be good to the girls. I've liked them almost from the beginning. That part of it . . . . I took that part very seriously. They're better, you've noticed that. Pansy speaks up now. She'll say what she thinks . . . . And Violet is so good. She tries so hard to mind." My voice trails away. I'm pleading with him to approve of me. "Are you going to let me stay?"

He looks at me, then away. "Of course."

"Why did you make me go tonight? If you had said I was sick . . . ."

"I'm not sure. I guess I thought it might be fun. I wanted to see you in a different way, maybe."

"What about Emily?" I ask. "She will find out. I'm sure she will." And then . . . .

He's stirring sugar into his coffee, adding milk, tasting it, adding a pinch more sugar. He considers carefully before he answers, and then he says, "I guess I didn't care if she found out. I guess I still don't." His eyes meet mine. "You know, Lucilla, whether you realize it or not, you've had an effect on this household. On me. Six months ago, I never would have done what we did tonight."

This is not a compliment. Thanks to Lucky Wilta, The Honorable ain't quite so honorable anymore.

"I'm sorry," I mutter again. "I learned to survive by cheating my way into things."

He nods. "It's never been my way, though."

Like he has to tell me that.

He stands abruptly and carries the coffee cups to the sink. "I'm tired, Lucilla. This was an exhausting evening." He stands there thinking for a minute, looking around at the kitchen light with its broken glass globe, the worn out linoleum, the ridiculous green painted chairs against the wall.

He shakes his head sadly, a hopeless gesture. "I suppose I'll get rid of this place eventually," he says. His hands are gripping the edge of the sink, and he's looking out the window at the black night. "You know, living here isn't going to bring your father back."

My voice catches in my throat. "I know that."

"Even when we were hiking, when you mentioned him, I could hear something . . . ."

"I miss him," I say, and it comes out wobbly.

He looks back at me; there's sympathy all over his face. "What I might do," he says, "what I think I'll do . . . ." He stops, looks out the window again at the black night, the pinpricks of stars far away and up high, and I can't see the expression on his face. But his words, when he finally says them, are clear and definite. "I'll split the profits with you, Lucilla. Fifty-fifty. As much or as little as they are. Half for Smithson's heir; half for Todd's. When the castle sells."

I stare at his back. Money. Profits. It doesn't feel right to me. It feels like a buy-out, and I blink back the tears stinging my eyes.

He turns around, and he looks at me again. Not smiling, not a joke. And not a buy-out, after all. A serious offer of forgiveness. "I can do that much for you, at least."

It's exactly what I would have loved to hear just months ago. In spite of my deception, I can stay in the castle; I can share the profits if it sells. It's more than fair. It's generous. It's typical of Charles Fitzham Smithson.

I don't know why I hoped for so much more.

# 24

I FEEL AN UNEXPECTED SENSE of gratitude now that Charles knows who I am and who my father was. He could so easily have tossed me into the street, but he didn't. I came here to destroy him, and he knows that and still allows me to stay. He has freed me to be myself: the Good, the Bad, the Ugly.

I've never known anyone like him before.

I call the Garloffs to make them understand. I try to connect with Mrs. Garloff, but I get Ippy, and he makes me feel like a hopeless derelict. He's sympathetic and gives me a fatherly lecture on the hazards of a life of crime, but, thanks no, he's still not interested. He never really tells me I'm deceitful and malicious, but I know what he's thinking. Or maybe it's me that's thinking that.

I make a decision not to share Charles' and my heartfelt conversation with Lionel. For one thing, I feel sorry and embarrassed that I put Charles through it, and for another, it's not Lionel's business. If Charles wants to tell him who I really am, that's up to him. It won't be coming from me.

I continue to search for the secret room, going over the same ground I've already covered. Smithson still doesn't know that I'm looking for treasure, and I ask myself why I didn't just tell him. Well, I know why, of course: My search is too important to me. It's the thing I have based my whole life on, and if I'm not exploring the castle, hoping to find the cache of diamonds my father promised me, then what am I doing here?

So I keep it to myself. I know my hope for revenge was wrong, but how can I change the whole person I am? Who will I be if I lose the goal I've nurtured all these years?

And, even though my haunts through the castle are beginning to look like a fool's game, I've decided to be magnanimous. If I do find treasure, I'll split it with Charles, halfsies, and enjoy the look of pleased surprise on his face. He doesn't need the money, of course. But the gesture makes me feel generous, and I haven't felt that way in a long time. I want him to see me that way.

It does occur to me that Charles may already have found the diamonds; maybe that's where his fortune came from in the first place, and it's possible that's why he was so quick to offer me half of the profits when the castle sells. Maybe he's not generous at all. Maybe he owes me more than I ever dreamed.

But maybe not.

So I keep searching.

Lionel is quite taken with a new acquaintance named Shelly Neverstone, so he's not much help. In a way, it's a relief to wander through the familiar corridors alone, to pass chambers and unlikely corners that have already given up all their secrets to me, to simply sit in familiar dusty rooms staring out familiar cracked windows at familiar dead shrubs.

I once thought I would love the castle. I realize now that I love it in the way one loves familiar things. With all their flaws, with a nervousness that comes of wondering what might replace them. I don't love the castle itself; I know that now. But if not here, where? If not this, what?

◇◇◇

Lionel shows up early one afternoon, when I've just rocked a moody, sniffly Pansy to sleep and Violet is coloring happily in her bed. I'm in the corridor outside their rooms when he suddenly appears, startling me.

"How do you get in here every day?" I ask him. "Doesn't Charles ever remember to lock the door?" Lionel just laughs and grabs my hand, pulling me up the hallway. We do a little halfhearted exploring together, and our enthusiasm is conspicuously absent until we come across a stubborn door in a shadowy corner of an unused bedroom. Neither of us can remember whether we've ever seen inside it before. Lionel's eyes are gleaming like two reflective moons.

I tell him that I've seen every inch of the castle, that there can't be anything here because the room on the other side just wouldn't allow for it, but he's Lionel: always hopeful, always willing, always immersed in greedy boredom.

So I let him get the keys, and he unlocks the door to reveal a shallow series of damp, moldy shelves piled high with damp, moldy linens. We remove them, shaking them out and watching most of them crumble into tatters at our feet. We pat all the walls, wrinkling our noses at the rancid mustiness of the space, and finally we agree that it's exactly what it seems to be - a rotting linen closet. Just one more smelly closet that Charles will never suspect I've examined.

Finding it, exploring it, wasn't even that much fun.

Charles still disappears most days, and it bothers me that he still makes it such a mystery. After all, I 'fessed up to him; he should 'fess up to me. I have the phone number he gave me months ago, and one day I decide to call, just to see who answers. "Chuck's Canned Squid Company," they'll say, or "Smithson's Quickie Tattoo Art." I figure I'll hang up quickly or claim a wrong number. But at least I'll know.

What really surprises me is that he answers himself. "Lucilla. What's wrong?"

"Um . . . er . . . ." Why didn't it occur to me that he'd have Caller ID? "Sorry I bothered you," I say crisply. "I think I have a handle on it now."

"Are the girls all right?" There's absolutely no background noise on his end. No voices talking, no television blaring, no machinery, vehicles, appliances, animals. No nearby airport sounds. No telltale gun blasts or factory whistles. Apparently, each morning he goes off into a deep black hole.

"Yes, everything's fine," I say. "Sorry."

"Do I need to come home?"

"No, no. I think we're fine."

"All right." He sounds distracted and annoyed now, and he hangs up quickly.

Relieved, I slide the telephone receiver into its cradle. What am I doing? What difference does it make where he goes and what he does? I did not come here to learn the scoop on Sir Charles Fitzham Smithson the Second. I came here to find my secret room.

And then? After the secret room reveals itself, the treasure is counted and shared? Or, if not that, after Charles sells the castle, gives me my half, and I move my gear out? Then what? Then I set myself up in some swanky little apartment in a nicer part of town, I guess. I go back to college maybe and finish a degree. Maybe I become a chef. Or a neurophysicist. Oh, sure, I keep up with Pilot and Vansy for a while, but eventually I forget about them, and they about me. They're little. They'll adjust.

Lionel, my flitting candle moth, comes over some evenings, and while Mr. Smithson furrows his brow over folders and documents or does some serious bonding with his two little girls, Lionel and I do some bonding of our own. Lionel lives by the adage 'Out of sight, out of mind.' And this applies to Shelly Neverstone as much as it applies to Lucky Wilta. So, as long as I supply the beer, I'll do, and he's in love with me, and his skinny little frame never puts on an ounce, even though we sometimes go through a six pack in an evening. His four to my two. Once in a while, he doubles that, and sometimes he's already fairly wasted when I let him in the door.

Smithson frowns in disapproval and tells me I'm crazy to let him in the door at all.

The two of us, or sometimes the three of us, watch television or rent a movie, or just talk sometimes, and I find out again and again that Lionel can be devoted and amusing when he's sober, downright crude when he's not. A couple of times, I have to force him, staggering and swearing, out into the dark in the wee hours, and I despise the looks The Holy One gives me when I come back in and start turning out lights.

"I hope you know what you're doing," Charles says to me.

"As much as you do," I retort.

Lionel asks me to spend a weekend with him on his boat, and, after I negotiate him down to a single afternoon, of course I say yes. Lucky Wilta does not get invitations like this every day. We set a date, my next afternoon off, and agree that there will be no drinking on board. Lionel argues for moderation; I insist on abstinence.

Through it all, Charles gives me disappointed, scornful looks.

"That sounds like a poor idea," he warns.

Well, excuse me, Your Stuffiness. Why don't you ask me to your own boat? I'm not all that particular; I'd go.

It doesn't surprise me, but it is a little uncomfortable when Charles receives a note from Emily Cheseworthy of the Cheseworthy-Tafts. He meanders into the laundry room one day while I'm dumping little jumpers and big shirts into the washer, and stands there looking at me for a few minutes.

"Yes, Yore Grace?" I say.

No smile. He just hands me this flimsy, scented paper, which I take.

"Read it," he says, so I do.

She's a little dismayed to find out that he spent three days vacationing in Maine without letting her know. And why is she hearing rumors that he attended some art reception in Glens

Falls with someone who was introduced as Mrs. Smithson? Was it a joke? Was she misinformed? He hasn't been answering her calls lately either. She's a little concerned about this, and he has some explaining to do. She'll be in New York for the next few days to do some shopping, and, after that, will be expecting to hear from him.

"What do you think?" he asks me.

"She's peeved," I say. "Good luck." I'm not taking responsibility for this. He forced me to go to Maine with him, and he cajoled me into attending that reception. No way is any of this my fault.

"She says she's expecting to hear from me."

"Right."

"I have a feeling that if I don't get in touch with her, she leaves me. It's over."

"Sounds like it." I shake out a stained tablecloth and add it to the load.

"I think I could explain the reception to her pretty easily. She would understand about needing to unload the castle."

"Probably."

"Of course she might be shocked that we pretended to be married. It wasn't fair to her. She's always known me to be honest about things."

"I'm sure that's true," I say. "I suppose you could tell her I was a bad influence."

"Yes, yes, I could do that. And then there's Maine. That might be a little harder to explain."

"You could just tell the truth," I advise him. "That we wanted to get away from her for a while."

"That would go over well," he muses. "I actually wanted to watch the girls run in the waves," he adds righteously, "to give them an ocean experience. And to get some space from all of life's stresses." He looks over to see how I'm taking this.

"Right," I say.

He's thoughtful for a moment. "I told her that foolish story, the one about Old King Charles that the girls seem to like so much."

I measure out laundry detergent and pour it over the clothes.

"I told her how worried they seem. I wanted to talk with her about it."

"And?"

237

He shrugs. "She didn't get it. She didn't seem to care. It made me wonder if she'll be able to read them, you know? Understand their moods, that kind of thing. I think that's why we went to Maine. I needed some time to think about that." He grows quiet. Me, too. I mean, how can I answer this? I glance over and, yes, he's still standing there, quiet, pondering, and I glance at his face. Why is he looking at me that way?

"Lucilla," he says thoughtfully, "I don't believe I'll answer this note." I pause in what I'm doing and watch him tear the scented sheet into pretty fragments that drift down into the wastebasket. It's a nice, symbolic gesture, so much more poignant than deleting a text. It's one of the perks of living in the heart of the Adirondacks.

"You're going to have to talk to her sometime," I say.

"Yes, she deserves that much, at least."

I glance into the wastebasket; the scent of Emily's notepaper drifts up at me.

"Where are the girls?" he asks me.

I gesture out the window. "On the swings."

He leaves the room, never knowing that I collapse in relief against the front of the washing machine. I do not whoop for joy, nor do I do a little dance on the laundry room floor. I just close the washer and start the cycle, then look out the window and see him pushing his little girls on swings, first one, then the other.

Good man.

# 25

LIONEL HAS PULLED my arm through his and is half walking, half running beside me along the dock at the marina. His eyes are glinting, and he's keeping up a peppy monologue while I eye every boat in a long line, searching for Mandi's Kiss.

"No, not that one," he assures me as I grimace at a hokey-looking painted craft with a makeshift flagpole sticking out the front. We pass vessels, big and bigger, mostly showy white fiberglass with decks and glassed-in viewing areas and glossy polished wood interiors visible through open doors. They're lined up like slick sardines, cramped to the wooden docks, each in its slotted space. Some have whimsical names: Fuelish Pleasure; Sink or Swim; On The Rocks; Shores Fun.

"Are you sure this is a good day to go out?" I ask Lionel. My glance keeps lifting toward the dark sky where black, roiling clouds tumble and crash together, then drift angrily apart.

"A perfect day," he assures me. "There's nothing as majestic as a storm over the lake, especially from the safety of a boat like mine." He pauses in his speech, and, as if taking their cue, his feet stop, too. "Thar she blows," he says affectionately, and he looks at my face to see my first reaction to Mandi's Kiss.

I'm appalled.

I've visited Lionel's brand new log cabin and seen his beautifully landscaped grounds. I've had dinner with him, cooking out on his Argentinian-style wood-burning grill and eating steaks on his extensive, layered stone patio. I've gone for breezy rides in his BMW, taken stock of the classy clothes he wears, and admired his new Titleist golf clubs.

So how can this be Lionel's boat?

It's listing to one side, faded and ramshackle. It's about thirty feet long and built of plywood once painted white. The peeling paint, badly repaired deck, and faded, patched sails don't exactly boost my confidence.

"So this is Mandi's Kiss," I say, trying to muster up enthusiasm. "Mandi must be so pleased." I glance at my watch.

One o'clock. The afternoon is very, very young.

"She's a lot more seaworthy than she looks," says Lionel, seeing my doubting face. "Don't be fooled by the sails. There's an auxiliary motor, too. She moves great."

I flick at the wood side of the craft, and a long sliver of old paint comes off in my hand.

Lionel is getting anxious. "Come on," he says. "Step aboard." I try the short gangplank tentatively. It seems to hold, so I step onto the boat. "None too soon," Lionel says with great satisfaction, as the first hard raindrops splat on Mandi's Kiss.

I have to duck my head to get inside. It's no better in here. There are cupboards and cabinets, a door at one end, and thin, shallow drawers all painted a sickly green that's peeling and blistered with age. A grimy stove and small refrigerator are shoved together in one corner, a built-in nest of benches surrounds a splintered board that pretends to be a table, and an open door reveals a tiny bathroom with old built-in fixtures. Worn indoor-outdoor carpeting that might once have been orange covers the floor.

Even Lucky Wilta is disgusted.

"How long have you owned this thing, Lionel?" I ask.

"Four years, almost five. I bought it from a friend who was sick of taking care of it."

I'm pulling aside the musty curtain that covers one dirt-streaked window. Clouds of dust billow. A nervous centipede races into a crack. "Are you sick of taking care of it?" I ask.

Lionel grins. "I don't know yet. I haven't started."

Like I couldn't tell.

"Lionel," I say gently, "when you invited me to spend the afternoon on your boat, I pictured something a little more elegant."

"Ah, Lucky," he says, his eyes gleaming. "Don't let first appearances deceive you." He goes back outside to free us from the dock. Through the scratched, cloudy windows, I can't help noticing that other boats are coming in to the marina, tying up. No one else seems to be leaving.

"Is this a good idea, Lionel?" I yell to him. I clunk my head on the door trying to peer outside. Throbbing begins, low and rhythmic. In seconds, Lionel is back by my side, his arm affectionately around my waist.

"Be comfortable, Lucky," he says and steers me to the plastic bench. "Sit right here and wait for me." He propels us out toward deeper waters, and I dutifully watch our progress through a scratched plastic window. Vessels pass us, every one glad to reach the shore, glad to dock, glad to button up and get out of the storm.

But not Mandi's Kiss. On we go, chugging bravely out onto the choppy lake.

Suddenly the motor cuts. I assume Lionel has anchored the boat. But maybe not. Maybe we're just drifting, waiting for a whimsical breeze to crash us against a rocky shoreline. I can hear thunder outside and some pretty stiff lapping of water.

"Well," says Lionel, standing in the doorway. The top of his head doesn't even reach the doorframe that almost knocked my block off. He must be five inches shorter than yours truly. "Well," he repeats, grinning, "what do you think of Mandi's Kiss?"

"I think it's dreary and ugly."

He throws his head back and laughs loudly. "Lucky," he says, "be kind. Have you ever been on a boat like this before?"

"No, but I've been in a few cheap, furnished rooms, and this is worse. Shouldn't you be out there steering this thing?"

"We're anchored," he says. He peers outside. "There don't seem to be any other boats out anyway."

Gosh, I wonder why.

He comes to sit beside me and his strong, wiry arms slither around my waist. "Lucky," he whispers, "I've waited a long time to see you here on my boat. This is a dream come true for me."

I can't help raising my eyebrows a little. A dream come true? A nightmare. I extricate myself from his arms and start exploring the cabin. "Mind if I look around?" I ask.

"No, treat it as your own."

"Thanks, no, Lionel. I'll just look around." A drawer is rattling and I pull on the sticky handle. Inside, a haphazard mess of lipsticks, tubes of blush, combs, and hair ties are clumped together. The boat sways and everything slides to one end. I look at Lionel quizzically, and he laughs.

"A lot of women have enjoyed themselves on Mandi's Kiss," he says. "They almost always forget something." He leans back on the hard built-in sofa, clasping his hands behind his head, grinning. "Lots of women, Lucky, appealing women."

Which is why he invited me, I'm sure.

"You're an appealing woman, Lucky. Did you know that?"

"Shore thing," I reply. I can still hear thunder rumbling and feel the tilt of the boat as it sways in the choppy water. "Lionel, are you sure this thing is safe?" I'm looking at a glinting stream seeping down the wall next to the grubby stainless steel sink.

"Completely safe," he assures me. "That's just rain water. Come and sit by me, Lucky."

I don't. Frankly, Sister, I'm not interested in Lionel Hawthorne. In fact, right now I'm disappointed and annoyed. "Lionel," I say, "I thought we had this all straightened out between us. You're fun and amusing, but you're short, and you drink too much. And I'm sarcastic and tacky and no Miss Universe. Let's just leave it at that."

"So we should feel grateful we found each other," he says. He comes up behind me, massaging my shoulders with his strong hands. "Come on, let's just have some fun."

"Lionel, knock it off." This is really frosting me. I definitely am not interested in this kind of attention from Lionel, and he knows that.

He ignores me and steers me to the closed door, then flings it open. I have no choice but to stare inside.

My Kansas house has just plopped down on the yellow brick road, and suddenly the world is all in color. Can this little room really be part of Lionel Hawthorne's filthy boat?

The walls are burnished gold wood, polished to a sheen, and the bed takes up almost the whole space. It's made up with a blue satin coverlet, and a variety of soft pillows are tossed casually against the glowing headboard. On shelves above, behind turned wooden railings, bottles of liquor and wine are stowed. They sparkle in the subdued light, polished garnet and amber, most of them full, some corked and already sampled. Below them, glasses hang, swinging gently with the waves made by the wind. Hidden recessed lighting bathes everything in a golden glow. It's a beautiful, inviting space, and Lionel is looking at me hopefully.

I slam the door firmly. The room disappears and I lean against the door with murder in my eyes.

"Oh, come on, Lucky," he wheedles. "It's the best part of the boat. We'll be a lot more comfortable in there."

"I'm perfectly comfortable out here," I say.

"It's filthy out here," he reminds me.

"I like filth. I'm used to it." I'm still leaning against the door, not budging.

He sits down on the plastic bench, looking slightly defeated. "Your friend Kitty wouldn't be saying no to me."

"I'm sure you're right about that."

"That's the problem," he muses. "Kitty's so eager, so willing. And Shelly. She was thrilled when I brought her out on the boat last week. But I'm finding that I love women who play hard to get."

Then he must really love Lucilla T. Wilta, except that if it's a game, I'm truthfully not playing.

He sits watching me, and I decide to explore a little more. I peer into a closet and find a shoebox pushed neatly against the wall. I lift the cover: a pearly barrette, a couple of cheap tangled gold chains, two or three toothbrushes, an earring, an odd high-heeled sandal. "Lionel, for heaven's sake. Whose stuff is all this?" I ask him.

He shrugs. "Lots of people's. That's the overflow." He comes toward me and starts steering me gently toward the bedroom again. "Come on, Lucky. Time's a'wasting."

"Is that all you use this boat for?" I ask him. "Don't you need to use this limited storage for necessary things? Paper towels? Bait? Maybe a few boat bailers?" I shake out of his hands. "Lionel," I tell him firmly, "we're here for a boat ride. To enjoy the water and the wind on our faces."

"It's storming."

"You knew that when we started."

He places a hand on my neck and turns me toward him gently.

"I'm not kidding, Lionel," I snap. "Take your hands off me."

He does and then stands there looking irritated. "You know what, Lucky," he says sullenly. "There will come a day when you wake up and kick yourself for refusing me."

"I'll let you know when that day arrives," I tell him. "Here's a deck of cards, Lionel. Let's play Fish." I force him down at one end of the rickety table, take the seat opposite, and begin dealing.

"Fish?" He sounds suspicious, but hopeful. Maybe he thinks Fish is some kinky parlor game. It's not.

"You know. Give me all your threes."

"Lucky!" He sweeps aside the cards I've dealt him. They scatter on the floor and then slide to the wall as the boat pitches. "Lucky, that is not what I asked you here for."

"I know that, Lionel." Poor guy. It must be a real blow to a man's ego to be turned down by Lucilla Wilta, washerwoman. I pick up the spilled cards and redeal. "Give me all your kings, Lionel."

He won't play. He sits sulking, looking out at the rain, a little humiliated, mostly annoyed. "Life isn't fair," he proclaims finally.

"No kidding." I have two pairs already, and if he would just take his turn I'd be on my way to a winning hand.

"Don't you ever wish you were born different, Lucky?"

"Every minute of every day. Pick up your cards, Lionel. Give me all your kings."

He turns back to the table and reluctantly picks up his cards. He raises one eyebrow, slightly interested. "A hundred a hand?"

"A hundred? Isn't that a little steep?"

"Seventy-five then." He's checking out his hand, glancing at me with furtive eyes.

"Ten maybe," I say.

"Ten? Hardly worth it." He places his cards face down on the table, a ceremonious gesture of refusal.

"Lionel, I'm just a poor waitress."

"Ha!" It's an exclamation of contempt. "I know how much you make, Lucky. Twenty."

"Fifteen," I say. "Final offer. Give me all your kings."

Rain splatters against the windows, creeping in here and there. He picks up his hand and tosses down a king. "If I looked like Charles, you wouldn't be making me play Fish right now," he says.

"If you looked like Charles, you'd have somebody besides Lucky Wilta on your leaky boat," I say.

We play in silence for a few minutes. I lay down a pair of jacks, four sevens, and a pair of threes. He plays two pairs, nines and tens.

"He's lost a lot of money, you know," Lionel says finally.

"Who?"

"Charles."

"Really?" I erase the look of concern that I know must have flashed across my face.

"He's lost quite a bit on some investments lately. His investment advisor isn't exactly a crook, but he's no Einstein either."

"Is that Keith?" I ask.

"I don't know any Keith. His name's Ferdy Wilson. Charles fired him."

"Give me all your fives," I say. "He's not broke, is he?" Broke - meaning no more salary for Lucky Wilta.

"Getting there. Sixes." I hand over a six. He lays it on the table, making a nice, neat row with all his other cards.

"Eights," I say. Lionel can probably guess that this is extremely bad news to me, but I compose my face into a mask of boredom, stretch my arms in a great big yawn, and lean back. The wall behind me is wet. Water soaks into my shirt, and I hunch forward again and shiver.

"Go fish," he says.

I do, and I draw an eight. "I win, Lionel," I tell him. "You owe me twenty bucks."

"We agreed on fifteen, Lucky."

"Fine," I say. Well, Sister, it was worth a try, wasn't it? If Smithson's millions are dissipating into thin air, I need to grab all the change I can. "Want to play again?" I ask Lionel.

I can still feel the cold, wet spot on my shirt from the dribble of water slipping down the wall behind me. "God, Lionel," I say, "this boat is a disaster."

"I know. I should really sell it. Mandi won't even speak to me anymore since I named it after her."

I can't help laughing. "You are so low."

"I fixed up the bedroom, but I never put any money into the rest of it, which is why it's falling apart."

"Well, why don't you? You have enough."

"I guess I like the look of surprise whenever I open the bedroom door."

"One day it will sink while you're in there."

Lionel grimaces, then shrugs. "That wouldn't be such a bad way to go."

I smile at him. "Should I deal again, Lionel?"

He thinks for a minute, then goes out to the upper deck. The rain is still coming down, sliding over the dull windows and in through the cracks. He pokes his head back in. "We'd better head back before the boat really does sink. Lucky?"

"What?"

"Do you think you could leave something? Maybe that barrette you have in your hair?" He disappears again.

Leave something? I can't help it; I have to laugh at Lionel. I think about it, then pull off one of my socks. Phew! Lionel's next guest won't know what hit her. The drawer of lipsticks is rattling with the motion of the yacht, but my dirty sock makes a nice, cushiony buffer in there.

I wonder about Charles losing money, though. That's something he didn't share with me, yet somehow Lionel knows. Lionel seems to know a lot about Charles that I don't. Trustful

Chuckles must confide in Lionel a lot more than he confides in me, not that I blame him, of course. I decide I'll give this more thought once I'm off this awful vessel and away from Lionel's curious eyes.

Mandi's Kiss. A disaster. A catastrophe. An insult.

Whoever Mandi is, I feel sorry for her.

◇◇◇

"How did you like Lionel's boat?" Smithson asks me with a superior smile.

"Loved it," I say, and I close the dialogue and concentrate on spooning chicken and vegetables onto Violet's plate.

He sits there digesting my answer, then snorts deep in his throat. Violet is pushing two fingers into her mound of mashed potatoes, and her father suddenly hollers at her. "Violet, stop that."

"But I'm trying to-"

"Stop playing with your food!" he repeats.

She keeps digging in. "You don't have to holler," she whines, "I'm making a-"

He jumps up and grabs her plate. "If you can't eat like a human being, then don't eat." The plate crashes into the sink and cracks, and Violet starts to sniffle. Pansy sits still, frightened. "Well, really," Charles says, glaring at me. "Their manners are atrocious."

"It's not worth breaking dishes over," I say.

"I'm not hungry," he mutters. He tosses his napkin on the table, stalks out of the room, and disappears. An untouched serving of chicken fricassee begins congealing on his plate.

A long round of golf does him good, and he comes back in a better frame of mind. I pity the golf ball. I'm feeling miffed that he ruined the nice dinner I made, and I decide not to tell him that I've saved his portion in the refrigerator. He finds it anyway, and I hear him in the kitchen clattering silverware and dishes while he reheats his food.

Mr. Moody. It sure is a pain to live with such a peevish, impossible man.

He brings his plate, a glass, and a bottle of wine into the living room, where I'm curled comfortably on the sofa with a dimestore detective novel I found in the library. I watch him eat and drink for a minute until he looks at me and catches my eye.

246

"The food's good," he says. "Sorry I stormed off before."

"Why did you?"

"Just a lot of things getting to me. Nothing in particular."

"You didn't say good night to your daughters. That wouldn't sit well with their grandparents."

He shrugs. "Well, I'm sure you did. It's just as well, anyway. I think I scared them. I feel bad about that. I'll talk to them tomorrow."

"You know, their table manners are actually not bad for a three and four year old. Dr. Harvard says-"

"Sometimes I get sick of Dr. Harvard."

"Oh? I wasn't aware you'd read him."

"I don't need to," he says. "You quote him constantly."

Touchy, touchy. It seems there is no safe topic this evening. He's determined to be fractious.

"Are you planning to drink that whole bottle of wine tonight?" I ask. "You don't drink that often."

He puts his fork down thoughtfully and looks at me. "Gee, Miss Wilta, Miss Todd, I didn't know you were keeping track." He leaves and returns with another wine glass, fills it, and hands it to me silently. I gaze around the room. No moonlight in here, and my host definitely isn't in the mood to caress my head on his soothing, comforting shoulder.

I guess I'm safe.

The wine is delicious, a lightly chilled sparkling burgundy the color of rubies.

"I didn't even know we had this," I say.

"Or you and Lionel surely would have polished it off."

I put my glass on the table and glare at him. "Not necessarily. If you resent a bottle of beer now and then, maybe you should say so."

"No, of course I don't," he says contritely.

I pick up my burgundy and sip.

Smithson chews his belated dinner for a few minutes, chasing it down with the wine, then asks in the pleasantest tone he can muster, "What did you really think of Lionel's boat?"

"I told you, it was fine."

"You thought it was fine?" He stops eating. "Did he show you all of it?"

"Every inch. I enjoyed myself completely."

"Hmph." That's what he really says. I don't know, maybe he has chicken fricassee stuck in his throat. Then, while he carefully studies a forkful of potatoes, he says, "Do you suppose you'll go with him again?" Sir Charles Fitzham Smithson the Subtle.

"I haven't been asked," I say. "I doubt I will be."

"Why's that?" He's waiting patiently for me to tell all.

Finally I give in. "We played Go Fish."

"The kids' card game?"

"I won fifteen dollars. It wasn't exactly what Lionel had in mind."

"No, I'd guess not." He takes my empty glass and refills it. Isn't he nice to reward me for my good behavior. "Well, that's good, Lucilla," he says slowly. "That was a good decision."

"It's such a relief to have your approval."

He glances at me, slightly annoyed, finishes his food, sets the plate on the coffee table, and leans back thoughtfully against the cushions of the old sofa. The light hits the polished tabletop, accenting the water rings made by Lionel's many glasses and beer bottles. Ah, memories.

I try to get back into my novel, but it's hard to concentrate with Good Time Charlie sitting silent and preoccupied beside me. I close my book and swirl the wine in my glass, making little bubbles pop on the surface. "Charles," I say at last, "are you running out of money?"

His eyebrows go up, and he gives me a curious look.

I start explaining. "You're not usually short-tempered with the girls. There's something on your mind, right?"

"I have a lot of things on my mind," he says. "I always do."

"Including financial troubles?"

There's a silence before he says, "Where did you get that idea?" He waits for me to answer, but I don't. Finally he says, "I wouldn't say I'm running out of money. But I can count it now."

I smile slightly. "So there's enough then."

He leans back more comfortably, sipping. "Enough for what, Lucilla?"

"Everything," I say vaguely. "That broken pipe Bob just repaired upstairs, the upkeep on the castle, new clothes for the girls, all your other expenses." I don't say 'my salary,' but I'm thinking it.

"There's always been plenty," he says. "I made a fortune by investing what my mother left me. I was lucky, and I had good advice. It seemed endless. Just spend, spend, fritter, and spend."

"And now? Not that it's my business . . . ."

His mouth is a straight line. "Well that's certainly never

stopped you before."

I persist. "So now there's a dent in it?"

"A dent, yes." He corks the bottle of wine and stands up with his plate and glass. "Guess what," he says from the doorway. "I got another hole in one tonight, the second in my life. I don't suppose I'll ever get another. And there wasn't anyone there to see it." He lifts his empty glass in a toast and heads for the kitchen. Well, I had wondered if he was any good at golf. Guess so.

If Smithson gets a hole in one, and there's no one there to see it, is he still a moody member of the upper crust? I uncork the bottle and pour myself another glass of wine, while I consider. I can't help wondering just how big the dent is.

He's back in the doorway, looking at me, and I do him the favor of looking up.

"Don't go back to that boat, Lucilla," he says. "He may ask you, and I'd recommend that you say no."

"I'm a big girl, Charles," I tell him.

He nods and looks sad, as if he knows it isn't his business anyway.

It isn't.

And I don't bother to elaborate. But, just for the record, Sister, I wouldn't revisit Mandi's Kiss for all the diamonds in the castle.

# 26

PANSY AND VIOLET and I spend our days hanging out together in the castle. We cook together, draw pictures, clean, scrub, and polish, and reward ourselves by taking picnics into the woods or driving into town for ice cream, or, on rainy days, smashing out rollicking jive on the out-of-tune piano.

I sift through the sheet music in the cupboard and come up with two or three that I think I can resurrect. The girls aren't too particular about rhythm or tone quality. They dance and sway happily, and we sing in loud, lusty voices.

Today I'm dust mopping the floor around the front staircase, and little tufts of gray-blue fuzz are flitting around my face. I don't remember ever cleaning this particular spot before, so I'm attacking those black and white marble squares vigorously and in earnest.

Pansy is lying on the floor nearby trying to sound out words in a picture book. She's not doing too badly either, has already pieced out CAT and RAT. Any moment now, she'll be trading in her Dr. Seuss for James Michener. It occurs to me that Charles could start her in kindergarten early, since she shows unusual promise, but he vetoes that. He wants to have her around a little longer, he says.

I've suggested that he could have the best of both worlds if he has her schooled at home. Not that I could do that, but somebody else could. I'm thinking back to my own public school days. I recall the long bus ride from the castle to school, from school back to the castle. The ride seemed interminable, and the days at school even worse.

I didn't have many friends, and no one ever seemed to have time to help me with homework. Nancy certainly did her best, but often I seemed to know more than she did. Our study sessions were clever mimes of real learning experiences.

When Jimmy started coming around, Nancy's face would flush and her eyes would grow brilliant. She would talk in excited tones the whole time he was visiting, then tug on the front of her sweater and watch from the front terrace until he was completely out of her sight before she returned to the castle to resume her chores. I wonder sometimes if Jimmy actually became a chef, a bumbling one I'm thinking, or if Nancy ended up writing greeting card taglines. Not likely. Maybe they found some even more zestful future. Anyway, I hope they are together polishing their stars. I know now that Nancy loved him. She wouldn't have left me otherwise.

I lean on my dust mop, thinking.

Was that why my life turned upside down? Maybe it had more to do with losing Nancy and my father than with losing the castle.

"Lucky, what's a P and a I and a G?" Pansy asks me now. She's pointing to the letters in her book with one pudgy finger.

"Pig," I tell her. "You don't know about short I's yet, Pansy. Just look for A words."

"Angel," says Violet. "Acorn. Ape. Ate."

"The ape ate the acorn," Pansy adds irrelevantly.

"Apes don't eat acorns," laughs Violet. "Do they, Lucky? Do apes eat acorns?" She's sitting on the banister straddling Marion, hanging onto his sharp mane and digging her heels into the newel post below.

"No idea," I tell her. And it happens to be the truth.

"Watch this, Lucky," she says, and I glance up to see her fling her arms wide and slip over sideways, just her bony knees keeping her from banging her head on the step below.

"Violet!" I drop the mop and rush over.

She doesn't need me. She rights herself and starts laughing again. "Watch, I'll do it one more time."

"No, you won't," I say. And I pull on her, trying to remove her from her perch. She tightens her legs around the post and digs in hard.

"Violet, let go. Get down from there," I say. "You'll get hurt fooling around like that."

"But I wanna stay with Marion," she whines.

"Fine, then," I tell her. "Stay with Marion, but no more stunts." I go back to my dust mop.

Pansy can't resist. She approaches her sister and grabs her left leg. "Yeah," she says. "No more stunts."

"Get away," Violet hollers. She kicks at Pansy and clutches Marion more fiercely. "Get away, Pansy!" she yells. She's grabbing poor Marion's mane savagely and jabbering at Pansy to leave her alone, and Pansy is chanting, "No more stunts, Violet!" in a bossy voice.

"Violet," I start, "quit being a pain in the neck. Pansy, come on-" but I never finish.

My eyes are widening in disbelief as I catch a motion out of the corner of my eye. I turn slightly to stare at the staircase in front of me. One of the steps has sprung open.

It's the sixth one from the bottom, at my eye level, but out of Pansy and Violet's view. They're still busy arguing. Pansy is pulling nastily on Violet's legs, and Violet is shrieking and kicking.

I eye the sixth step. I am not imagining this. The tread has lifted about two inches and sits there, inviting me to take a closer look.

"Okay," I say with sudden authority, "it's time to get down. Marion needs a rest." I summon up superhuman strength and lift a fighting Violet and a flailing Pansy from the stairs, and set them down in the doorway that leads to the back of the castle. "There are cookies on the kitchen counter," I say breathlessly. Can they hear my heart pounding in my throat? "You may each have three if you sit in chairs at the table, and if you promise not to fight." They begin to whirl away, but I catch the backs of their shirts and stop their progress. "You have to use napkins, and um . . . ." What other time-consuming requirements can I attach to an impromptu afternoon snack? "Take small bites. One bite at a time and chew it all up before the next one. And you have to promise to stay there until I call you." A very important if. "Do you understand?"

They do, I let go, and they race each other to the back of the house and disappear.

There must be a hidden latch, something in Marion's mane or on his face, and I almost can't decide what I want to do first. My time is limited; how long can it take to eat three cookies? Marion, I decide, will have to wait. I know my first priority must be to explore inside the sixth step.

I approach cautiously. I have a grave fear that the tread will suddenly slam down hard if I'm not careful. I kneel carefully on the third step and peek cautiously into that dark, mysterious space.

I can't see anything so I place my hands, ever so carefully, under the tread. I grasp firmly and I grit my teeth, more in fervent prayer than for strength. Gently, I pull up on the step.

It comes. It opens with a dry, creaking noise until it's almost straight up, and I look inside to see if the diamonds I never truly gave up on are here, rolling around brightly in this unexpected place.

They aren't, and I breathe out in disappointment, but also curiosity. For there inside the sixth step, nestled on a bed of thick brocaded fabric, lies a china teacup. And next to it sits a key.

It's a very small key, made of cheap brass, the kind of key that must be sold by the thousands for little girls' diaries or small keepsake boxes. In fact, it looks very much like a key I own, the pressed key to a jewelry case I use for hair clips and bobby pins.

I reach for it with shaking fingers and pick it up. It's lightweight and a bit tarnished. And I wonder how long it's been here and what it could open. It certainly isn't a door key; it's too small and too frivolous. But it's just the kind of key to unlock a treasure box filled with, say, a nice assortment of diamonds and emeralds.

My heart is beating fast. Somehow, sometime, this little key will lead me to my treasure. I'm sure of it.

The teacup is light and fragile in my hands, and I examine the design painted on it, swirls of soft, delicate purple flowers. The cup is rimmed in flaking gold. I set it down carefully.

Cautiously, I pick up the fragment of cloth and unfold it. The piece is about three feet long and a foot wide, folded under and around itself to make a good cushion for a wispy teacup and a tiny key. Black bears cavort on the fabric, and ferns and tiger lilies sway while deer drink from a pool of faded blue. And as I remove it from the step, I recognize it and look behind me. Yes, I'm holding the edge of the tapestry that hangs here in the foyer. I know that if I were to hold this remnant up against that tattered edge, I would have a completed picture.

There's nothing else in the compartment.

A nagging thought returns to me, and I feel that familiar anticipation as I cross the foyer to read Lewie Forsythe's poem again.

*Live with honor; refrain from lion.*
*The mane thing is to cease your sighin'.*
*If my orthography leaves you scowling,*
*Imagine my secretary weeping and howling.*

This little poem led to the secretary and to Marion, and

Marion led to this key and teacup. But there's more; there has to be more.

I return the piece of fabric, tucking it carefully along old folds. I memorize the design on the teacup and replace it inside the step.

But this little Woolworth key, I decide, will remain mine.

I find my handbag in the closet and drop the key into my shabby change purse, along with my nickels and pennies and a button from one of Violet's shirts. No one needs to know about it but me.

I close the step carefully and hear a tiny click when it becomes solid again. I go to Marion and feel carefully, all over his eyes and tongue and mane, until I recognize a tiny bubble in the wood. I press it carefully and nothing happens. I try it again. Two hard presses and the sixth step pops slightly open again.

I know that Violet has once again opened a secret space. But this time she will never know.

Whoever hid Marion in Borstrom's bedroom had a purpose after all - to prevent this puzzling little key from ever being found. Or maybe we were meant to find it.

What does it open?

Something small, I know.

I've been searching for a secret room. Well, maybe it's time to change my tactics. I think of all the old jars, bottles, boxes, and canisters in every room of the castle. Thousands of them, on tops of dressers, crammed on shelves, stuffed into closets and cupboards. I think of the many china receptacles, vases and little tubs, porcelain boxes, cups and dishes. Were any of them swirled with gentle purple flowers?

My snooping is about to begin again in earnest.

I close the step again and know that from now on, while Pansy and Violet sleep, I will revert to the old Lucky Wilta, Eager, Anxious, Greedy. I visualize myself casually handing a little box full of diamonds to Charles at lunch someday.

"Oh, yes, half of these are yours," I'll say.

"What?"

"For you. I found them in the secret room."

Chortling with glee, I go to the kitchen, where Violet has already fallen asleep at the table. Pansy looks up guiltily. There are a lot more than six cookies missing from the platter, and the remains of them are clinging to Pansy's damp chin.

"Violet didn't want hers-" she starts.

I pick up Violet and take Pansy's hand.

"Okay, my precious moon beetle, upstairs. It's time for naps."

"I'm getting too old for naps, Lucky," Pansy argues. "I'm not even tired."

I look at her. She's right. I've been here almost half a year, and a lot has changed. These girls are not babies anymore.

"Then get a broom," I tell her, "I'll take Violet up and then I'll teach you what we do here every day while the little ones sleep."

And while Pansy happily wields her uncooperative broom in the kitchen, I press the button on Marion's mane, watch the sixth step open, and then place my fingertips under the lip of every single stair tread. And I yank - hard. I'm not satisfied until I try all the steps, and I refuse to give up until I'm convinced that not one of them will yield to my feverish, prying hands.

# 27

WHEN EMILY SHOWS UP, her eyes are blazing. She slams her car door and marches to the front terrace where I'm trying to read in a well-worn hammock. I've never been able to get the hang of these things, and my legs are all twisted together while the canvas cloth wraps me up in a stifling cocoon. Emily stands staring while I turn upside down briefly, right myself, and finally manage to wriggle out of my bindings. "Hello, Emily," I say.

There is simply no time for courtesy. "Is Mr. Smithson at home?" she demands.

I hook a casual thumb toward the back. "On the rear terrace, I believe."

She stalks around the side of the building, and I follow at a little distance. He's back there with pieces of lawnmower motor scattered around him. His hands are greasy and he's sweating under the hot sun. The project isn't going well.

Poor Emily. I could have warned her that I myself bolted to the front of the house to escape the wrath of a man done in by his lawnmower. Well, she just didn't have time to listen.

"Charles!" Her first word is biting and sharp.

He looks up and stands hurriedly.

I stop along the side wall, just under the windows of the west bedrooms. I'll hear the girls if they need me, and I'm still in view of the exciting scene unfolding on the terrace. I pick up a pair of garden clippers left rusting in the grass and dash up the steps to the stone balcony overhanging the pavement below. I busy myself over a pot of long-dead geraniums the girls and I planted one day in a fit of summer.

She's chewing him out good. How could she possibly marry a man who didn't have even the common decency to explain his unacceptable behavior to her? Did he bother to read her note? Did he think she would devote her life to a man who lacked even the basic good breeding to answer it? She was only doing it for him, after all, blah, blah, blah.

She turns slightly and sees me there, eavesdropping. I peer under a yellowed leaf and snip at a stiff, brown flower.

"And her," she says, her voice lowered slightly. "Did you seriously take her to Maine for three days to watch the children?"

He nods. "It's hard for me to watch them myself-" he starts.

"Yes," she says in exasperation. "I have come to realize how very hard it is for you to keep track of things around here. Have you become blind suddenly? This home of yours looks worse than it ever did before, Charles, even after Mrs. Frocks left. Look around you!"

Obediently, he gazes up at the dirty windows and at me performing my useless chore on the balcony.

"What has she accomplished since she's been here, Charles?" Emily's voice is demanding, and he, of course, has no satisfactory answer.

A big pause descends, and then Emily checks her voice and becomes his soothing helpmate. "I've been removing things from the castle Charles, valuable things, trying to keep them safe." She steals another look at me and can't help herself; the temptation to speak her mind is just too enticing. She lowers her voice, but not enough, for I hear her say, ". . . safe from her grasping, little, low-class hands."

I'm surprised to hear him say, "Lucilla wouldn't steal," in a most sincere tone. How does he know that? Why would he even think it? Myself, I believe Emily has made a number of excellent points.

"Oh, really Charles, you are so naïve," she says now. "Why else is she here?" Her gestures are excited and perturbed. She flicks a hand to her perfect, shiny, black hair, jerks her head sideways, and tries another tack. Her voice is modulated now, an attempt to be reasonable. "Did it occur to you that I might be humiliated to hear that you took someone else on vacation to watch the children?"

"I'm sorry, Emily. You're absolutely right. I should have told you I was going."

Wrong answer. "Told me! Told me! No, Charles, you should not have gone in the first place! How do you suppose it looks . . . ."

Poor Charles. I can't help darting a sympathetic glance in his direction, he looks so guilty and uncomfortable.

"And this gallery reception," she's saying now. "Who were those people, Charles?"

"They were thinking of buying the castle," he begins.

Emily starts. "They were? Are they going to?"

"No, they-"

She shrugs off his explanations, impatient and annoyed. "If you had a buyer for the castle, why didn't I know about it?"

"They weren't serious about it, Emily, they were-"

She's practically screeching. "Then why did you go all that way to their gallery reception? *Without me!*" She lowers her voice again. Her eyes are bright, accusatory. She jams a thumb in my direction and seethes at him, "You took *her*, didn't you."

"It was just kind of a joke," he says lamely. Why doesn't he tell her about my valiant scheme not to sell the castle? How I screwed it all up, how I sabotaged the single most important thing, not counting keeping the girls breathing, that he's ever asked me to do?

I've stopped stabbing at dead flowers and am leaning against the balcony wall, listening carefully.

". . . just the kind of event I enjoy," she's wailing, "and you know that, Charles, but it never dawned on you that I might like to meet these new friends of yours? That I have a stake in selling this horrible old house, too? Am I supposed to simply swallow my pride and accept . . . ."

All he has to do is say he's sorry, beg her forgiveness. I can tell by the whimpering way she's going on that she's dying to forgive him.

His emotions are clear on his face; he feels wretched. I watch him listen to her intently for a moment, but he doesn't say anything. His shoulders hunch and he puts a guilty hand on her arm and turns her around, heading her back over the side lawn, towards the driveway. "You've been a good friend for a long time," I hear him say. "I hope I haven't destroyed that, Emily."

"All right, Charles," she says, her voice calmer, "we'll work this out; we'll-"

But he interrupts her. "We can't work it out, Emily. I tried, but I was wrong to think we could be more than friends."

She's struck dumb. She can't figure out what just happened. What does she do now? Begin begging him?

"I can't do it," he says simply.

"Charles," she says suddenly, staring at him, "I love you. Are you just going to throw that away?"

Charles looks taken aback. His eyes blink and his face turns pale. "What?" he says, "No, no you don't. That's not what we said."

"What we said has nothing to do with it," Emily replies. "Really, do you think I would have suggested we marry otherwise?"

He looks absolutely dumbfounded. "You were just doing me a favor," he says.

She twists away from him. "Well, there was a little more to it than that." She's angry again. "Why are men always so idiotic?"

This is something I have wondered myself from time to time. I realize that Emily Cheseworthy and I do have something in common after all.

Charles stares at her for a moment and then looks down at the sleeve he's been clutching. His face registers sudden horror as he sees the spot of grease he's left on her blouse, and his words trip all over themselves as he apologizes for ruining her clothes. He pulls a rag out of his back pocket, swipes ineffectually at the stain, and then wipes his hands on the rag. Emily watches, speechless.

He guides her back to the front of the castle. "Emily, I'm so sorry," he murmurs as they pass me. "I should have realized. I screwed up."

I can tell he feels bad about this. They've been friends since childhood, and he's hurt her. He glances up at me, maybe hoping for a cheery thumbs up, maybe wishing I'd mouth some magic words he could use to soothe her. He gets neither, just my dumb face staring back. I bury my face in weeds and clip rapidly.

Emily follows his glance, sees me hiding behind the geraniums and looks back at him. She remains silent, at a loss for words; the only sound is the snip-snipping of my garden clippers. Then, suddenly, her face collapses; her look turns from righteous and indignant to suddenly slack. When she speaks, the words come out slowly, like a revelation, and her voice is so low I can hardly make it out. "You have got to be kidding me."

She makes a motion toward her car, then I see her turn back to him. She musters up a last bit of dignity and says so quietly I can barely hear, "For God's sake, Charles, all you had to do was tell me."

"Emily, I'm sorry," he chokes out.

In nervous satisfaction, or maybe it's horror, or maybe relief, or maybe it's plain old shock, I lean against the pot of geraniums I've been massacring. There's not much left of the plant itself, but the clay pot slips off the edge of the wall and crashes on the untidy terrace below. Dry dirt scatters in lumps on the pavement. Charles and Emily both look back, she rolls her eyes at my incompetence this one last time, and I scoot down to make myself busy picking up the broken fragments.

I glance up in time to catch the sun glinting off the wheels of her Mercedes, bright orbs leaving the driveway of the castle, familiar wheels turning out of our lives for the last time.

I look around to see how Charles is reacting to the drama that just took place. He's gone. But I can hear him, out back, clanking lawnmower parts together in the searing afternoon sun.

◇◇◇

Do you want me to try to get your stuff back?" I ask Mr. Smithson later, as we stroll the grounds, skipping over bits of lawnmower strewn on the grass. The August sun feels warm on my face, and the woods look enticing, deep and cool. "I'm afraid she's a kleptomaniac," I continue. "It might have been very difficult to keep that out of the press."

"Lucilla, she took things to keep them away from you." He shakes his head slightly, as if this is the most ridiculous thing he's ever heard. "She wasn't really stealing."

"I could write up a list for you if you want."

He looks at me sideways. "That won't be necessary. She's welcome to whatever she took."

"I wonder if she really bought those ties she gave you. You may not be her only victim."

"How do you know about my ties?"

"I'm thick with your daughters. And all those dolls, Charles. You might have thousands of dollars worth of contraband in your house right this minute."

"I'm a coward," he says. His face is tied up in one of those self-deprecating knots that's become so familiar to me.

"What?"

"I should have called her or talked to her. She shouldn't have had to storm the castle like that."

"Emily kind of enjoys storming, though."

He chuckles a little. "I'm not sure she enjoyed it that much."

We can hear Pansy and Violet playing in the sandbox, some kind of complicated game that involves a lot of arguing over who had the last turn and who gets the next turn and whose turn it is right now. Lionel is with them, digging in the dirt with a big metal spoon and ordering the girls around like servants. He settles the argument about turns and sets about showing them how to run their cars on the ramp he's created down the side of the enclosure.

He might be a decent father someday, I think to myself. He only needs about twenty more years to grow up.

"This way," Charles says, and he steers me toward the woods. I follow along. The sun is climbing higher, and we're approaching noon. Soon, I'll need to bring the girls in for lunch. Or bring lunch out for the girls. Yes, that's a better idea.

"Doesn't this put you in a tight spot with your wife's family?" I ask him. "Wives are high on their priority list."

"I have time to come up with something else," he says. "As far as they're concerned, I'm engaged and we're waiting to sell the castle. They'll be at bay for a while."

"For a lifetime," I agree, glancing back at the wreck we call home.

"Oh, it will sell eventually." He shrugs. "Even if it doesn't, I can't keep living here. It's ridiculous to have all those rooms, and the repairs and upkeep cost a fortune. Besides, Pansy seems to have colds all the time."

"You could buy a new place," I say. "Something modern and cozy."

He inclines his head slightly, noncommittal. I wonder if he's heard me. "This place just eats money," he says.

I nod. "It's probably Bob's influence."

"I could just close it up, let it decay into one of those intriguing abandoned castles that teenagers go to for partying."

"Yes, the Adirondacks are just full of those."

I can tell he's not really listening to me. "Lucilla," he says suddenly, "there is something I'd like to show you." He glances back at the lawn, at the sandbox. Lionel is standing in the sand, waving his spoon at Violet, giving instructions. He isn't giving us a thought.

"Do you think they'll be okay with him?" I ask.

"Sure, they'll be fine."

"I know you've been friends a long time, but sometimes Lionel seems so . . . frivolous."

Charles looks blankly at me and stifles whatever remark he might have been thinking of saying.

I shrug. "Well, you know what Dr. Harvard says." I glance at him; his expression doesn't change. I've about given up on getting him to read Dr. Harvard.

"They'll be all right with Lionel," he assures me.

He turns around and yells to Lionel, letting him know we're going for a walk. Lionel waves us off with the back of his hand. He's engrossed in sandbox playtime.

"Where are we going?" I ask.

We trudge into the woods, out of earshot of the others, until little girls' excited voices give way to birdsong and the scampering of chipmunks. Quick, light breezes pull the August leaves. Our shoes crunch on dead leaves and needles as we walk, and Charles looks agitated, more agitated than any simple walk in the woods warrants. "You used to ask me where I went every day," he says now. "Do you still want to know?"

"You betchum."

He almost smiles. We cross a rutted road and pass a clearing of fruit trees. We disturb a family of field mice, who shoot off in all directions, and we keep on walking, further into the woods than I've ever gone.

The undergrowth is getting thicker, and the trees are tall. Sparse sunlight peeks through the gently moving top branches. He seems to know exactly where he's going, but as far as I can see, we aren't on any kind of path. I could never find my way back if I had to.

"Right over here," he says after a while and veers to the left.

I don't get it. "You spend your days in the woods?" I say. It would explain his muddy boots and the casual clothes he usually wears. But what could he do in here all day long?

"Not in the woods," he says. "In there." I look where he's gazing and see through the trees a little house sitting by itself in a clearing, drenched in sun. Pine needles and old leaves make a path to the door; ancient trees tower above and around. We walk closer, into the grassy clearing dotted with timothy and Queen Anne's lace. The house itself is clapboard painted white. Its shingled roof is pointed and sturdy, a brick chimney climbs one wall, and there are two windows above, on a second floor. It's quaint and small and tidy. It looks nothing like the castle. I love it.

"You spend your days here?" I ask. "Doing what?" I'm very confused. I can see liking to be here; it's peaceful and picturesque, but wouldn't a man go crazy just sitting in a little house in the woods day after day?

"Sit down here, Lucilla," he says, and he indicates a dry,

grassy place. We both sit, and I force myself to clamp my mouth shut. He will tell me what this is about when he's ready. "We're about two miles from the castle," he tells me. "Sometimes I walk, when the weather is nice. Other days I drive. There's a dirt road that loops around the property and comes out on the other side of those trees over there." He smiles. "I treated you to the long version."

"You own this," I say.

"It's a guest house or summer house. A lot of these old places have them. Or it might have been the gardener's cottage. I'm not really sure. I had it winterized, though. I thought I might move in here with the girls last year, then I decided to hire Mrs. Frocks instead."

"The girls have told me a little about Mrs. Frocks."

"She's nice enough, but too old and set in her ways to take care of my daughters. They needed someone livelier."

A nice way of putting it.

"They're really good kids," I say, and my sincere enthusiasm surprises even me.

He nods. "You've been an excellent influence." And believe it or not, he's serious. "I shouldn't have left them with Mrs. Frocks all those months," he says. "That was a mistake."

"We all make mistakes. Some of us make big ones. What did you do all that time in Europe?"

He glances at me, surprised. "How do you know I went back to Europe?"

I feel a little sheepish, but I've decided that from now on, Chuck F. Smithson gets only the truth from me. I'm sick of keeping track of circles of lies and half truths and fabrications. All the game-playing just gets unwieldy after a while. "Lionel told me," I say.

"My, you and Lionel certainly cover every topic, don't you?"

"You're not answering, Charles. What did you do?"

He shrugs. "Wandered around. I don't know what I was looking for."

I snort in suspicion, and he turns me to look him full in the face. "Why? What do you think I did, Lucilla? Had the Grand Tour to celebrate my wife's death and deception?"

"No, of course not," I stammer. "I didn't . . . I mean, I didn't think anything. I just wondered," I finish contritely.

"I wrote it all down," he says shortly. "That's what I did. I can't show it to you because I destroyed it. My symbolic destruction of a year's worth of rage and grief and guilt." He looks at me. No pretense. No pretending. "Any other questions?"

I shake my head. Only an idiot would ask him to relive that time. And anyway, it isn't my business.

To my surprise, he continues. "When I came back, I was appalled at how bad things were at the castle. Everything so run down. Then I realized I didn't even care. I didn't have the energy or interest to get things fixed. I just . . . escaped."

I can see agitation on his face. And sorrow. The look of a man who keeps losing things, letting them slip away. Poor Mr. Smithson.

"Don't look at me that way," he says. "I've seen you buried in books every chance you get."

"So? I like to read."

"You like to escape," he corrects me.

Escape? Is that what I've been doing?

"There's nothing wrong with it," he adds. "We all do it, right?"

He stands up and breathes in deeply, glancing up at the eaves of his summer house, taking in the general lines of the cottage. I'm surprised to see the distressed look drop away as he looks at the little house. It pleases him, I can tell.

A thought that has been burning in me suddenly makes its way to my tongue and trips right on out, thoughtlessly. Why do I do these things, Sister?

"Charles?"

"What?" He looks down at me where I'm still sitting on the grass.

"Emily would have forgiven you. She wanted to."

My words hang in the quiet for a few minutes. He's definitely heard me; he's staring right at me. Then he interrupts the silence by murmuring, "I know."

"Why did you let her leave then?"

He extends a hand to help me up, surprised and impatient. "You know why. Come on, are you ready?"

I am. I'm ready to find out what Charles Smithson does whenever he leaves the castle, and I'm ready to accept it, whatever it is.

We walk up the grassy path. He puts a key in the front lock, and I detect something in his eyes, in his movements. A tremble. A nervousness. It reminds me of that quick flicker of fear I saw the day I tried to follow him. But why? What could be in here?

The house is small and a little shabby, a living room, big kitchen and bathroom downstairs, two bedrooms and a tiny bath upstairs. It takes two minutes to see the whole thing. It's sparsely furnished and needs paint and new carpeting, but it isn't the furniture or decor that I'm looking at as he shows me through.

It's the paintings.

Hundreds of canvases lean against walls and hang wherever he could fit them. Tables are cluttered with brushes and tubes of paint, solvents, rags, and sketchbooks. The oily smells of paint and turpentine cut the air.

"Most of them aren't very good," he tells me. "Try not to be too critical."

He's wrong. I'm no art critic, as he well knows, but I can tell beauty when I see it. Believe me, I've lived without it long enough to know.

"I kind of like this one," he says, and props up a city street scene, hazy people gathering on corners, traffic lights. It's a night scene, pulsating with the energy of a city coming alive in darkness.

"It's beautiful," I say.

He grins at me. "No, not beautiful, but better than some of the others."

Pictures of deer in forests, ocean scenes, mountains sweeping up into crystal white peaks. Pictures of dunes and beaches, cafés and street markets, snapdragons bursting in shades of purple, pink, and yellow. Boats and lobster traps crowding a familiar coastal pier. Scenes of Paris, and of a tiny village poised on a hillside overlooking the sea. A record of places he's seen and imagined.

"You painted the pictures in the dining room," I say.

"Rose wanted to hang them there. She encouraged me a little. Tell the truth, Lucilla. Do you think any of these are any good?" He's watching my face intently and I realize - he's *afraid* of my reaction.

"I think . . . I think," I say. I can't even tell him what I think. So this explains his daily absences, his daughters' flair and creativity. His reticence to talk to a nosy stranger about his passion. "But you said you were a business major," I say. "I thought . . . ."

He shrugs. "I hated it."

We go up the stairs, and everywhere there are paintings. Years worth of sweat and talent, stored carefully in this place that no one ever comes to. "Don't you show these or sell them or something?" I ask him.

He laughs ruefully. "I've never needed the money, and I wouldn't handle the rejection very well, I'm afraid."

"But, Charles, you wouldn't be rejected. Other people can't do this. These are beautiful."

He shrugs. "It's kind of a useless talent."

"Who knows about this?" I ask him. "Your children? Or Emily?"

He shakes his head, frowning. "My wife knew," he says. "She would come down to see what I was working on. But she respected my privacy. She never even told her family." He smiles a little. "She did love me, you know, in spite of everything."

I don't respond. What can I say? For nineteen years, while I was creating a monster in my head, Charles Fitzham Smithson was making gentle pictures, hidden away in a house in the woods.

We're in the smaller of the two bedrooms upstairs, and he's showing me a picture of the castle, a good likeness, but with softer contours than it really has, a more balanced proportion than Marsuvius Borstrom ever imagined. "That isn't the castle," I say to him. "That's what you wish the castle looked like."

He laughs and replaces the canvas against the painted wall. I notice a picture hanging to my left, a pretty scene of a flower garden and two little girls with their faces upturned to the sun. They've been caught in the act of throwing daisies over their heads, and their laughter is almost audible.

"Charles, could we take this one home?" I ask him. "The girls should see this. They should know about all this."

"No," he says, and he's adamant. "I'm not ready for people to know about this. They'll start questioning me and showing up in little groups to show off. I don't need the criticism."

"But the girls-"

"The girls don't need to know everything."

I'm still looking at the painting, at the golden glow around the little heads, the laughing mouths opened to the summer air. Everything I love about his daughters is captured in this one picture.

Charles is watching me, and something in my face must make him change his mind. "Well, all right, I guess we could take just this one," he says finally. "Anonymously." He reaches behind and loosens the wire from a nail in the wall, and the nail falls to the floor. Light filters through the hole, and I squint, confused.

"Are these walls that thin?" I ask. "There's sunlight coming through here."

Charles chuckles. "No, that's not the outside wall. There's a little space back there. A sealed off secret room."

I'm staring at him, and I feel as if my heart is in my throat. "A secret room?"

"There's no big mystery, Lucilla. Someone partitioned off this area to make a small third bedroom, then eventually it got sealed over. It's hardly big enough for a single bed. Why are you staring like that?"

And the words come tumbling out. I tell him the whole thing, about my father's diary, and the mice, and my searches through the castle with Lionel. About Margaret's note to Clymna. About destroying closets and forcing doors. The moldy linens, the measuring, the pacing, the hoping. The diamonds of a thousand brilliant colors and the hidden treasure that must be *here*. "The *treasure,* Charles," I say, "There's a treasure behind that wall. Diamonds, maybe. I'm sure of it."

"Lucilla, your father was just being dramatic. There's nothing back there. I've been in there. In fact, I paint in there sometimes when I want a certain light."

"How? How could you get in there if it's sealed up?"

He takes my arm gently. "Someone cut a door." And he leads me into the tiny hallway, really just a narrow passageway between rooms. He pushes aside a tall, heavy wardrobe.

There *is* a door. So he really has been in the secret room, another thing of mine that he already possesses.

"And diamonds, too," he says with a small smile. "Lucilla, I'm sorry. If I had known you were looking for this . . . ." He opens the door and ushers me through.

I find myself standing in the secret room I've been searching for. The sun breaks into fragments, blues, greens, reds, yellows, all brilliant, all filtered through the window high up in the wall, the unique, exquisite, diamond-shaped stained glass window made up of dozens of tiny diamond-shaped panes. Each pane is a different color, the rich hues of the paint tubes scattered on the tables below. The colors stream in, rays of magenta, silver, indigo, and purple pulsating on the whitewashed walls. Pinks, golds, lavenders, blues, shivering slivers breaking apart and dancing like prisms.

*Diamonds of a thousand brilliant colors,* my father wrote.

And in my greed, I never knew he meant a window.

My heart sinks. The secret room is no big secret. There are no diamonds.

I look around. A sturdy table with a painting propped up on it, a few brushes and tubes of paint. A chair, rags, a lamp, a coffee mug. A couple of empty bottles stuck in the corner. Lots of sunshine. No little boxes, no mysterious containers begging to be unlocked with my small, secret, cheap metal key.

I feel like howling in disappointment. It only takes one glance to be sure; as far as treasure is concerned, the secret room is completely and enormously empty.

# 28

TWO DAYS LATER, I'm in the castle kitchen, beating chocolate cake batter within an inch of its life. I've tried hard to shove my sick disappointment over the secret room to the back of my mind. There's no point, absolutely no point, in feeling bad at the loss of something that was never mine to begin with.

I've asked Charles if he remembers any small locked boxes or other items that might have been in there. He told me no, he never took anything out of that space. There was nothing to take.

"Why, Lucilla?" he asked me. "What do you think should be there?"

I didn't bother to explain.

The cake batter is flying around the kitchen, and little chocolate dots are landing on the countertop, the wall, and the front of my shirt. I slam my wooden spoon down and lean over the countertop, propping myself with both hands. I take a deep breath.

I can hear Pansy and Violet in the foyer. I've been ignoring them all morning, and I know I have a job to do. I square my shoulders, swallow my sadness, stalk to the foyer, and smile brightly at Charles Smithson's kids. I peel Violet off Marion, where she has perched herself waiting for her shoes to be tied, and I reach for the laces.

I have things to get done. I can't wallow in misery even if my soul is screaming in pain so real that it hurts.

◇◇◇

The girls and I go into Tupper Lake to do a few errands, and we stop to chat with Bob about the bathtub faucet trickle that's becoming a thin stream. We pick up a large, economy size bottle of cough syrup on sale and some fresh raspberries for a pie, then check out the poster paints in the local craft shop. Dr. Harvard says paints are very good for kids.

Pansy asks if she can paint on the walls of the playroom, and

I don't object. Why would I? It's not my castle. It has taken me a while to admit this, but I'm coming to believe it's true. And I figure she's artistic, so where's the harm? She selects a big flat stone in the wall and splashes it with yellow paint, then dabs green polka dots on top of that. The polka dots become little turtles, and Pansy nods as she admires her work. Violet can't be left out, so she paints a rather lifelike rat and then, to our relief, cages it behind squiggly orange lines.

It looks like fun, and I could use some fun. I only hesitate for a minute before I pick up a paintbrush and carefully look over the wall, selecting a stone high up and almost out of reach. A crimson flower with a royal blue stem. Weird, but cheery. I choose another stone, lower down, and pause for a moment, thinking, then do my own unique rendition of a Maine sand castle. *I* can tell what it is. I'm not sure, however, that the general public would know.

I step back to admire our work. "What do you think?" I ask.

"It's beautiful," says Violet dreamily.

It's not, but we go ahead and color a few more stones. We can't make this room much uglier.

I wonder if their father will mind. He doesn't seem to, just looks at the wall, looks at his daughters, looks at me, and walks out again.

Lionel comes for dinner, and I look forward to having him around for the evening. I'll admit, I could use a little cheering up, and Lionel's goofy personality is bound to do a good job distracting me. He compliments me lavishly in French, or maybe it's Italian, and jumps up politely when Kitty shows up unexpectedly. They do a furtive dance around each other, and the next thing I know, they've left together. I watch them go down the porch steps, Kitty's short, swingy skirt swishing provocatively.

Lionel is tripping over his own feet in anticipation.

When I close the door and turn around, Charles is there and I almost bump into him. He meets my eyes and smirks at me. "Good old Lionel," he says.

Who cares.

I go up to my room and experiment with the cosmetics Violet and Pansy helped me pick out in town today. Pink Rose on my lips. Toasted Caramel on my eyelids. I tilt my head this way and that. Maybe I should get my hair cut some new, exciting way, or have it highlighted. Maybe I should have a face transplant.

I feel frustrated and unhappy, but I know Lionel Hawthorne is not the problem. I am the problem. I spend my days searching for riches that don't exist. I can't pass by a mirror without wishing I looked like Kitty Nellahopkiss. Or Emily Cheseworthy. Or a thousand other women I've passed by chance on the street or stood next to in the Post Office or handed my lettuce to at the grocer's cash register. Wishing I had grace and poise and something called class that keeps eluding me. Wishing I were someone else.

Anyone else.

I dust powder blush lightly over my cheeks, and then I pick up my hairbrush and give my long hair a few careful strokes. I tie it loosely in a frothy pink ribbon and head back downstairs.

His Grace is stretched out on the old sofa, the television remote extended in his hand. He's switching channels briskly, so fast he can't possibly know what he's seeing. He doesn't take his eyes from the screen. "I warned you about Lionel," he says. Images fly by. "He's not your type. And he'll never change. Are the girls asleep?"

"No, they're making a fort under your bed."

He sighs; it's like the good old days. "Lucilla, I told you I don't like them doing that."

I shrug, helpless. "Don't tell me; tell them."

Finally he looks at me. "Don't take it out on me if your feelings got hurt."

"By Lionel? Don't make me laugh."

He gets up and stomps upstairs. In a few minutes he's back, standing in the living room doorway, exasperated. "Why do you do that?"

"Do what?" My eyes are glued to the television. There's a game show on, and I'm really eager to see which prize the contestant picks. Will it be the cruise? The car? The matching luggage?

"They're sound asleep," he says. "There's no fort."

"Oh, I was jest joken widja."

He rolls his eyes and goes up to bed.

He didn't even notice how enticing I look.

# 29

SEPTEMBER ARRIVES, and with it a cold snap that sends me burrowing through closets for warm sweaters for Pansy and Violet. I'm awakened early one morning by a frightening, violent howl, and I fling on my robe and race to the kitchen to find Charles doubled over against the counter, snorting with laughter. His hands are dirty and there's a streak of grease across his face. The persistent banging almost drowns out his words.

"I turned the furnace on," he shouts, grinning crazily. "I'll give Bob a call." He walks out of the room, shaking his head, smiling like a madman.

It isn't until later that I find the painted stone, almost at eye level in the playroom. It's surrounded by the bright orange, red, blue, and green stones the girls and I painted, the sand castle, the caged rat, and Pansy's eerie, futuristic bottle of cough medicine. I smile when I see it, a perfect likeness of Bob Cobb, his worried forehead wrinkled into confusion, his sincere eyes begging for work, begging.

Everybody likes to paint the castle.

Our tree fort is coming along great. The girls and I have decided to add a balcony and a tower, and there's a lot of disagreement about the length of the balcony and the height of the tower. I win because I'm biggest. We spend a lot of time lying on the floor drawing up complicated plans and sketches. The actual physical work may start any day now. If we plan well, we might be able to put it off 'til spring.

Now that I've found the secret room, my days are long and useful. I have lots of time to cook great suppers, and I do. I make stuffed peppers one night, and rigatoni with meatballs the next. We have some pretty fancy omelets and one Sunday a whole turkey with all the trimmings. Everybody eats everything. This family excels at eating.

I still search for the little lock that fits my little key and for china with painted purple flowers, but my quest entails picking through all the items in the castle, one by one, a tedious and boring job. So far, I've gleaned only disappointment, but I keep plugging away. *All* my dreams can't fade into nothing.

One day I decide to polish all the silver plated trays and candlesticks and condiment dishes, and I collect them in front of the big spotted mirror over the dining room buffet and light it with a dozen candles. Charles' eyebrows go up when he sees the display, and the girls ooh and ah. We eat dinner that night on the finest Borstrom china, with twelve candles glinting.

I've finally chosen just the right spot for the painting of Pansy and Violet. It's in a place of honor in the living room, over a nice old walnut table, and they squeal with delight when they see it. "Somebody took our picture," says Pansy.

"No, somebody painted that picture," I tell them. "It almost looks like you two, doesn't it?" They're very impressed.

Charles comes in the back door for dinner, tracking dirt to the sink where I'm cutting and peeling vegetables. He waits patiently for a spot at the sink and laughs when I put a tomato and a serrated knife into his hands.

"I pay good money not to do this," he says, handing them back. I can see traces of blue paint on his hands. He has been in the guest house, where he has always been. While I searched deliriously for my diamonds, he took them for granted, worked in their brilliant light, and enjoyed their vibrant colors, never realizing what a fool he hired for a housekeeper.

I sigh and step aside so he can wash his hands before he goes upstairs to change.

"Why so glum, chum?" he says. He looks at me expectantly, hoping I'll laugh.

I wouldn't give him the satisfaction. *I'm* the one who says irritating things when other people are feeling low. I ignore him and sweep into the dining room with a bowl of baked beans.

Lionel comes by after dinner, and the girls can't wait to show him the new picture.

"Did you do this, Lucky?" he asks.

"You know I don't have any talents, Lionel. Charles brought it home." Home from the little house in the woods, from right outside the secret room that I never bothered to tell Lionel about. Well, why should I? How can I, without telling about the paintings and breaking Charles' trust in me? Lionel is right; things certainly have changed in the Smithson household.

"What do you think of it?" I ask.

"I can see why he bought it; it could be Pansy and Violet. Or did he have it commissioned? The kids must be pleased."

"But do you like the painting, Lionel? Do you think it's good?"

He's looking at me through suspicious, slitted eyes. "You did it, didn't you," he accuses me.

"No," I scoff. "I just wondered if you think it's good."

He gazes at it for a few minutes. "I think it's great, but what do I know?"

"Would you pay money for it?"

"Are you selling it?"

"No, of course not. It's not mine to sell."

He settles down on the bumpy sofa and watches me straighten the painting. I step back to see it more clearly. Maybe when I leave, Charles would give me one of his pictures. I would pick the one of the pier in Maine. Would I have the guts to ask him? As a token of friendship, symbol of an absence of malice.

I'm not sure when the thought of leaving first came to me, and it doesn't make me feel good, but the more I think it over, the surer I am that it's where I'm headed. My reasons for working here were stupid, greedy, and dishonest, and I can't stay on indefinitely. My year is half over, I feel like a cheat, and who knows if Charles might be having second thoughts about the extravagant salary I humbly collect every week? I do have some pride. Why wait around to see him legally hooked up with the next Emily Cheseworthy? I might stay just long enough to see the girls safely into kindergarten. Or maybe I'll split before then. I'll let the circumstances dictate the time.

Who could have guessed that the secret room would be just one more empty space after so many empty spaces, that the hidden place under the sixth step would offer nothing but a cheap, worthless key, a faded teacup. What I expected, of course, was real, glittering diamonds that I could run through my fingers like beach sand. Or money. Moolah. Greenbacks that I could share with The Honorable Charles Fitzham Smithson the Second. To show my True Colors.

Who am I kidding? Even if there had been a treasure, it was his to share, not mine. It takes guts for me to admit I've been stumbling around in a fantasy world.

Okay, I admit it, Sister. Another first for Lucky T. Wilta.

Lionel is still leaning back on the velvet sofa, settled comfortably with his after dinner drink, something brown and fizzing in a tall glass. "You know what, Lucky?" he's saying, "In some ways I envy Charles."

"Really, Lionel?" This surprises me. Lionel of the many acres, the log cabin, the BMW, the plethora of leisure time, and a long string of willing women is jealous of a lonely widower who lives in a leaky, run-down house that he can't get rid of.

"It's his daughters, I think," he says thoughtfully. "I hope I have children someday."

I smile at him. "You will," I say. "Cute ones, too. With row upon row of little teeth."

He grins. "I could offer a lot to a wife. She'd never lack for anything. And I'd stop running around, too, if I had the right woman. Someone steady and trustworthy, someone who's not afraid to have fun, but intelligent, too. Not like Kitty or the others. Someone I'd want to come home to."

"You'll find her, Lionel."

"I have found her." Something in his tone of voice makes me take notice, and I look at him, startled. He reaches up a hand and pulls me down beside him. His elf eyes gaze into mine. "I want you to move in with me, Lucky. I'm not talking about a romp on the boat; I mean permanently. I think we would be great together. We could even get married if you want."

"Lionel," I say. I'm flabbergasted. This is not something I expected, and I try to laugh it off. "I told you no before, remember?" I grin at him and twist out of his arms. "I even hurled my beer at you to christen the decision." Marry him! This crazy, childish excuse for a man? How could I marry someone who's content to play in the sandbox for hours on end?

"I mean it this time, Lucky. I'm not just fooling around. And I'm sober."

"And I'm the Queen of Sheba," I say. "And I'm not really ugly, right?"

"Did I say that?" He looks embarrassed.

"You say all kinds of obnoxious things." I hit him over the head with a cushion. "You're just seeing me with new interest because I wouldn't sleep with you on the boat. You're looking for a name for your next vessel. Lucky's Lunacy."

"Lucky, you're not taking me seriously." I look into his eyes and am shocked to see real sincerity there. Lionel isn't kidding. "Think of all I could offer you," he says. "This game you're playing isn't going to last forever, you know. Maybe you'll never find your diamond haul. Maybe it never existed. Or maybe Charles has already found it."

I stare at him. I've thought of this before, of course. Would Chuckles toss me the pretty colored window as a red herring?

I dismiss this thought. If Charles had found my diamonds, he would have said so. If I know anything, I know the kind of man he is.

At least, I think I do.

"And as for Charles," Lionel says quietly, "if you're thinking about him, he's not-"

"Thinking about Charles!" I say. "Don't be a moron, Lionel. He's just my employer."

He nods. "And losing money fast. Don't forget that. Honey, it'll be a miracle if Charles can even afford to keep you on for the full year." Lionel finds my hand and holds it, caressing my fingers with his own. "So what happens after your contract expires, Lucky? You go back to waitressing?"

I gulp. "I'll have more money by then. I'm saving up."

"For what?" He laughs. "A bigger room, a fancier refrigerator in the corner? Lucky, I can give you a hundred rooms and anything else you want. At my house, you won't have to sneak around looking for some hidden treasure so you can buy yourself new hair clips-"

"Lionel, you're being ridiculous. You don't love me."

"No." He pulls me gently to him again. "But I like you; I have fun with you. And I'll learn to love you. I'm sick of my life, Lucky. I want what other men have. You might even love me after a while. I do have some endearing traits."

I can't help laughing. Lionel playing Simon Says with the girls on the lawn, racing toy cars in the sandbox, his head poked into the refrigerator to root out yet another drink. That grin he has that says, 'Forgive me, I'm just wacky Lionel Hawthorne. I don't take myself very seriously, so why should you?'

"I want children, Lucky, and a companion. Someone I can trust when the chips are down."

"When you're down, you mean, on the floor, passed out."

"Someone who'll pick me up and fling me into bed."

"Lionel-" I don't get to finish because he plants his lips on mine and kisses me. It's a friendly kiss, not unpleasant, and to my surprise, I like it. Before I know what I'm doing, I'm kissing him back, and we're both giggling, kissing there on the lumpy sofa, and he's saying, "Don't answer right now. But think about it."

I do like Lionel, and he makes me laugh. Is that enough to

base a lifetime on? "Okay," I finally give in, "I'll think about it. It'll be fun to think about it."

So I think about it, Sister. After he drives off, I go up to my room and try to crank open one of the windows, but the thing is so rusty it won't budge. So I peer through wavy, distorted glass at the moonlight and the stars and the silver leaves starting to swirl down from the trees.

Is this the star I've been searching for?

Marry Lionel. He's proposed twice, and the first time was a humiliating mockery. He was drunk, and when he's drunk, he's not very nice. Maybe if I moved in with him, he would stop drinking, settle into a happy home life with me and the girls . . . .

Wait a minute, the girls don't have anything to do with this. I won't be responsible for them once I marry Lionel. No, *if* I marry Lionel.

I think he's sincere, but does he realize what he's offering? To spend his whole life with me, even if someone more appealing comes along, as she surely will. To share everything with me. This is worth thinking about. In Lionel's case, everything is quite a lot. His stuff is actually his best attribute.

I'd never have to scrub and polish, or sweat over steamy ironing. I could cook when and if I feel like it and spend my days trying out new makeover techniques. Be realistic, I tell myself. I'd probably spend my days plotting ways to keep Lionel faithful.

Maybe I wouldn't care if he was unfaithful. It's not as though I love him. Maybe all that money would more than make up for . . . .

I get up from the window seat and walk over to the rippled mirror hanging above my dresser. Take a good look at yourself, Miss Wilta, I tell myself. You are seriously contemplating moving in with, even marrying, a man you don't love.

For money.

You are adding up all his financial assets and liking what you see. You are about to commit yourself to a phony union based on greed. You are a gold digger.

Haven't you learned anything living in the castle all these months?

My sharp little chin is beginning to quiver, and I stand there staring at the weak-willed person for whom money is life's most important love.

I *have* learned something, and it has nothing to do with Lionel Hawthorne. What a fool I am. I've spent all this time falling for the wrong guy. And it frightens me. And I know I have to get out.

It's time to move on. The secret room has turned out to be a stale joke, and the little key a cheap, sideshow gyp. Time I packed my duds and took a cruisin'. I ain't needed. Chuck can find someone else for Pilot and Vansy to abuse.

When the castle sells, he'll send me my half of the money. When Christmas rolls around, I'll Federal Express some decent ornaments for their tree. We'll all part friends.

I swipe at the ugly tears forming in my eyes.

Shore thing. This li'l adventure is over.

◇◇◇

When Michelangelo passes my room on his way to breakfast, he takes one look in and stops in his tracks. He stares at my empty suitcases.

"Lucilla, what are these things all over your floor and dressers?"

"My stuff. You know- clothes, hairspray, my electric toothbrush."

"I don't understand."

"Don't worry, Chaz. I'd never take anything that didn't belong to me. I'm no Emily Cheseworthy."

"Are you going somewhere?"

"Yessiree Bob, I am." I pick up a suitcase and start stuffing things in. It's amazing how much one accumulates in a period of just a few months. It's true what they say, I guess. If you have a small space, you crowd it up. If you have a big space, you crowd it up crowdeder.

"Wait a minute, Lucilla. Where are you going, and why? Do the girls know?"

"Not yet. You don't think I'd leave without saying good-bye to them, do you?"

"How long will you be gone?" He sounds bewildered.

"My life, no more, no less." What did I do with that new curling iron I bought last week? It works great. In a matter of seconds, I can create tight ringlets or loose, sexy waves. It's easy to control and gives super results. I start yanking out dresser drawers.

"Lucilla!" he says, a trifle impatient. "Stop packing things and talk to me! What is this about? Is this . . ." He pauses and an

278

incredulous look passes over his face. "Is this because of the business about the diamonds?"

"Don't be a fool," I mutter.

"Is it?" He's getting angry. "The big treasure you destroyed my home for didn't materialize, so you're leaving?" His eyes are black clouds.

"No!" I shout indignantly. "It has nothing to do with that!"

"Then what? Did someone do something or say something? Did I do something?"

"No," I say with a sick grin, "Lionel did. He asked me to move in with him last night. To marry him, even." Even as I say it aloud, I know how ridiculous the whole idea is.

"Lionel! And you're going with him? Now?" His voice is almost screechy.

"Of course not."

He looks relieved. "Lionel," he scoffs. "That doesn't mean anything."

Right, nobody could seriously propose to Lucilla Todd Wilta. I look at him belligerently. Pompous fool. "It sounded pretty sincere to me."

"Well, you told him no, didn't you?"

"I told him I'd think about it."

"What!" He laughs, one of those unbelieving laughs.

"You heard me, Sir Galahad. I told him maybe."

There's a large quiet moment while I continue zipping sweaters into duffel bags. Boy, I sure have bought a lot of useless junk lately. Give a girl a little dough, and she goes store-crazy. A regular mall maven. Bargain Basement Floozie. Shop 'til you Drop.

Charles is still watching me pack, and then he says calmly, "That doesn't explain why you're leaving or where you're going. You're not going to him, are you?"

"Core Snot." It was fun to say that. He doesn't even get it.

"I see," he says. "You're running away because you don't know how to tell him no. He's made you feel awkward." He makes his voice soothing. "Well, don't go. It isn't necessary. Just tell him you're not interested. With someone like Lionel, you have to be blunt." He picks up one of my bags and starts retrieving my clothes, stacking them in drawers and hanging them in the closet. "There's no reason to run off," he says, unpacking me efficiently. "In two days, Lionel won't even care anymore."

"Gee, thanks. That makes me feel special." I empty the drawer he has just filled and slip the jeans back into the suitcase.

"Lucilla! Stop this!"

I don't.

He stalks to me and grabs my arm roughly, turning me to look at him. "Stop," he says, and then more gently, "Stop packing. There is no reason on earth for you to leave here."

"Yes, there is," I tell him. I try to be glib, but it doesn't come out that way. I sound like one of his own whiny brats, about to cry for no reason. "I have to leave. I'm afraid if I stay, I'll say yes."

He lets my arm go and stares at me. "You'd marry Lionel? You don't love him, do you?"

"Sometimes people get married for other reasons."

He's just staring.

"Charles," I say bluntly, "look at me. Closely. Would you say I have a lot of other prospects?"

He looks away from my face and glances over the array of clothing and personal items strewn about my bed. "You are ridiculous," he says. "You have always been ridiculous, and this is the most ridiculous thing yet. Put these things away," he tells me. "The girls are expecting to go to the public library this morning. I'll start breakfast and see you downstairs in ten minutes."

Oh no, he won't. He will not see me downstairs in ten minutes or in any minutes.

Ridiculous, am I?

Angrily, I stuff the remaining things into suitcases, and then I pick up two of them, and I march downstairs with my nose in the air, a furious coldness in my eyes. I can hear one of the girls coughing in the next room, Pansy, I'm sure, and I curse this wretched castle that makes her sniffle all the time, and its pompous, egotistical owner who thinks he can dictate my every move. I stand in the downstairs hall and call a cab, not caring who hears me or whether or not it hurts them.

The cab arrives, and I throw my bags into the back. I start upstairs to get two more, and then, I don't. I'm so angry that I get into the cab and order it far, far away from the castle. *His* stupid castle.

I leave the rest of my bags piled up on the bed. I'll get them some other time if I think of it. Or maybe I won't even bother. Who needs all that junk anyway? Who needs any of it?

Not me. I'm Lucky Wilta. I don't need anything or anybody.

And I certainly don't need him.

I get bored with Kitty Nellahopkiss at Chez Fred's, and I like her even less in her tiny upper flat on Division Street. But I can't complain too much since she took me in yesterday when I had nowhere else to go. It wasn't hard to convince her. I wrote her a check for a whole month's rent ahead, just until I can get settled somewhere.

She's at work now, and I'm lounging on my rigged cot, staring at the cloudy ceiling. It's sure not like the castle. It's drier, for one thing, and warmer and a lot cleaner. And the walls are straight, too. I force myself to get out of bed, take a shower, and get dressed. I find a stale bagel and make some instant coffee, and then I spread out the flyer from the local community college.

Now, some of these courses sound interesting. This one, for instance: *Theory of Internal Combustion: Investigate the basic principles of internal combustion engines, study noise identification . . . .*

Hmm. Maybe something else would be more my cup of tea. *Embalming and Aseptic Techniques. Hydraulics. Sewage Treatment.* Ah, here's one that's right up my alley: *Advanced Juvenile Delinquency.*

I flip back to the first page of the flyer. Wow. Hundreds of dollars for just one course. The price sure has jumped since I was in school. You'd have to sell your castle for a very big profit to afford this. Maybe I can become a juvenile delinquent on my own.

I stuff the flyer into Kitty's overflowing magazine rack and heat water for a second cup of coffee.

One of my first orders of business this morning is to get in touch with Lionel Hawthorne. The Big Decision is whether to call or text, and I spend quite a bit of time weighing the pros and cons of each. Finally, I decide to text, and, yes, Sister, I know this is the ultimate of tawdry in romance etiquette. I refuse him, of course. Me, Lucky Wilta, being choosy. Anyway, I don't want kids with corn kernel teeth. It's a rule of mine.

Kitty can't believe I'd turn down Lionel. She remembers the good old days when he'd come into Chez Fred's and moon over her eggplant parmesan, when he gazed into her eyes at the castle and lost, she thought, his heart, when he sent roses to her at the restaurant, and Ancient Ella dumped them out and took the vase home. Those were the days, my friend. If only Lionel had proposed to Kitty. We'd have zippy, energetic Hawthornes, springing up like rabbits, populating the countryside.

I put the finishing touches on my text message, hit send, and fritter away the rest of my day. Eventually, I do take a taxi to the college campus, just to look around and see what's cooking. After my brief stint living in the lap of luxury, going back to waitressing doesn't feel like much of an option.

I look around at the impressive academic buildings and note the students scurrying to class. Yes, I might like to be part of this again. I thought I would look like the old woman in the shoe, but I don't. There are a lot of students with gray hair and hearing aids. Or no hair and midriff bulge. It makes me feel young again.

I wish I had been more successful the first time I tried getting educated. My failure was disappointing, especially to my mother, even though I went to classes, mostly, and I liked learning. It was fun to find out that *The Raven* only earned Edgar Allen Poe about ten dollars, and that one of the stars in the Big Dipper is actually two stars, and that Paul Revere had sixteen children. Not that anyone would be impressed by my knowledge of these useless facts.

Before she died, my mother made sure to tell me I wouldn't amount to anything unless I mended my ways, and I'm pretty sure she was right. Unfortunately, she never told me which ways I was supposed to mend.

It was hard to predict my mother. Nice to me one minute, jealous of my happy rapport with my father the next. Sometimes I think she even tried to drive a wedge between us.

It didn't work, though. Daddy was my anchor 'til the last.

I glance at my watch, a gold Rolex I bought with a couple of my early Smithson paychecks. Well, sure, it was pre-owned, Sister, but it's still ritzy and really shiny.

I see that it's going on three o'clock, and I know Kitty's shift is winding down. I might as well go back to the flat and find out how her day was. I'll be glad to cook her dinner, and she can let me know if my mug is still there. I hope I'm not in for a scuffle with Mack with the Beans in his hat. That guy was always trying to use my mug.

The taxi ride is quick, and I'm at the flat in no time. The door to the living room is unlocked, so Kitty must be home.

Oh, is she ever.

She's gushing and exclaiming, and primping in front of the mirror. She looks excited and distracted. And I see why. Turning slowly to face me, one hand stuck leisurely in the pocket of his khaki pants, is My Boss, The Honorable Sir Charles Fitzham Smithson the Second. Boy, does he look good. No wonder Kitty is flitting around the room, unable to contain herself.

I remain cool.

"Hi, Chuck," I say.

"Lucilla, will you please get your things?" he says. "My car is blocking the driveway to the bait shop next door."

"Nosiree Bob. I'm not going."

He crosses his arms over his chest and looks at me. "We have a contract. It doesn't expire for several months. At that time, you can do whatever you choose."

"The contract is null and void," I tell him. "I misrepresented myself. My signature's not worth the ink I wrote it with."

He just stands there, mulling over how to respond.

"And besides," I sneer, "I'm not sure you'll be able to come through with the rest of the cash anyway." God, what a low blow. He's right about me. I choose to be undignified. To be less than I am. To be cruel, classless.

It's quiet for a minute, except for Kitty's excited, ragged breathing. "He came to Fred's," she's telling me nervously. "He wanted to know where you were . . . ."

Smithson stands there; I stand here. Nobody moves.

He's talking to Kitty, but he's glaring at me. "Kitty, apparently there's an opening in my household after all. But I would need you to come immediately. The pay is more than generous, as Miss Wilta can tell you. Tell her how much you earn, Lucilla."

I swallow. This is some kind of trick, but he can't ruffle me. I tell her.

Kitty's eyes go wide and she flees to the bedroom to pack a few things. Charles' eyes haven't left my face.

"Wait a minute," I say. "She doesn't realize what she's getting into. Kitty!" She appears in the bedroom doorway. "You can't do this, Kitty. He hasn't been honest with you. You'll work twenty-four hours a day, all the cooking and cleaning, which you hate, and taking care of his two kids. You'll run the whole household. And if he says so, you'll even have to give up your days off . . . ."

"It sounds fine to me," Kitty says.

"And he'll never thank you," I say. "You'll never know whether he's happy with your work or not." I stare at him. "His kids might love you, but that won't even matter. Because he'll never tell you that he appreciates it."

"Of course I appreciate it," Charles says. "I should think that would be obvious."

Kitty is getting confused now. "I'll go pack my things," she says.

"No," I tell him. "You never tell me. And I try to make everything the way you want it. Especially since the Garloffs. I've tried so hard, Charles." Where are all these wimpy words coming from? I didn't intend to say any of them.

"I know that," he's saying. "Don't I say it?"

Kitty appears with an overnight bag, her coat slung over her arm. "All set!" she says brightly.

No one is paying any attention to her.

"You never say it," I tell him.

"Well I'm saying it now. Come back. Please." There's a little silence in the room while he watches my face to see what I'll do, and I watch his, begging him with my eyes to say more.

He doesn't.

"Kitty," I finally say, "he's right. I can't just walk out on a contract."

"That's not fair," Kitty starts.

"I'm sorry," Charles says to her. "My offer was premature. I guess the position's filled. How many bags do you have, Lucilla?"

I'm already grabbing up my suitcase from the living room corner where I shoved it last night. I hand it to Charles, then go into Kitty's bedroom and jab my belongings back into the bag in there. In two minutes, I'm ready.

"Well, let's go," I say belligerently. "What's everybody looking at?"

Charles holds the door and apologizes to Kitty once more, and I even remember to thank her for the overnight before the door slams behind us. Hell, she should be thanking me. I paid her a whole month's rent.

"Honestly, Lucilla, you-" begins Smithson as we head down the dreary stairway.

"No," I tell him. "Don't say anything." Final. Finished. "Forget it."

We throw the bags into his crookedly-parked car and he drives off. Back to the castle, the giddy eyesore that I embrace in my mind long before we arrive. My heart sings. My eyes tear up. Relief explodes inside me as I gaze out the window.

Whatever would I have done if he hadn't come after me?

# 30

A FEW DAYS LATER, I'm whistling as I stir pancake batter, keeping a careful ear tuned to the sounds of little girls playing Frisbee in the foyer beyond. Something crashes, and I stalk through the doorway to see Pansy bending over a smashed lamp, gingerly picking up glass fragments. She sees me and sneaks her hands behind her back.

"Into the trash," I tell her, holding out a wastebasket. Guiltily, she drops the glass shards in. "That, too," I tell her. Reluctantly, she lets the Frisbee go as well. Violet scrambles down from the chair she's standing on, looking as guilty as Pansy. "I told you guys not to do that in here," I remind them, "and especially not to touch broken glass. If you break something, leave it there and tell me." I check Pansy's hands for cuts, sweep up the splinters and send the girls to the music room to pound out some favorite tunes on the old piano.

When Charles comes in at lunchtime, he's carrying a big, square cardboard carton. He sets it down in the middle of the kitchen floor and goes out again, returning with another much longer, thinner box. I have to keep stepping over them to get lunch ready. "My, how inconvenient," I mention.

"I'll move them in a minute," he says. "Just don't touch them." He's sitting on the floor with his face buried in a lot of papers, and although I'm curious, I'm not going to ask. Finally, he looks up. "Do you know what's in these?" he asks.

"Diamonds?"

He grins. "A telescope. I'm going to set it up in the back yard, and teach the girls about the stars and planets. I think they'll like that, don't you?" He moves the bigger carton against the wall and begins slitting packing tape. Gently, he lifts out several big metallic pieces and shows me how they all fit together. Eureka. A pedestal. The second carton holds a big, round tube, four or five feet long. He fits this onto the pedestal and begins a lesson, right here and now, on Sky Patterns: Finding the Planets and Recognizing Constellations.

My Very Excellent Mother Just Slurped Up Nine Pineapples. Mars, or is it Mercury? Venus, Earth . . . .

We eat lunch with an accusatory telescope eyeing our every move.

"May I leave this here this afternoon?" he asks me. "Will it be in your way?" He seems to have forgotten whose house this is. He grabs his jacket from the closet next to the back door and I watch him striding off through the woods.

I trundle an overloaded basket of wash into the laundry room and drop it with a nasty thud on the hard stone floor, turn my back on the door, and start removing the last load of wet jeans and towels from the washing machine. I can hear the piano and those sweet, lusty voices singing a few rooms away, and then I gasp and jump involuntarily as a voice says, "I got your text."

What is Lionel doing here? He's lucky I don't wrap Chuck Smithson's damp jeans around his neck and strangle him for startling me like that.

"For Pete's sake, Lionel," I breathe. "Give a person a little warning when you do that." I lean back against the washer, my heart throbbing. "How did you get in here anyway?"

"The same way I always do," he answers easily.

"And what way is that, Lionel?" I ask. "You're always skulking around the castle. Do you sneak in through a broken window or something?"

He laughs happily. "Of course not, Lucky. I have a key."

"Charles gave you a key to the castle?" It must have been a long time ago. I don't think he would have done that since the Mandi's Kiss adventure.

Lionel grins serenely. "No, not Charles."

I'm fighting with a lint trap while we're talking, and it sure is frustrating. I'm trying to yank the lint trap out of the dryer, and it's made the way everything is made these days - cheap. It jerks and catches, and when I finally pull it free, thick gray dust flies all over, drifting up into my nostrils and making me sneeze.

I rub my nose and look at him. "What's that mean, 'not Charles?'"

He laughs again. "Lucky, you love to talk like trash from the squalid part of town, but you're really one of the most incredibly innocent babies I've ever known. Charles didn't give me the key; Rose did."

"Rose?" I say stupidly.

"His wife. Are you getting the picture?"

286

I'm just staring at him; I know I must look shocked.

Lionel isn't smiling so much now. In fact, he's looking at me pretty intently, wondering if he's going to have to spell this out for Silly Lucky Wilta. I have a dry, hard feeling in my stomach, and it amazes me that my words come out sounding so normal. "Does Charles know?" I finally say.

"He knows," Lionel says. "He certainly knows what his wife was."

I've dumped the thick pad of gray lint into the wastebasket, and I'm trying to force the trap back into its slot in the top of the machine. But I can't do it. My hands are beginning to tremble, and I suddenly realize that I'm not the least bit interested in drying clothes. I lean against the dryer, staring at Lionel, and he puts his hands on my shoulders. "Hey," he says, "this isn't anything for you to get upset about. This is nothing, Lucky. Charles never should have married her in the first place. She never took it very seriously."

I'm remembering back to my first weeks in the castle. *I'd like you to be more particular*, Charles had said to me. *I know him better than you do.*

And he still allows Lionel to roam the castle at will, still plays golf with him, eats meals with him, leaves his daughters alone with him. My stomach has developed a gnawing tension, and I shake Lionel's hands from me. "Lionel, please go home," I say. I'm not even sure if the words are audible or not. "Go home. Go away."

"Wait a minute," he says. "You sent me a polite little text refusing to take me seriously. I meant it when I asked you, Lucky. I don't make such a gesture to everybody, you know, and I think you owe me a little more-"

"I said. Go. Home," I repeat, one word at a time, my voice completely even, deadly, my eyes staring coldly into his.

He backs away, alarmed at my quiet seriousness. "Lucky," he says, "You don't have any right to judge me."

"You're his friend," I say, and suddenly I'm screaming. "His *friend*! How dare you! Get out! Go away!" I'm oblivious to the two children still singing nearby, ignorant of the lint trap which has finally clattered to the floor, lying dormant like some fuzzy dead animal. And I'm convinced, absolutely convinced, that Charles doesn't, couldn't possibly, know anything about this at all.

"Lucky, calm down! I only came over to talk," Lionel says. "I haven't done anything so bad-" I scrabble for the lint trap, and I hurl it at him. He dodges it, trips his way out of the room and down the hallway, and bolts out of the castle.

He hasn't done anything so bad? Seducing his best friend's wife isn't so bad? Traitor, I'm thinking. Scum. Slime. Filthy, unfaithful, disgusting slime. And I don't even know who I'm furious with, Rose or Lionel. Or maybe Nick Wilta.

I go about the rest of that day in a sickening fog. My stomach hurts, and every time I think of how close I came to pairing up with Lionel Hawthorne, I want to weep in shame.

And Charles. How can he tolerate having Lionel in his sight? How can he stand calmly by and accept such disloyalty and betrayal? Lionel is a hypocrite, a slithering, treacherous, repulsive serpent.

It must be that Charles doesn't know. He couldn't.

Or could he? Is he, after all, exactly what I thought him all those years? Weak and spineless, an object of ridicule. A chump, a terrible fool.

◇◇◇

I'm in my room after dinner when Violet knocks on my door and comes in without an invitation. "Lucky, come on," she urges. "We're going to look at stars with the phonoscope."

"Telescope," I correct her. "Is it all set up?"

"Yes, Daddy says to hurry up."

Lionel's words from this afternoon are still burning in my head, and the last thing I feel like doing is fraternizing with the Smithson family. But I have to go down. It will look funny if I don't go down.

I throw on a warm, fleece-lined jacket and zip it up to my chin, and we go to the back yard. It's hardly dark yet, and I'm wondering what all the rush is about. Pansy and her father are there, and the telescope, secure on its pedestal, is aimed up into the heavens. He's adjusting a knob, and Pansy is saying, "I can see all the planets."

"No you can't," he says, "but you might be able to see some of the moons of Jupiter if you look carefully."

"Other moons?" Pansy asks, impressed.

"Yes, look, Pansy. See that star over there that's bigger and brighter than all the others?" She nods. "I'll aim this right toward it. Now, look in here. Can you see it? It will look white against the sky, and you should be able to see the moons."

She can't at first, so he takes over the eyepiece and makes a few adjustments, then he holds her steady, right in front of it. Eventually, she squeals, "I do. I see it." Who knows whether she really does or not. At least she's convinced she does. And Violet, following suit, claims to see it, too.

When I finally get my turn, I discover it's not hard to spot, and the moons really are visible. I can even see the red spot. I've never looked through a telescope before, and Charles lets me fool around with it a little, pointing it in various directions and guessing what some of those bright shapes are.

"Look, Lucilla," he says. He turns the shaft slightly, looks through, and starts twisting the knob gently. "We're early enough, I think." He twists the knob a little more. "There, I think that's Venus. That bright one." His hand is resting casually on my shoulder, and I squirm away from him, disgusted at what I've learned today. I can't help it; he should have renounced Lionel. No friend deserves to be forgiven that much. He notices my jumpiness and removes his hand. I don't need to see the puzzled expression on his face. I have come to know it only too well.

I try to hold the telescope very still as I put my eye to the eyepiece, and I think I see what he's showing me, a little white disc, brighter even than Jupiter, bouncing around in the eyepiece.

"Can you make it hold still?" I ask.

"Not really," he says. "Just try not to touch it."

He wanders away and leaves me to admire Venus. It's very bright, achingly bright, and isn't Venus the goddess of love? *"Star light, star bright,"* I murmur, *"send a prince this very night. Send a prince to hold me tight . . . ."*

"Hang on, Violet." That's Charles, hoisting a sleepy Violet onto his back and saying, "Come on, you two, time to get up to bed." I hear him gathering them up while I keep on examining bright little Venus through the telescope. I turn once to watch them go toward the back door. "Stop wiggling, Violet," he's saying in exasperation.

"I don't wanna go to bed," she whines. "I wanna look through the phonoscope."

"Well, you can't anymore tonight," he insists. "It's time for bed. Come on, Pansy. Ouch! Violet, don't dig your knees into me." Smithson and his progeny disappear inside the castle.

I check back with Venus again. "No," I say aloud. "You

misunderstood me. I said a *prince*."

I give the telescope a gentle pat and watch it move slightly on its pedestal. The air is moving gently in the tops of the trees, and the black leaves are rustling, up high and out of sight. I walk around to the front of the castle, looking up at the lighted windows of Pansy and Violet's bedrooms. They're up there with their father. It has taken him six months to adopt the habit of putting his daughters to bed at night. It's a good change, healthy and wholesome.

I shiver in the evening air.

The porch swing creaks when I sit down on it, and I have to brush off some old pine needles and leaves blown in by the wind. The castle is the only residence for miles around, and the silence and encroaching darkness soothe me. I lean back, exhausted, and gaze up at the stars, far away and terribly out of reach, then close my eyes and let the motion of the swing and the creak of the chains lull me into a quiet calm. The knot I've carried inside all day begins to fray and loosen; the heaviness drains away.

I don't know how much time has gone by when Charles opens the front door and stands there for a minute, looking out over the front lawn, down toward the highway.

The swing creaks again and he looks over, then comes to join me. "There you are," he says. "I wasn't sure where you went."

I wish Charles' face in the moonlight would remain Charles' face. It doesn't, though. As I glance at him, I see Lionel's scheming, devil-may-care grin. I look away, but it doesn't fade.

"You're quiet tonight," Charles says at last. He waits for me to explain or deny. I do neither.

"You can still see Venus," he says. It's a tiny twinkling chip in the darkening sky. "The girls seemed to enjoy the telescope." I have no comment on that point either. Eventually he asks me, "Do you want to tell me what's wrong?"

"Did you know that Lionel has a key to the castle?" I don't even know I'm going to ask him until I say it.

Charles doesn't answer for a minute, and I concentrate on the creak, creak of the old swing. Then he says, "Yes, I knew that. Does it bother you?"

"It didn't," I say, "until he told me where he got it."

"I let him keep it. There didn't seem any harm in it. He used to check on things for me when Mrs. Frocks was here."

"And when I was here."

"I suppose so, at first. If you'd rather he didn't have it,

though, I'll ask for it back. It seemed like a good idea to have a friend I could rely on-"

Suddenly I'm sputtering. "Rely on, Charles? How can you even say that?"

"Well, he's not perfect, but-"

"No, he sure isn't," I snap. "And you, you're just as bad." I turn on him. "How could you? Play golf with him, and let him be here, hanging around all the time, even leaving Pansy and Violet with him. Letting him be such a big part of things." I don't even know how to put my fragmented feelings into words. I just know that I feel utterly disappointed. This man beside me is no knight in shining armor. He's a weak, sad excuse for a man, and I want nothing more than to run out of his sight and upstairs to my room. I wonder if I was too hasty in coming back to the castle, just because he asked me to.

"Lucilla," he says softly, "what is it that you're angry about?"

"I'm angry because you're not," I cry. "I'm angry because no one has the right to do what he did. You should be furious. And yet you treat him as a friend, Charles."

"He *is* a friend."

"No!" I cry. And I'm pushing away from the swing, jumping up, angry and uncontrolled. "Friends do not seduce one another's wives, Charles!"

"He didn't do that." I can see him looking up at me in the darkness. "You don't know what you're talking about. Lionel has a key to the castle because my wife gave it to him. That doesn't mean he slept with her."

"How do you know that?" I say. "He's always bragging about his latest conquests. I'm sure he saw her as just one more. The two of them-"

He interrupts sharply. "Don't say that." Then his words come quietly, a still breath. "I know because he told me," he says. "My wife gave him a key for her own reasons, whatever they were." I turn away, impatient with his flimsy excuses, the excuses that forgive and pardon Lionel Hawthorne.

"Well," he adds quietly, "I know what her reason was, I guess. To have an affair with Lionel."

"Yes," I sputter, "your *friend.*"

But it's as if he hasn't even heard me. "I've never said that out loud before. Well, it didn't kill me like I thought it might." He exhales a big breath and sits there, just staring up at the night sky.

What can I say? I say nothing.

"Anyway, that was her idea," he says. "Lionel says he never took advantage of it. Nothing ever happened between them."

"And because he told you that, you believe it?" He's dumber than I thought if he trusts anything Lionel Hawthorne says. How could he believe that lying, cheating . . . .

"Lucilla, I've known Lionel all my life, and I didn't really know my wife until after we were married. I was in too much of a hurry, and I built her up to be something she wasn't. In some ways, we were a terrible match."

"But Lionel-"

"Lionel is my friend, Lucilla, my best friend. I know him very well. He wouldn't lie to me." He says it so simply that I believe him. I want to believe him.

"But you told me," I begin, "you told me when I first came here that I should be more particular . . . that I didn't know him well enough. You warned me away from him." I sit down again, looking into his night-darkened face.

"And I meant it," he says. "He drinks too much, and he's a womanizer. You know that. He made a decision about Rose, and that was for my sake. But I was afraid he would take advantage of you."

I bristle at this. "Take advantage! I can look out for myself. No one has to-"

"Oh, Lucilla," he says wearily, leaning back on the swing. It stops moving. "You have a great act. The tough girl with a smart aleck answer to everything. I saw through that by our third conversation."

I swallow. What does he mean, he saw through that? That's the real me. Cool. Unflappable. Knowing and capable. If I'm not that, then what am I?

His voice softens. "There's something fragile in you, underneath the layers. I didn't want Lionel to spoil that innocent part of you."

Fragile? Innocent? I'm not those things. I've been beaten up by life and emerged whole. I've had pickle jars hurled at my head by the man who vowed to cherish me and the clothes off my back stolen out of the buck-a-load dryer at the Scrub-a-Duds Laundromat. I've cheated my way into Charles' home and lied to him every chance I got.

Fragile? He's making me feel like crying.

"Lucilla." He touches my hair softly, and gently tilts my chin up with one finger. His other arm goes around my shoulders, and his face comes in close to mine, big and handsome in the moonlight. I almost believe he's going to kiss me, and I almost want him to.

Instead, he presses my head gently against his chest and encircles me with both his arms. The anger, the righteousness, the fury I've been feeling against this very good man evaporate, and I allow myself to be held by him as we rock gently on the swing.

Why shouldn't he believe Lionel Hawthorne, his boyhood friend? Would anything be gained by severing their friendship?

A new understanding is seeping in. A Charles Smithson who has forgiven a dead wife, and believed in the loyalty of a lifelong friend. A Charles Smithson who knows all the most irritating habits and unforgivable flaws of Yours Truly, Lucilla Todd Wilta. And yet, here he sits, arms around me, helping me, by his silence and acceptance, to see something I have never seen before.

Maybe not wimpiness or weakness at all.

Maybe in some weird, quiet kind of way, the most amazing kind of strength.

The tears that I thought I felt like crying never come. In their place, a profound comfort envelops me. I tighten my arms around him, and I can feel his heart beating behind his shirt. When he leans away from me a little, I look up at him again. He tilts his head and smiles slightly as he gazes into my eyes.

"Okay?" he asks.

I nod in answer.

He holds me longer; we hear an owl screech, and we watch in silence as two deer wander into the yard and nibble softly at the dry autumn grass, then bound away into the woods.

Venus is still twinkling up there, and Charles is still holding me down here, and a year ago, never in my wildest imaginings could I have foreseen this picture.

When he does kiss me it's so honest and sweet that I don't even bother to become nervous or say something wise or wait for it to turn to passion. I accept it, an inevitable ending to six months of learning the truth about Charles F. Smithson, and also, the truth about myself.

The air around us is inky black, and the rough thatch of the lawn looks eerie where moonlight hits it. Lights from inside the castle make gold pools here and there. With his strong arms around me, I realize I haven't felt this safe in a long, long time.

The wind is picking up, and I shiver in my fleece jacket.

"You're cold," he says. "It's getting late, and it's been a very long day. I think we better go in."

I murmur an agreement.

"I'll put the telescope away and check on the girls. You should go in and warm up."

And the child in me, that fragile, innocent part, the part that has been hurt and broken, but, somehow in this bleak, cold castle, incredibly protected, nods gratefully and agreeably, and goes.

# 31

I'M WANDERING AROUND the guest house, up and down the stairs, in and out of rooms, looking at Charles' art and yelling back comments while he paints in the secret room. He's hired a nice woman from town, Mrs. Murdock, to look after the girls for a while, so I've agreed to come along. Of course I have; he's asked me to, and while I'm here, I might as well offer my opinion of his work. My opinions are all the same. I don't know art, but I like his paintings, all of them. And, for the record, Trayson-Ruge, excuse me, Renlatto, has nothing on Charles Smithson.

I can hear him humming to himself while he works, and I have to admit I like that sound. I may have lost my secret room, but I've gained something else- a Charles Smithson who hums instead of sighing, who talks to me instead of looking at me with something like bewilderment. Well, sometimes he still looks bewildered when I speak, but so does the rest of the world. Why should he be different?

"So, this is what you've been doing the whole time I've known you?" I yell in the direction of the secret room. "Just making art?" I run my finger over a windowsill in one of the bedrooms. A fine powder of silty dust comes away. This place is as bad as the castle, kind of run down and in need of some serious TLC.

"Yes, this is it," he replies.

"I still don't see how you could let your daughters live in the castle," I yell, "when they could have been here." We've talked about this a little. He claims he needed the privacy of the summer house for painting. What he doesn't say is that he was too afraid to let anyone in on what he was doing here.

"I assumed Mrs. Frocks would let me know if there was some reason they shouldn't be there." He's making his voice a little loud, and I realize it's probably distracting to have to holler while he's being creative, so I amble my way toward him.

"I've come to the conclusion that Mrs. Frocks was a little bit blind and a little bit deaf," I point out. I join him in the secret room and take a good look at the painting he's working on. A gray-blue background and some hazy lines. How this will become a landscape is a mystery to me. "Nice," I say. "It will look good downstairs right above that cabinet with all the broken hinges."

He chuckles. "There's a lot of stuff here that should probably be thrown out. I ought to sort through it all someday."

"Is it okay if I look around? Be nosy?" Gosh. Look at me. Lucky Wilta asking permission.

"Sure. Go ahead," he says. "Explore to your heart's content. Break down casements. Force doors."

Well, there are no doors to force, and why would I bother? The secret room ain't so secret anymore.

I turn away and glance up at my father's great little joke, the diamond-paned window high up in the wall, studded with color, a symbol of my own remorse. How foolish I was to waste my life aching for treasure that doesn't exist.

Here I am, standing right inside my secret room. I can't help feeling a little confounded. I expected a gloomy, mysterious dungeon, and it turned out to be one of the prettiest spots on the whole Smithson property. I look at the sun pouring in through the colors in the window, glinting off the oils in the pictures stacked around me and the empty wine bottles in the corner.

"Explain to me how alcohol helps the creative spirit, Chuck," I say. I pick up one of the bottles and glance at the label, wondering why he didn't just throw them out.

He stops painting and looks over at me. "We can get rid of those," he says. "They should be recycled. And just to set the record straight, I didn't drink them."

"Why are they here then?"

"They were under the floor. I started to replace a worn plank one day - See where that board is loose over there?"

He's right. A board by the far wall has been pulled up and tossed back down. I lift it up and peer into the empty space beneath. "Why would someone put bottles under the floor?"

"Don't know. I imagine somebody came here to have a grand old time and decided to hide the evidence. Probably your father."

I give him a disgusted look, but it's all wasted. He's squeezing a dollop of paint from a tube and mixing colors. "Sounds more like a Smithson stunt," I say. He at least has the good sense to laugh.

Something occurs to me, and I pick up the clear glass bottles, one in each hand. You wouldn't need a key to open them, so I know I'm being silly. I hold them up to the light anyway, and watch the colored prisms dance inside the glass. Both of the bottles are empty.

He sets down his paintbrush, comes over to me and takes one of the bottles. "I suppose these could be old; they might even be Borstrom bottles," he muses.

"More likely Smithson the First," I say tartly. "He probably came here drinking all the time. Don't forget he was inebriated the night he won the castle from my father."

"You don't know that," Charles scoffs. "What about your own father?"

"He was taken advantage of."

I sit on the floor and lean against the false wall, and Charles sits beside me. He holds the old bottle on his knees, tapping it distractedly with one finger. "Lucilla," he says, "every man who owned this castle got it in the same way, do you know that?"

"I've always thought the history was pretty spicy."

"First Borstrom lost it to Lowland to pay a gambling debt. He sounds irresponsible."

"He had built it for his wife, too," I say. "Clymna. She was so worried she started giving away her valuables. Imagine how she felt when he lost her home."

"Maybe relieved," Charles says.

"Probably," I agree. "My father said Clymna was on her deathbed when they moved out. She had TB. He read that in some old document he found." I think for a moment. "Then James Lowland signed the castle over to Harold Ruggins."

"And then *he* got rid of it," Charles adds. Then he looks at me quickly. "Do you think maybe they all *wanted* to lose it? The castle is ugly, Lucilla, ugly and cold and uncomfortable, and ridiculously expensive to keep up. Why assume anyone else liked it any better than we do?"

"I loved it when I lived there," I say simply.

He looks at me sympathetically. "You loved the safeness you felt there. You loved your father and Nancy; are you sure you loved the castle?"

"It was my home," I say.

"I understand that," Charles says, "but you were a child. I wonder if anyone who owned it, anyone who had to maintain it, ever really *wanted* it. Or maybe they liked it fine, but couldn't afford it. I know I'm sick of financing it." He gets up and returns to his table. I watch him mix colors.

"Especially now that there's a dent," I say.

"Why are you worrying about that?" he says. He dabs a bit of paint on the canvas, steps back, and looks critically at the painting, then back at me. "Is Lionel planting ideas in your head?"

"Well, he did say-"

He waves a hand impatiently. "Let me give you the facts. I made a lot of money a few years ago when the stock market was doing so well. A lot. Knowing a little about the business world helped, but it wasn't enough." He peers at me uncertainly. "I've never really worked, you know."

"Never?" It boggles the mind.

"I've never needed to. I was just lucky when the stocks did well. Then recently I had some setbacks, bad financial advice. I invested too much in some stocks that went belly up. I lost quite a bit, Lucilla, and I could lose more. But not everything. I'm not a pauper."

I'm looking at him, feeling a little scared for him, and he sees that on my face. He places the brush on the table top and comes to sit by me again. "Hey," he says gently, "I'm not even middle class yet, and if I get there, I'm sure I could get a job. So you can stop worrying about your next paycheck."

My next paycheck? I wasn't even thinking of that. It startles me to realize I was worrying for his sake, and not my own.

When did Lucky Wilta become unselfish?

"Anyway," he says, "I decided it was foolish to let someone else make decisions about my money, so I started studying up on investments myself, reading up on the stock market, finding out about bonds and mutual funds. Keith helped me a little. Or tried to." He grins, a lop-sided look. "It's just as boring now as when I was in college. I couldn't get enthusiastic about any of it. I could hardly pay attention when Keith was talking."

Yes, I recall those days. So it wasn't me driving him to giddy distraction, after all. He was simply bored to tears.

"I have to hire someone to do it for me, Lucilla. It's chancy, but I'm not going to spend my life thinking about money all the time."

"You only feel that way because you've always had it," I say.

"Maybe. Anyway, I don't plan to be poor, so you can stop wondering."

He stands up and stretches. "I need a break," he says. "Can you make some coffee while I clean up this stuff?"

I go down to the shabby summer house kitchen and rummage through cupboards until I find the coffee maker. It's the only thing in this kitchen that's new and probably the only thing that works. He may have brought in a spanking new coffee maker and winterized this building, but the whole place is just screaming for updates.

I take the coffee maker out, start the coffee and listen to the hiss and bubble as the brewing gets underway. The cupboards are chock full of junk, and while I search for mugs, I start removing things and piling them on the countertop. Biscuit cutters, a rusty can opener, assorted pans.

Ah, here we go. Mugs.

I remove two, thinking I'd better wash them before we drink from them, then I step back suddenly as my eye catches sight of something familiar, a soft swirl of purple peeking out from behind a pile of plates. I yank the plates out and clatter them to the countertop, then stand breathless, staring at seven delicate china teacups pressed against the back wall of the cupboard. They're stacked upside down - fragile, chipped, painted with vague purple flowers beneath flaking gold rims, an entire set matching the cup I found in the sixth step, the cup that accompanied the little key hidden in the folds of the ruined tapestry.

"Charles?" I say, but I know he can't hear me; my voice comes out a little squeak. Something, I think, must be hidden underneath these cups.

My fingers shake as I remove a top cup from the stacks. Then another and another until I've removed them all. And, no, there's nothing under the teacups, but there is something behind them. A panel about eight inches square is cut into the back of the space. It blends in so perfectly that at first I can't even see how to open it. Fortunately, I have a lot of practice at this kind of thing, so I peer and press and wipe away grit, and then I see the two tiny latches. I work the latches until the entire cut-out falls forward into my hands. I set the slice of wood aside.

I've revealed a slim compartment about an inch deep, just big enough to fit the small leather book standing upright before me. I reach for it and feel the supple leather under my fingers, but when I try to open the cover, it won't budge. Then I notice the tiny keyhole, filled with grit and dust, and the three initials looking back at me, curved and fancy: *C.F.S.*

"Charles!" I call. "Charles, come down here!" My breath is coming shallowly and my heart starts beating fast as I hold the little book so tightly that veins pop up on my hand. "Charles!" I'm trying to remain calm, but my voice ends up a screech.

I can hear him on the stairs, racing down, but it's a blurred sound, as if it's happening at some other time, in some other place.

He reaches the kitchen and sees me standing there. "I thought you were hurt." He peers into my face. "Are you hurt? Why did you holler like that?"

My hand is shaking as I pass the book to him. "It was in that cupboard. Look, C.F.S."

He takes it from me and examines it. "Huh, it must be my father's," he says. "It looks like a diary."

"Another one?" I ask.

"It must have been a popular idea." He's pulling gently at the cover, realizing the journal is frozen shut.

"It's locked, Charles," I tell him.

"I can probably force it open with a knife." He pulls out a drawer and starts rummaging, but I already know that won't be necessary.

"Wait," I tell him. "I don't think you'll need to." I grab up my handbag and dump it out on the kitchen countertop. He watches curiously as my lipsticks, pens, shopping lists, and dirty, rumpled tissues settle in among mugs and plates, spatulas and frying pans, and a whole set of pretty, spindly teacups. I grab up my change purse and dig through quickly. Quarters and dimes, odd displaced buttons, a one-of-a-kind earring I'm always optimistic I'll find the mate to. And a small, cheap, flat brass key.

Triumphantly, I hold it up.

His face falls in disbelief. "You have a key for this?"

"I meant to tell you," I start. Then I correct that. "No, I never meant to tell you, but I never expected to use it either." I correct myself again. "No, I did plan to use it," I say. "I searched everywhere, but I thought it would be a box, not a book. Oh!" I feel that familiar old sense of disappointment flood through me. "A box of diamonds, Charles."

"What?" He looks confused.

"Oh, it's stupid. I was going to split them with you. I wanted to surprise you, but it's just a diary."

"Lucilla . . . ." He's shaking his head slowly.

"But I know there's something in this; there has to be."

"Something? I don't understand."

"They were all clues, Charles! The lion's head, and this key. There was a teacup with it. That's how I knew-"

"Lucilla, I don't know what you're talking about."

"Oh, never mind. Here." Into his hand I willingly place the key. His key.

He looks down at it. "But where did you get this? How . . . ?" He's standing there with his hand out, cradling the key between us, his face tinged with confusion.

"It was in one of the steps in the foyer," I say. "There was a secret latch, and the step sprang up-"

"You're kidding. How?" His eyes are scrunched up and he's still staring blankly at the key.

"It will fit this book," I tell him. "I'm sure of it. Try it, Charles." I gesture eagerly toward the key.

"Lucilla, how do you-"

"Violet found it," I tell him. "She doesn't even know."

"How could she not know?" The confusion on his face is growing more pronounced.

"It was on Marion. I'll show you later," I tell him impatiently. "Open it, Charles."

"Marion? I don't understand." He takes a step back and looks at me curiously. "Explain it to me now."

So I tell him about Violet and Marion and the tiny, magical button in Marion's mane, the sixth step, the teacup. I tell him about Forsythe's poem, which he's ignored all these years. Charles takes it all in, then, "Lucilla, you never . . . . You should have . . . ." He stops, then, and just looks, first at me and then down at the book in his hand. "Never mind," he says. He wipes a thin layer of dust off the journal, examines the cover, and blows dirt out of the little keyhole. He uses the point of the key and digs gently, loosening grime, letting it fall away. Then he inserts the key, turns it, and opens the book.

# 32

WE REMOVE THE PAINTINGS piled on the lumpy living room couch, then we sit down and peer over the first page of the journal together.

"I can't read his writing," I say. "Read it aloud."

"*I, Charles F. Smithson,*" he reads. "It seems funny to read that in someone else's handwriting, Lucilla."

"Just read it, Charles."

"*I, Charles F. Smithson, being of sound mind and body . . . .*"

"It's a will," I say. "Maybe there are diamonds after all. Maybe your father found them and left them to you."

"You're imagining things, Lucilla," he says distractedly. "There aren't any diamonds. And it isn't a will. It's some notes about the castle . . . ."

That sounds promising. I lean in eagerly.

". . . and then a letter - to me." He sounds surprised and maybe a little pleased.

He flips through a few pages to see what lies ahead. The journal appears to be full of writing, every page complete. He turns back to the beginning, and starts to read.

"*. . . being of sound mind and body, am setting down in these pages my personal . . .* something, 'commentaries' I think *. . . regarding a certain truth learned in this summer house.* Oh, he calls it a summer house."

Who cares about that? "A truth, huh?" I ask him. "I wonder what he means." I try to get a better look. I can't make out some of the words. Charles is doing a lot better at reading this miserable script than I am. And this is without those dapper reading glasses he wears for his money studies.

He bends lower, squinting over the journal. "*You found this book, so presumably you also found the key to open it and the lion's head for the banister. But you aren't finished yet.* What does that mean?" Charles asks.

"I bet it means there are more clues," I say. "Cool. I bet this journal is going to give us a lot of other clues."

"Really?" He sounds skeptical.

"Yes, for diamonds. It's what I've been telling you right along." Well, right along might be a stretch. But I did come clean, sort of, the day he showed me the secret room.

I can hear the coffee pot hissing in the kitchen. "Don't read one more word," I say. "The coffee's done. I'll go get it. Wait for me." I practically break my neck racing into the kitchen and I slosh coffee around trying to pour it as fast as possible into mugs that I have decided are clean enough. When I come back to the living room, Mister Impatience is busily plunging ahead in his father's journal, not waiting for me at all.

"It's family stuff," he says. "My father's grandfather bought the castle with a couple of friends in 1930 to make it into a hotel."

"Wait, that can't be right," I say. "Your great grandfather couldn't have bought it, Charles. You know your father won it from mine in a card game."

"Well, we've always thought that, but maybe it wasn't true. Maybe your family was just renting it."

Renting it? My home? Land of my happy dreams? Secret shrine to my dazzling future? No way.

He tells me more, summarizing what he's read. "They built the summer house in 1931 and the three friends stayed here while they oversaw renovations and improvements to the castle. The Depression hit and they had to abandon the idea of a hotel." He bends over the book and reads. "*Forsythe . . . .*"

"Forsythe," I say. "The guy who wrote the poem. And I remember that name from my father's journal, too. He was one of the friends?"

"Shh," says Charles.

I give him a miffed look, but he doesn't see it. He's plowing on and if I want to hear it, I had better be quiet.

"*Forsythe served when war was declared . . . .*" Charles reads, then he looks up. "Lewie Forsythe was a friend of my father's. They owned the castle together, but this Forsythe is two generations earlier. I remember meeting Lewie; he was a really nice guy. In fact, he signed his share of the castle over to my mother when I was in college. He was living in Florida, had made a mint, and really didn't care about the castle. It must have been handed down to Lewie and my father."

"That doesn't make sense, Charles. *My* father owned the castle." I tap the book impatiently. "Yours won it in a card game. You keep forgetting that fact."

303

He shrugs and opens the book again, reading silently. "Apparently the friends owned it together for years," he says, "then they decided not to leave it to their sons, who were older and already well-established, but to their grandsons. That would be my father's generation." He reads a little more, then a smile breaks out on his face. "Oh, of course. You'll like this, Lucilla. . . . *the group decided to leave the castle, not to their sons . . . but to their grandsons: Lewie, Luke, and I.*"

He doesn't even finish out the last word because I'm up off the sofa and high-fiving the air. "Luke! You said *Luke*, didn't you?"

"Calm down, you'll shatter the paintings." He pulls me back down beside him. "Yes, I said Luke. That must be your father. Your great grandfather was the third friend. Smithson, Todd, and Forsythe. The three of them left it to our fathers."

"So we did own it. Renting, indeed!" I'm up and dancing around the living room, smiling big and wide; I can't help it. I knock into a painting and catch it before it smashes to the floor. "I knew it was my castle. I knew it!"

He's leaning back lazily, looking at me patiently. "So, would you like me to read more of this?"

"Fer Sher, Yore Grace." I sit obediently.

"*After the Depression, the castle was vacant for many years, but never entirely abandoned. Now and then, someone would come for a picnic or use it as a summer retreat. At some point, modern bathrooms were put in. And the three families began using it as a dumping ground. If it doesn't work but it's too good to throw away, why not take it to the castle? It was well-furnished with an odd assortment of mismatched furniture, discarded dishes, and lamps in need of rewiring. Of course, old Borstrom's cast-off belongings were still there, too, and Ruggins' and Lowland's . . . .*"

"Well, that explains a lot," I interject. "It never had decent furnishings to begin with."

"*The three of us inherited, and we realized we needed to make a plan,*" Charles reads. "*Our first meeting was an event I'll never forget. Luke's wit kept us laughing throughout. Both he and Lewie are generous to a fault, constantly giving to causes, trying to improve life for everyone they know. We met, we ate, we drank. We played cards, joked, and talked. We discovered we had a lot in common, and we became friends. We discussed the future of the property left to us, and we tried to decide how we felt about owning a castle together."*

Charles stops reading and looks at me. "Did you know this? That our fathers were friends, that they owned the castle together?"

"No, I thought my father hated yours."

"I suppose if either of them had lived longer, we might've known."

"Let's keep going," I tell him.

*"The idea came to us when Luke mentioned that the castle had always changed hands because of a reckless wager.*

*"It might have been Lewie who first suggested the Castle Game. His law school education was a bonus. Why not make a pact that every five years we would meet for a weekend and relive the fun of that first encounter. We'd eat, drink, and play poker, and the wager for the two day poker game would be the castle. Possession would change hands immediately. It would be legal and binding. For five years, any improvements you care to make, any entertaining you care to do - the castle is yours. Move right in or come for vacations. But at the end of five years, if the current caretaker lost the wager, he would agree to move out immediately."*

"So we were right," I say in amazement. "Your father did win it from mine in a card game, but a friendly one, all planned and executed in a businesslike way."

"And they did it for almost twenty years, Lucilla. It was a way to honor the castle's strange history."

"And to keep any one person from having to support it alone. It makes sense that things are so ramshackle. No one would want to put a lot of money into it and then give it up a few years later."

Charles' lips are pursed and he's bending over the diary, reading quickly. "Lewie won first, then your father. Lewie was happy to be out, it says. He didn't like it much."

"That doesn't surprise me."

"So your father won twice," Charles says.

"We must have moved in when I was born," I say. "My father had inherited a lot of money, Charles, so he could afford to live here making crafts and doing his woodworking. We moved out when I was ten."

"And that's when my father won. And I've been here ever since."

"Well if they did it every five years-" I start.

"But my father died unexpectedly," Charles reminds me, "in

305

that motorcycle accident. "We had been here four years. Luke and Lewie must have skipped that year out of respect for my mother. It would have been heartless to make us move."

"And then a few years later, my father died," I add. "Forsythe couldn't continue with the wagers alone; their game just died a natural death. But Charles," I grin, "I do own a third of the castle."

He hesitates just a little before he responds. "Well, actually, you don't. When Lewie Forsythe deeded my mother his share of the property, it was two-thirds. I own it all."

I let out a small groan. "That's so unfair, Charles. But how did Forsythe get my father's third?" And then it comes to me. My father's unexpected gift of a thirty thousand dollar check after my wedding to that creep, Nick Wilta. He said he had some legal things to tie up, and suddenly we had money. It all becomes clear in a flash, and I sit back heavily.

"He threw away all his money taking care of my mother," I tell Charles, "then he watched me marry Nick. He tried to talk me out of it, but I wouldn't listen. He realized Nick was never going to get a job, so he got Forsythe to give him thirty thousand dollars for his share of the castle. That got us through that first year when I was earning minimum wage."

The knowledge is sudden and confusing.

"Charles, my father sold his third of the castle to a man who didn't even want it. We know he didn't; he turned right around and gave the property to your mother. My father must have talked Forsythe into that," I say, "begged him maybe. The money Nick and I lived on was a handout from Lewie Forsythe."

Charles is holding the journal, his finger marking the page. "I think it might be the other way around, Lucilla," he says thoughtfully. "I'm betting it was Lewie Forsythe's idea, that he came up with that plan to help your father precisely because he needed the money. I don't think your father had to talk him into doing anything. Your father wanted to make sure you were okay, and Lewie wanted to help him."

"He was dying," I moan. "He had cancer and he knew he wouldn't survive it. He didn't want that money for himself. He only needed it for me." My face is screwed up and I feel like bawling.

Charles gives a sympathetic laugh. "Sometimes," he says, "men do very weird things for their daughters."

# 33

HE'S IMMERSED in what he's reading, his head bent over his father's journal again.

"What does it say?" I ask.

"Well, it's this letter," he says.

Oh. Right. The letter that Charles Fitzham Smithson the First wrote in his personal diary to Charles Fitzham Smithson the Second. I suppose this is private, and my impeccable manners dictate that I let him read it in seclusion.

Delicately, as if I'm used to doing the polite thing, I suggest, "Well, there sure are a lot more paintings here that I haven't even begun to critique yet. Why don't I just yell back my thoughts to you while you go ahead and read your letter." I stand up, ready to wander off.

No one can fault my artful good breeding.

He doesn't even look up from his reading, just grabs my arm and pulls me back. "You stay right here."

"Maybe I should go back to the castle and check on the girls?"

"Thanks, but I'm sure Mrs. Murdock is doing just fine."

"Make you a snack? Get your pipe? Fetch your slippers?"

Finally, he looks up and laughs. He still has a grip on my sleeve, so I guess I'm not going anywhere. I sit back down.

"The first thing is a date," he says. "I was twelve when he wrote this."

And then he begins to read me the letter.

"*This letter is for you, son. And if someone else finds it, I know it will be a Todd or a Forsythe, who will deliver it to you. Unless you hacked this book open, you've discovered the key to this book and the newel post lion . . . .*"

Charles says what I'm merely thinking. "Actually, Lucilla, you were the one who found those things."

What would he do without me? I grin at him.

"*What you've just read is a testament to the power of friendship, a treasure that can last a whole life,*" he reads. "*I am a lucky man, Charles. Besides your mother and you, I also have two true friends, more than many men have in a lifetime."*

"That's weird," I say. "My father wrote almost the same thing." Of course, I thought he meant the other kind of treasure. Gems you can bite down hard on to see if they crack. Or if your teeth crack.

*"When Luke Todd, Lewie Forsythe, and I met, none of us had any idea how powerful the bonds would become. The castle was the thread that brought and bound us together, but it was only a symbol for something much bigger. In the last twenty years, we've been together only a handful of times, yet the trust and honor among us has been unflinching. That's the truth of the Castle Game; that's the prize we treasure."*

"Is he saying that's the treasure?" I say. "No. Wait."

He keeps plowing on. *"Lewie is ready to start his own law firm in Florida, but I know he will still show up every five years to wager the castle. It's tradition; he wouldn't forego it."*

"But is he saying there isn't a treasure, Charles?"

"It sounds that way," he agrees. He starts flipping pages. "It gets boring through here, Lucilla. You don't care about everybody's finances, do you? Wow," he adds, "your father had a lot of money, Lucilla. It's kind of scary the way he lost it all."

He looks up and stares at the far wall. "It's like my father to write about their fortunes, though. I think he spent a lot of time thinking about money. All week, he manipulated money and numbers and figures, right down to the last penny, and on weekends he showed off on a motorcycle and bet on races. He was a funny man."

"Old King Charles," I murmur with nostalgia.

He pulls his attention back to the diary, reads a few pages quickly, then squints to see the words better. "Listen," he says, "this is about your father. *Luke knocked his glass to the floor and bent to retrieve it. Of course, we'd all had more than enough to drink."*

"This must be one of their five-year get-togethers," I decide.

Charles holds up a hand. "Just listen. *A mouse scampered under the wardrobe and disappeared. Even in his fuzzy mental state, Luke was suspicious. He cocked one rheumy eye to the wardrobe's foot . . . ."*

I arch away from Charles. "Well, isn't this demeaning," I mutter. "A drunk sprawled out on the floor. He's talking about my father!"

"He says it well, though, don't you think?"

I give him a scathing look.

". . . *and found a door*. It's the secret room, Lucilla! He's describing the very night they discovered it. *He motioned us to join him. Lewie and I stumbled to him, and with manly heroism, we three pushed aside the ancient wardrobe and beat down the door to discover our secret room* . . . . It's just like your father wrote; he really did follow a mouse in there."

"They sound a little silly to me," I say righteously. "If it's the same wardrobe, it took three of them to push it aside; I recall that you did it alone the day you showed me the room."

"One of the perks of sobriety," he says. "But listen . . . *a perfect place to store our empties. Have you found them yet, under the floorboards, Charles? It started as a joke. When Lewie found a loose board and stuffed an empty bottle under, it made us laugh, so we made it our practice. What's the point of having good friends if you don't share a few secrets?*"

"Well, now we know how the bottles got there," I say.

Our fathers had fun, all right. Three rich guys without a care in the world, and their legacy is a little disappointing. Empty bottles under the floorboards, a stained glass window, and a cheap dimestore key. Not exactly what Lucky Wilta had in mind. I'm watching Charles intently as he reads on in the diary, enjoying himself, immersed in the wacky, madcap past we share.

Finally, he looks at me curiously. "How did you end up with your father's journal? Did you find it hidden somewhere?"

"No, it was with his papers when he died. There's not much to it, anyway," I say. "He probably wanted to keep a journal because his friend Chuckie Smithson had one. He gave up after half a dozen entries. You know, I always thought that it was leaving the castle that started my father's downfall."

He dismisses that. "Losing the castle didn't hurt your father. After living in it, you know better. I'm sure he didn't mind being rid of it. He had hard luck later, but you heard the diary. He was generous to a fault. That's not such a bad thing." Charles looks thoughtful. "I bet my father would have helped your family out if he'd known, if he'd lived longer. Then everything between you and me would have been completely different."

That's true. Very different. In what ways? To what end? I don't dare look at him.

I'm recalling the words from my father's own diary. *My little Lucilla will stumble on that room one day - and the treasure hidden there.* I lean back against the tattered sofa, beaten and disappointed. "They found a pretty window, and they hid a lot of stupid things," I say. I really thought there'd be a treasure, Charles."

"Treasure," Charles muses. "That's a funny word. It can mean so many different things. There's the window, for starters." He smiles at me. "And for our fathers, the real treasure was their friendship, wasn't it?"

I nod. I know I'm grimacing. And, yes, I feel guilty, Sister, but, oh, how I'd hoped to find sparkling rocks. But I concede that their friendship was impressive. Three good friends who made a commitment to keep a date every fifth year come hell or high water. And they did it. The only thing that kept them away was death.

There's something kind of admirable in that.

◇◇◇

Charles is flipping through the journal again, arrested now and then by a particular line or paragraph. A few of these he reads to me. Soft light from a floor lamp spills onto the faded pages open before him.

"I guess I should call the castle," I sigh, "and see how Mrs. Murdock is getting along."

He doesn't answer, just looks through the last few pages of his father's journal. The amber lamplight is making soft shadows on his face. He finishes reading and gazes before him for a moment. His fingers come to rest between the last two pages and he looks at me.

"What?"

"I almost hate to show you this," he says, "cuz you'll go all nuts. But it doesn't make sense. Maybe you'll get it."

I lean into him and peer at the last page of the diary. *Charles,* it says, *the love and trust of your family and friends are far more valuable than any fortune I might leave you. The summer house can be a symbol of that for you. The real treasure is the people around you.*

"Well, obviously," I mutter. And then I read the last line, and I can feel my face furrow into a puzzled frown. *But keep in mind: It's also up high and down low.*

"Up high and down low?" I repeat. "What is? I have no idea what that means, Charles. But he's definitely talking about something we'll want to find. Maybe there *is* a treasure somewhere." I reread the lines. "Yes, there must be."

"Well, there's something anyway," Charles says. "And what's this thing?" He peels a small silver hook from inside the back cover where his father taped it to keep it secure. The hook is about four inches long and the handle is ornately carved.

"It looks like a button hook," I say. "One of those old-fashioned ones they used to button up shoes back in the day."

"Or gloves sometimes. But why here?"

I'm shaking my head. I have no idea. But I know without a doubt that my days are about to become full and exciting again. If I have to dig out every shoe in the castle, every glove, the ones up high and the ones down low, I'm going to figure out why Charles Smithson Senior left his son a weird, cryptic message and a nineteenth century button hook, hidden behind a secret panel in the summer house kitchen.

# 34

I NEED MORE SPACE," Smithson says. We're in the summer house again and he's organizing pictures, trying not to smear those that are still wet, piling up some older ones against the walls, preparing to cart them all downstairs. I'm admiring the painting he was working on last time I was here. Vague, hazy lines have become a nice landscape, a lake, soaring mountains, a misty haze over the water, two little canoes floating near the shore. What a guy. He can make beauty out of nothing. Who'd a thunk it?

"Removing this false wall will enlarge the bedroom and let in a lot more light," he's telling me. "It will be so much nicer up here."

He disappears down the stairs with a couple of paintings and I follow. "You'd really destroy my secret room?" I say plaintively.

"It wouldn't be such a great loss, would it?" he asks. "Besides, I'd like to have that window visible. It's a work of art."

So we move all the pictures and his painting supplies to the living room, and he finds a stack of faded bedsheets and begins draping them over everything. "There's likely to be a lot of dust flying," he says.

He can hardly hire a professional to start tearing down walls in the guest house; after all, he has his secret vice to think of. So I've agreed to help him, and he's hired Mrs. Murdock again. She's at the castle right now with Pansy and Violet. They like her a lot, and she has promised a possibility of ice cream later if they behave well this afternoon. Bribery. I wonder why I never thought of that myself.

Locating and examining all the shoes and gloves in the castle turned out to be a lot more work than I expected. You have no idea, Sister, how many old shoes there are in the castle, buried in closets and hidden away in trunks. And even though buttoning up old high-tops and long, vintage ladies' gloves with the button hook was fun the first few times, it got old fast, and I can say with authority that none of the shoes in the castle yielded anything more than a musty, old-feet smell and tattered fabric and leather that fell apart when I became too enthusiastic in my investigation. Gloves, likewise.

Yes, I searched high - the attic, the ceilings, every top shelf and crown molding and chandelier in the castle - and yes, I searched low - in the cellar, under the carpets, and beneath all the rocks in the foundation that were loose enough to move. And no, I don't have any idea what Charles Smithson the First had in mind when he left such a strange, perplexing message and such a strange, useless tool.

Charles the Second and I have even talked this over, and both of us are stumped. He was willing to make a few random guesses - all of which I had already considered - but that's where his interest ends. It was up to me to find and examine all the shoes and gloves, and I persisted, even when I could hear him chuckling quietly behind his newspaper.

He's right, though, about revealing the window, and I feel almost excited as we shove furniture aside and begin demolishing with gusto. The work goes quickly, the wall comes down easily, and soon we're left with a second floor full of rubble. Gorgeous color spills in from the window, transforming all the debris into piles of broken, ashy jewels.

Charles is pitching chunks of old plaster into a big trash can and dragging bags of refuse downstairs and out the door. I find a broom and start to sweep up fragments of wood and wallboard. Already, it seems lighter and roomier up here, and the light from the odd window lends a happy brilliance to this end of the house.

When he returns, he finds me standing, leaning on my broom. I'm staring up at the diamond-shaped window, and I can't help it; a big heaving sigh escapes me. "I do love this window," I say.

"You don't sound as if you do." He saunters over and stands next to me. We both stare up.

"No, I do. It's beautiful and everything. But it's not what I expected, and it sure wasn't what I wanted." I shrug. "I don't think that button hook is going to amount to anything, Charles. I think our fathers pulled a fast one on us."

"I know you're disappointed," Charles says, "but really, how likely was it that there'd be some treasure hidden in the castle? Or here, for that matter? They're just old houses, and not nearly as nice as some old houses." He looks around and corrects himself. "As any other old houses."

I'm only half listening.

Leaks and drips. Mold and cold. A falling down castle with a screaming furnace, and a bright, sunny secret room that Smithson found long ago. I hate to give it up, and I look into his eyes, imagining, imploring. "It's possible I missed something, though," I say. "Maybe down the old well or cemented into the terrace floor, maybe on the roof . . . ." *Up high and down low . . . .*

"Lucilla," he says gently, "whatever treasure there was, we've found it. Let it go. Even if we do find something more, you know it will just be a disappointment."

I look at him, and I know he's right. It's silly to spend one's whole life seeking imaginary riches.

"Come downstairs with me," he says. He takes my hand and we go down together. "You wait here. This time I'll make the coffee." He leaves me there, brooding on the old couch, and returns a few minutes later with two mugs of very strong coffee.

"Did you find anything?" I ask as he sits next to me. I try to smile. "Another journal maybe? A clue? Another hint? An old fashioned boot with a hundred buttons?"

"No." He moves closer to me on the sofa, and I can feel his arm around my shoulders, strong and affectionate. He kisses the top of my head. "Just this delicious coffee."

"But *diamonds*, Charles," I say. "It's so hard to forget all about them."

"Diamonds," he scoffs. "That's so unimportant, Lucilla. And you know that."

"They say they're a girl's best friend, though."

He's quiet for a minute, sipping coffee, and then he says almost casually, "Well, I have one I can give you if you'd want it."

A diamond he can give me? I laugh and it comes out a nervous little burble.

He's looking at me, a frank look. "My mother's engagement ring. Two carats. Is that enough? If you want it, it's yours. Or we could buy a new one if you'd rather."

Now I have suspected lately that this could happen, Sister, have even dreamed of it and practiced for it. In truth, it shouldn't surprise me at all. I know him so well, you see. But none of that seems to matter. There is no such thing as practicing for events that knock your socks off. I can practically feel my heart fluttering, and suddenly I'm very conscious of that arm resting so snugly over my shoulders.

314

"Lucilla?"

"What?" I can hardly get the word out, but I manage to turn my face to him. He's smiling, pretty sure of himself.

"I suppose I could court you in the traditional way, but that seems a little silly since we live in the same house and share all the same silverware and furniture and soap. Anyway, I think we both know what we want." He pulls me closer to him, grinning. "This is a good little house," he says, looking around. "A family could make a nice home out of this."

"Yes, they could," I say. Can he hear my heart, pounding so loudly in the stillness? Does my hair look all right? I'm wondering if I should maybe hide my fingernails; they're pretty grimy from all that poking around in the rubble upstairs. And chipped, too. Damn! Why didn't I keep them nicely filed in preparation for this moment? Why didn't I polish them?

"We can have the whole thing redone," he's saying. "Everything painted and repaired, a whole new kitchen, whatever you like. We could even add on." He indicates a lifetime of paintings. "I'll move all this stuff to the castle. Won't the girls be surprised?" He grimaces a little.

Then another thought takes hold. "We could have an out-of-this-world garage sale, Lucilla, with all the trays and tarnished candlesticks and tables and outdated light fixtures. In fact, turning the castle into a hotel isn't a bad idea either. A bed and breakfast, maybe." He glances around the room. "I'd rather live right here, though, wouldn't you?"

Well, I sure can't answer. My glib old tongue is cleaving to the roof of my mouth like a melted gumdrop. For one of the few times in her life, Lucky Wilta has nothing to say.

"Lucilla," he says finally, his voice dripping with patience, "this is a marriage proposal. You understand that, don't you?"

I find my voice. "I thought maybe it was."

"Well?"

And then I can't believe I say this. Pressing my luck. But I have to. I have to get all my cards out on the table. No subterfuge, no secrets.

"I couldn't marry anyone who doesn't really love me," I say. "If it's for Pansy and Violet, for Rose's family . . . ."

"Rose's family? Of course not. They won't even approve of you, Lucilla. No, it's for the girls and me - all of us. You know we need you."

It's not enough. I want to say yes so desperately, but it isn't

315

enough.

"I didn't like it when you left us," he says. "I want you here - with me." He's searching my eyes. "I mean that, you know."

"And do you love me?" It comes out a whisper, a little whimpering wish.

He puts his head sideways for a minute, examining my face. I wish he wouldn't do that. It could ruin everything. Finally, he smiles. "Of course I love you. Don't you know that yet, Lucilla?"

Actually, I do. I sure don't understand it, but I know it, and I've known it for a while. But sometimes, a girl just needs to hear it.

I lean back against him and I close my eyes. I can't help smiling. All I'm seeing is me in a white satin dress with flowers in my hair, and all I'm thinking is that for the first time, I truly deserve my name.

"Lucilla?" His hand finds a stray wisp of my hair and smoothes it behind my ear. It's so quiet in the room that all I can hear is his even breathing. "Is that a yes?"

It's all I can do to get the words out. My response is a tiny, quiet breath. "You betchum," I whisper.

I throw my arms around him, and he tightens his. I let him kiss me, our second kiss, and this is nothing like kissing Lionel Hawthorne.

A thousand perfect hidden diamonds crumble into soft dust. A secret room folds in upon itself, collapsing brightly. A castle falls, rock upon rock, thudding, shaking the earth, then resting in a quiet, spent pile.

Like yesterday's newspaper.

Old. Forgotten.

Trivial.

At last. At last, I'm home.

# 35

THE CONTRACTORS will be here tomorrow, and the plans the architect and Charles and I have come up with for the summer house would captivate even your most jaded diner waitress. Talk about your wow factor! They will be adding on rooms, renovating bathrooms, restructuring the entire kitchen and building a studio for Charles. We've agreed that the only thing they may not touch is the diamond-paned window; it's the thing that brought us together, after all.

I told Charles it seemed like too much, that after living in the castle, small seems homey and easy. He agreed, sort of, but hey, a man's home is his castle, and if he wants more rooms, he shall have them.

We are engaged - officially. Lionel grimaced at first and told me I was making a big mistake, then he thought it over and told me marrying him would have been the big mistake. Which I already knew. Kitty showed up with a really nice clock, an engagement present. She threw her arms around me in a big hug and got all teary-eyed. This surprised me, and I wasn't even sure how to act. I still wonder how many paychecks she had to save to afford that clock. I never knew we were friends exactly, but I guess we are, and maybe we always were. I think I'm going to ask her to be my maid of honor. Go figure.

She'll probably grab all the attention away from the bride, but I don't much care. I get to keep the groom.

The girls are pretty excited, especially since they will get to share a bedroom, their lifelong dream. And they get me, of course.

I am deliriously happy. And I mean that when I say it. Charles acts happy, too, and I just hope he doesn't awaken one morning, slap himself upside the head, and realize what a bad bargain he's making. That would be a bummer.

I decided to stop searching for treasure. Who needs it? I have my treasure. The real thing. I mean, if jewels drop into my lap, I won't complain, but I have so many delicious plans to make that

I don't really have time to be skulking around looking for diamonds. Jeesh. What a waste of a life that would be.

Charles is downstairs trying to decide if Bob Cobb is going to need to run more pipes for the plumbing, and I am upstairs in what used to be my secret room, sweeping up debris. It isn't really fair to make the contractors deal with the mess we left here, and after Charles proposed, well, things just got too exciting to be moving pictures and hauling trash.

I grab up a couple of broken boards studded with bent nails and toss them into an overflowing plastic wastebasket.

Charles comes up and busies himself battling cobwebs that have taken root on some of his earlier pictures. "All these should go to the castle," he says.

"Yup. We can come back with the car and get them later."

"I'll take these bags down so we can clear more space in here." He hoists several filled plastic garbage bags, turns away, and clatters down the stairs.

I pick up my broom and make a fresh attack on the rubble in what used to be the secret room, sweeping old dirt and debris into dusty piles. I'm working with such zeal that I hardly notice that it's getting darker and darker in here. When I look up, I realize that the room is ensconced in a gray, fuzzy haze and the diamond-paned window is so coated with dust that the sun is having a little trouble penetrating. Well, I can easily remedy that, and I think what a nice surprise it will be for Charles to see that window really sparkling. I bet he hasn't cleaned it in years.

I find a ladder and haul it over to the window. It's a bit rickety, but it will do, and I gather up some rags and a bucket of warm, soapy water and climb up to give a little TLC to the window.

The jewel tones of the glass fragments burst with color, one by one, as I wipe the grit and grime from them. I do love this window, *our* window, and I smile to myself as I think of my father's journal entry that led me here. *Diamonds of a thousand brilliant colors . . . .*

I'm wiping the wooden windowsill, when I pass my hand over a small imperfection in the wood, a little bump. I peer at the windowsill more carefully and find a tiny, almost invisible metal loop projecting from the wood. I'm thinking about getting a claw hammer to pry the metal out, but the loop is so small that I don't think the claw could grasp it. I try twisting it out with my hand, which is too big and awkward, and that's when I realize that the metal loop is grounded in a section of the wood that's been cut out, like a little trapdoor.

I need something smaller, a little piece of wire. And I shiver all over as I realize that I know exactly what to use. "Charles?" I yell. "Could you bring that button hook up here, please?" It's right in the kitchen, where it's been all these years, back inside the journal, just waiting.

He shows up a minute later with the button hook in his hand and a questioning look on his face. I'm grinning from ear to ear. "You are not going to believe this. I think I figured out the 'up high' part."

He joins me on the ladder. It's a little crowded, but kind of nice, too, all balanced together there in front of our special window. We grin at each other like fools and he works the button hook into the loop and pries the wooden piece away from the windowsill.

"My goodness, Lucilla," he says. "Being married to you is going to be one adventure after another."

"Yep," I say. "I can promise you it will never be dull." I peer into the tiny space. I can see a little scroll of paper in the recess and use the button hook to fish it out. The scroll is tied with a piece of string, and I untie it and then unfurl the paper carefully. The printing inside is clear and readable, and I read it aloud.

*"Don't be too hasty carting away the bottles. Your fathers, Charles, Luke & Lewie."*

◇◇◇

That's all that's written on the slip of paper, and for a split second I stand there on the ladder, stock still, my mind working furiously. I can feel my eyes widen and my breath coming in quick gasps, then I nearly fall off the ladder. "The bottles! All this time, it was the bottles!" I flail about in my anxiety to get to floor level. My feet tangle and I feel myself plunging, but luckily Charles is quick. He grabs me and we stumble down from the ladder together.

The slip of paper is still clutched in my hand. *"Down low,* Charles. They mean under the floor." Charles takes it from me and reads it again, standing near me as I hunker down, grabbing at floorboards with my bare hands.

"All right, come back up here," Charles says. He grips my arm and pulls me to him, but he loses his balance and lets go of

319

me, and I fall to the floor with a sudden thud. Fortunately, I land sitting.

I look up at him, and he sinks to the floor with me. He smiles a little and puts both arms around me. "Are you hurt?" he says.

"No."

He nuzzles his face in my hair and I know he's grinning over the funny antics of his fiancée, Lucky T. Wilta.

"They're telling us to look in the bottles, Charles," I say. "There must be something in them - a clue at least, or maybe the bottles themselves. They might be antiques, valuable collectibles." I'm babbling on, trying to get loose, and he's smiling a small smile, holding onto me.

"That can wait a minute," he says. "You're going off the deep end again, Lucilla. I thought we agreed that that kind of treasure can't hold a candle to-"

"But, Charles, dear, there may be diamonds under the floor!" Well, sure I said that Charles is the real treasure, and I certainly meant it, but the excitement of the search is on me again. I mean, isn't this why I came here in the first place?

"I gave you a diamond, Lucilla, a beautiful one. Isn't that enough?"

I glance down at my dazzling ring, his mother's engagement ring. I reach up and kiss him. "Yes, of course it is," I say. But is he crazy? Didn't he hear what I just read?

He leans back lazily and reaches for me again. "Okay, then," he says. "Let's not go crazy." He looks at me almost shyly. "Kiss me again," he says. "I'd like that."

Well, I'd like that, too, of course, and I sink into his embrace. He kisses me once, twice. The room spins. No romance novel heroine ever had it as good as Lucky Wilta.

But there's treasure here, I'm sure of it, right under this floor we're sprawled on. Seriously, this new wrinkle is so exciting that I don't know why we aren't hacking up this floor as quickly as possible.

And then I hear the low chuckle, and I open my eyes and peer at him. He's looking at me, trapping me with his devotion.

I jump out of his arms, clutch his hand, and pull him up. "Come on, Charles!"

He gets up, holding my hand tightly, and looks around at the rubble all over the floor. "Let's just gather up some of this garbage, Lucilla, and get it out of here first."

I stare at him through slitted eyes. Very, very funny.

He puts down the trash he has picked up, leans in, and kisses me again, a long, lingering kiss, which does help me to put treasure under the floorboards into some kind of perspective. Then he smiles at me and asks, "So, Lucilla, do you intend to control *everything* in this marriage? We might as well straighten that out right now."

"What do *you* think?" I say breathlessly, leaning away from him. I mean, it's obvious.

Isn't it?

He laughs and pulls me closer. "Life with you is going to be very entertaining," he says.

"Yes, side-splitting," I retort, "and very short if we don't check out those bottles *now*, Mr. Smithson."

"Okay, okay," he says. He puts his hands up in a sign of surrender, but I'm already across the room and grabbing up a hammer. My glance darts wildly about. Where do we begin? Charles strolls to my side and we look at each other. I hunker down on the floor, ready to rip and tear in all directions at once.

"Let's do this in an organized way," he says. "We'll start over there with the board that's already up, then move clockwise."

I roll my eyes at him and let go with the hammer, smashing the board under his feet until he yelps and moves aside.

Our search has officially begun. Finally.

◇◇◇

I want to grab, yank, and toss bottles as quickly as I can find them, but Charles puts a gently restraining hand on my arm. "Lucilla, hold on. As you said yourself, it might be the bottles themselves that are valuable. Let's treat them a little more carefully, shall we?"

He's right, of course, so I force myself to slow the pace a little. After all, it's not as though we don't have the rest of our lives.

We've pried up a few boards, and along with a lot of dust and some mouse droppings, we've found three more empty bottles, green ones, whereas the first two were clear glass. I find myself wondering idly what the happy trio liked to drink on their once-every-five-years binges. I start reading labels, a nice variety, and nothing particularly interesting. Some wine, a few hard liquor, some beer bottles, too. I'm looking the bottles over pretty carefully now, and I don't see any distinguishing marks. Varied shapes, some a little taller, one has a number on the bottom; one is a little misshapen.

Charles takes them from me and holds them up to the light, peering carefully. It's a little disappointing. One empty bottle looks a lot like another.

As we continue to pry, peek, lift, and examine, we make a nice little arrangement of bottles in the corner of the summer house floor.

"You go ahead and check this area," Charles tells me. "I'll go over there and see what I find."

Fine with me. The more territory we cover, the quicker we find our stash.

For a while there's little progress. We're trying not to destroy a perfectly good floor, and most boards don't have bottles underneath anyway. But every now and then we strike gold and find two or three bottles placed neatly below the floor, lip to bottom. Then empty spaces again. Another bottle or two. We hold them up to the light, empty, empty, empty. They join the hoard lined up neatly, ready to be bagged for recycling.

"I don't think these bottles have any value, Charles," I say. "They're not that unusual."

"I'm sure you're right. But, just in case . . . ."

And then he says, "Here's something," and I'm at his side in a flash. "There's something in this one," he says. And he can't fool me; he sounds as excited as I am.

It's one of the green bottles, but with a difference. This one has a cork, and inside the bottle is what looks like a small tube of crumpled paper.

Charles pries the cork out and upends the bottle, but the paper doesn't pour out. It gets caught in the hole.

"Wait a minute." He fishes a thin artist's brush from one of the tables. "I always hoped these brushes would someday have a practical purpose," he says. He pokes it into the bottle and uses it to coax the paper through the hole. Gently, he pulls, and the paper comes grudgingly. But something else scatters backward down into the bottom of the bottle.

We both gasp. He lifts the bottle and pours it out into my shaking, waiting hand - a necklace, stone after glimmering stone, shining like a string of stars on a long, slim chain. And they sure look like diamonds to me.

"Oh," I breathe, "I can't believe it." Clymna's jewels; they must be. They lie there in a sparkling heap in my palm, catching the light and glowing richly.

Charles lifts the chain from me and holds it in two hands, examining it. Then he fools with the clasp, steps behind me, places it around my neck and fastens it.

I can feel it, heavy, cold, and glittering against my grubby tee shirt.

He's gazing at me, and then at the necklace. Back at me again. "You look just as pretty without it as with it, Lucilla."

"Pretty?" I grimace at him, and he laughs softly.

"You are," he says. He gazes thoughtfully into my dirty face, "in an unconventional sort of way." The dazzling light from the stones must be blinding him. I start to argue when he puts a finger to my lips. "No, no more of that. You do that too much. I will not hear my bride insulted."

So I spare him the words I'm thinking, and I walk to the dirty mirror hanging on the far wall. My eyes become misty, a faraway look. The Lucilla Wilta gazing back at me with her smudged face and unkempt hair, her eyes too wide apart and nose too long, her neck decorated with a stunning, throbbing diamond chain, is, if I squint my eyes a little until they tear over and blur, not a beautiful, but maybe a pretty woman.

Charles wants to see me that way, so who am I to argue?

He has unfolded the rumply paper wrapper and comes over to me.

"*Congratulations,*" he reads, "*You've won the Castle Game!*

"*We found these jewels under Borstrom's secretary in the east wing. He left no heirs; there's no-one to contact, and we don't need them.*

"*We intend to keep up our every five years Castle Game weekend to give all of you a chance to win these jewels. The better we play at cards, the more likely you are to live in the castle, the more likely to find this bit of wampum.*

"*We created this game, a treasure hunt to lead you here, and we all agree: Finders Keepers. No questions asked. And this signed paper will be proof if you ever need it. You needn't contact the others. The necklace is yours. But if you do want to get together to sell the jewels and share the proceeds, we feel convinced that the friendship among you might become more valuable to you than these diamonds ever could.*

"*But- it's your decision. Do with the necklace whatever you decide. It's real.*"

I glance at the paper Charles is holding and see the three

distinctly different signatures at the bottom. *"With love from your fathers, Lewie Forsythe, Charles Smithson, & Luke Todd."*

I put my hand to the necklace and touch its stones gently. "This is Clymna's," I say. "The wedding gift she hid so that Borstrom wouldn't lose it in a wager. She was dying when they moved out, Charles, so she never took it with her."

"Well, it's yours now," Charles says.

"I suppose we could contact Lewie Forsythe," I say, "if you think we should . . . ."

"He must have had kids," Charles finishes my thought. "The note sounds that way, so I'll find out where he is, just to be fair. But we don't have to, you know. It's pretty clear that we don't have to."

"True." I shrug, staring at the diamonds sparkling back at me from the mirror.

"I think we should assume, Lucilla, that this necklace is yours."

"Mine." The gems are beautiful, stunning, winking gloriously back at me. They're exactly what I hoped for, precisely what I imagined, and I'm struck dumb that my quest is over.

I see the look Charles is giving me, standing behind me in front of the mirror, and I can't help grinning from ear to ear. Diamonds or no diamonds, nobody has a right to expect that much.

"There really is a treasure; can you believe it?" I say.

"You were right all along, Lucilla," Charles says. "Now we know why my father wanted me to stay in the castle. They must have had a great time planning all this. Each clue leads to another one and then another one."

"What if someone else had found this, though?" I ask. "A cleaning lady, a contractor, the Garloffs . . . . What if I hadn't bullied my way in and disrupted your life?"

I don't care about the necklace, I realize in mild surprise, but would I still have Charles? Any other future hurts too much to consider, and I look away.

He turns me to face him and kisses me softly. "We would have arrived at exactly the same place, Lucilla, and I know that. We might not have the diamonds, and we might have come here by a different route, but I would have found you."

And he would have. I don't know why I believe that, but I do.

I smile and turn back to the mirror to see my million dollar baubles winking at me. Charles Smithson the Second is still standing behind me, and I see our two reflections there.

One Todd, one Smithson. Together. Forever. Forever and ever. Amen.

He puts his hand on my shoulder and turns me to him gently. "Hey," he says, "how long am I going to have to stand here competing with that thing?"

"You will never have to compete, Charles," I say. I throw my arms around his neck. He kisses me and smiles at my happiness.

"Let's bust outta this joint," I tell him. Suddenly I'm finding words to say, all kinds of words. My mind is blasting ahead, making all kinds of plans. "We can finish up here later. We've got kiddies back at the castle. Wait 'til they get a look at these rocks! I can't wait to let them try them on."

Charles laughs. "Sure, I can just see Violet all doubled over, dragging out to the sandbox."

"Plus," I add, "I need to spend some time trying out our fine new gems with a few of my favorite outfits."

Charles gives me a confused look. "Your outfits are all the same, Lucilla- jeans and a tee shirt."

"Exactly. And these will dress them up big time."

He takes my hand, and, weighted down in awe by the treasure around my neck, the treasure next to me, I walk beside The Honorable Charles Fitzham Smithson the Second out of the summer house, through the woods, and back to the castle.

# 36

SO THAT'S IT," I tell Sister Mary Phyllis. "That's how I ended up sitting here talking to you. That's the story of the castle, Sister, the story of Charles and me. My story. Our story. You asked me why we made the decision we did, what led up to it. Now you know. We're more than ready to let the castle go.

"I hope you'll be happy here, Sister. I know the diocese has had its eye out for a good spot for an intergenerational care facility, a place for kids and seniors. I know that you and the other sisters were hoping for a quiet place away from the noise and chaos of city life, where you could live and work and pray and do all those good works you're famous for.

"You'll find it here, I think, just as I did. Well, maybe I wasn't so much into the good works. And there wasn't nearly as much praying as there should have been. Well, not much work either.

"But it's a place that could lend itself to all those things. And, believe me, you'll find lots of reasons to pray," I tell her. "Every day when the furnace kicks on, and with every leaky faucet and defunct bit of wiring, you'll raise your eyes to heaven and say a prayer."

"Yes, a prayer of thanks," she says.

Well, that wasn't exactly what I meant.

"So while you're praying, Sister," I say, "think of us now and then. We'll be right over there, through the woods, looking at life through a rose-colored window.

"I can picture it, Sister, kiddies and old folks all tangled up at the castle, being cared for by a staff of pros. You're likely to have shared songs and storytelling, picnics on the lawn, probably a lot of laughing and playing games in the sun. It sounds like fun. I might even stop by myself and join in.

"I have so many plans to make, Sister, and so much to do. First thing tomorrow, I need to take a trip into town. We need groceries, and there are bills to be paid. We owe Bob Cobb hundreds of dollars, hundreds; we always do. I've got my class tomorrow, too. I found a good one: Interior Home Decorating. I know it doesn't seem like a perfect fit, but you should see some of the things I'm doing to the summer house. Charles is very impressed. In fact, he's speechless.

"Did I tell you he's thinking about exhibiting his paintings? I'm going to call Mrs. Garloff. She might be able to tell me how to set it up. Anyway, I think she and I could get along. She's peculiar, but I'm the first to admit that I, too, every once in a while, act in unusual ways."

Sister Mary Phyllis is nodding like crazy. She gets it. She seems to understand me. That makes two people.

It boggles the mind.

"I have to take a whole bundle of tasteless ties to the Good Will people, too," I continue. "What does an artist need with ties? He can wear whatever he wants to. And the girls are leaving you a roomful of dolls for the kids you'll have here. That will give you a good start.

"I need to buy some blueberries for a great cobbler recipe I just found. I'll get you some, Sister. And I need to make a quick stop at the toy store for glitter and glue. Dr. Harvard says glitter and glue are very good for children. I can't wait to dig in, and of course I'm inviting Lionel."

I pause for a second, thinking something over.

"I think I'll drop the name Lucky," I say. "It's a little silly for a grown married woman with two daughters of her own. From now on, I'm Lucilla, Lucilla Smithson, or Mom, to some people.

"You know, Sister, I've regretted a million times my rash behavior with Ippy and the missus, even though it couldn't have turned out better. If I could have foreseen the future, I'd have done everything differently. I don't know why I always have to experience things before I realize what bad ideas some of them turn out to be.

"My father was a darn good father. He taught me what's important, even though I never caught on until he'd been dead nine years. He taught me to value what I have."

Sister Mary Phyllis peers at me from behind her little round glasses. "It's good," she says with a smile, "that you realize all that you have. So many people don't, and you do have a lot."

I nod emphatically and begin cataloguing. "What I have, Sister, is a hideous castle that I once thought I wanted. I've had so much fun finding an outrageous diamond necklace that I still can't believe really exists. I also have a buyer for the castle who did turn out to be exactly right." I smile at her. Yes, my smile is still way too wide, but I've decided to stop worrying about that. I like smiling. I like feeling happy.

"I have mold, mildew, dust, and rubble," I tell her. "Broken plaster, splintered doors, mice, moths, and millipedes. Soon, Sister, they will all belong to you."

She laughs, and it's so contagious that I join in.

"I also have a habit," I admit, "of sometimes saying stupid things before I think. Okay, usually. But I'm working on that.

"And I have so much more." I want to list all the rest for her, but I see Charles standing in the doorway to what used to be the girls' playroom, a soft smile on his face. "They must be ready for us," I tell Sister Mary Phyllis.

The old rock walls of the castle look just as dreary and forbidding as they did the day I had my interview here well over two years ago, but something has changed. Not on the outside, not what you can see, but on the inside.

"Sister?" says Charles, "The lawyers are ready. Everything is all set with the trust, so you should have plenty of money to get you and all the sisters through for more years than you could possibly hope to live. And enough left over for whatever you want to do here."

Sister Mary Phyllis looks back at him and smiles a beatific little smile.

She's not moving in sight unseen. She's visited us a few times, and she knows what she's doing. When I took her to Marsuvius Borstrom's creepy old room and showed her the hidden compartment under the desk, she jumped right in. I got in, too, of course, and we lounged in the dirt and dust for a while, like two bathing beauties in a hot tub.

"Hang on," I remember saying. I ran downstairs and grabbed a bottle of wine and a couple of Borstrom's finest glasses, with just a few little chips on the rims.

Sister looked unsure at first, then accepted the glass I held out to her. "Well, I guess a small one wouldn't hurt," she said.

I like her.

She's older than I am by about fifteen years, but we're becoming good friends. And she still has a good long time to settle in to the castle and relive her own good times in this place.

It should work out perfectly. Lewie Forsythe is intending to foot the bill.

Forsythe lost the castle to my father, but Lewie's daughter

had had her run of the place for a number of years before they left. Apparently, she was saintly even then- She told me how she made a First Communion outfit for her favorite doll, that it matched hers exactly. It was only because her devoutness outranked her love for that doll that she didn't carry it up to the Communion rail on the big day.

She told me she used to climb the circular stairs to what later became my playroom- just to be alone. Peace and silence would overtake her there, and that was where she began to recognize her calling.

She left the castle at age fifteen, when we moved in, but it never quite left her. When Charles contacted Lewie Forsythe about the necklace - of course, he had to; he wouldn't be Charles otherwise - we learned that Lewie did have one child, his daughter Phyllis. Wealthy in his own right, Lewie contacted Phyllis to see if she wanted to fight over the diamonds of Marsuvius Borstrom. She didn't, of course, but his letter pricked her memory and started a landslide of legal and religious decisions ending in Lewie's greatest act of mercy - buying the castle to be converted into a residence and workplace for Sister Mary Phyllis and the sisters she lives with. He's already started a trust fund that will cover repairs, maintenance, and whatever purchases the sisters need to make, and he's hired a contractor to fix all that stuff that we couldn't be bothered to take care of.

And he's getting a deal, a rock bottom price.

The sisters are eager to make this move. Sister Louise Joseph plays a mean piano; she'll be pleased to try out her own rollicking jive on the old grand in the music room. And Sister Florence has a knack with a hammer and saw. She'll never lack for projects.

Sister Elizabeth loves to garden, and here she can garden to her heart's content. This place will be blazing with color when she gets through. She's also planning to plant a huge vegetable garden and some fruit trees, and will even try to coax back the old grape arbor. She says she'll share the results with us, and I can't wait.

It's a good move.

Sister Mary Phyllis is pushing back her chair, eager to sign the papers and get on with it. "It's very exciting!" she says. I know the feeling. She's back in her castle, wishing her father were able to be here to see this day.

"Why are you smiling like that?" she asks me in her gentle, cultured voice.

"I'm smiling," I say, 'because I'm thinking how strange it is that you've become my friend - a sister, of all things!'

She smiles, too. "Well, our fathers were buddies," she says. "Why shouldn't we be? And we'll be neighbors, as well."

I follow her into the playroom, devoid now of its little wicker couches and chairs, its plastic toys, and shelves of dolls. We all sit down around a big, scratched table Charles and Lionel dragged in, and the lawyers shuffle some stacks of papers. A rat caged behind orange squiggles and a mammoth bottle of cough syrup decorate the rocks around us. The lawyers ignore them politely, but Sister Mary Phyllis takes a good look and I'm sure I hear her snicker under her breath.

"Ready?" says an attorney.

"Ready," we all say at once.

Smithson, Todd and Forsythe, together again.

Forever and ever, Amen.

Some might call this providence.

Sister glances over at me, her pen poised in her hand. She's ready to sign, but first she slides a small envelope over to me. "It's nothing, really," she says, "just a little thank you note."

I can see Charles smiling on the other side of the table. He leans back and taps his pen on the tabletop. "It wasn't easy, Sister," he says. "I had to wrestle it away from her while she slept."

"That's a lie," I say.

He laughs. "Yes, it is. It shocked me as much as anyone. After all that searching and carrying on, I couldn't believe you'd just up and give it away."

I shrug. "Well, they'll need it. Can you think of a better use for Borstrom's gems?"

Someone on the internet paid me a fortune for that snazzy diamond necklace, and the money went straight into Lewie Forsythe's trust fund. It's no big deal. It didn't do justice to my favorite jeans anyway. And once you find out about real treasure - once you *know* - any other treasure, even one as brilliant as that one, pales in comparison.

"You were telling me the things you have," Sister Mary Phyllis says thoughtfully, "when your husband interrupted. You said there were more. What were you thinking of?"

"Well, a couple of things," I tell her. "I have a new name that sounds like a snake that can't get going."

Charles laughs again, and I'm glad to say that he does that a lot more lately. At me, or with me, what difference does it make? I love the sound.

"I have a flower garden of little girls, and I have their father. That's the truly amazing part."

She smiles. "Yes, that would be the best thing."

I pat the tiny bump that's just beginning to show. I don't mind admitting I'll be running to Dr. Harvard more than ever. Charles still refuses to read him, and maybe he's only doing that for old times' sake, but he seems to be feeling pretty confident. Me? I find myself keeling over with delirium, scared to death, but eager, too, and anxious to try to do everything right.

"If it's a boy," I tell her, "we're going to name him-"

"Clover," murmurs Charles, "in keeping with the theme."

"No," I scowl, dismissing that, "Charles the Third, of course, after his father."

I suddenly think of something. "Do you know what he said to me, Sister? That he intends to keep his stars polished. To me, he said that. He remembered what I told him when we were hiking. Not only remembered, but knew exactly what it meant. You gotta love a guy like that."

Charles is grinning at me.

I grin back. "So let's get this deal done. And you can bring out the polish, too, Yore Grace," I say. "I'm ready."

And, I think to myself, I'm something else that I never thought I'd be. Lucky.

Man, am I lucky.

# A NOTE FROM THE AUTHOR

I love setting fiction in the Adirondack Mountains. It's challenging and entertaining to use real places and infuse a dash of local color, but intersperse my own made up place names and elements (a big stone castle, for instance) that are a little bit at odds with how things really are up here.

Chez Fred's is entirely my own invention, as is the castle. But Esther Mountain is real and the trail is much as I've described it. It was my husband's last hike when he became an Adirondack 46er (achieved by climbing all 46 of New York State's High Peaks), and we took two toddlers up the mountain for the celebration with family and friends at the top. The kids were troupers, and did so much running ahead and running back that they actually climbed Esther twice that day. Tupper Lake, of course, exists, but Duck Vly and Hunting Fork do not, although those are just the kinds of names you'd find here for tiny towns with not much in them.

I had fun writing about Lucky Wilta, Bob Cobb, Pansy & Violet, the Garloffs, Lionel, Charles, Kitty, Emily, the whole gang. None of them is based on any real person, and, in some ways, they are more caricatures than characters. If you felt they acted a bit zany at times, well, that's the fun of fiction. I enjoyed inventing them all.

Whether you call it a romantic comedy or a modern fairy tale, I hope you enjoyed reading CASTLE GAMES, that you found a reason to smile, and that the book left you feeling happy for the bright future ahead for my main characters. If you enjoyed the book, please tell your friends and leave a review on Amazon. I also invite you to contact me at janpresto@gmail.com.

I'm looking forward to your comments. I love to hear from readers!

Jan Prestopnik
August 2016

# THANK YOU

-to my sister, Amy Sponenberg, for always taking on my books with enthusiasm and humor and for finding things that everybody else misses.

-to my daughter, Emily Prestopnik, for giving me excellent insights into the 'late-twenties to early thirty-something' psyche and for taking the time to read CASTLE GAMES even though she never had more than two spare minutes a day.

-to my critique partner, Rosemarie Sheperd, for her relentless enthusiasm for writing, for finding the fun in mulling over one phrase for an hour, and for brewing lots of excellent coffee.

-to my friend Edie Meikle, for reading an early draft and asking great questions, and for liking Lucky right from the start.

-to my son, Nate Prestopnik, for making useful suggestions even though he was 'off-duty' as a reader, and, especially, for designing the perfect cover (again) and making it look effortless.

-to my husband, Rich Prestopnik, for always helping with the technical aspects, for knowing a lot about many things, and for being so much fun to live with.


All of these people are fine writers themselves, and their comments and questions helped me enormously. Without any one of them, CASTLE GAMES would be a different book and a lesser one.

. . . Thanks to all of you, plus to my wonderful family, and to readers who made my day by telling me they were looking forward to my next release. This is for you!

**JAN PRESTOPNIK**, a retired teacher of college, high school, and middle school English and writing, is married and the mother of three grown children. Camping, traveling, teaching, performing, reading great books, and savoring the atmosphere of her beloved Adirondack Mountains are some of the things that have influenced her writing.

# TITLES BY THIS AUTHOR:

**Captive** (2014)
*Available in Kindle, Paperback, and Large Print editions*

**Quarter Past Midnight** (2015)
*Available in Kindle, Paperback, and Large Print editions*

**Castle Games: A Rocky Romance** (2016)
*Available in Kindle and Paperback editions*

Made in the USA
Middletown, DE
18 August 2017